D0992077

Also by Gregory Bean

No Comfort in Victory
Long Shadows in Victory

▼▼▼

A DEATH
IN VICTORY

▲▲▲

GREGORY BEAN

ST. MARTIN'S PRESS

NEW YORK

A THOMAS DUNNE BOOK.
An imprint of St. Martin's Press.

Library of Congress Cataloging-in-Publication Data

Bean, Gregory
    A death in victory : a Harry Starbranch mystery / by
Gregory Bean.—1st ed.
      p.   cm.
    "A Thomas Dunne book."
    ISBN 0-312-15512-3
    I. Title.
PS3552.E1525D4   1997
813'.54—dc21   96-54502
                                                        CIP

First Edition: June 1997

10 9 8 7 6 5 4 3 2 1

In memory of
the beautiful Elizabeth Weed

Acknowledgments

▲▲▲

I owe several people my heartfelt thanks for their help in the preparation and writing of this book, starting with Rich Grosz of the U.S. Fish and Game Wildlife Service for his help with information on Wyoming poaching and the Asian medicinal market. Thanks also to Chief Matt Bider of the Rock Springs Police Department, and Rich Moses, a sergeant in the San Francisco Police Department's gang task-force unit, who provided background on Asian gangs in that city. My appreciation also goes to Linda Zellmer, head of the University of Wyoming's Geology Library, for her help with research on Wyoming jade. Dan Housel and Ray Harris, both with the U.S. Geological Survey, also helped in that area.

Special thanks to my good friend and mentor Richard Fleck, who not only encouraged me as a fledgling writer, but whose memory of things we learned together on the Wind River Reservation was better than my own; to "Bear Claws" Patti, a dependable partner on a rocky trail, a fair shot, and self-proclaimed expert on every John Wayne movie ever made; and to my brother Russ, an attorney who answers my literary legal questions for free.

As always, my love and thanks go to my beautiful wife Linda, who not only makes it possible for me to write, but whose eye for detail on the San Francisco segments of this book was indispensable.

The characters in this novel are products of my imagination, and any resemblance to real people, alive or otherwise, is purely coincidental. Factual mistakes, as always, are mine alone.

Every normal man must be tempted at times to spit on
his hands, hoist the black flag, and begin slitting throats.
—H. L. MENCKEN

Think twice before you speak to a friend in need.
—AMBROSE BIERCE

A DEATH
IN VICTORY

1

Ursus horribilis, the North American grizzly, is an omnivore—a fifty-cent word that means he'll eat anything. The animal whose tracks we'd been studying was a mature bear, a behemoth weighing up to 600 pounds, strong enough to kill a horse with a single swipe of his giant paw. For all his majestic size, however, he was incredibly sloppy and had scattered the remains of his last meal across a hundred square yards of the Snowy Range foothills.

I was sitting on a granite boulder warm from the noonday sun, looking out over a long slope dotted with lodgepole pine and aspen, glacial rubble, and razor-sharp scree. To my left, in a small stand of sage, a leg dangled upside down from a thick branch, bloody at the haunch, long bones visible, the foot still encased in a white Reebok sneaker. We'd found a left arm about thirty yards downslope, the other arm gnawed to the bone and left on the black earth at the side of a game trail running horizontally across the steep slope. We were still looking for the victim's other leg, his torso, and his head.

My name is Harry Starbranch and I'm the chief of police in Victory, Wyoming, a small town of 650 souls at the foot of the Snowies, about six miles from where I was sitting. Technically, my jurisdiction ends at the border of town, but this is the West, and out here everyone pitches in when there's trouble—which is why Frankie Tall Bull, a six-foot three-inch Teton Sioux and the only officer on my small force, and I were helping members of the Albany County Sheriff's Office, the state Game and Fish Department, and the county coroner's office scour the area for parts of the victim's corpse.

The body parts had been discovered earlier that morning by Colin "Three Fingers" Fitzpatrick, a local rancher who was herding cows up the mountain to their summer range and saw the afore-mentioned leg and foot in the brush. He spotted grizzly tracks in the vicinity, rode back down the mountain as fast as his old horse would carry him, and called my office to report his discovery. I'd no-tified the sheriff's office, the Game and Fish, and jumped into my new Jeep CJ-5 with Frankie to head up the mountain.

We arrived a good half hour before anyone else, and while the bear responsible for the carnage was nowhere to be seen, it gave me the willies hanging around with only my .357 and Frankie's .44 mag-num for protection. I imagine those weapons would stop a full-grown grizzly, but they might not put him down before he had a chance to do us serious damage. There were plenty of times in that nervous half hour when my fingers cramped on the butt of my re-volver and I watched the underbrush, cursing my stupidity for fail-ing to bring along a .30-06, or better yet, my old ten-gauge loaded with double-aught buck.

Down the slope, I could see a cluster of three sheriff's deputies and Albany County Coroner James Bowen, the tails of his black suit coat flapping in the wind, poking through the section of deadfall timber where we'd found the man's left arm. The tangle of dead wood was sprinkled with droplets of blood, pieces of flesh, and torn frag-ments of the victim's shirt and pants. Carefully, the deputies culled artifacts from the jumble and handed them to Bowen, who cataloged the gory bits and stored them in individual plastic bags. As he worked, Bowen muttered to himself and frequently wiped beads of sweat from his balding skull.

Twenty yards away, Frankie Bull scoured a deeply fissured gran-ite outcrop where we believed the killing had taken place. I had gone over the same ground with him before and knew what evidence was there—a large granite boulder splashed with blood, most likely the result of the bear's initial attack, more smidgens of bone and flesh, some of it brain matter, and drag marks in the earth leading from the rocks to the place where Bowen and the deputies were gathered.

It looked as if the bear had killed the victim in the rocks, mauled him considerably, and lugged the body a short distance before beginning to consume it.

In the rocks at the outcropping, we'd found a light windbreaker, a Phoenix Diamondbacks ball cap, and a half-pint bottle of Jack Daniel's bourbon with most of the liquor gone. We'd also found a wallet with $95 in cash, a few credit cards, and a California driver's license issued to Liam O'Bannion of 349 Prospect, San Francisco. The license said O'Bannion was thirty-four years old, stood five feet eleven inches, and had dark-brown hair and hazel eyes. He weighed a hundred and seventy pounds and was listed as an organ donor.

He was also a woman-hitting son of a bitch, although that information wasn't included on his driver's license.

The last time I'd seen Liam O'Bannion was two days previously, when he was getting his ass whipped by J. B. "Curly" Ahearn, my best friend and the mayor of Victory. As I knew from talking to my friend, O'Bannion and Curly's estranged daughter, Faith, had been living together for the better part of two years in San Francisco and had come to Victory in part so Faith could mend fences with her family but in greater part because the trip would give O'Bannion a chance to catch up on some business he had in Rock Springs.

O'Bannion and Faith stayed in Curly's guest bedroom, and the visit had apparently gone relatively well until two days before, when Faith and O'Bannion went to an early dinner with Curly and his wife, Madelaine, at the Trails End, one of the two huge steak houses on Victory's main drag.

I said hello to the foursome when they came in and declined their offer to give up my seat at the bar and join them for dinner. I saw them to their table and went back to my prime rib. I didn't hear from them for a half hour or so, just enough time for them to finish their shrimp cocktails. Before their main course arrived, however, a loud argument broke out between O'Bannion and Faith over a comment O'Bannion made about the casual way Faith had dressed for dinner. It culminated when O'Bannion backhanded Curly's daughter so hard she was knocked from her chair—the absolute wrong thing to do in front of Curly Ahearn. Next thing anyone knew, Curly had lunged across the table and came up with his fingers locked around O'Bannion's throat, his face a hardened mask of rage.

From that point on, the fight was a humdinger, with the women screaming, Curly advancing with savage determination, pummeling the shocked and cringing O'Bannion with his expensive cowboy hat, and O'Bannion backpedaling as fast as he could go. Curly hat-whipped O'Bannion all the way through the restaurant and didn't quit until he got to the top of the stairs leading to the front door. He only stopped then because O'Bannion fell down the stairs backward and didn't finish tumbling until he lay in a heap in front of the glass door.

That's when Curly dragged him outside and put boots to the man with a single-minded viciousness that might have ended in murder if I hadn't intervened. I came outside just as Curly delivered a kick to O'Bannion's side that made something pop. The young man curled up in a ball and couldn't have protected himself from the next kick, which Curly was aiming at his temple. I grabbed my friend just in time and held him back until he cooled off.

Although he was humiliated by the public beating and might have had a cracked rib, O'Bannion was not injured seriously enough to require hospitalization. And despite the fact that numerous local ordinances had been violated, none of the foursome seemed inclined to press charges against any of the others, so no arrests were in order.

After threatening to kill O'Bannion if he ever showed his face in Victory again, Curly finally went back inside to finish his meal and console his sobbing daughter.

For his part, Liam O'Bannion was almost relieved when I advised him to take off and start putting some miles between himself and Victory before my friend got a notion to finish what he'd started. Last I saw of O'Bannion, he was peeling out of the parking lot in his rented sedan—a car we'd found two miles from his body in the parking lot of a Forest Service campground—his rear tires kicking up a storm of gravel.

Now he was dead, the apparent victim of a marauding grizzly. I wondered how he'd ended up in the mountains instead of on a plane back to San Francisco. At that point, though, I didn't wonder long. I was more interested in the exceedingly unusual circumstances of his death.

It's not that grizzly attacks are unheard of in Wyoming, because they aren't. Every summer, it seems, there's at least one or two incidents between bears and tourists in Yellowstone Park to the northwest, and sometimes others in the surrounding mountain ranges— the Absarokas near Cody, the Tetons, and the Jim Bridger Forest between Jackson Hole and Dubois. For the most part, though, grizzlies shun human company, and it's only the occasional rogue that causes trouble.

Not only that, but the Snowies haven't been prime grizzly range since before the turn of the century, the large bears having been shot and trapped out by the first settlers to the area, along with most of the other large predators like wolves and cougars. Obviously there's nothing to stop a determined grizzly from wandering through this part of the Snowy Range if he gets the urge, but seeing one here would be a rare and unique occurrence—a once in a lifetime deal, no pun intended.

For Liam O'Bannion to have run into a rogue bear in country grizzlies haven't inhabited for nearly a century was entirely possible, but I estimated that the odds against it were at least a million to one.

As I told Frankie, the man had horrible luck.

Frankie Bull pulled the wide brim of his black Stetson low on his forehead, folded his mirrored sunglasses away in the pocket of his leather motorcycle vest, and leaned back against the trunk of a lodgepole pine. He balanced a can of soda on his knee with one hand and used a red bandanna to mop his brow with the other. It was a little after noon, and the temperature had just nudged seventy-five degrees. Early June in the Rocky Mountains, and the dry air was sweet with the scent of juniper, willow, and sage, the hills dotted with a profusion of wildflowers—Colorado columbine, larkspur, salt-bush, chickweed, and chamiso. Two gray jays in the branches of the tree above Frankie's head watched him eat the brown-bag lunch delivered by a late-arriving deputy sheriff, hoping for crumbs. If they didn't get a share soon, I figured one of the thieving birds would screw up the courage to swoop down and steal something from his hands. Gray jays—known as camp robbers in these parts—aren't known for their patience.

We'd broken for lunch without finding Liam O'Bannion's missing parts and had spent the last half hour in the shade of the lodgepole pines, trying to fine-tune a plan for the afternoon. According to Bowen, it looked as if our bear had made his kill the day before and had spent a long time dismembering and consuming the victim. Frankie, who found tracks and drag marks leading northwest from the killing ground, thought the bear had probably left sometime last night, maybe early that morning, taking the remains of Liam O'Bannion along to eat at leisure.

After lunch, we all knew we'd have to follow those tracks, and none of us were looking forward to it. I watched with interest as Craig Donaldson, a warden with the state Game and Fish, squeezed fat cartridges into the magazine of a 7-mm magnum hunting rifle, pushed the bolt home, and checked the safety. Two sheriff's deputies were also carrying heavy rifles, locked and loaded. The three of them would cover the rest of us—twelve in all—as we spread out over the mountainside and continued our search. If the bear still had most of O'Bannion's corpse, none of us expected him to give it up without a fight.

I finished my own lunch, wadded the bag into a ball, and stood to stretch my aching, forty-something legs. We had to cover some rough ground that afternoon, and I knew that by night I'd need plenty of liniment to soothe my muscles. My knee crunched like an old gear box filled with sand and I ground my teeth against the pain. I've got a bum knee, thanks to a right-wing fanatic who'd smashed it the previous year before I put a bullet through his heart. I leaned my weight against the blackthorn walking stick I use as a cane and stretched until I'd worked out the worst of the kinks. Then

I adjusted the .357 Blackhawk on my hip and made sure the safety strap was in place. The heavy weight of the revolver was reassuring.

"So here's the plan," Donaldson said, squatting down among us. Donaldson's face was flushed, almost as red as the wisps of hair that peeked out from under the sides of his brown cap. There were smudges of dirt on his cheeks and forehead, a long mud stain on the knee of his green trousers. Using a sharpened willow branch, he drew an *X* in the dirt at his feet and pointed at it. "Here's where we are," Donaldson said. He leaned forward and drew a circle about two feet from the *X*. "And this," he said, "is Whiskey Ridge, about a mile away. I figure the bear went to ground somewhere between here and there."

We couldn't see Whiskey Ridge from where we were sitting, but I could picture the intervening terrain in my mind—a deep valley so thickly timbered it was nearly impossible to move, with a small stream meandering through the bottom. The valley was a popular hiding place for big game—elk and deer—because the dense timber provided a nearly impenetrable haven, a safe place to hole up during the daylight hours. Whiskey Ridge was a knife-edged ribbon of rocky ground at the top of the valley's far slope.

"We'll spread out at thirty-yard intervals," Donaldson said, "and make a lot of noise so the bear will hear us coming and have plenty of time to get away." He paused to make sure we were all listening. "By the time we get to Whiskey Ridge, I imagine we'll have found the bear, or what's left of Liam O'Bannion—or both."

One of the sheriff's deputies, a lanky young man in his mid-twenties named Dennis Heffner, stroked his thin mustache nervously while he listened to Donaldson talk. When Donaldson was finished, Heffner cleared his throat self-consciously. "Warden?" he asked tentatively.

The game warden shouldered his rifle, motioned for Heffner to go on.

"What happens if we come across that bear?" the deputy asked. "What do we do then?"

Donaldson nodded as if he'd been considering that question himself. "Well, Deputy," he said, "if you come across that old bear, here's what I suggest. I suggest you stand up as tall as you can, wave your arms over your head, and holler as loud as you can. Like as not, you'll scare him off."

Heffner's Adam's apple bobbed while he imagined that prospect. His tongue darted over dry lips. "And if that doesn't work," he began, "you'll shoot him, right?"

Donaldson frowned, pursed his lips, and shot a glance in Frankie's direction to see if he was paying attention. "Nope, I won't shoot him," he said matter-of-factly. "If that doesn't work, I'll just run."

Heffner looked confused, stood first on one foot, then the other. The muscles of his jaw seemed to twitch and a deep frown line creased his young face. "Come on, Warden," he said finally. "You really think you can outrun a grizzly? They run pretty fast, don't they?"

Donaldson's face broke into a wide grin, as did Frankie Bull's. They both knew what was coming. "We don't have to outrun no bear, Deputy Heffner," the game warden beamed, breaking the tension. "We just have to outrun *you*."

It's one thing to see a grizzly behind bars at the local zoo. It's another to see one less than fifty feet away from you in dense timber and notice that he's got his fangs clamped around a human leg.

The bear was a large male almost cinnamon in color, his hump thick and muscled. The thick fur on his snout and chest was crusted with dried blood. He grunted like a pig when Frankie and I entered the small grove of willows where he'd been hiding, and at first I only saw his huge head framed between branches of the tree. Then he stood on his hind legs to get a better look at us, and my heart began to pound so loudly in my chest that I was sure the animal could hear it. He towered over us, his massive body thick as a barrel. He kept the leg in his jaws as he snuffled loudly and sniffed the slight breeze, trying to identify us. The air was spiked with his musky smell.

Frankie and I had formed the right end of the line as our search party worked its way down the near side of the valley, crossed the stream, and began working up the far side toward Whiskey Ridge. I tore my eyes from the imposing sight of the enormous bear and tried to spot another member of our group, preferably someone with a rifle, but visibility in the heavy timber was less than thirty yards. Outside of Frankie, who stood as still as a stone a few feet to my right, the forest seemed to have swallowed everyone up.

I tried to communicate with Frankie using just my eyes, and there was no way he could misinterpret my message: What the hell do we do now? His shoulders moved in an almost imperceptible shrug and he slowly reached down to unsnap the safety strap of his .44. Gently, he lifted the long-barreled weapon from the holster, took it in a two-handed shooter's grip, the bore pointed in the general direction of the bear. Cautiously, he used his thumb to pull the hammer back. It caught with a dry, metallic click.

When Frankie was ready, I drew my own weapon and thumbed the hammer back. For safety's sake, I never carry a round under the hammer, so only five of the six chambers on my .357 carried live rounds. Roughly five ounces of lead against a 600-pound brute who could cover the sparse ground between us within seconds. If he wanted me, I doubted I could fire more than twice before it was too late. I held the weapon in the best grip I could muster, but my hands were shaking badly. I had trouble catching my breath.

In the willow grove, the bear came down off his hind legs and dropped the leg from his mouth. He grunted angrily and used his chest to bull his way through the undergrowth that had hidden most of him from view. The leaves hissed against his fur and the young branches snapped as he passed. When he was out of the foliage, there was nothing between us but a scattering of downed timber and a short run of empty ground. He planted his front legs like a linebacker and huffed again, his cheeks puffing with the great gouts of air he blew from his lungs. I didn't know much about bear body language, but his intent was unmistakable. He was about to charge.

"Shoot high," Frankie whispered as the bear took a first tentative step. "Don't kill him unless you have to."

I remember the next few seconds as a series of stop-action images. The bear taking another slow-motion step toward us. The roar of Frankie's .44 as he fired two quick shots. The recoil of the .357 as it bucked in my hand once, twice, then again. The startled look on the animal's face as it tried to comprehend the source of the ungodly racket. Its look of uncertainty, then almost disgust as it stopped its forward motion, turned slowly, and ambled away from us and the willow grove toward the top of Whiskey Ridge. The almost overwhelming sense of relief as I realized that my friend and I were safe, at least for the time being.

I could still see the bear's reddish rump moving through the undergrowth like the caboose on a ponderous train when Donaldson burst through the timber to my left, a crazed look on his ruddy face, the hunting rifle at port arms. When he saw the bear, he knelt on one knee in a shooter's position, flipped the safety, and brought his scope to bear on the animal's spine. I could almost feel the tension in his finger as it began to squeeze the trigger.

"Craig, don't," I shouted.

He gave me a quizzical sideways glance but did not lower the weapon. I didn't want him to shoot the bear for a couple of reasons. First, the animal might have killed Liam O'Bannion, but it wasn't acting aggressively toward us, so there was no immediate danger. Second, he didn't have an especially clear shot, and ran some risk of simply injuring the animal. In such inhospitable terrain, the last thing I wanted to think about was a wounded and angry grizzly. "Let it go," I demanded. My voice sounded strange in my throat, raspy and coarse.

Almost reluctantly, Donaldson lowered the weapon. It wasn't that he was bloodthirsty, but he knew the man killer would have to be taken eventually and that if he didn't do it now he'd have to come back later. Still, he certainly realized the danger of taking a shot that might not bring a quick kill. He didn't relish the idea of following a wounded grizzly into the bush any more than I did. He'd wait for a better opportunity. He set the safety on the 7-mm and planted the butt of the rifle in the ground at his feet. "He have O'Bannion with him when he left?" Donaldson asked. "I couldn't see . . ."

I shook my head. "Nah," I said, pointing at the willows where we'd first spotted the animal. "Dropped a leg up there."

"Well then, that's where we'll find the rest of him, too," Donaldson said. He grunted with fatigue and stood. I noticed that he didn't shoulder the rifle but kept it in his hands. He looked through the canopy of trees at the sun, then at his watch. It was almost two in the afternoon; maybe six hours of daylight left. None of us wanted to be there after dark. "We better get it over with," he growled, looking anxiously in the direction the bear had gone, "before that mother humper decides to come back."

The remains of Liam O'Bannion were half buried in the small stand of willows, although if I hadn't known what I was looking at, I would've been hard pressed to identify the amorphous blob of flesh, hair, and bone as human.

Cautiously, I brushed some moist earth and leaves away from the mass of flesh and studied it long enough to identify what was left of O'Bannion's torso and head. His eyes were gone, as was most of the skin from the lower face. The lips were torn away and teeth were visible in the mess of gore. Half his scalp had also been ripped away, so one side of his skull was still covered with longish brown hair; the other was shiny bone with muscle and bits of gristle still attached.

As those details registered, I felt the gorge rising in my throat and the muscles of my stomach begin to constrict. I turned away quickly, pushed past Frankie Bull, who'd been standing behind me, and braced myself against the trunk of a tall willow. I closed my eyes and took deep breaths until my equilibrium returned and my stomach settled.

Before I moved to Victory, I worked in the Denver Police Department and spent most of my time as a homicide detective, so I've seen plenty of bodies in various stages of dismemberment and decay. But outside of one corpse that had been disposed of in a fifty-gallon barrel of acid, I don't think I've ever seen anything as macabre and unsettling as O'Bannion's mangled, half-eaten body. It was like a prop from a horror movie, not something that would be found in the natural world.

Donaldson and Frankie Bull responded in much the same way and turned from the corpse after a quick glance, Donaldson pale, lips tightly compressed, Frankie tight-jawed and scowling. Together, we stood facing away from the body and let the breeze cool our faces as we waited for the others to arrive, listened to the sound of birds in the valley, the rattling of the leaves on the branches. At one point, Donaldson pulled a metal flask from his fanny pack, took a long drink, and offered it to Frankie. Frankie shook his head no, but I accepted the offer. I swallowed gratefully, closed my eyes, and felt the whiskey burning all the way to my belly.

"Damn," Donaldson muttered when I'd had my fill of his bourbon. "That's something I'll be seeing in my nightmares for a while."

I grunted assent, patted my shirt pocket for a cigarette, and cursed mentally when I remembered that I was trying to quit smoking, for about the millionth time in the last three years. Instead of a cigarette, I found a piece of butterscotch hard candy and popped it into my mouth. The combination of whiskey and butterscotch made me pucker. "I wonder what he was doing out here alone?" I asked no one in particular.

Frankie began to mutter a reply, but just as he started to speak he was interrupted by the noise of Bowen and the rest of the search team crashing through the underbrush toward us. When they saw the three of us sitting around the trunk of the willow, they pulled up short, eyes wild, chests heaving.

"What the fuck is going on over here?" Bowen wheezed. There was a long rip in the right knee of his suit pants and his brown wing tips were caked with mud. His hair was so wild that it looked as if his head had exploded. "Sounded like a goddamned war."

Donaldson shrugged and pointed at Frankie and me. "Those two were doing the shooting," he explained. "Scaring off that bear."

A look of surprise crossed Bowen's long face. "You found him?" he asked. "Where?"

I hooked a finger over my shoulder. "The bear took off," I told him. "What's left of O'Bannion is right over there."

Bowen showed none of the squeamishness the rest of us had exhibited, and began a rigorous examination of the corpse immediately, poking here, probing there. From where we were sitting, the undergrowth obscured our view of the body, but Bowen's head and shoulders were clearly visible as he squatted down to work. He took a white reporter's notebook from the front pocket of his suit jacket and occasionally he'd stop poking or prodding to note something of importance. His long face was pinched in concentration, and he kept up a nearly continual patter to himself as he worked, although none of us could understand a word he said.

After a while, I decided to ignore Bowen's mumbling and relax until he put Liam O'Bannion in a body bag and we could all go home. Frankie and a few deputies had stretched out on the ground with their arms behind their heads and closed their eyes. Within minutes, Heffner and a couple others were snoring softly. I sat with my back against the trunk of a willow, pulled my own hat brim down over my eyes, and let the warm afternoon sun filtering through the foliage warm my tired bones.

The way things were going, I imagined we'd have O'Bannion ready to transport in a half hour, maybe less. After that, it would take us an hour or so to walk back to our vehicles and another thirty minutes to drive off the mountain, which would put me back in Victory around five, five-thirty.

As was my habit on most nights, I'd probably drop in for a couple of beers at the Silver Dollar Saloon (owned by Curly Ahearn), then I'd either stop for dinner at Ginny Larsen's Country Kitchen in Victory or head back out to my farmhouse and rustle up a meal for myself. I tried to remember what provisions I had in my larder— it was a while since I'd gone grocery shopping—and finally decided it would probably be best to stop at Ginny's and order something nutritious. Chicken-fried steak, cream gravy, and biscuits, perhaps. Maybe some meat loaf and mashed potatoes. Top it off with a thick slice of deep-dish apple pie and a seventy-five-cent cigar. Yes, I thought happily as my stomach began to rumble, that was the best plan, since my alternative at home would likely be a grilled-cheese sandwich and a bowl of soup.

While I was certainly sorry Liam O'Bannion had died so violently, I figured his end was probably some sort of cosmic repayment for the way he'd lived his life, and felt no guilt at contemplating my gullet while Bowen continued his grisly explorations a few feet away. Frankie and I had already done our part by helping to find O'Bannion's body. After that, our responsibilities ended. Bowen would perform the postmortem and prepare the body for burial. The sheriff's department would contact the next of kin. Donaldson and his colleagues in the Game and Fish would hunt down the rogue bear.

I wondered idly whether the mauling would have any impact on the current tourist season, but I doubted it. Every summer thousands of out-of-state travelers pass through Victory, many of them headed for camping and fishing excursions in the Snowy Range, and most of them come with the knowledge that there's a certain element of risk involved in any worthwhile outdoor adventure. Every summer we take part in search and rescue operations for tourists who get themselves lost in the mountains, and every summer a few people go home with broken bones, stitches, burns, scrapes, bruises, and the occasional perforation from a misplaced fishhook. Once in a while someone even dies, but none of those misadventures reduce the flood of visitors significantly.

I imagined the news of O'Bannion's demise would make the newspapers and have a temporary impact, might even keep a few people out of the mountains. In a week or two, however, his death would be forgotten and things would be back to normal, especially if the Game and Fish managed to kill or capture the grizzly.

As I ruminated, I was aware that the level of Bowen's muttering and consternation was gradually increasing, and I could begin to make out specific words, most of them of the four-letter variety. I left him to his examination, though, and finally heard him rustling through the brush in my direction. When I peeked out from under the brim of my hat, he was sitting beside me, shaking his head in obvious disgust.

"Bad one, huh?" I asked sympathetically.

He gave me a distracted nod of agreement, looked around at our group, and leaned toward me. I had the distinct impression that he had something to say and didn't want to be overheard. "We've got a problem, Harry," he whispered urgently.

I sat up, pushed my hat back on my head, and leaned toward him conspiratorially. My curiosity was piqued. "What kind of problem?"

Bowen licked his dry lips and nodded over his shoulder toward where O'Bannion's body was waiting to be bagged. "I think you ought to have one of these deputies hoof it on back to the vehicles and get on the horn," he said. "If they get started right away, we can have a forensics team from the sheriff's department in Laramie out here in a couple of hours, still have a little daylight to work with."

"Forensics team?" I asked skeptically. "What do you need one of those for? You gathering evidence on that bear, James? Gonna charge him with murder?"

"No, Harry," Bowen sighed, "but they're gonna want to charge *somebody*."

Despite the uneasy feeling in the pit of my stomach, I didn't know what the hell he was talking about, so I just kept quiet and waited for him to go on. Eventually, he did. "That bear didn't kill O'Bannion," he explained. "It must have come on the body after O'Bannion was already dead."

Already dead? I looked at him stupidly for a moment as the meaning of his words sank in. I realized that our long day had just gotten a lot longer. "O'Bannion was—" I began tentatively.

"Murdered, Harry," he broke in. He formed his thumb and forefinger in the shape of a pistol, put it to his temple, and pantomimed firing a shot. He smiled grimly. "Someone put a bullet through the poor bastard's skull."

2

The sun was down by the time we finished bagging Liam O'Bannion and headed off the mountain—the timber-dark hillsides bathed in the silver light of the hunter's moon hanging just above the horizon, the cool, pine-smelling night air blowing through the open windows of the Jeep. Once the sun sets in the Rockies, the temperature drops quickly and while the breeze was invigorating, I wished I'd brought a jacket along. I scrunched down in the seat and tried to pull myself into a smaller, heat-conserving package for the six-mile trip to town.

Frankie and I were leading the convoy, and in my rearview mirror I could see the headlights of the other rescue vehicles, the flashing red beacon of the ambulance bearing O'Bannion's body. In the jump seat, Frankie's angular face was outlined by the glow of the dashboard lights, his square jaw tight with worry and fatigue, the breeze through the window ruffling his long, braided hair. I flipped the radio on to KOWB—they were playing Chris Ledoux—and turned it up loud. I felt low and used-up myself, the way I always do when I see the aftermath of violent death. Maybe the music would pump some energy into my veins and do something about the sense of foreboding that was gathering about me like storm clouds over the granite peak of Bald Mountain.

We'd both had several hours to think about Liam O'Bannion's demise while the forensics team from Laramie worked the murder scene, and we both realized that Curly Ahearn, our boss, was likely to be a primary suspect. I don't think either of us believed Curly was capable of cold-blooded murder, but we knew our opinion was unlikely to hold much sway with the sheriff's department, which had jurisdiction in the case. I knew there was little I could do to protect my friend from the unpleasantness headed his way, but I wanted to do something.

I'd told the deputies at the scene about O'Bannion's recent fight with Curly—there were numerous witnesses, so there was no way it would stay secret—and figured I had less than a half hour if I wanted to speak with Curly before the sheriff showed up. I stepped on the gas as we came out of a tight switchback turn and accelerated away from the convoy. Within seconds, the forest hid them from view, and Frankie and I had the road to ourselves, speeding toward Victory.

Less than five minutes later, we crossed the city limits, passed the old white Ford with the red coffee can bolted to the roof—our unmanned traffic-control device. We park the Ford at the edge of town and it usually tricks tourists into slowing down while they travel the three-block length of Main Street. By the time they realize they've been hoodwinked, they're on their way out of town and someone else's problem.

It was a Tuesday evening, and the streets of Victory were nearly deserted. Clusters of automobiles and pickups formed small islands beneath the mercury vapor lamps in the huge parking lots at the Trails End and Gus Alzonakis's steak houses. The community's single traffic light went about its business forlornly, bathing the asphalt in a sequential red, green, and yellow glow. A young couple strolled hand in hand down Main, stopping to window-shop at Shapiro's Hardware, where the owner had set up a display of patio furniture in the front window.

There were three or four pickups and a couple of Harley-Davidsons parked in front of Curly's saloon, the Silver Dollar. I pulled into a parking space behind the motorcycles and killed the engine. The neon Budweiser sign in the window turned our faces blue as we creaked our tired bones out of the Jeep and headed through the door. Inside, a lanky cowboy and a short woman with tight pants and a silver concho belt danced to the Patsy Cline on the old Wurlitzer. A group of lumberjacks had taken two tables at the back of the bar, where they drank pitchers of beer and threw darts. The motorcycle riders, dressed in black leather and lots of chain, hunched over shots of whiskey and beer chasers at the bar, served by Curly's assistant manager, Lou McGrew, who was sporting plenty of cleavage and a new permanent in her blindingly blond hair.

When she saw us, she gave Frankie and me a happy wave and pointed to the end of the bar, where His Nibs was washing glasses, a white towel draped over his shoulder, a Colorado Rockies cap covering the crown of his bald noggin, and the remainder of his dark-brown fringe of hair combed carefully so that it fell behind his ears in waves. Dangling from the corner of his mouth was a long strand of red licorice, the vice he'd chosen to replace tobacco when he quit smoking six weeks ago. So far he'd stayed off cigarettes, but he'd gotten two cavities and gained fifteen pounds, which hung poorly on his five-foot-eleven frame. The extra weight made his cheeks look chubby and cheerful, but his jeans were so tight around his belly that it looked as if they might be cutting off the circulation below his waist.

He pulled two frosted glasses from the freezer and started drawing beers for us before we'd even gotten comfortable on our stools. While he poured, he nodded in the direction of the police scanner he keeps on the backbar. "I been tryin' to listen to the radio traffic all afternoon," he said. "This is gonna play hell with the tourist trade."

I nodded grimly and took a sip of my beer, beer so cold it almost froze my tongue. "That it might, Curly," I agreed, my heart heavy with what I was about to say. Curly, after all, was not only my employer but my best friend.

He'd hired me shortly after I quit the Denver police department, a middle-aged wreck of a man with plenty of vices, no discernible future, and enough psychological baggage to fill a Pullman car. There are times when I'm convinced that he saved my life by believing in me in that black period, a time when no one else did, least of all myself. He'd helped me make a new life in Victory to replace the one I'd left behind—and in the years since, we'd been through plenty. I hoped we would make it through what was coming next.

"You hear who we found?" I asked him, looking into the brown eyes that animate his pudgy face.

He shrugged his shoulders and began wiping a fresh glass. "Nah," he said. "I only caught bits and pieces. Heard a lot of jabber about a bear attack this afternoon. Later on, some traffic from the ambulance crew, a couple of deputies calling for forensics." He paused, set the glass on the bar. "What was that about anyway? Why'd they want forensics?" he asked.

I didn't answer, looked down at my hands. Beside me, Frankie stood up from his stool, leaned his elbows on the counter.

Curly studied us closely, reached across the bar, and put a warm hand on my shoulder. "Man, from the way you two look, it must be real bad news," he said. "Was it someone local? If it was, we'd better get hold of the family. We don't want them to hear it—"

"It was no one local," I broke in. I looked him in the face. "It was Liam O'Bannion."

Curly looked as if he'd been punched in the stomach. He stood up, his hands wrapped around the glass so tightly I thought it might break. "Oh Jesus," he whispered. "You're sure it was him?"

When I told him I was sure, Curly's face seemed to melt. He whistled through his teeth, shook his head in disbelief. "Poor Faith," he said. "This'll break her heart." He laid his bar rag on the counter, turned away, and reached for the phone on the wall. "I'd better call her before she—"

I stood up, reached across the bar, and grabbed his wrist. His face registered confusion as he eased the receiver back on the hook and turned toward us. "He was murdered, Curly," I said softly. "Bowen found a bullet hole in his head."

Curly's upper body clenched and he backed away from me, resting himself against the backbar. "This is horrible," he muttered. "What was he doing on that mountain? And who the hell would have done something like that?"

I couldn't respond. I felt like I was caught in the middle of a bad dream—the kind where there's a train coming and you can't move. There was no way I could change what was about to happen to us all, and that knowledge made me almost physically ill—the same way I imagine a heavyweight boxer feels when he steps in the ring and knows that, win or lose, he's gonna take some nasty punches.

"Come on, Harry, tell me," he said, so excited the nerves under his eyes were twitching. "Do they have any idea who—"

"If they don't have an idea now, they will shortly," I said sadly. The words seemed to stick in my throat. "Unless it turns out the dumb son of a bitch plugged himself, they're gonna think it was you."

The back room of the Silver Dollar, which doubles as Curly's office, was stacked floor to ceiling with cases of warm beer and liquor, empty metal kegs, cleaning supplies, and the assorted detritus of thirty years in business. Old beer posters featuring impossibly beautiful models dressed in string bikinis, T-shirts that barely covered their breasts, Halloween costumes, and emerald-green St. Patrick's Day attire papered the walls. In one corner were a couple of battered filing cabinets and a gunmetal-gray desk covered with receipts, bank statements, and who knows what else. Every surface in the room, with the exception of the beer cases, was coated with dust, and the place smelled of stale beer and the atomic residue of around a million cigarettes.

When Curly led us out of the bar and into his office, Frankie and I found seats on the stacked beer cases and Curly cleared a corner of the desk and sat down. His legs didn't quite reach the floor and he beat an agitated tattoo against the metal of the desk with the heels of his boots.

He listened restlessly while I told him about the discovery and condition of O'Bannion's body, Bowen's examination of the man's torso and head, and the fact that O'Bannion was apparently killed by a large-caliber bullet to the brain. Bowen had discovered powder burns on O'Bannion's right temple, which led him to conclude that the round that killed him had been fired at extremely close range. The bullet had liquefied a good part of his brain before it exited the top left side of his skull, completely shattering the parietal bone. The forensics team hadn't recovered the slug, despite looking for several hours. Still, Bowen surmised that the fatal wound had been made by a pistol, and I agreed. As devastating as the wound was, a big-bore rifle would have made a much larger hole in the man's head.

"Any idea when he died?" Curly asked when I'd finished. My friend's ruddy complexion looked gray in the fluorescent lights, and there was a sheen of perspiration on his forehead. He wiped it away with the back of his hand.

I shrugged. "Autopsy won't be done until tomorrow at least," I said. "Until then, there's no way to be certain, but Bowen thinks he was dead for at least thirty-six hours before we found him."

That news almost deflated him completely. It appeared that O'Bannion had been murdered the day he and Curly fought at the restaurant. Lots of people had heard Curly threaten to kill O'Bannion. Lots of people had seen him try. It wasn't a great leap to conclude that Curly had simply finished what he'd started.

I didn't believe it, though—not for a second. There had to be a better explanation. I leaned forward on my beer-case seat. "Let's assume he was killed the night of the fight," I said tentatively. "All we have to do is prove you couldn't have done it."

A look of hope crossed his face and he nodded energetically. "That shouldn't be too hard," he said. "I didn't see the son of a bitch again after he left the restaurant."

I thought back to the fight, after which we all went back inside, where Curly spent a half hour calming his wife and Faith, and I finished my meal. "You left the restaurant, what . . . a half hour after O'Bannion did? Around six-thirty?" I asked, seeking to confirm my own memory of events.

Curly agreed. "Yeah," he said. "Maybe a little less."

Frankie Bull pulled a small notebook from the pocket of his black leather vest and the stub of a pencil from his shirt. He opened the notebook, licked the tip of the pencil—one of his few bad habits—and got ready to take notes. "What'd you do then?" he asked.

Curly's face crinkled in concentration while he thought. "I took Faith and Madelaine home, and decided I needed a little recreational therapy," he explained. "I threw my fly rod in the car and drove out to the Little Laramie River, fished until after dark. Then I fell asleep in the front seat of the vehicle for a couple of hours. Made it home a little after midnight."

"Anybody go with you?" Frankie asked eagerly. "Anybody see you?"

"No," Curly said, shaking his head. He paused, nodded at me. "I called to see if Harry wanted to go along, but he wasn't home."

I frowned, rubbed the sides of my head with my fingers. I was getting a dull headache that would likely become a world-class banger before the night was over. I wasn't home when Curly called because I'd driven over to Laramie after Sunday dinner to take in a movie. If I'd only been around to accept his invitation to go fishing, I could have accounted for Curly's whereabouts on the night of the murder myself.

"That's gonna be a problem, isn't it, Harry?" Curly said. It wasn't really a question, but I answered it anyway.

"Maybe," I agreed. "You made the threat. You've got no alibi. Yeah, I guess it could be a problem."

Curly stood up from the desk and began to pace the small room. The soles of his sneakers made annoying squeaking noises on the tiled floor. We watched him pace for a couple of minutes and then he stopped in front of me, his hands on his hips and a measure of certainty in his voice that hadn't been there before. "Listen, you guys," he said emphatically, "I know I threatened to kill O'Bannion at the restaurant, and there might even have been a couple minutes then I actually wanted to. But I calmed down. I didn't do it."

He looked from me to Frankie, trying to read our expressions. "You believe that, don't you?" he asked. When we didn't answer right away, he asked again more forcefully. "Do you two think I did it?"

Frankie made a face that said the notion of Curly as a murderer was ridiculous and went back to scribbling in his notebook. I answered for both of us. "Of course we don't think you did it," I said. "But what we think ain't gonna mean shit to Tony Baldi, and you know it."

Curly nodded miserably at the truth in that observation. Tony Baldi—in addition to being the sheriff of Albany County—is a twenty-four-carat, gold-plated prick. I hated him for a host of personal and professional reasons, beginning with the lies he told about me when we were briefly opponents in the race for the sheriff's job almost two years earlier. It's no secret that I indulge in an occasional drink and my love life is in a state of continual chaos, but he made me out to be the biggest drunk and whoremonger west of the Arkansas. In a fit of common sense, I eventually dropped out of the race and left the job to Baldi, who's distinguished himself by becoming universally loathed in these parts. In the years since he was elected, lots of people have discovered what I knew all along: Tony Baldi is not only almost criminally inept as a lawman, he's a bully to his men, the people he arrests, and the citizens who put him in office.

Our personal enmity has only increased since he's been sheriff, largely because he's taken every opportunity to get in my face, step on my jurisdictional toes, and screw up my professional life. I imagined the mere thought of arresting my best friend for murder—whether he was guilty or not—would have Baldi nearly wetting his tent-size khakis with glee.

Curly knew that as well as I did, and the prospect of being questioned by the sheriff threatened to throw him into a state of clinical depression. He sat back down on the desk heavily and stared at his feet, biting his lower lip so hard I was afraid it would bleed. When he'd confronted the prospect of Tony Baldi for as long as he could stand it, he looked up at me. "So what do we do, Harry?" he asked.

"I'll do anything I can," I told him honestly. "But since the murder didn't take place in my jurisdiction, it's gonna be tough." The air-conditioner wasn't doing much in the back room, and the air wa hot and muggy. I pulled a handkerchief from my back pocket and mopped my forehead. There were half-moons of perspiration under my arms and my shirt was sticking to my back. I jammed the handkerchief back into my pocket and smoothed my hair with my hands. "You could start by telling me what you know about Liam O'Bannion."

Curly shrugged. "Not a hell of a lot," he said. "He and Faith met in San Francisco a little over two years ago and found out they had at least one thing in common: Faith grew up in Wyoming, and O'Bannion visited here occasionally on business." He frowned. "I guess that was enough for a start," he said bitterly. "They moved in together right after that and have been living together since."

"What kind of business dealings?" Frankie asked.

"He was working with a couple of people over in Rock Springs," Curly said. "Selling Wyoming jade to Chinese jewelry makers on the West Coast. There's apparently a market for the stuff, and O'Bannion was acting as a middleman between the Wyoming suppliers and the California buyers."

It's a little-known fact that outside of the Orient and India, certain areas of Wyoming—like the Laramie Mountains and a few others—are the only places on the planet where jade is found in significant quantities. It's not particularly difficult to find if you know what you're looking for, and although the market had been soft for over a decade, I'd heard that decent pieces could bring as much as $300 a pound. That's more than enough to maintain the interest of local rock hounds and weekend treasure hunters. Still, I didn't think there was enough demand to provide an income for someone like Liam O'Bannion. "What else was he into?" I asked.

"I don't know for sure," Curly said. "He lived pretty well, and I got the sense that jade was only one of the ventures he was involved in. He was vague about it when I asked him, but my impression was it was mostly import-export. He brought stuff over from the Orient for the Chinese community in San Francisco, sold American products in China and the Far East." He stopped, thought for a minute. "Sorry, Harry," he said finally, "but I just don't know the details. Guess I wasn't that interested."

"He have any enemies you know of?" I asked.

Curly laughed weakly. "Yeah, me," he said. "Beyond that, I don't have a clue. I'll tell you this much—I never trusted the shifty-eyed bastard. When he looked around my house, it was like he was appraising the value of the silverware. He reminded me of a hustler, Harry, one of those guys you see on television selling time shares in Florida—all kinds of fake sincerity and no soul behind the eyes."

It wasn't much to work with, but it was better than nothing. "I'll check it out," I told him. "Talk to Faith, see what she knows."

Curly's face softened. "Go easy on her, Harry," he said. "She's not a strong girl."

I told him not to worry about Faith, and we all stood up. I figured we'd go back to the bar, have a beer, and wait for Tony Baldi to show up and start throwing his weight around. I wanted to be handy when that happened, provide moral support for Curly and make sure Baldi played it by the book. Before we got to the door, though, a troubling thought made the skin on the back of my neck tingle. I turned back to my friend, a knot of anxiety growing in my belly. "You have a pistol, don't you, Curly?" I asked. "A thirty-eight?"

He blinked rapidly and the lines on his forehead deepened. "You know I do, Harry," he said incredulously. "You were with me when I bought it . . . snub-nosed Smith & Wesson with black rubber grips." He looked at me as if he didn't understand what was going on. "Why the hell do you ask?"

I waved him off and opened the door. The twangy country music coming from the jukebox would make it difficult for Lou McGrew or any of the patrons to overhear us, but nearly everyone began to stare curiously as soon as they saw us in the doorway. I leaned toward Curly. "Never mind that," I said quietly. "Where is it?"

He leaned away from me, eyes wide with surprise. "Right where it's always been," he said, pointing in the general direction of the bar. "In a locked drawer right under the bourbon shelf. If the lumberjacks who come in here get so rowdy I can't discourage them with my baseball bat, I want to—"

"Show me," I interrupted. I turned away from him and tromped toward the bar, Curly and Frankie Bull legging it behind. When we got to the bar, Frankie and I hiked ourselves onto stools while Curly went behind the bar and rummaged behind a jar of pickled eggs until he came up with a set of keys on a ring. He held them up to the light from a neon beer sign until he identified the one he wanted, then he jammed it in the lock and jiggled it until it opened.

His back was between us and the drawer, but I could see the reflection of his face in the mirror as he opened it and reached in for the weapon. The muscles of his face constricted in shock, then horror, and I knew what had happened before he turned around— hands painfully empty—and gave us the worst news I could imagine.

"It's not here, Harry," he whispered. "The damned pistol's gone."

Sheriff Tony Baldi and three of his deputies blew through the front door of the Silver Dollar five minutes later like a plague of badge-wearing pork.

Baldi hadn't been on the mountain where we discovered O'Bannion's corpse, but as soon as Bowen pronounced the death a murder, Tony's deputies got on the radio and tracked their boss down in Saratoga, where he was playing golf at Old Baldy. Once he heard that Curly had threatened O'Bannion's life in public the day he died, Tony scurried off the green, hopped into the sheriff's department Blazer, and made the drive over the mountain to Victory in record time.

When he saw Frankie and me perched on barstools talking to Curly, Baldi made a face like he'd just taken a bite of something rancid, turned to his deputies with an exaggerated "See what I have to put up with?" look, and sauntered toward us, the flesh of his massive belly jiggling like blood pudding beneath his tightly stretched uniform shirt. When he got to the bar, he left his deputies standing and took the stool next to mine, nodded dismissively at Curly and

Frankie Bull, and leaned toward me, a phony grin on his face that came short of reaching his eyes. I could smell onions on his breath, and the sickening acid tang of body odor, but I tried not to let my revulsion show. "Well, Harry Starbranch," he sneered. "I should have known I'd find you here."

I looked Baldi in the eyes, just long enough to let him know I wasn't afraid of him. "Fuck you, Tony," I said, swiveling away from him on my stool. When my back was to Baldi, I winked at Frankie and Curly, gave them a faint smile. If the deputies saw it, they didn't let on. "Public office hasn't done a thing for the sheriff's personality," I said, loud enough so everyone could hear. "But it seems to have increased his waistline." I swung back around to face Tony. "You've gained what . . . fifty, sixty pounds since you been in office?"

Tony's neck started turning red at the insult, but he didn't answer. I watched the blush as it worked its way up his cheeks, then pasted on my most earnest expression and stung him again. "Not for nothin', Tony," I said with all the fake sincerity I could muster, just one good friend concerned about another, "but you oughta think about skippin' a snack once in a while." I looked down at his stomach hanging over his belt and clucked my tongue. He kept staring at me, so angry his eyes were tearing at the corners. "If you aren't careful . . ." I said, snapping my fingers, "someday the old ticker's just gonna explode. One minute you're happy as a clam. Next minute . . . boom . . . face down in your tub of fettuccine."

I probably shouldn't have been so mean, but in my own defense, at least it was true (although Miss Manners would call me rude for pointing it out). When I first came to Victory, Tony Baldi was a fairly lean 190—which he wore well on his six-foot frame—but he'd gone downhill in the intervening years. These days, he probably goes 265, most of it in his gut and three chins. He's lost what's left of his hair except for the wings on the side that he slicks down with a quart or so of gel, and his clothes are always wrinkled, ill-fitting, and bear traces of several of his most recent meals. He's a slob, is what he is, and a mean one into the bargain. He doesn't scare me though, and one day I may just have to kick his ass.

Judging from the look on his face, however, Curly hoped I wouldn't do it right then. As a matter of fact, I got the distinct impression he wished I'd just shut up before I made matters worse.

Frankie, on the other hand, was trying valiantly to stifle a laugh. He choked most of it down, but a couple of little hmmphs leaked out through his nose. He'd enjoy watching me clean Baldi's clock, and he'd have made sure the three deputies stayed out of it. On their best day, those deputies would have been no match for Frankie Bull—a fact understood by everyone in the room.

Baldi puffed up his chest and tried to salvage a little dignity. "Thanks for the concern, asshole," he growled, looking over his shoulder at his deputies for support. "It makes my heart sing to know the drunks of the world are worried about my welfare."

In the old days, that would have been the moment I kicked him in the balls. Thankfully, I've matured. I like to savor my anger, let it grow and fester before I take it out for a walk. Delayed gratification, that's the Starbranch motto. I shrugged to let him know his barb was water off my back. "No problem, podna," I said cheerfully. "That's what friends are for."

Tony bit back another inane reply, stood up, and adjusted his gun belt. It was cutting so deeply into the flab around his waist, I'm sure it was painful. When he thought he looked appropriately officious, he rested his hand on the butt of his revolver, looked at Curly, and spoke loud enough to be heard by everyone in the bar. "Speaking of friends," he said. "I need to talk to yours." He looked me square in the eye. "In private."

I held my hands out, palms forward. "Don't worry, Tony," I said. "You can talk in front of us. No secrets here."

He ignored me, pointed a sausage-size finger at Curly, then hooked his thumb toward the back room. "I said private," Baldi snapped. "Either we do it here," he said to Curly, "or we can throw your butt in the cruiser and drive over to Laramie." He paused to let that sink in. "Your call, Ahearn, but make it quick."

Curly took the bar rag off his shoulder and used it to dry his hands, which I noticed were shaking almost imperceptibly. "Mind telling me what you want to talk about?" he asked. He spoke so softly, we had to strain to hear him over the music.

Baldi chortled, looked at Frankie and me with malevolence, then back at Curly. "I think you know what I want to talk about," he said. "I've got a murder on my hands, and it turns out the guy who got himself murdered . . . Well, you were threatening to kill him that very afternoon. I'd say that makes you the number-one suspect, pal." He paused for dramatic effect. "*That's* what I want to talk about."

"You're wasting your time, Tony," I said reasonably. "He didn't do it."

Baldi laughed. "What are you?" he asked sarcastically. "The man's mouthpiece? He can't talk for himself?"

I stood up and motioned for Frankie to follow. "I'm sure he can," I told Baldi. "But I think Officer Bull and I may listen in on the conversation just the same—make sure everything is by the book." I waited a beat. "You may have heard of those, Tony. They're something you read."

Beside me, Frankie got off his stool and stood up to his full height. He towered over everyone in the room, his expression as cold and foreboding as a granite mask. One of his hands rested on the butt of his .44 magnum, the other on the hilt of the huge Bowie knife he carries in a beaded leather sheath. He looked like someone who eats raw meat and sleeps on a mattress of iron spikes.

Baldi looked at Frankie and grimaced. "Butt out, Starbranch," he said tautly. "You've got no business sticking your nose in here. This is a county murder investigation, and if I think you need to know anything I'll damned sure—"

"It may be a county investigation, Tony," I broke in. "But look around you, podna." I picked up my blackthorn walking stick and held it in two hands. I leaned toward him, got in his face. "Right now, you're smack dab in the middle of Victory—my jurisdiction—and that makes it my business. If I say I'm gonna sit in on an investigation or an interview taking place in my jurisdiction, then I'm by God gonna sit in. And if you don't like it, Sheriff, then I'll suggest something I've suggested to you on more than one occasion: Get back in your car and get your ass out of *my* town."

Tony's Adam's apple was bouncing in his throat and his face was so red it looked as if it might catch fire. I'm not sure what mine looked like, but I think both of us realized that within seconds one of us would throw a punch and shortly thereafter Tony would start to bleed. I'm not particularly proud to report it, but that knowledge made me happier than I'd been in months, strangely liberated. Suddenly, I could hardly wait to break his fat nose—the hell with delayed gratification. Then I'd arrest him for disturbing the peace and assaulting a police officer—me. Let the courts sort it out.

Curly got between us before I got the chance. He put his hands on my shoulders and pushed me away from Baldi, gently shaking his head to let me know he didn't want a fight, his brown eyes almost pleading.

It took a few seconds for me to recognize my friend's face through the haze of anger in my field of vision, a few more to gain control of myself and the adrenaline pumping through my veins like high-octane jet fuel. Finally, the haze dissolved, the roaring of blood in my ears subsided. I took a deep breath and backed off reluctantly, my heart racing and my fists still gripping the blackthorn like a bat. My eyes and Baldi's were still locked in a savage glare.

"All right, Tony, we'll talk in private," Curly said over his shoulder, a lot more flint in his voice than had been there just minutes ago. "But it's gonna be the world's shortest conversation, because I didn't kill Liam O'Bannion." He turned back to me, smiling thinly, then leaned forward and whispered in my ear: "Even though the cocksucker deserved it."

Anthony Baldi's interrogation of Curly Ahearn may not have been the shortest conversation in the world, but it was no marathon, either. Twenty minutes after Tony and his deputies led Curly into the back room and closed the door, Baldi emerged with a scowl on his face and enormous circles of perspiration around the armpits of his shirt. He glowered at Frankie and me and stomped off toward the front door of the Silver Dollar, his deputies following like tubby goslings.

Curly trudged out on their heels, wrinkled and sweaty but looking stronger than he had when he went in. Unlike the apprehensive and jittery Curly Ahearn who had gone into the interrogation, the one who came out was sure of himself, pumped by righteous anger.

While Curly was in the back room with Baldi and the deputies, Lou McGrew had closed the Silver Dollar early, sent the bikers and lumberjacks home. Now the four of us had the place to ourselves and the mayor was in full throat, waxing ferocious about the sheriff's manner, or lack of same. "The man is without doubt the lamest dickhead I ever met," Curly announced to the group at large. "I'd like to toss his carcass in a wood chipper. Grind him up, real small. Use him to fertilize my tomato plants."

I laughed, and it felt fine. "Nah you wouldn't, Curly," I said. "You *love* those tomatoes."

Curly considered that, then nodded agreement. "You're right, Harry," he said thoughtfully. "It wouldn't be good for the plants." He pondered for a moment. "Hogs then," he said. "I'll feed him to the hogs."

While Lou checked the doors, turned off lights, and began her closing-time cleanup, Curly set us all up with fresh draft beers and bowls of pretzels and chips. Frankie—who, among other talents, is a gourmet chef—ransacked Curly's stocks of meat and vegetables until he came up with the ingredients for a decent stir-fry, which he intended to cook on the bar grill. I watched hungrily as he stropped a knife and cut paper-thin strips of steak and chicken, then sliced red and green bell peppers, onions, tomatoes, carrots, and celery, whistling the *William Tell Overture* as he worked.

By the time the food was on the grill, filling the air with a wonderful steamy aroma, Curly had finished counting the day's take and filling out a bank deposit for the morning. He pulled the cork on a bottle of Chardonnay to sip with our dinner, then hiked himself up on the stool next to mine and pulled a stick of red licorice from his shirt pocket. He studied it for several seconds before shaking his head disgustedly and throwing the candy into the trash.

"To hell with that," he said. He reached behind the bar and came up with a thin cigar, which he lit and inhaled with gusto. "You gonna be long with the grub?" he called to Frankie. "I need to be getting home."

"Five minutes," Frankie grumbled over his shoulder. "I'm not making your greasy heart-attack burgers here, Mayor. I'm creating *art*."

While we waited for the meal, Curly filled me in on everything he'd told Tony Baldi, which wasn't much. He'd told him about O'Bannion and his relationship with his daughter; told him about the fight at the steak house; told him what he'd done afterward, and that there was no one who could confirm his alibi.

"You tell him about the gun?" I asked when he'd finished.

"Nah," he said through a cloud of smoke. "He didn't ask about a gun, so I didn't mention it."

I questioned him about his apparent change of attitude during the interrogation. Curly had gone into the back room shaky and nervous but had come out sure of himself and mad as a cornered badger.

Curly knocked the ash from his cigar, jammed the cheroot into the corner of his mouth. "Baldi pissed me off," he explained simply. "I went in there worried he'd continue to think I was guilty of murder, and what that might mean in my life . . . and the more we talked, the more it became clear he's convinced I'm guilty, no matter what I have to say. He's got this preconceived notion I killed O'Bannion, and he'll arrest me for it sooner or later. He *wants* to arrest me, Harry—it'll make great newspaper copy." He sat out four glasses and began pouring our wine. "I can smell ambition on the man, and it stinks."

I certainly couldn't quibble with that. I knew Tony Baldi well enough to know he was practically drooling at the mouth over the publicity he'd get if he arrested a county mayor for murder. It would be page-one news in the *Laramie Daily Boomerang* for weeks; the wire services would pick it up, maybe even the big Denver dailies. A story like that might even knock the ultraliberal environmental tomes off the front page of the *Casper Star-Tribune*, which bills itself as Wyoming's largest newspaper.

"He didn't arrest you today, though," I said, stating the obvious.

Curly chortled. "That's because there isn't enough evidence, even for Tony Baldi," he said. "He'll be back to get me, though . . . bet on it."

That's a wager I wouldn't take, and told him so.

Curly put his wineglass to his mouth and drained it. "In that case," he said, smacking his lips, "you better find the real killer before that nitwit does something stupid, like ruin my life."

I stared morosely into the depths of my glass. Before I became a small-town cop, I was a homicide detective—a good one. And while I was a few years out of the game, I still had the talent. But I couldn't shake the nagging suspicion that I wouldn't be good enough to keep Curly out of jail, and that the whole situation would get worse before it got better. Maybe much worse.

Turns out I was right.

3

▲▲▲

I woke the next morning with the taste of a stable in my mouth and a brainpan full of lacy cobwebs. I'd neglected to set the alarm and the sun was well up, streaming through the open venetian blinds at my window. The bedroom was uncomfortably warm, so I threw the sheets off and stared at the ceiling until I summoned the strength to stumble into the kitchen and put on a pot of coffee. While it perked, I ran the shower as hot as I could stand and let it beat the top of my head until my body was functioning well enough for me to get out and dry off. Then I poured a mug of boiling black coffee and sat naked at the kitchen table to sip while I took stock of the day.

Frankie and I had left the Silver Dollar a little after midnight, then taken a quick tour of Victory to make sure it was buttoned down for the night. I made it home to the farmhouse I rent on the outskirts of town at about one, poured myself a double shot of Rebel Yell, and drank it on the front porch, counting shooting stars in the heavens above the Snowy Range. Then I crawled into bed and tossed and turned for hours—my head full of Liam O'Bannion and his bloody corpse, my general sense of foreboding growing by the hour. I agreed with Curly that Tony Baldi wanted to arrest him for the murder, and unless something popped up to clear my friend soon, there was little I could do to prevent it from happening. I felt frustrated and powerless, the way I always feel in the darkest, lonely hours of night, and my brain was a muddle of half-baked plans and theories, none of which I could follow to a conclusion. With the first false light of dawn, I finally drifted off and got a few hours of fitful rest.

Now I was feeling spent and slightly nauseous, my body running on nerves and my mind barely able to form coherent thoughts. The first half cup of coffee primed my physical and mental engines, but I knew that as the day wore on I'd only feel worse. When I was a youngster—say thirty or thirty-five—I could stay up drinking and tom-catting all night, then get up for work the next morning with spunk to spare. Not anymore. The day I turned forty, I noticed it took twice as long to rejuvenate from even medium-intensity debauchery as it once did. Lose a night's sleep, pay for the next forty-eight hours. It gets worse every year, and by the time I'm fifty I figure I'll need twenty-three hours to recover from my morning ablutions.

Through the open window I could see Edna Cook, my ancient landlady and the only ninety-year-old person I know who has more energy than your average teenager, feeding the three horses she keeps around because they're too lazy and mean to send to the glue plant. Dressed in her usual summer work outfit—denim overalls, knee-high rubber boots, work gloves, and a T-shirt—she cursed and cooed in turn to the old nags she seems to love more than the raft of children, grandchildren, and great-grandchildren who turn up from time to time in hopes of getting her to give them the farm so they can sell it. I laughed as her mangy Shetland pony stuck its wet nose down the back of her coveralls to see if Edna had any treats hidden in her britches. Edna jumped at the intrusion, unleashed a stream of invective that would make Andrew Dice Clay blush, whacked the pony's snout, and went back to feeding without missing a beat.

Edna Cook is a tough old bird, and one of my best friends. I'd lived as a tenant on Edna's farm since I first moved to Victory and became the local chief of police, paying token rent in exchange for companionship and the occasional favor. Once in a while, I stop by the feed and seed store in Victory on my way home to pick up some food for her chickens and horses. When I make the thirty-mile trip from Victory to the big city of Laramie (population 26,967) to do my laundry or grocery shopping, I occasionally swing by the video-rental emporium and rent her a copy of the latest Tom Selleck or Sylvester Stallone action movie so she can lust after her favorite actors. In addition to those practical considerations, she uses my proximity as leverage in her never-ending dispute with her money-grubbing family, who'd like to move her off the farm and into a nursing home. Her large house sits next to my smaller one, and as long as the chief of police lives next door, she reasons, they don't have to worry about her well-being. We figure we can keep them at bay with that argument, at least until Edna turns one hundred.

In return, she gives me privacy, her fierce loyalty, and the best place to live a man in my circumstances can imagine—all for $150 a month.

The year before, Frankie and I had a deadly confrontation with some white extremists that left blood (some of it mine, some Frankie's, most of it theirs) and bodies all over Victory. I'm not proud of it, but I sold my story of that adventure to the tabloids and one of those pseudo-news programs on cable for a nice pile of change. Early the past spring, I'd dipped into that nest egg, taken out a loan at the bank, and purchased twenty acres of land from Edna atop Coyote Butte, a small knoll covered by sagebrush and scrub pines about 400 yards from the farmhouse. It was there that I was building my dream home, a three-bedroom log-construction house with a huge kitchen, cathedral ceilings, two stone fireplaces, and a redwood-paneled room where I planned to put a hot tub and a sauna.

Workmen had been busy on the place all summer, and at the rate they were going I figured I could move in by fall. When the Château Starbranch was complete, I'd sit on the wraparound veranda in a heavy wool sweater, sip coffee, and feed the chipmunks and mule deer while I watched the leaves change color throughout the whole Laramie River valley. It would, I knew, be a fine place to grow old in.

When I'd started building, it had been in my mind that it would also be a perfect home for me, my ex-wife, and my three sons. At that time, Nicole and I were in the midst of one of our many mini-reconciliations and talking about getting remarried. She had even expressed a grudging willingness to give up her job as a court stenographer in Denver and move to Victory, try to find a job at the courthouse in Laramie. Before long, however, our marital schooner ran hard aground.

A few weeks after we began making plans for an October wedding, Nicole, faced with the looming prospect of the bucolic life of Victory—over a hundred miles away from decent live theater and a symphony orchestra—came down with a severe case of cold feet and gave me an ultimatum: Move back to civilization and find a job that pays more than $30,000 a year or give up any immediate hope of reuniting my family.

Much as I wanted my family back together, there was no way I could do what she demanded and still maintain a firm grip on my sanity. I'd finally come to terms with the fact that I was a small-town cop with not much of a future, if you measure success by the traditional yardsticks of money and career advancement. But I was happy, well fed, and relatively healthy. Despite Tony Baldi's assertions to the contrary, I wasn't an alcoholic. I had friends who needed me, an entire community to protect.

I planned to run out my career in Victory, grow old in view of the Snowy Range, and die a contented man. And if I had to do it alone in a three-bedroom log cabin with nothing but chipmunks, elk, mule deer, rattlesnakes, and the occasional badger for company, so be it. It was a more attractive alternative than the one I feared awaited me if I tried to ride it out as a big-city homicide detective: cirrhosis of the liver and a taste of my own service revolver. I'd seen that happen to enough of my friends who'd waited too long to escape. I wouldn't let it happen to me.

Besides, I held fast to the hope that Nicole would see things my way if I just gave her time to realize that she can't really live without me, not forever anyway. So far, I'd given her more than five years. If I had to, I could give her five more. And five more after that.

When Edna had finished feeding her horses and chickens and gone back inside her house, I choked down a couple slices of toast with peanut butter while I finished my coffee. Then I rummaged through my closet until I found a clean pair of blue jeans, a freshly laundered uniform shirt, and my new pair of Justin calfskin cowboy boots. I dressed, then strapped on my Ruger Blackhawk .357 magnum, jammed a wide-brimmed hat on my head, and stepped out into the bright morning sunshine. I inhaled deeply and smiled at the cacophony of summer scents in the air—fragrant sage, columbine, prickly poppy, bitterroot, Indian paintbrush, and a hundred others I couldn't classify. I worked up a light sweat as I took the top off the Jeep, then I climbed into the sun-warmed leather seat and turned the engine over. It caught immediately, a muscle-bound workhorse straining at the bit. I eased the stick shift into reverse, backed out of the dusty gravel driveway, and pointed the Jeep toward the blacktop highway leading to Victory. It was only a ten-minute drive from my farmhouse to Curly's place in the foothills of the Snowy Range—the first tentative step in a journey I hoped would lead me to Liam O'Bannion's killer.

Time to go to work, Starbranch, I told myself as I began to pick up speed, the Jeep's knobby tires singing on the asphalt. Time to do what you do best.

Curly Ahearn's huge ranch-style house sits on a rise overlooking a small spring-fed stream full of brook trout, its banks crowded with chokecherry, bitterbrush, thimbleberry, and wild raspberry. His two dogs—an ugly red bulldog and a German shepherd—lolled on the wooden deck with their tongues out. When I pulled up in the driveway, they looked up and gave me a few desultory wags of their tails but didn't bother coming down the stairs to say hello. If I hadn't been such a frequent visitor to the place, I knew my reception would have been a bit more spirited. If fact, they wouldn't have let me out of the vehicle without Curly's permission but would have made me wait there all day and eaten me if I ran.

I trudged up the steps, patted each of the hounds, and let myself into the kitchen without knocking. Curly and Madelaine were at the table, still dressed in their bathrobes and nursing mugs of coffee. The air smelled of the bacon they'd eaten for breakfast, and their dishes were stacked neatly at the side of the sink. There was a half-empty bottle of Jack Daniel's on the sideboard, which I imagined Curly had been drinking the night before.

The mayor looked as if he'd slept even less than I had. The thin hair on the sides of his otherwise bald head looked as if it had been combed with a Weed Eater, his skin was an unhealthy gray color, and there were droopy bags under his eyes. I could tell he was still angry, though, and controlling it through sheer force of will.

Madelaine looked a little better than her husband, but not much. A strikingly handsome woman whose black hair was shot with streaks of silver, she looked every one of her forty-eight years that morning. She wasn't wearing makeup and her cheeks and lips were pale. Her eyes were red, either from crying or lack of rest. The worry lines on her forehead were deeper than I'd ever seen them, the muscles of her jaw tighter than guitar strings.

I sat my hat on the counter and put my hands on her shoulders. She stood, and I wrapped my arms around her, pulled her to me, felt her heart beating against my chest. "Thanks for coming, Harry," she said, her husky voice cracking with emotion. "It looks like we're gonna need some help."

I didn't respond, just held her until the trembling stopped, stroking the back of her head with my rough hands. When I let her go, she gave me a peck on the cheek and a thin smile, then poured me a mug of coffee from her electric coffeemaker. It was the bottom of the pot and the thick brew tasted like hell, but I sipped it anyway, pretending it was good.

Curly nodded at the bottle of bourbon. "You want something to sweeten that with?" he asked. I imagined he'd already poured a dollop into his own coffee, but I shook my head. I figured he needed a bracer, considering what he and his family were going through, but the days when I drank before lunch are long gone. "Just as well," he mumbled, swallowing the dregs from his own mug. He grimaced, stood up, and cinched the belt of his robe. "I guess you're here to see Faith."

It wasn't a question, so I didn't answer, just waited until he went on. "She's downstairs, Harry," he said. His eyes softened and he laid his hand on my forearm. "She's taking this pretty hard. You won't—"

"I won't upset her any more than I have to," I broke in. "But I've still got to talk to her about O'Bannion, see if she can give me a place to start. Did she tell you anything?"

A pained look crossed his face and he shook his head. "I'm afraid not," he said sadly. "She's not telling me much of anything. As a matter of fact, she's not talking to me at all."

My heart went out to him then. At twenty-four, Faith Ahearn was the youngest of two children born to Curly and Madelaine while Curly was still in college at the University of Wyoming. Her older brother died at three from pneumonia, and, as a result, Curly had become almost overbearing in his protectiveness for his remaining child, smothered her so completely that Faith left home as soon as she finished high school and didn't quit running until she hit the Pacific Ocean. From lots of beery late-night conversations, I knew Curly considered their broken relationship the great tragedy of his life, even greater than the death of his infant son. There was nothing he could do to prevent the boy's death, he knew, but he could have done everything to prevent his daughter's disaffection.

He'd viewed her homecoming as a chance to start over, an opportunity to let her know that he could let go, let her live life on her own terms. He'd hoped to regain even a portion of the love he'd seen in her eyes as a child. Now that chance was slipping away, and he clearly didn't know what to do.

"She doesn't think you killed him, does she?" I asked softly. "She can't believe that."

His eyes were misting at the corners, and it looked as if he was having trouble swallowing. "I don't know what she believes," he said mournfully. "But I expect she believes the worst."

There were no lamps burning in the basement, and the weak sunlight coming through the ground-level windows did little to cut the gloom. On the walls, I could barely see the collection of Jim Bama prints Curly is so proud of, the mounted head of the six-point bull elk he took in exchange for some local nimrod's bar tab, the pool table in the corner of the room, the imposing outline of his bigscreen television. The temperature in the basement was at least ten degrees cooler than upstairs, and I savored the slight chill as I stood quietly in the doorway, waiting for my eyes to adjust to the change in light.

Faith Ahearn was curled up on the overstuffed leather couch, the bottom half of her small body wrapped in a colorful knitted afghan, her long hair falling across her face. I crossed to the table at the end of the couch and turned on a lamp, then I pushed aside some of the wadded tissues she'd been using to soak up her tears, sat down beside her, and looked at her face.

By any definition, Faith Ahearn was a beautiful young woman, the kind you see in a theater or strolling down the street and remember in your dreams for weeks afterward. A doll collector by trade, her thick hair, jet-black and lustrous, fell to the middle of her back, framing a face that might have been taken from a Botticelli painting. Her skin was creamy pale, her cheeks nearly always rosy with a natural blush. A fine spray of freckles crossed the straight line of her nose, her lips were soft and full, her eyes gray and large. She came in a small package—five one, maybe a hundred pounds sopping wet—but with a streak of spunky Irish fighting spirit that had enabled her to leave her secure home at twenty and move halfway across the continent.

In spite of her spirit, she seemed to be a poor judge of character, hooking up with a creep like O'Bannion. I wondered if the incident at the steak house was the first time he'd raised his hand to her. Considering the insignificant reason for his anger—the fact that he didn't like the way she was dressed—I doubted it. If he cuffed her for such a stupid reason in front of her father, I cringed to think of what he probably did in private. I wondered what she'd seen in him in the first place, and why she'd stayed. With her father's Celtic blood in her veins, it's a wonder she hadn't slit his miserable throat while he slept.

Nobody deserves to be murdered, I thought uncharitably, but the world was a better place without Liam O'Bannion. If he'd punched my daughter, I'd have wanted to kill him, too.

I'd met Faith Ahearn on a couple of occasions since I moved to Victory—once when she came home to visit at Christmas and I was a guest at Curly's for their traditional roast-goose dinner, once at the restaurant the day she was slapped by Liam O'Bannion. I was her father's friend, and therefore the object of some suspicion. She'd been formally polite the times we'd spoken, but I could tell she'd had no desire to take our relationship beyond superficial pleasantries.

I wasn't surprised that she didn't acknowledge me when I sat beside her on the couch, seeming to retreat even deeper inside herself. Her eyes were closed but puffy around the edges, swollen from crying. She was still dressed in a sheer peach-colored nightgown that left her arms and shoulders bare. There were goose bumps on the skin of her forearms and she shivered from the cool, belowground air. I tucked the afghan around her shoulders, then I reached out and held her small hand. She didn't draw away, but she didn't respond, either. It was as if I weren't really there, just another bit of irrelevant stimuli blocked out by the heavy veil of her grief.

"I'm sorry for your loss, Faith," I said gently. She groaned but didn't answer. I continued to hold her hand, felt it warming gradually, stared at my feet, and tried to find words that wouldn't sound hollow. I needed her help, but first I had to make a connection, pull her back from the edge. I didn't know where to start, so I told her a basic truth. "I don't know you very well," I began, "but I want you to know something about me."

She didn't answer, didn't open her eyes, but I had the feeling that at some level at least, she was listening. I went on. "I was a homicide detective for a long time . . . and I saw firsthand almost every cruel thing one human being can do to another," I said. "I saw husbands kill their wives, wives kill their husbands, mothers kill their children, crack addicts kill total strangers for the loose change in their pockets. It was a dark period of my life, Faith, and all that killing snuffed a part of me as well, the naive part that assumes people are basically good. Because of that, I don't make friends easily . . ."

I paused, watching her face for a reaction. Save for a gradual slowing of her breathing, there was none. "In fact," I continued, "outside of my immediate family there are maybe three or four people on the face of this earth I can truly claim as friends, people who have proven themselves to me, people I would trust with anything I have—even my life, the lives of my children. I trust them because I've come to know them as well as I know myself. I know their strengths. I know their weaknesses. I know they're dependable and loyal. But most of all, I know they're men and women of honor. It sounds corny, but I believe in the integrity of those few people as surely as I believe the sun will come up in the morning."

She opened one gray eye but seemed to have trouble focusing. She was breathing through her mouth, still shivering. With my free hand, I reached over to brush a strand of damp hair away from her forehead. She flinched from my touch. "Your father is one of those people, Faith," I said quietly. "I know him, I know what he's made of. He had nothing to do with Liam O'Bannion's death. He would have torn O'Bannion limb from limb at the restaurant to protect you, but he's not capable of cold-blooded murder."

She looked into my eyes, and I could feel a slight tightening of her grip. "He's your father—you know him as well as I do," I said. "You know what I'm saying is true."

She took a deep breath, held it for a long moment, and exhaled in a sigh. She closed her eyes again, her lips trembling. She nodded her head as if it hurt to agree with me. "Then who—" she said finally, her voice choking. She couldn't finish the question because the dam of her emotion broke and her small body was overcome by a wave of fresh sorrow. She sat up and put her arms around me, and we held each other without talking for a long time, until she'd cried herself out, until her breathing returned to normal. Then I eased her back down on the couch, supplied her with fresh tissues, and went into the bathroom for a glass of water.

When I came back, she'd blown her nose and wiped her eyes. She took the glass and sipped gratefully.

"Your dad didn't kill O'Bannion," I told her when she'd composed herself, "but the sheriff thinks otherwise." I let that sink in. "I've got to figure out a way to get your father out of this mess, and the only way is to find the real killer. To do that, I'm gonna need your help."

Faith bit her lower lip, then took a fresh tissue from the box and wadded it into a ball. "I don't know how I can help you," she said weakly. "I've been thinking about it all night, and besides my father, I have no idea who might have wanted him dead."

"I didn't think you did," I said. I found a pen and pulled a small notebook from my back pocket, opening it on my knee so I could take notes. "But you're the only one around here who knows anything about O'Bannion. You just tell me everything you know about him, Faith. I'll take it from there."

In the next half hour, I learned enough about the dead man to make me suspect that there were others in the world who would not exactly mourn his passing. According to Faith, who told the story in fits and starts, their first year together in San Francisco had been wonderful. O'Bannion was an attentive and romantic lover who brought flowers for no reason, lavished her with praise and long weekend drives through the wine country of northern California. Even though he was always short of money, they'd talked about marriage in those days, she said, about children, a home with a view of the Golden Gate Bridge.

"He was a very attractive man," she said. "A little dangerous. You know, the type all the women look at secretly when he walks into a restaurant? He could have had anyone he wanted, but he said he wanted me, begged me to move in with him. He had big plans for us, told me that in just a little while he'd have enough money to support us for the rest of our lives. He even talked about buying his sister a house in San Francisco so she could be close to us. She was his only family."

A year ago, she said, it all began to fall apart. Although he never discussed the specifics of his business with her, the revenue from his import-export ventures dropped off dramatically. And to make matters worse, she discovered he'd been gambling away the little they had. He owed a lot of people money, people who called the house at all hours, waited for him on the street. Several times, he came home with black eyes, bruises. He never told her how he got them, but he'd cleaned out their savings, the money in their checking account, run her charge cards up to the limit, even sold a few of her dolls without telling her about it until she noticed they were gone.

"Two weeks before he and Daddy fought at the restaurant, he told me to pack for a trip to Wyoming," she said. "He thought it would be a good chance for me to bury the hatchet with my family while he did a little business in Rock Springs. Maybe you knew he bought jade there.

"That was the plan, at least," she said. "But right before we left for the restaurant that day, he talked to someone on the phone who made him incredibly angry. After that, he told me he wouldn't be going to Rock Springs after all, and we should plan on flying back to San Francisco as soon as possible."

She wrestled with the memory of that conversation on the last day of her lover's life. "He was still angry about it when we got to the restaurant," she said. "That's probably why he hit me. Just taking it out on the person closest to him. That's all it was. He didn't mean to hurt me."

She was rationalizing, but there was nothing to gain by bludgeoning her with the truth. I needed to keep her focused and talking. "Do you know who he was working with in Rock Springs?" I asked. "Who he might have been going to see?"

Her forehead wrinkled in concentration. "Sorry, Mr. Starbranch," she said. "He never mentioned a name."

A knot of frustration was growing in my belly, and I had the feeling she was holding back, not telling me everything she knew. I couldn't press her hard, though, for fear of losing her. "Can you tell me anything about his business in Wyoming?" I asked. "Anything at all?"

She thought for a moment, then shrugged her shoulders. "Only one thing," she said tentatively. "I don't know if it's important . . ."

I nodded eagerly, waiting for her to continue. When she didn't, I prodded gently. "I'll take anything at this point, Faith," I said. "Why don't you tell me what you know, and I'll figure out if it means anything."

She thought about it for a few seconds, then went on hesitantly. "After his last trip to Rock Springs, I found a motel receipt in his suitcase," she said. "He stayed for three days at the Golden Spike Inn. Does that help?"

I knew the place she was talking about, a large motel that served the truckers and tourists coming off Interstate 80. I'd stayed there once at a law-enforcement seminar, and I remembered an Olympic-size outdoor pool, a huge restaurant, and a trendy nightclub with a jungle motif. There were plenty of hookers hanging around the well-stocked bar. Guys with folding knives on their belts slogging beers and gnawing bloody steaks. Lots of polyester on the traveling salesmen. "I don't know," I said, writing the name of the motel in my notebook. "I'll check it out."

I asked her if she'd seen O'Bannion or spoken to him after the fight at the restaurant, but she said she hadn't. By the time she and her parents got home, she said, he'd already been back, packed up his clothes, and taken off in their rented car. The next she heard of him, it was to learn of his horrible end, although it was clear from talking to her that Curly had spared her most of the gruesome details of O'Bannion's communion with the bear.

Before I left, I asked her if she had a photo of Liam. She nodded, reached under her pillow, and handed me a snapshot of the two of them taken on the beach. They were wearing bathing suits and huge grins. Kids were flying kites in the background. A few sailing boats were on the water. "Mind if I take this," I asked. "Make some copies?"

She agreed reluctantly. "Please give it back to me when you're done," she said sadly, her heart obviously breaking. "It's the only photo of him I have. . . . At least the only one where he's happy."

It was barely ten-thirty when I finished at Curly's, and I decided that if I hurried I could make the 200-mile drive to Rock Springs by late afternoon. It was there I'd start looking into O'Bannion's business connections, see if I could find out who might have wanted him dead. I only had a small lead, but it was more than I'd had a few hours before. I'd follow that faint trail and hope it led to a better one.

I drove to the farmhouse to throw some fresh clothes into my old leather doctor's bag and check in with Edna and the workmen at my new house. Then I cruised into Victory to see Frankie Bull at the office.

I found him at his desk, hunched over his latest sculpture—a bellowing buffalo cow and her calf, beset by hungry wolves on the open prairie. Frankie was a sculptor long before he became a cop, and I've always known that he's only in law enforcement to pay the bills until he starts selling enough artwork to make a decent living. Lately, his pieces have begun to catch on with the regional Western art collectors, and he's made a half-dozen semilucrative sales. I figure it won't be long before his art makes him rich and I can say I knew him when. Until that happens, I'm happy to have him around. Tell the truth, I don't even mind that he works on his art at the office when things are slack. It's a hell of a lot more productive use of downtime than the way I use most of mine—tying trout flies, reading seedy mystery novels, and stuffing my gullet with high-calorie food at Ginny Larsen's Country Kitchen. (Victory's finest restaurant, in my humble opinion. Ginny makes chicken-fried steak with cream gravy to die for.)

Frankie looked up when I came in and greeted me with the barest nod, then went back to the fine detail work he was doing on his sculpture, the etching tool virtually lost in his ham-size fist. He continued to work while I poured a cup of coffee, but when I'd gotten myself situated at my desk, he put the tool down and filled me in on Victory's goings-on over the course of the morning. There wasn't much to report. He'd written a couple of speeding tickets to tourists who didn't slow down for our unmanned traffic-control device. Both tourists threatened major lawsuits for police harassment, but both had ended up paying their $35 fines before leaving town. After that, he'd jump-started a fisherman's four-wheel drive that was stalled on Main, and acted as a referee between Howard Shapiro, who owns the local hardware store, and a customer who thought Howard ought to replace his chain saw for free, even though the customer had been running it without benefit of oil and using it to cut railroad ties—with spikes.

"That's pretty much it in the way of police business," he said, grinning as he finished the account. "Phone's been ringing off the hook, though."

I raised an eyebrow in question, sipped some of the deadly coffee.

"Reporters mostly," he explained. "One from the *Daily Boomerang* over in Laramie, a guy from the Associated Press—and Sally Sheridan from the *Casper Star-Tribune*. They all wanted to know about finding O'Bannion's body yesterday."

I'd groaned at the mention of Sally Sheridan, the local correspondent for the state's largest newspaper and a red-headed harridan of a woman who's made my life miserable since I first set foot in Victory. "Well shit," I mumbled. "Do I have to call her back?"

"Nah," Frankie said, a wide smile breaking on his brown face. "I sicced her on Tony Baldi. Told her it was his case."

"Thanks," I said gratefully. "Anybody else?"

"Your ex-wife," he said. "Wanted to remind you to drop the child support in the mail. Said to have you call her this evening if you got a chance."

I smiled at that one. I hadn't spoken to Nicole for over a week and I missed her, missed the husky sound of her voice. I'd call her that evening from the motel, maybe try to talk her into a little long-distance phone sex. Since we weren't having it in person at that particular point in our lives, I was willing to take whatever I could get.

I told Frankie about my plan to spend a day or so in Rock Springs trying to learn something about Liam O'Bannion, and he said that sounded like a fine idea. While I was gone, he'd get in touch with the coroner regarding the autopsy results and tap a few friendly contacts in the sheriff's department to see if they'd found any physical evidence of interest at the crime scene.

Before I hit the highway, though, I had one quick phone call to make, so I punched out the numbers and listened to the wires crackle until Danny King answered. King works as an investigator for the Laramie police department and does the odd favor for me in exchange for hand-tied trout flies and an occasional fishing excursion in search of lunker rainbows.

Most frequently, what I need from him is access to the National Crime Information Center, or NCIC, a national database administered by the Federal Bureau of Investigation that lists everybody who's been arrested for crimes in the twenty or so member states. The sheriff's department has access to the NCIC, and so does the Laramie P.D. Victory's too small to afford the computer equipment for a linkup, so that's what I needed before I left for Rock Springs. I wanted King to punch Liam O'Bannion's name into the computer, see what it spit back.

King answered on the third ring, his voice raspy from the two packs of unfiltered Pall Malls he smokes every day. When I identified myself, he perked up immediately. "Hey, Hollywood," he said brightly. "How they hangin'?"

"Hollywood?" I asked. "The hell you talkin' about, Danny?"

"Hollywood," he said again, as if that explained everything. "I saw the show about you on television, Harry . . . the one where you shot that neo-Nazi, or whatever the hell he was. You looked cute as a june bug."

"It was a re-creation, Danny," I said patiently. If he was going to tease me, I'd just have to suck it up and play along. Getting mad would only encourage him. "They used an actor to play me."

He laughed again. "Yeah, we *all* know that, podna . . . kind of an Ed Harris type. Not a bad resemblance, though, if you take into account that actor's pants were a couple sizes smaller than yours through the waist."

"He gets paid to look like that," I grumbled. "I don't."

"Me neither," he said cheerfully. "Guess we're all gettin' older, Harry. I could use a bit more exercise myself."

We chatted for a few minutes before I asked him to run O'Bannion's name through the NCIC, then we talked while we waited for the information to come back, made plans for a weekend fishing trip to the Snowies as soon as the snowpack finished melting, maybe the first week in July.

I heard his computer beep when it received the information he'd requested and then I listened in silence while he read what was there. When he was finished, he whistled through his teeth. "Got a hit here, Harry," he said. "A whole laundry list."

"O'Bannion's got a record." I said, stating the obvious. "What for?"

"Take your pick, podna," he said. "Arrested twice for grand theft . . . looks like he romanced old ladies, then relieved them of their most expensive jewelry. He got popped once for credit-card fraud. Three times for receiving stolen merchandise. Once for hiding a baggie full of opiated hashish in his luggage on a plane ride back from Thailand."

"He do time?" I asked.

"Not much," King said. "The grand theft and fencing charges were eventually dropped for lack of evidence, and in one case the district attorney gave up when the primary witness disappeared . . . so was the credit-card charge when he made restitution. Did a year and a half on the drug charge, though. Got out of the state pen in California in 1991."

I scribbled the information in my notebook. "Anything recent?" I asked.

"Nah," King said. "As far as the NCIC knows, he's been clean since the drug thing." He paused, and I could hear him lighting a cigarette, inhaling deeply. "I don't believe it, though—do you, Harry? He probably just got a little smarter, at least smart enough not to get caught."

"He wasn't smart enough to stay alive," I told him. "He wasn't that bright."

King was quiet until he made the connection. "That's right," he said. "O'Bannion was the guy they found on the mountain yesterday, wasn't he? It was in all the morning papers."

"One and the same," I said. "You think you could send me a copy of his fingerprints?"

He whistled through his teeth again. "No problem," he said. "But tell me this, Harry . . . what was a West Coast mutt like Liam O'Bannion doing in Victory?"

I don't think he expected an answer, so I didn't even try.

4

It's a good thing Interstate 80, the transcontinental highway that follows the route of the old Overland Trail, goes through the southernmost part of Wyoming; otherwise there'd be more people living here than there are in New Jersey.

The trip's not bad on the short hop from Laramie to Elk Mountain, which sits in the foothills of the Medicine Bow Range, but after that it's pretty much interminable stretches of arid badlands, all of it in varying shades of brown. Once you pass Rawlins, a gritty little town whose claim to fame is an oil refinery and the state prison, there aren't even any settlements for 110 miles, unless you count the wide spot in the road at Wamsutter, which sits at the far eastern edge of the Red Desert.

People from the green states aren't used to that much open space. The vast landscape makes them feel so small and insignificant that their bodies have a visceral reaction to the overwhelming emptiness, and that unpleasant reaction scares the bejesus out of them. They're so accustomed to a horizon that ends at the tree line in their backyards, they don't know how to respond when they can suddenly see for fifty miles or more, which you can do on I–80 because there is little in the entire Great Divide basin but the occasional craggy geologic formation to break the monotony—very few trees, no impressive plant life besides sage and tumbleweed; nothing but miles and miles of ramrod-straight blacktop where the majority of traffic fatalities are one-car rollovers caused by drivers who got so bored they fell asleep and never woke up.

Lots of tourists who travel west mistakenly assume that the dry country cut by I–80 is representative of the whole state. Because of that, they can't wait to see it in their rearview mirror—which is fine with most of us who live here. If the tourists knew what incredible beauty and diversity awaited them once they got off the interstate, they might want to hang around, which would just crowd the countryside and ruin the fishing.

I like the drive, though, having discovered years ago that in its own way the desert is every bit as beautiful as the mountain country Wyoming is famous for. While it looks inhospitable to everything but reptiles (of which there are plenty), the hardscrabble countryside is actually full of wildlife: pronghorn antelope, deer, a few elk, mountain lions, coyotes, birds, and one of the largest herds of free-running wild horses in the nation.

Usually I take my time crossing the desert, pack a few sandwiches and a jug of iced tea, get off the blacktop at Bitter Creek and see if I can find the muscular palomino stallion I've been watching off and on for the last few years. Not your average mustang, he looks like a full-blooded quarter horse that likely escaped one of the ranches bordering the desert before striking out on his own. These days he's got a little harem of a dozen mares and a few foals, and the sight of him running flat-out—long mane and tail flying, thick haunch muscles bunching, sharp hooves pounding the packed ground—is enough to take my breath away.

That day, though, I was in a hurry, so I popped a Charlie Daniels tape in the player and pressed the accelerator to the floor, didn't even stop at Crested Junction for my usual cache of beef jerky and root beer. I passed the city-limit sign, heading into Rock Springs just as the sun was setting over White Mountain, and was struck anew by the tremendous ugliness of the place.

Nestled in a barren gorge, Rock Springs grew up next to the Union Pacific railroad line that cut the nation in the late 1800s, and hung on because of the railroad and because of the massive amounts of coal in the area, much of it mined under the town itself (a fact that occasionally leads to someone's home sinking into an abandoned shaft). The town was settled by immigrants—miners, mostly—from almost every country in the world, and the rich cultural heritage of the Springs is the best thing it has going.

On the downside is a dark and bloody boomtown past that kicked into overdrive in 1885, when a bunch of Anglo miners slaughtered thirty Chinese workers they claimed were scabs at one of the local coal mines—a dispute that resulted in occupation by government troops until the end of the century. The most recent manifestation was during the boom years of the mid-1970s, when energy construction and mining for extractive minerals drew a new tide of immigrants, this time unemployed hard cases from the American heartland who came for the good wages and brought along a taste for liquor, drugs, whores, and brutality.

The energy boom is only a memory in Wyoming. Oil prices went through the floor, uranium mining is all but over, and other states are becoming more competitive for coal. That means things are quieter in Rock Springs these days, but you always sense the potential for violence simmering just beneath the surface. I guess it's not fair to the good people who live there, but when I visit I always feel I should be looking over my shoulder to see what's lurking in the shadows.

I wanted to start digging into Liam O'Bannion's link to the town as soon as possible, so before I checked into the Golden Spike I swung down K Street and stopped at a print shop, where I had them run off fifty copies of the photo of O'Bannion that Faith Ahearn had so reluctantly provided. Then I drove to the motel and got a room overlooking the pool. The room had little in the way of charm—a granite-hard bed with a stained and gaudy flower-patterned spread, a color television with no remote, a couple of uninspired bargain-basement prints depicting desert flora bolted to the wall, and a Gideon Bible inside the nightstand with the first fifty pages missing. At least the air-conditioning worked. I ordered a couple cans of cold Coors from room service and drank them on the balcony while I watched a family of tourists splash in the pool, then I stripped off my clothes and stood in the shower until I'd washed the trail dust away.

Around eight, I found a Chinese restaurant that served excellent oyster duck and passed O'Bannion's photo around to the staff when I finished my meal. They all looked at the photo politely, and although the manager hesitated for a few seconds, as if he might have recognized Liam, they all said they'd never seen him before. It was just a shot in the dark—if the man visited Rock Springs on business, he had to eat somewhere—so I thanked them and left my room number at the motel in case anyone had a sudden flash of memory.

I stopped at a couple other restaurants after dinner, but it was no good. Nobody recognized Liam O'Bannion.

For a while, I thought it was going to be the same story at the bar off the lobby of the Golden Spike, where I spent the next hour sitting on an uncomfortable stool smoking a cigar while I sipped club sodas and tried to chat up the bartender. A stout-looking specimen with a name tag that said he was Stan, he wore a crewcut and a long handlebar mustache that made him look as if he had wings growing from his nose. Dressed in black slacks and a black vest, he was wearing a short-sleeved white shirt that gave me a look at the tattoos on both of his arms. They were good-size tattoos, but I couldn't tell exactly what they were because they were old, blotchy, and poorly done. One might have been a tugboat, another a freight train. One of them was shaped just like the state of Idaho, with a cancerous-looking mole right where Pocatello should have been. Very attractive.

Whatever the motif he'd chosen to decorate his thick forearms, the man had a vocabulary that excluded all but one-syllable words, and he glowered at me every time he looked at my glass of club soda. As if I were taking space that should have been reserved for real men, the kind who drank shots of whiskey with beer chasers. Not that there were many of those around. Of the thirty or so tables in the dark and cavernous room, only five or six were occupied, and besides a couple of traveling salesmen involved in a serious conversation about hospital supplies, I was the only person sitting at the bar.

When I showed O'Bannion's photo to Stan, he held it in his fingers as if it might be contaminated and glanced at it for about a tenth of a second before sailing it back in my direction. He didn't care whether I caught it or not. "Never seen him," he growled before steaming off to complete some job that was vastly more important than talking to me. Polishing his church keys, perhaps.

Once, I looked down the bar to see him talking on the phone, and because he was looking in my general direction, I had the uneasy feeling he was talking about me. I dismissed that as paranoia and went back to my club sodas, trying to avoid eavesdropping on the hospital-equipment salesmen. I couldn't imagine a job that required me to drive around the country all year selling bed pans, but to listen to them talk, the profession had all the drama and intrigue of international espionage. If I had to hang around with those two for more than a day, I thought, I'd drive my Jeep off a cliff.

Around eleven, business started to pick up, if you can call three truckers, the tourist couple who had been cavorting in the pool, and two heavily made up women in high heels, miniskirts, and form-fitting halter tops a crowd. Thankfully, the truckers and the tourists—a beefy man and his road-weary wife, both of them wearing matching Hawaiian shirts and Bermuda shorts—sat at tables. The two women, whom I pegged as hookers, sat next to me at the bar. My magnetic personality, I suppose. I had a look at them while the bartender made their drinks, Stoli sea breezes with a twist of lime.

One, a saggy brunette whose thick pancake makeup didn't hide the pockmarks on her cheeks, looked to be in her early thirties. She smoked long brown cigarettes and had curving, bright-red fingernails she could have used to eviscerate customers who came up puny on her payment. She looked me over for a few seconds, then arched her thin eyebrow in an expression that said she'd already made me for a cop. After that, she broke eye contact and looked away, but

I could tell she was still watching my reflection in the backbar mirror.

Her companion, the one sitting next to me, was in her mid-twenties. About five five and slender, she had blond hair with dark roots, wary-looking brown eyes, and a tan so even it probably came from a bottle. She had nice legs encased in black hose, and she crossed them provocatively when she caught me looking, gave me a little smile that brought out her dimples. There was lipstick on her front teeth, one of which sort of overlapped the other. There was something familiar about her that made me a little uncomfortable, and then I realized what it was. Take away the makeup and the tight clothes, give her light-brown hair instead of blond, and she looked a lot like my niece Carolyn, the daughter of my ex-wife's older sister. I quit staring and looked into the depths of my club soda, but I could feel her studying me as she took a first sip of her drink.

The brunette whispered something into her ear and then hopped off her stool to plug a few quarters into the jukebox. It took her a long time to make her selections, all of them slow blues numbers you might hear in a strip joint. She stood in front of the juke, swaying her hips in time to the music for most of the first song, then she came back to the bar and climbed back on her perch. Gave me a little look to see if I'd been watching the performance, and smiled to herself when she saw that I had. I turned my head away self-consciously.

"It's real dead in here tonight, but they have live music on the weekends," the blonde said.

I looked back over and, sure enough, she was talking to me. "Pardon?" I said. I'd heard her the first time, but I was stalling a little. Guess I'm out of practice when it comes to pickup patter.

"Music, on the weekends," she repeated. Her voice was soft, and she had a slight lisp. "Country-and-western, mostly." She paused to make sure I was listening. "You like country?" she asked, as if my boots, jeans, and snap-button shirt weren't a giveaway. Personally, I figured her for a rocker. Pearl Jam, U2, that kind of thing.

"You bet," I said, smiling. "But I like Ry Cooder better, and Van Morrison best of all."

Her eyes got a little wider. "Who?" she asked.

I laughed and shook my head. "Never mind," I said. "They're not from your generation."

Our appreciation of music didn't give us much in common, but it was enough for her. She held out her hand and I noticed there were rings on every finger, even a wide silver band on her thumb. "Name's Cherry," she said. I imagined her real name was something much more mundane.

We shook. "Harry Starbranch," I said, remembering a line from a movie I'd seen recently on video. "People call me Harry Starbranch."

She took a long sip of her drink, gave me a meaningful look over the rim. "Don't think I've ever known a Harry," she said, heavy emphasis on the word *known*.

"There are lots of people who'd say you haven't missed much," I said lamely. Harry Starbranch, conversational genius, hiding his light under a barrel. My cheeks felt a bit hot, and I thought I was probably blushing.

"I bet they're wrong," she said, leaning toward me. She was inclining so far forward I was afraid her breasts would spill out the top of her low-cut halter, and then I'd really blush. She put one hand on top of mine, but I pulled my hand away. That close, I could smell her perfume. Something spicy.

I sat up straight and put my hands in my lap, looked around the room to see how much of a spectacle we were making. None, apparently. Everyone was lost in their own conversations, except the brunette, who was watching us with bemused interest, and the bartender, who was still glaring at the end of the bar. I motioned him for a refill of soda and tapped my feet nervously as he grudgingly filled a clean glass with his bar gun. He sat it in front of me on a fresh coaster and made a face as he took another seventy-five cents from my stack of change. Big spender, his look said.

The blonde wasn't quite ready to give up. She'd give it one more shot before she moved on to the salesmen and truckers. "You're not from around here, are you, Harry?" she asked. She came in here often enough and already knew the answer.

"Nope," I said. "I'm from Victory. Just over here checking out the territory."

She gave me a knowing look and licked her lips. "You looking for anything in particular?" she asked. She sounded breathy, trying for seductive. It was a blatant invitation, but I'd had enough of flirting with whores. Besides, I figured if I stayed in the bar another thirty minutes I'd have to choke that surly bartender. Either that or beat him with my blackthorn walking stick.

I reached into my pocket for one of O'Bannion's pictures and laid it on the bar between us. "As a matter of fact I am, but not what you think," I said, pointing at the photo. "I'm looking for that man there. You ever see him around?"

A look of disappointment crossed Cherry's face briefly, but she recovered quickly and took a long look at the photograph, the brunette peeking over her shoulder. At one point, I think Cherry looked at the bartender and saw something she didn't like. "No," she said finally, shaking her head. "I'm afraid I've never seen him before."

"Me either," the brunette chimed in. She took a long and dramatic drag on her cigarette, blew a noxious cloud of smoke in my direction. I waved it away, blew her a couple puffs of my cigar, enough to make her grimace.

The brunette was still wreathed in cigar smoke when I stood up and waved the bartender over, told him to give me a six-pack of Coors to go. "That's too bad," I told them. "Think it over, though. If you've got any information on that man, I'll make it worth your while. I'm in room 327."

They nodded and went back to their drinks, Cherry already taking stock of the truckers' reflections in the mirror. I held the beer under my arm and threw a ten on the bar to cover my tab. I put another picture of O'Bannion beside the ten spot and laid a twenty on top of that. "Show the photo around if you think of it," I told the sour barkeep. "There's another twenty in it for you if anything pans out."

He didn't say yes or no, just gave me a smirk and slipped the folded bill into his shirt pocket. I turned to walk away and didn't look back until I was at the door.

The chucklehead was already throwing O'Bannion's photo into the trash.

I thought about calling Nicole when I got back to the room, but it was too late. With nothing better to do, I pulled off my boots and shirt, plumped the pillows on the bed, and drank two of the beers while I watched Letterman and laid out a game plan for the next morning. I fell asleep in my boxers a little after one, the air conditioner going full blast and the comforter pulled up to my chin for warmth.

When the first knock came at the door, I was having a dream that involved full-frontal nudity and wasn't exactly anxious to wake up. The second knock was more insistent. I groaned and looked over at the luminescent numbers of the digital alarm on the nightstand. Two-fifteen. The bar downstairs had just closed.

I had a feeling who was on the other side of the door, but I tumbled out of bed and turned on the light, reached into my bag for the .357, and held the weapon at my side as I peered through the peephole. Her face was close to the peephole and the glass distorted it grotesquely, but I could still tell it was Cherry.

I told her to wait a minute while I put the revolver back into the bag and hobbled into my jeans. I caught my reflection in the mirror as I walked by. It wasn't pretty, but there was no help for that. I gave my hair a couple perfunctory pats, then I opened the door and waved her inside.

I imagine Cherry had been in that very room before, but she took a few seconds to look it over when she came in. Then she tossed her purse on the bed and sat down beside it. She kicked her right shoe off, crossed her leg, and began massaging her foot, getting comfortable like she planned to stay.

"I thought I might be seeing you again," I told her. I didn't sit beside her on the bed. Instead, I took one of the chairs beside the writing table.

She was obviously tired, not as quick to smile as she'd been earlier. "Yeah, well, it's a slow night out there," she said, as if that explained everything. She finished massaging her right foot, kicked off her left shoe, and started working on that foot. She looked at me curiously, peered over at my bag, and saw the handle of the Blackhawk sticking out. "You're a cop, right? That's what Stan and Shawna say."

"Stan and Shawna?" I asked. "That'd be the bartender and your pal?"

She nodded that I was correct. "I'm a cop all right," I agreed. Her face started to fall. "But not a local cop." She perked up again. "Like I told you earlier," I said, "I'm from Victory."

She mulled that over for a couple minutes, long enough to convince herself that I had no jurisdiction or reason to arrest her on her home ground. She pointed to the remaining beers. "May I?" she asked.

I told her to go ahead, so she took one and popped the tab, making a little face when she discovered it was warm. Then she tucked the can between her thighs. We were quiet for a while, and I realized she was staring at the small puckered scar on my left shoulder. I'd taken a bullet there the year before and it was almost healed, but still pink and tender. The exit wound in back looked much worse.

"That what I think it is?" she asked, a trace of excitement in her voice. Some girls really go for scars. Maybe she was one of them.

"Yeah, Cherry," I said, reaching for my shirt. I slipped it on and buttoned the bottom buttons. "I ran into a bad man a while back." I didn't want to talk about Kit Duerr, the white supremacist I'd killed in a shoot-out in a small cabin in the Snowy Range. I seldom want to talk about Duerr—and never with strangers—so I left it at that. But Cherry wasn't finished.

She looked at my blackthorn walking stick, propped up against the nightstand. "He do your leg?" she asked softly.

I nodded. "Smashed my knee up good," I said. "But it's better now. Just a little limp."

"And your nose?"

"Yep," I said. "He broke that, too."

She studied my face for a few seconds and then came to a conclusion. "It looks cute," she said. "Gives your face some character."

I finished buttoning my shirt, didn't bother tucking it in. "Thanks," I said. "My face always needed more character." Mr. Suave. I looked at the clock. Two-twenty. Outside, I could hear a big diesel engine warming up. One of the truckers taking off.

Cherry took another drink of her beer and fiddled with the comforter, bunching it up and smoothing it out. She waited a minute or so before she came to the real point of her visit. "That guy whose photo you were showing around?" she said, making it a question. "I may know something about him after all."

No surprise there, I thought. I didn't want to scare her off, so I tried to sound friendly. Sincere. "I sort of figured you didn't want to talk about it in the bar," I said. I waited for her to go on.

It didn't take long to name terms. "I generally get a hundred bucks an hour, Harry," she said hesitantly. "And like I said, it's been a slow night."

I doubted that she got a hundred bucks an hour, but I was interested in what she knew. I found my wallet and counted out a fifty, two twenties, a five, and five singles. I handed it to her in a jumble. She straightened the bills and recounted the money, made it disappear inside her purse. When she was comfortable again, she picked up one of O'Bannion's photos from the stack on the nightstand and looked it over. "I met him about a year ago," she said. "He stayed here for a week on business and we ended up partying." She paused. "Pretty nice guy, I guess. Good-looking. Not too kinky."

Hell of a recommendation. "Care to elaborate on that?" I asked.

Cherry gave me a scowl. "What I mean is, he didn't want anything that involved animals or rubber body suits," she said. "He seemed satisfied with the usual—you know, oral sex, screwing from behind, that kind of thing. At one point, he asked if he could tie me to the bed, but he didn't gripe when I told him no. Even gave me a twenty-dollar tip when we were finished."

"Do you know what O'Bannion was doing in Rock Springs?" I asked.

She looked up as if she hadn't understood the question. "*O'Bannion?*" she asked.

"Yeah," I said. "Liam O'Bannion."

She seemed crestfallen. "He told me his name was Holden," she said. "Bill Holden."

I would have told her William Holden was an actor who played in movies before she was born, but I didn't want to get sidetracked. "What was he doing in Rock Springs, Cherry?" I asked again.

Cherry looked guarded, her arms crossed under her breasts, trying to figure out how much information my hundred bucks was worth. "I don't know exactly," she said. "He didn't talk much business when he was with me." Her way of letting me know they'd spent most of their time in bed.

I was growing a little impatient, but I tried not to let it show. "Then just tell me what you know, Cherry. Who did he meet here? Who'd he hang around with?"

Cherry looked around the room nervously, as if there might be bugs in the ductwork. She looked down, and I could hardly hear her when she spoke. "I saw him having dinner with Sam Pantaleo in the restaurant a couple times. Two other men with them. I think they work for Sam."

I'd heard Pantaleo's name before. "Pantaleo. As in Pantaleo Trucking?" I asked, even though I knew the answer. Pantaleo Trucking is one of the biggest freight-hauling companies in the state. I saw his rigs everywhere. I'd run into them on highways as far west as California. Once, I even saw one in Boston. Over the years, I'd heard rumors that Pantaleo was involved in other businesses as well, not exactly legal. I didn't pay them much attention, though. When people look at a prosperous man, lots of them immediately assume that he didn't come by his success legitimately. I normally write these speculations off as badly concealed envy.

Cherry nodded. "That's right," she said. "Pantaleo Trucking."

At one level, the connection made sense. If O'Bannion had been dabbling in the import-export business, he'd need a way to transport his goods. Still, it didn't seem likely such a small-timer would be doing business with the big boss. I doubted that O'Bannion was shipping enough jade to warrant Pantaleo's personal attention. It takes a bunch of jade to fill a tractor-trailer.

Cherry may have read my mind. "Sam's in lots of things besides trucks," she said, a teacher explaining a difficult concept to a dim student.

"Like what?" I asked. The makeup on her face was starting to wear thin, and for the first time I noticed the red irritation around her nostrils. I thought I knew the answer, at least part of it. Had to be cocaine. Maybe speed. I wondered how much she had in her purse.

Cherry, however, wasn't about to commit. "That's all I know," she said, closing up.

I probably should have pressed harder, but my sixth sense usually tells me when it won't do any good. I had the feeling Cherry had already told me more than she'd intended. I had one more question, though—a throwaway. "Stan doesn't work for Pantaleo by any chance?" I asked.

She looked up again. Scared. "Just odd jobs," she said, her voice almost a whisper. She swallowed, licked her lips, and looked at the empty ice bucket on the dresser. "You don't suppose I could have a soda, Harry?" she asked. "A little ice?"

I told her of course and pulled on my boots. There were soda and ice machines at the end of the hall. I picked up a dollar in change from the dresser, but before I left the room I made sure I had my wallet—and the .357, tucked in the waistband of my jeans.

When I came back, Cherry was naked, lying on the bed with her back propped on a stack of pillows, her clothing folded neatly on the chair. She was a nice-looking young woman, but soft, a layer of baby fat around her middle. She had a tasteful rose tattoo high on the inside of her right thigh. Sharp tan lines, curves in all the right places. In spite of myself, I felt a familiar stirring in my groin.

It was all wrong.

I turned my back and busied myself filling a glass with ice, then poured her soda. It fizzed over the rim. "What are you doing, Cherry?" I asked. I was embarrassed and a little angry. She heard it in my voice.

"Well, we're done talking," she said defensively. Then her tone brightened. "But you've still got time on the meter," she added.

When I didn't respond, she went on, trying to talk me into it. "It's two forty-five, Harry. Too late to drive home," she said. "Why don't I just stay here with you till morning?"

I shook my head no.

"Don't worry," she said, a sarcastic edge in her voice, the real Cherry coming out. "I won't charge you extra."

I turned around, went to the chair, and picked up her clothing. Dropped it beside her on the bed. She scowled as if I was throwing her out into a blizzard and plucked the pile of clothes to her chest. "Thanks for the offer, Cherry," I said, as kindly as possible. "Maybe another time."

Harry Starbranch. Master of self-discipline.

The next morning I woke at about nine-fifteen with the smell of Cherry's perfume still on my pillow. The thick motel drapes kept the room dark, so I dozed and stretched for a half hour until I was fully awake. I called room service for a pot of coffee and then took my cup into the bathroom and let the hot shower beat on me until the caffeine started kicking in. When I was finished, I pulled on fresh clothes, lit a cigar, and sat down at the phone to make a few calls.

First I dialed Nicole's number in Denver, even though I knew she'd already left for work. None of the boys were home either, so I left a message on the machine with the number at the motel and a request that she give me a buzz that evening.

Then I called Frankie Bull at the office in Victory to find out what was going on and fill him in on what I'd learned so far about O'Bannion. Victory was quiet, he said, although things might pick up around noon. That's when Tony Baldi was driving over from Laramie to interview Curly again, and he'd asked that Curly's family make themselves available as well. Baldi had apparently checked with the state and discovered that Curly had purchased a .38 revolver in the not-too-distant past. He told Curly he wanted to have a look at the weapon when he came by. I told Frankie to keep me posted, and that I'd probably be back in Victory before long. So far, I'd had incredibly good luck, and I didn't think I'd need to stay in Rock Springs much more than another day. Two at the most. In the meantime, I told him to advise Curly to hire a lawyer. I thought he was going to need one.

When I finished with Frankie, I pulled the slim Rock Springs phone book out of the nightstand drawer and looked up the number of the police department. I identified myself to the receptionist and asked her to patch me through to the chief, a man named Al Kincaid. I'd never met him personally, but he had a decent reputation in the law-enforcement community, having made several impressive drug and homicide busts in his five-year tenure on the job. He answered on the second ring. His voice was scratchy, with a trace of southern accent—Texas, maybe Missouri. I told him who I was and what I wanted—information on Liam O'Bannion and Sam Pantaleo. He didn't sound at all surprised.

"Tell you what," Kincaid said when I'd finished. "I been out most of the night on stakeout and I'm pretty whipped. Why don't I let you buy me breakfast, and I'll tell you what I can."

We made arrangements to meet in a half hour at a little diner a few blocks from the high school. I'd recognize him when he came in, he said, because he'd be the only person in the place wearing a silver, pearl-handled .45 automatic in a shoulder holster. "At least I ought to be the only person wearing one," he said, chuckling. "Although in Rock Springs you can never be sure."

Less than an hour later, we were both digging into big plates of ham and eggs; side orders of buttered toast and home fries with chunks of onion and green pepper. The fries were thick and juicy, and we smothered them with spicy Mexican salsa that was hot enough to make your eyes water.

A man of medium height with salt-and-pepper hair cut short, leathery skin, and eyes that looked as if he'd just finished telling a good joke, Kincaid was the type of man who attacks life with relish. And yes, he was the only person in the joint wearing a pearl-handled .45.

He sawed a big hunk of ham with his knife, speared it with his fork, tossed it into his mouth, and beamed with the fantastic pleasure of it all. I thought I could grow to like Al Kincaid immensely. He chewed his meat for a while, smacked his lips, and gestured at me with the tip of his fork. "Now," he said happily. "I don't know a damned thing about this Liam O'Bannion you're so interested in, but what can I tell you about my good friend Sam Pantaleo?"

I figured he wasn't serious. "Your good friend?"

"Sure," he said, grinning. "It's a small town, we're all good friends here. I see him all the time. Football games. Restaurants. The Elks Club. You know how it is." He waited while that sank in, watching my reaction. "I won't drink with him, though," he said, stabbing a fresh hunk of ham. It was impossible to miss the disapproval in his voice. "And I sure as hell wouldn't let him buy me breakfast."

I asked Kincaid about the rumors that Pantaleo was involved in criminal activity, and he just grinned. "He makes enough money in the trucking business he shouldn't have to cross the line," he said. "But he does, all the time." He frowned. "I just can't catch him at it."

I mopped up some egg yolk with a piece of toast. "What's his scheme?" I asked.

Kincaid shrugged. "I hear the same stories everybody else does," he said. "Drugs, smuggling, prostitution—you name it. I just hear them more often." He laughed to himself. "The DEA calls me about him every six months. The FBI, the Bureau of Alcohol, Tobacco, and Firearms—they think he has mob connections. Hell, I even got a call the other day from a guy named Becker with the U.S. Fish and

Wildlife Service. He thinks Pantaleo might be trafficking illegal animal parts."

"Say what?" I asked. That one caught me off guard.

"Sounded pretty weird to me, too," he said. "Becker thinks he might be mixed up in selling elk antlers, bear gall bladders, paws, and who knows what else to the Asian market in San Francisco. Lot of money in that, you know." He looked at me thoughtfully. "I'd never heard that about Pantaleo before, but who knows? I guess it could be true."

I took out my notebook and scribbled until I had it down. "Any idea where I can find this Becker?" I asked.

Kincaid shook his head. "Last I heard he was working a few miles out of town," he said. "Out past Point of Rocks. Something about eagles. I suppose you'd have to check with the office in Casper or Cheyenne to be sure."

"How about Pantaleo?"

Kincaid took a final bite of ham and pushed his plate aside. "That one's easy," he said. "He shows up for work at the trucking company every morning at six o'clock. All you have to do is drop by. If he's feeling social, he'll give you a few minutes."

I finished my own breakfast and picked up the check. "Thanks," I said, standing. "That gives me a place to start." I shook his gnarled hand, picked up my hat, and started looking for the waitress to take the bill. I gave her a twenty, and she winked at Kincaid and sashayed off to make change.

He sat his own hat on his head and took a few steps toward the door. Before he got there, he stopped and turned around. "One more thing, Harry," he said. "A bit of advice."

I looked at him curiously.

"Pantaleo has an 'associate' name of Harvey Stone, calls himself Junior," he said. "Disfigured facial features. No neck or nose to speak of. Looks like a fire hydrant on steroids."

I nodded for him to go on.

He gave me the kind of grin skydiving instructors must give their pupils just before they shove them out of the plane on their maiden jump. "An ill-tempered sort, Junior is," he said. "If he's around, watch his ears. If they start turning red, I suggest you run like hell."

"Run?"

"You betcha, Buckwheat," he said. He laughed again, his eyes dancing with glee. "Old Junior's so mean it won't do a damn bit of good to shoot him."

5

The grounds of Pantaleo Trucking were a hive of activity when I arrived at about eleven-thirty. A geriatric security guard stationed in a shack at the entrance took down my license number and asked me who I'd come to see. When I told him, he lifted the wooden gate and pointed me toward the visitors section of the parking lot in front of a squat, two-story administration building made of the same red brick you see in schoolhouses built in the 1950s.

The windows of the building were treated so that they looked like mirrored sunglasses. You couldn't see inside, but every window gave you a reflection of the pale, rocky slopes of White Mountain in the distance, the busy highway in the middle ground, and the parking lot up close. I got out of the Jeep and waved at my image in one of the ground-floor windows. I was happy when my reflection waved back.

Beyond the administration building and taking up several acres was the warehouse complex, the place where incoming truckers dumped their loads and outgoing teamsters picked up freight for their next outbound haul. There was a twelve-foot chain-link fence topped with barbed wire separating the administration parking lot from the warehouse, where maybe fifteen big rigs—all of them sporting the Pantaleo Trucking logo—were backed up to tall bay doors that provided access to the loading docks. Crews of two or three laborers with dollies scurried in and out of the various trailers, backs straining against their heavy loads. Truckers stood in front of some of the rigs, smoking, drinking sodas, and chatting with their colleagues while they waited for the dock crews to finish. A few sat on the docks, dangling their legs off the side and soaking up the mid-day sunshine. The smell of diesel was heavy in the air, and the deep-throated rumble of all those idling engines seemed to make the asphalt beneath my feet vibrate.

I ambled up the sidewalk toward the administration building, past the flagpole with the Stars and Stripes and the Wyoming state flag, and through the wide glass double doors leading to the lobby. It was so dark inside that it took my eyes a couple of minutes to adjust to the change in light. When they did, I found myself in a large but oppressive waiting room with dreary, dirty-brown wood paneling on the walls, lots of dusty fake plants in woven basket pots, and a cou-ple of kelly-green sofas a few years past their prime. The walls were hung with framed color photos of Pantaleo trucks in various parts of the nation—zooming through the red mesa country of Arizona, crossing the George Washington Bridge in New York, a Pantaleo rig pulling a steep grade someplace with lots of blazing fall color, may-be Vermont, a close-up of a Pantaleo Kenworth with a grinning man behind the wheel I recognized as the last governor of the state.

There were plenty more, but I didn't get a chance to look at them because I was distracted by the receptionist, who asked in a cheer-ful voice who I'd come to see. Seated behind a large walnut desk with a computer and the nerve center for the company's telephone sys-tem on its top, she was maybe twenty-one and much too attractive to be spending her life in such dismal surroundings. She was decked out in the kind of gauzy red dress with bright tropical flowers they don't sell within 500 miles of Rock Springs, with a pearl necklace around her slender throat, and her thick dark-brown hair fell to her shoulders in a riot of curls. Her wide hazel eyes sparkled with cu-riosity and good humor, and her smile offset a mouthful of perfect white teeth. She was wearing a wedding band and a diamond en-gagement ring the size of a quail egg on her left hand and an im-pressive dinner ring on her right with a large stone that looked like a high-grade ruby. Beside her computer were a couple five-by-seven photos in sterling-silver frames, one of her holding a small baby and one with a good-looking dark-haired man who had his arm draped around her shoulders, both of them in party clothes, red and green Christmas decorations in the background.

I pasted on my most nonthreatening smile and told her who I was and that I'd come to see Sam Pantaleo. I'd left my revolver in the Jeep and I wasn't wearing a badge, so I hoped that maybe she'd just figure I was a friend or a business associate and point me toward his office so I could drop by unannounced. No such luck.

She looked at her appointment book and started running her lacquered fingernail down a list of names under that day's date. She was looking for Harry Starbranch, but naturally I wasn't there. She frowned when she got to the bottom of the list, looked up, and gave me the once-over. She didn't look so cheerful anymore. "You have an appointment, of course," she said, letting me know that without one I had about as much chance of making it past her desk as I had of making it into the Pentagon.

"As a matter of fact, I don't," I said. I took off my hat and held it at my waist, looking beyond her down a long hallway with office doors leading off to each side. The hallway was empty except for two people—a man wearing black jeans and a white short-sleeved shirt and tie, and a woman in a navy-blue dress and flats—who were leaning up against the wall, talking quietly while they sipped coffee from Styrofoam cups. "I just need a couple minutes of his time."

She'd heard that one before. "I guess you're here about a job," she said. She swiveled her chair away from me and reached down to pull open a deep drawer at the side of her desk, rifled a file folder, and came up with a form. "I've got applications here," she said over her shoulder. She nodded at one of the couches. "You can sit over there and fill it out."

I shook my head and chuckled. "I'm not here about a job," I said. "But I do need to see Sam Pantaleo."

The young woman held the form toward me for a couple of seconds, as if I might have been joking. When I didn't take it, she jammed it back into the folder and gave the drawer a slam. "Then might I ask what you need to see him about?" she asked, irritated. A little pout now, not her most enchanting expression.

I shrugged. "A personal matter," I said. Gave her another smile. "Only take a second."

She didn't like it, but she waved me toward the couches. "You can wait there," she said. "I'll see if he's in."

When I was settled, she picked up the phone and punched in the three-digit extension of someone in the building, glancing in my direction every few seconds to make sure I stayed put. I couldn't hear much of the conversation because she spoke so quietly, but a couple of times I distinctly heard the word *daddy*. Sam Pantaleo's daughter. It explained a few things, like her expensive taste in clothes and jewelry. I wondered if her husband worked for Sam, too—part of the family business.

When she got off the phone, she gave a Who knows? wiggle of her eyebrows. "He says make yourself comfortable," she said. A little disappointed I hadn't been asked to leave. "He'll be with you in a while."

Her switchboard got busy then, so I watched her talk on the phone for ten minutes, then I spent another twenty leafing through the stack of year-old *Newsweek* and *Sports Illustrated* magazines someone had thoughtfully left on the table beside the couch. I think there must be a company that does nothing but provide ancient periodicals for waiting rooms, because I'd seen those same magazines the last time I visited my dentist. I'm good at waiting, though, especially if I've got a swimsuit edition to ogle, so that's what I did until a quarter after twelve, when I finally heard the sound of heels on the tiled floor of the hallway.

The man who introduced himself as Sam Pantaleo seconds later was the kind who'd studied me well enough while he walked the few yards across the waiting room to have formed a first impression so strong it would probably last a lifetime. I don't think he liked what he saw. As he drew closer, he reached out a beefy hand, but his sleepy eyes were narrow and cold and the smile on his face so brittle I thought it might break.

In his late fifties, Pantaleo was maybe five ten and portly. He had a belly that came from forty years of high-calorie food, but you could sense the power lingering beneath the fat. He had the kind of hair most middle-aged men would kill for—still full, wavy, and mostly black, shot through with gray on top, with wide streaks of silver on the sides, like wings on the sides of the Minnesota Vikings' helmets.

I stood up, shifted my blackthorn walking stick to my left hand, and reached out to shake. Pantaleo took my hand and squeezed, hard. I felt my bones shifting around in there, and pain shot up to my elbow. Frankie taught me a karate move to use in situations like that—one where you grind the knuckle of the middle finger on your free hand into the back of your opponent's hand until he lets go— but I resisted the urge. I've got a fairly high tolerance for pain, so I sucked it up and grinned like a morphine-crazed idiot. Didn't fool Pantaleo, though. He knew he'd hurt me. I could see in his eyes he'd meant to.

The narrow smile on his face when he finally let go assured me that there was plenty of pain where that came from. But before I could utter the curse that was starting to build in my throat and whap him in the *cojones* with the business end of my blackthorn, he'd turned around and hooked a finger over his shoulder for me to follow. I clenched my throbbing hand and did what he wanted. When we passed his daughter, the smug look on her face did nothing to improve my mood. My dad can whup your sorry butt, it said.

I followed Pantaleo down the long, sterile hallway until we came to the end. He turned right and opened a heavy maple door with a brass plaque that said SAM PANTALEO, PRESIDENT, and held it open so I could follow him in.

While the parts of the administration building I'd seen so far looked as if they'd been decorated by the same people who decorate most mobile homes, Pantaleo's office would have done a bank president proud. There wasn't a bit of the heavy paneling that festooned the rest of the building. The walls were clean and white; all of the furnishings were done in matte black. Pantaleo's glass-topped desk was big enough to serve as the deck of an aircraft carrier, and all his office bric-a-brac was brass and crystal. The overstuffed couch was made of the same soft black leather as his high-backed chair and the two wing-backs on either side of the desk. There were two Art Deco glass coffee tables, and in one corner of the room was a three-foot free-form blown-glass sculpture of nothing I recognized. Might have been a ballerina. Maybe an oil derrick. The only splashes of color were an original Conrad Schwering oil painting of the Tetons on one wall and a twenty-four-inch apple-green jade dragon on a crystal stand atop a black bookshelf. The dragon was obviously Oriental, and not to my particular taste. To me, the thing looked like it belonged in a comic book. Still, it was probably worth more than I take home in a year.

On the side of his desk were two photos in expensive black frames. One showed Pantaleo with his wife and family—a handsome gray-haired woman I took to be his wife and three young women I assumed were his daughters. The receptionist was the middle child. The other photo showed a much younger Sam Pantaleo with a bunch of heavily armed young men in what looked like Special Forces uniforms. The backdrop was an airfield in the tropics. Vietnam?

I was glad to see that Pantaleo was alone in his office. At least I wouldn't have to worry about Junior Stone and his red ears.

Pantaleo motioned me to one of the wing-backs, and I obliged him, leaned back, and—just to see how far his courtesy extended—took one of the thin cigars from my shirt pocket. I put it into my mouth, licked it a couple of times, and looked at him expectantly. There wasn't an ashtray in the room, and he didn't invite me to light up, just gave me a look that said he considered cigars on a par with picking your nose in public, and pretended to ignore my cold stogie. I talked around it.

"Thanks for taking time to see me," I said. I waved my hand in an expansive gesture toward his window, through which he had a view of the warehouse. "It looks like you're a busy man."

Pantaleo grunted something that might have been agreement, then shot his cuff and made a big deal of glancing at the gold Rolex on his wrist. Let me know I was keeping him from lunch. "What can I do for you, Mr. Starbranch?" he asked, all business. He had the dry, scratchy voice of a longtime smoker, and I wondered how long it had been since he quit. "My daughter says you wouldn't tell her what you need to talk to me about."

I pulled my shield out of my back pocket and held it open for him to see. I doubted I was the first cop who'd come to visit him, but his eyebrows wrinkled in question when he saw where I was from. "Victory?" he said. He cracked a smile that didn't make it to his eyes. "I swear to God, I paid that parking ticket, Mr. Starbranch. I know I did," he said. He wasn't even trying to mask the condescension in his voice—the big-shot trucking-company executive having a little fun with Andy of Mayberry. Next, he'd ask to see the single bullet in my shirt pocket.

I decided to nip that bullshit in the bud. I took one of O'Bannion's photos from my shirt pocket and laid it on his desk with a slap. "I came to see you about this man," I said. "Fellow by the name of Liam O'Bannion."

He looked at the photo for a second, but his face was a mask—no reaction whatever. I figured he'd make a hell of a poker player. Pantaleo pushed the picture back toward me, then leaned forward and made a little tent of his thick fingers. "You looking for him?" he asked.

I shook my head. "No, I know exactly where he is," I said. He'd succeeded in making me angry, but I tried not to let it show. "Right now, his body is in the Albany County morgue."

Pantaleo clucked his tongue sympathetically. "I'm sorry to hear that," he said, "but I'm afraid it doesn't mean much to me. To my knowledge, I never met the man."

I picked up the photo and returned it to my pocket, looked into his eyes. They looked like black marbles. "I'm looking into his death," I said. "I was told you were business associates."

"Business associates?" he asked. "Who told you that?"

"Not important," I said. "But O'Bannion shipped jade out of Wyoming to San Francisco, and I think he probably used your trucks. I was just hoping you could tell me a little more about him."

Pantaleo gave me a look that said I was wasting his time. "I ship merchandise for thousands of people," he said. "That doesn't mean I know them all personally—and it doesn't mean we're 'business associates,' except in the strictest interpretation of the term. If he used my trucking company to ship his merchandise, he wasn't one of my biggest customers. Believe me, Mr. Starbranch, I would have paid more attention to him if he was anything but small potatoes." He caught himself. "Small potatoes . . . as a customer, of course. I'm sure he was a fine gentleman."

He stood up from his chair and rested his knuckles on the top of his desk, letting me know the interview was over. "Sorry I can't be more help," he said. "If you think it would be useful, though, I can call down to accounting and see if we have any paperwork on this O'Bannion. Just take a couple minutes."

If Cherry had been right when she said she'd seen O'Bannion and Pantaleo together at the Golden Spike, Pantaleo was lying. I believed Cherry, but I couldn't prove it. Yet.

I leaned back in the chair and crossed my legs. Settling in. "He was murdered, Mr. Pantaleo," I said. "He might have been small potatoes, but someone put a bullet through his brain." I let that statement hang in the air.

Pantaleo rolled his eyes, like he couldn't believe what he was hearing. "Is that why you're here?" he asked incredulously. "You think I had something to do with it?"

I shrugged my shoulders. "I'm going to find out who did," I said simply. It was a challenge, and a warning.

The change in Pantaleo's demeanor was instantaneous. A dark shadow seemed to pass over his face, his jaw tightened, and his small eyes narrowed. He looked at me the way a rattlesnake looks at a mouse. When he spoke, there was menace in his voice, and I had the feeling it was hard for him to keep it in check. "I certainly hope you do," Pantaleo said. "But I'd be very careful who you drag into this, and what kind of accusations you throw around. Like I told you, I never met the man."

He came around the desk and walked to the door of his office, opened it, and held it open for me. "Now, if you'll excuse me, I'm late for a luncheon engagement," he said, back in control now, but barely. "If you want to wait in the lobby for a few minutes, I'll have my people check Mr. O'Bannion's shipping records and give you a copy."

"Fine," I said. I stood and walked through the door into the long hallway, the copper tip of my blackthorn walking stick clacking on the tile. When I'd taken a couple of steps, I turned back. "I imagine I'll be talking to you again," I told him.

Pantaleo didn't miss a beat. "I'll look forward to it, Mr. Starbranch," he said. He gave me another alligator smile. *You* shouldn't look forward to it at all, that smile said. "But next time, you need to have an appointment"—his voice dropped an octave—"or a warrant."

Then he closed the door in my face.

When I got back to the motel, I called Frankie to see if Bowen had released O'Bannion's autopsy report yet. He hadn't, but Frankie had one tidbit of interesting news. He had talked to Larry Rawls, one of the few deputies in the sheriff's department I was still friendly with, and learned that Baldi had sent his evidence technicians back to the murder scene that morning. Somehow, they'd managed to come up with the bullet that killed O'Bannion.

"Apparently, Baldi was real proud of himself," Frankie said. "He's having ballistics tests run on it now."

"He *should* be proud of himself," I said grumpily. "It's the first bit of real police work he's done since he took office." I picked the phone up in my hand and carried it over to the air-conditioning unit on the far wall, kicked the AC on, and peered through the drapes of the room. A couple of teenage girls in string bikinis were baking themselves on plastic lounge chairs at the side of the pool. Their nut-brown skin glistened from suntan oil and a fine sheen of perspiration. "Is Baldi interviewing Curly now?" I asked.

"Far as I know," Frankie said. "I haven't checked in with the mayor for a while. I guess I ought to do that pretty soon."

"Do me a favor," I said. "When you talk to Curly, see if you can get him to go to the phone company as soon as he can and find out if any long-distance calls were made from his house while O'Bannion was staying there. If there were, tell him to get me a copy of the numbers where calls were placed."

I listened to the long-distance connection hum while Frankie wrote down my request. "You onto something, Harry?" he asked when he finished.

"I don't know yet," I said. "Maybe."

When I finished talking to Frankie, I called the U.S. Fish and Wildlife Service's main office in Cheyenne, and finally worked my way up through the chain of command to a supervisor who gave me the cellular phone number of Leo Becker, the investigator who'd been interested in Pantaleo. I dialed the number and listened to it ring for a long time. When Becker finally answered, the connection was weak, his voice fading in and out.

I told him who I was and where I'd heard his name, asked him why he thought Pantaleo might be involved in trafficking parts from illegally killed animals. Becker didn't feel comfortable talking on the cell phone, "because you never know who's listening in," but he gave me directions to his camp near Point of Rocks and said I could come out that evening and he'd be glad to fill me in.

I drew myself a map from his directions, and made arrangements to meet him around sundown.

"Come at seven and I'll throw a steak on the grill for you," he said. "You're a meat eater, aren't you, Starbranch?"

"As long as it isn't moving," I laughed, ringing off.

I spent the next few hours driving around to the five rock shops in the county—two of them in Rock Springs and three in the outlying areas—to pass O'Bannion's photo around and see if I could find out where he'd been buying his jade. Turned out Liam O'Bannion was an equal-opportunity customer, and the owners of all five businesses had sold him rough jade over the last few years.

With their information, I drew a pretty good picture of O'Bannion's jade business in Wyoming, and it was no big surprise. While the owners of the rock shops had sold Liam high-quality jade in a variety of quantities, none of them had sold him more than $5,000 worth in a three-year period. He was a model customer, they said, and he was always interested in good material for the artisans he supplied on the West Coast. He seldom haggled over price, and he always paid cash.

While most of the men admitted a certain discomfort in his presence—nothing they could put their fingers on, just a vague sense of unease—the women all remarked on his dark good looks and the way he had of looking at them that made them feel he was flirting, just a little bit. One even called him "dangerous." The one thing they all agreed on was the mystery of how he managed to stay in business. Because he paid top dollar, they figured his profit margin couldn't have been higher than 10 percent, tops. Adding up all the jade he'd purchased in the county, that meant he'd made around $2,000 profit, give or take a couple hundred.

At that rate, he lost money—lots of it—since round-trip plane tickets from San Francisco to Rock Springs go for around $500 a pop, and I doubted that he lived on the budget plan once he got here.

To me, O'Bannion's jade business smelled like a cover, and I was anxious to find out what really kept him coming back to Wyoming.

At my last stop—at a place called Mike and Marge's Rock Haven on Dewar Drive—the couple offered me a cold drink after telling me about O'Bannion, and I accepted. I stood around on the sidewalk while Mike locked the front door of the storefront, flipping the sign on the door from OPEN to CLOSED. Then I followed them around to the back of the business and across the gravel alleyway to the lot where their mobile home was parked under a couple of mature poplars.

Mike and I sat at a picnic table in the shade and smoked cigars until Marge came back outside with a pitcher of fresh lemonade and tall glasses filled with crushed ice. Mike and Marge had taken over the rock shop six years earlier, when Mike retired from the Union Pacific Railroad, and I got the impression they were glad to have company. I sipped the tart lemonade and listened politely while Marge told me about her particular area of expertise—fossils—and Mike rambled on about the exciting and dangerous world of rock sales. The year before, he told me, he'd finally discovered what a 500-pound boulder in the corner of the shop was, and it scared him silly.

"The damned thing was solid uranium," he said, clouds of smoke from his cigar puffing around his head like a steam engine on a winter day. "Sitting over there giving out death rays and who knows what else. Wonder we haven't come down with cancer."

Considering the cheap black cigars he smoked, I doubted it would be long, but I didn't mention that. Just nodded my head sagely and listened to them babble. I'd finished my second glass of lemonade before I finally got them back to the topic I was most interested in.

"What can you tell me about O'Bannion?" I asked.

Mike took a thoughtful puff. "Maybe you should ask my wife," he said, nodding at Marge. "She liked him a lot better than I did. Thought he was cute."

Marge snorted derision. They'd had this talk before.

"Any particular reason you disliked him?"

Mike laughed. "Well, I tend to dislike people from California on general principle," he said, "but with him it was more than that. O'Bannion was the kind of guy who was impressed with himself and wanted you to be impressed with him, too. You know the type— handsome guy who carries a big roll of money, but you suspect that beneath the couple of hundreds on top there's nothing but ones?"

"You didn't trust him?"

"Not much," he said. "For one thing, he usually had a gun in his waistband, and what kind of rock buyer needs a gun?"

I shrugged my shoulders.

"For another," he continued, "I'm pretty sure he stole stuff from the store a few times when I turned my back on him. Small stuff, stuff he could have paid for easy, worth less than a buck—no reason to take it but bad character. I never said nothin' because he paid good for the jade, but I always felt a lot better after he left."

I digested that information for a minute. "When O'Bannion came to buy jade," I asked, "did he come alone?"

"Yeah, he did," Mike said. "Different rental car every time."

"Except for once," Marge said. There was a twinkle in her eye, as if she enjoyed knowing more than her husband did. "He came once when you were off with those rock-hound pals of yours from Green River. Bought a nice piece of jade and a bunch of Apache teardrops, said he was gonna have 'em made into a necklace. Before he left, I even talked him into a couple of—"

"He was with someone?" I broke in. "Do you know who it was?"

"Nah," she said, a little miffed that I hadn't let her finish her story. "The guy sat out in O'Bannion's car the whole time. I only got a quick look at him as they were leaving. But there was one thing . . ."

She seemed to lose her train of thought and her eyes got dreamy, as if she was reliving the whole experience. After a few seconds, she shuddered perceptibly.

"What was it, Marge?" I asked.

She leaned forward conspiratorially, laid her wizened hand on my arm, her arthritic knuckles as big as walnuts. "It was his face," she said, her eyes widening with the memory.

"What about it?"

"It was real ugly, Mr. Starbranch . . . ," Marge said. "Looked like somebody smacked him upside the head with a sack of bricks."

I didn't have to think hard for a name to match that description, since I'd heard it just that morning at breakfast.

The man Al Kincaid had warned me about. Sam Pantaleo's "associate," Junior Stone.

It was nearly six o'clock when I turned off I–80 at Point of Rocks and headed north toward Leo Becker's camp.

In the old days, Point of Rocks was a stop for the stagecoaches coming down the rocky South Pass stage route, or heading in the opposite direction toward the gold fields in the mountains near Atlantic and South Pass Cities. These days, it's mostly a watering hole for the hundreds of workers from the hulking Jim Bridger power plant about five miles north of the main highway.

With the sun sinking behind Steamboat Mountain to the northwest, I followed the secondary blacktop road past the power plant— its tall stacks belching great clouds of steam into the turquoise sky—until I came to the rutted trail at Deadman Creek Becker had described.

I turned off the blacktop and stopped to drop the Jeep into four-wheel drive, then I angled north at less than ten miles an hour. The air was full of alkali dust that billowed out from under the Jeep's big tires and followed me in a gritty cloud. I thought about stopping again to put the top on, but it wasn't far, so I pulled a bandanna over my mouth and nose, squinted through the grime, and tried to keep from high-centering on the ruts.

Now and then the wind shifted long enough to blow the dust cloud in a different direction, and in those brief moments I savored the spectacular view. To the west the sun was just below Spring Butte and Hatcher Mesa, turning the foothills into a palette of greens, browns, and purples. To the east, soft early-evening light fell across the Great Divide Basin, its floor parched and cracked, speckled with stands of sage, scrub cedar, and rabbitbrush. Overhead, a couple of hawks circled on the warm air currents, their sharp eyes peeled for a jackrabbit or a mouse skittering along the edges of a ravine or the sandy bottom of a dry streambed.

As I crossed a small draw, a three-point mule-deer buck popped up from his bed and hopped over the ridgeline, his sharp hooves clacking on the shale. Small bunches of Pronghorn antelope stood open and exposed on the flats. Their large black eyes peered at me suspiciously as I approached, and then the animals streaked away at full tilt, their white rumps bolls of raw cotton against the brown desert landscape.

It was seven miles to Becker's camp on the Continental Divide, and it took me the better part of an hour to get there. I thought it would take a good deal longer on the way back to Point of Rocks, and I'd have to be careful. I'd eased over a hundred half-submerged boulders in the chewed-up trail that could easily destroy my oil pan. If that happened, I'd be in for a long walk in the dark.

Becker's canvas wall tent was pitched at the foot of a tall mesa, next to a pool of water from a natural spring. His four-wheel-drive Dodge pickup was tucked into a little arbor beneath some lodge-pole pines, and I found him sitting at a folding metal table between the tent and the pool. As promised, he already had the charcoal going in his hibachi, and was sipping a cold beer. I stopped the Jeep and hopped out, took a deep breath of the cool, piney air drifting down the slopes of the divide, air tanged with sage and the wonderful aroma of grilling meat.

A rawboned man whose long legs were bowed from spending lots of time on horseback, Becker was maybe fifty, with thinning hair and a pleasantly trail-worn face tanned the color of a new saddle. He was dressed casually in worn hiking boots, jeans, and a gray sweatshirt with the sleeves cut off at the elbows. I'd noticed a scoped bolt-action .30-06 racked in the Dodge, and he was wearing a 9-mm Beretta in a leather belt holster on his waist. When he saw me, his mouth curved in a wide smile and he waved me over, indicating an empty lawn chair beside the grill.

We made our introductions, and he pulled a beer for me from the ice in his cooler. I sipped it and we made small talk while Becker tended our steaks. I told him about the exciting life of a policeman in a town of 650 souls, and a little bit about the murder case that had brought me to Rock Springs. He reciprocated by telling me about his current project for the U.S. Fish and Wildlife Service, a bald-eagle investigation he'd been working on and off for most of the year.

Bald eagles have made an incredible comeback in the West, after going through a rough stretch in the '70s. In those dark years, some ranchers—convinced the eagles were killing off their lambs and calves—paid bounty hunters in helicopters to blow our national birds out of the sky at such an alarming rate that the federal wildlife people were worried the species might be rubbed out altogether. The feds put enough of the bounty hunters in jail to discourage the worst of the slaughter, and the birds have responded by procreating themselves off the endangered list.

These days, there are lots of bald eagles in Wyoming, but they're still a tempting target for gunners anxious to pluck their distinctive and valuable wing and tail feathers for use in hat decorations and the like. Native Americans, who use the feathers in religious cere-monies, can harvest a few of the birds, but for everyone else it's a crime.

Which explained why Becker was camped on Deadman Creek. There were several aeries in the rough country leading to the Con-tinental Divide, and he believed poachers—maybe shift workers from the power plant—were stalking the great raptors. He'd made two arrests so far that summer, but he suspected there was still one active group of poachers working the area. In the last week, he'd found three eagle carcasses—all of the birds killed by gunshot, all stripped of feathers.

"I'll get the bastards," he vowed as he pulled the slabs of meat off the coals and slapped them down on metal plates. "And you know how?" he asked, his words full of flinty determination. "I'll get them because I've got patience. All the patience in the world."

The steaks were blood-rare and tender, and we ate them while night settled on the Great Divide Basin. Then we washed our dishes in a metal wash basin by the light of a propane lantern, dried them with paper towels, and leaned back in our lawn chairs as we sipped fresh coffee and lit cigars.

We smoked in silence for a while before Becker broached the rea-son for my visit. "I've enjoyed the company, Harry, but I know you came out here to ask about Sam Pantaleo." He chuckled lightly.

"Hope you're not mad when I tell you I kinda brought you here on a wild-goose chase."

My eyes narrowed and I bit down on the stogie. "Care to explain that, Leo?" I asked. "That was a hell of a long drive for a hunk of steak."

"But you'll have to admit it was an excellent steak," he said, laughing. It was hard to be annoyed at the man, but I did my best. I mumbled an unintelligible answer and scowled until he went on. "Fact is, I just called Al Kincaid for information about Pantaleo because another investigator requested it, fella by the name of Andy Patti," Becker said. "He's stuck in the backcountry on the border of the Wind River Reservation and thought Kincaid might be more receptive to me because we know each other."

The law-enforcement community in Wyoming is a small one, but I'd never heard of Andy Patti. "Do you know why he was interested in Pantaleo?" I asked.

"I know a little," Becker said. He puffed on his cigar until the tip glowed cherry red and his head was wreathed in a cloud of smoke. "Pantaleo's was one of a couple names that cropped up in regard to some bear-poaching activities Patti's been investigating for the last six months." He looked at me thoughtfully. "You familiar with the trade in illegal bear parts, Harry?" he asked.

"I know the basics," I said. "Don't some Asian cultures use bear bladders for aphrodisiacs?"

Becker nodded. "That's part of it," he said. "But not all." He leaned forward and clasped his rough hands on his knees. "Here's how it works. Say you're a poacher, and say you've just shot a nice black bear and want to make some money. You cut off the bear's paws, slice out his gall bladder, and put them on ice. If you know the right person, he might pay you a hundred bucks and take those bear parts off your hands."

While the thought of slaughtering an animal for its paws and gall bladder has always enraged me on a personal level, it didn't sound like the sort of thing Sam Pantaleo would be interested in. Not only was it too messy, and too risky, but there wasn't enough money involved to get the attention of a man like Pantaleo. I interrupted Becker's story to express my doubts.

"Well, you're probably right, a hundred bucks isn't enough to prime Pantaleo's pump," he said. Becker's eyes began to gleam in the lamplight. "But what if I told you the right middleman could turn around and sell that same gall bladder in Japan, or Korea, or even to the Asian community in San Francisco—where the gall will be collected for medicine and the bladders dried and sold by the ounce to treat everything from arthritis and asthma to some old geezer with a young wife and a limp johnson—for *ten thousand dollars*? We talking about enough money to interest a guy like Pantaleo then? What if that middleman had twenty gall bladders? What if he had fifty?"

I blew air through my teeth. "That's serious money," I said.

Becker smiled around the stump of his cigar. "Damned right it is," he said. "And it's easy."

"Easy?" I asked skeptically.

"Sure," he said. "It's a snap to move illegal bear parts around the country, especially if you own a trucking company. All you need is Asians interested in buying the bear parts once you get to the delivery point."

I mulled that over. "What happens if you—"

"Get caught?" he broke in. He held his thumb and forefinger about an inch apart. "Not much," he said. "Even if you get caught and they throw the book at you, you're looking at a Lacy Act violation that could get you five years in the slam, max," he said. "Maybe a $250,000 fine, although it'd be rare to get both. Usually the lawyers just plead the cases out. The people involved pay a little fine and get a slap on the wrist. Go back out and do it again."

He shook his head and spit on the coals of the fire, and they sizzled angrily. "Stinking shame if you ask me."

I stared up at the sky, thinking about a half-million dollars' worth of gall bladders. You could fit them into a small cooler with dry ice. Take up less space than a suitcase. "Patti thinks Pantaleo might be a middleman?" I asked.

Becker shrugged. "I don't know. Like I said, his name came up."

I decided I needed to talk to Andy Patti, and I needed to do it soon. I asked Becker how I could contact the investigator.

"That could be a problem," he said, laughing. "He's got a camp in the backcountry of the Wind Rivers, and he's even more suspicious about talking on the cell phone than I am. I imagine you'd have to go see him in person."

I stubbed my cigar in an ashtray. "You think you could set it up?" I asked. "Call Patti and make the introduction?"

Becker nodded agreeably. "No problem," he said. "Get back to me tomorrow evening, and I'll have some details."

"I'd appreciate that," I said. I stood up and stretched my legs, shook his hand, and thanked him for dinner. Then I ambled away from the lamplight in the direction of the Jeep. Before I got there, I turned back and called out from the darkness. "Hey, Leo, one more thing," I said.

Becker looked in my direction and squinted. His eyes were used to the light, and he couldn't see me in the shadows. "What is it?" he asked.

"You said Patti told you Sam Pantaleo's name was one of a couple that came up in the course of his investigation. You remember the other one?"

A frown crossed Becker's face, and he patted his shirt pocket as if there might be something there he'd misplaced. He looked up sheepishly. "Sorry, Harry. I've got it written down somewhere." He patted the shirt pocket again and stuck his hands inside the pockets of his jeans. They came out empty. "You want to hang around for a while? I'm sure I can find it," he said. He didn't sound hopeful.

"That won't be necessary," I told him. I climbed behind the wheel and put the key into the ignition. "It wasn't O'Bannion, was it?" I called back. "Liam O'Bannion?"

Becker shielded his eyes with his hand, peering out from the pool of lantern light. "Isn't that the guy whose murder you told me you were looking into?" he asked.

"One and the same," I said. I turned the key and the Jeep's engine rumbled to life.

Becker slapped his forehead with the palm of his hand and cursed. "I knew that name sounded familiar when you mentioned it earlier," he hollered. "O'Bannion. That's the other name all right, the one Patti asked me to check out."

A small piece of the puzzle dropped into place.

6

△△△

That night, someone slashed all four tires on the Jeep—long gashes in the sidewall of the oversize radials that would be impossible to patch. The bastard even cut the spare.

I discovered the vehicular carnage moments after I checked out of the Golden Spike at about six-thirty in the morning and walked out to the parking lot to throw my gear in the backseat and head down the blacktop toward Victory. The Jeep was sitting on its rims in a parking space visible from the front desk of the motel, directly under a large mercury vapor lamp so bright you could read by it at midnight. The mutilated tires puddled out from under the chrome rims like pools of molten rubber and my sporty bright red off-roader looked forlorn, even a little embarrassed at its pitiful circumstances.

I cursed and punched my fist into the spare tire so hard I barked my knuckles. Then I stormed back into the lobby of the motel and confronted the desk clerk, a gangly kid with a bad haircut and three rings in each ear who looked all of nineteen. I must have seemed a little rabid, because the pimple-faced kid started backing up as soon as he saw me barreling across the lobby, putting as much space between us as possible. When I got to the desk, I slammed my blackthorn stick down on the countertop so hard the Formica cracked. Even in the spacious lobby, the noise sounded like a bolt of lightning. "What the hell happened to my tires?" I growled between clenched teeth.

The kid was desperately eyeballing the check-in counter between us wondering if that chest-high obstacle would keep me from vaulting over and slapping him senseless. His glance frequently flicked to my gun, which he likely expected me to pull any second. Finally, he tore his eyes away from me and looked out the glass front doors of the motel in the direction I was pointing. His eyes grew even wider. I think it was the first time he'd noticed the vandalism. "I don't know anything about it," he sputtered. "I just came on a half hour ago."

"Then where's the manager?" I said. "I want to talk to whoever was on desk duty last night. The person who slashed those tires did it right under your goddamned noses."

The kid squirmed and shifted his weight from foot to foot, as if every one of his nerve endings was screaming at him to bolt. "Listen, mister," he said, "I *really* don't know what happened to your tires." He was almost crying now, a mouse with his tail in a trap and a twenty-pound tomcat creeping down the stairway. "And the manager won't be here till ten."

I saw the truth in his face and immediately regretted my churlish behavior. It wasn't his fault after all, and the worst thing he was guilty of was failing to notice the damage when he came in.

I was still seething, but I made the effort to modulate my voice and paste a smile on my face. The smile hurt the muscles around my mouth, and I flinched when I caught my reflection in the wall mirror behind the desk. I looked like a shark in a bathtub full of mackerel. "Don't worry about it," I said, a statement that had absolutely no positive effect on his state of mind.

I left the kid to calm down while I used the pay phones in the lobby to call a service station, where the manager told me he had two tires that would fit the Jeep, but not five. For that, he said, I'd have to wait until the tire dealership opened at nine. It was the same story at the three other stations I called, so at about seven I hiked down to a pancake house a couple blocks from the motel, bought every newspaper in the racks out front, and went inside to stoke up on black coffee and a heavy breakfast of pancakes, scrambled eggs, and Canadian bacon.

That took about a half hour, and it was all I could do to keep from climbing the walls until the tire dealership opened. By three minutes after nine, a truck from the dealership was on its way to the motel, where they put the car on jacks, pulled the wheels, and took them back to the shop to be fitted with new tires. Then they drove back and slapped the wheels back on. I was ready to roll by ten-thirty—and it only cost me a little over 400 bucks.

The truck from the tire dealership was between me and the parking spaces directly in front of the motel office, so I didn't see the gray Lincoln town car parked there until I'd finished signing the credit-card receipt for the tires and the mechanic had driven away. Even then, I didn't notice anything until the driver got out. Then I couldn't help but stare.

The man who folded his stocky frame out of the Lincoln was only about five eight, but he had a dense and powerful wrestler's body and a low center of gravity. I figured he weighed well over 200 pounds, but he was so squat that his frame was foreshortened, like a reflection in a fun-house mirror. The expensive blue pin-striped suit he was wearing was startling in its incongruity to his body—a Neanderthal torso that would have appeared more natural draped in animal skins and a bone necklace.

It was his face, though, that drew my attention and made the short hairs on the back of my neck stand up—the same reaction I have to black widows and most snakes.

His stringy black hair was cut short and unevenly, his skin was pale and lifeless, his cold blue eyes small, spaced closely together. The man had obviously been in some horrible fight or accident, and had healed without benefit of reconstructive surgery. His whole face looked out of whack, his cheekbones lumpy and unbalanced, his lantern jaw jutting, crooked in its lines, his brow ridges heavy and protruding. Large jug ears stood out from the sides of his head, their bulbous lobes distended and doughy. There was a white scar through the right corner of his upper lip that gave him a perpetual sneer. His most disquieting feature was his nose, or what was left of it after someone removed all the cartilage, leaving him nothing but an amorphous glob of flesh around his nostrils that looked like the snout of a boar.

The overall effect was not quite human, like Caliban, an almost otherworldly cross between real and surreal, man and monster. The bogeyman, I thought. Either that or the poster boy for those environmentalists who are always harping about the dangers of nuclear power.

He had to be Junior Stone, and from the look on his face he was fairly amused at my circumstances. He was grinning—at least his mouth was contorted in what passed for a grin on his ruined face. He clucked his tongue in fake sympathy.

My sixth sense told me I'd found the person who slashed my tires. The only question was why.

I took my Stetson off and sat it on the front seat, then stood facing him with one hand on the blackthorn walking stick and the other on the roll bar. Our eyes locked for several seconds before he spoke, a couple of junkyard dogs taking each other's measure. I was a few inches taller than Stone and in pretty good shape for a man in his mid-forties, but he outweighed me by at least thirty pounds and I imagined his bulk came from muscle, not fat. If it came to a fight, the outcome was a crapshoot. I imagined it wouldn't be pretty.

"I don't know what's happening to this neighborhood," Stone said. His contemptuous voice didn't belong with his body. It was high-pitched and adolescent, like a teenager in the middle stages of puberty, a voice like Mike Tyson's. "You can't trust anybody around here these days."

"I don't imagine the neighborhood's responsible," I said. "I've got a feeling we're dealing with one specific asshole." He started walking toward me, hands in the pockets of his pants, not a care in the world. "You wouldn't know anything about this, would you, Junior?" I asked.

We hadn't been introduced, but he showed no curiosity when I used his name. Maybe he figured everybody in the world knew Junior Stone already, or ought to. He shrugged his square shoulders nonchalantly. "Why would I know anything about it?" he asked.

"Maybe you got enemies, mister. Maybe one a them did it. Maybe they was tryin' to send you a message."

"And what message would that be?" I asked. We were only a couple feet apart then, and up close he looked even more hideous than he did at a distance. His teeth were yellow and crooked; the large pores in his skin were oily, peppered with blackheads. He smelled as if he'd doused himself in a gallon of Brut cologne.

"How should I know?" he asked. He took his hands out of his pockets, and I got a look at his knuckles. They were enlarged from being broken, crisscrossed with scar tissue. "I'm only guessin' here, but maybe they were tellin' you not to put your nose in other people's business. Maybe they were tellin' you to go back to Podunkville where you belong." His grin grew wider. "Then again, maybe it was just some punk kid with nothin' better to do. Who knows?"

I was gripping the walking stick so hard my right hand began to hurt, and I could feel the first hit of adrenaline shifting my nervous system into overdrive. "I don't think it was a punk kid," I said. My voice sounded strange, guttural. "I think it was a message from Sam Pantaleo."

Stone's eyes widened in mock surprise. "Who?" he asked.

"Sam Pantaleo," I said again. "The arrogant prick you work for . . . And I've got a message for him, too." I took my left hand off the roll bar, curled my fist in a ball. "You can tell that *disgraziato figlio di putana* the next time he has something to say to me he should say it to my face instead of sending his piss boy to do the dirty work."

The insult was the only one I knew in Sicilian, courtesy of my old homicide partner, John Bruno. I don't even know if I pronounced it correctly, or whether Stone had been around enough people who spoke Italian to know what it meant, but I found out one thing in a hurry: Al Kincaid was right—Junior Stone's ears turned red when he got mad.

He didn't hit me, even though I'm sure he wanted to. Instead he took his car keys out of his coat pocket, held one between his thumb and forefinger like the tip of a knife, and scraped it down the back fender of the Jeep. The key scored a deep gouge in the red paint, ruined the finish on the whole quarter panel. Stone's face was ice-cold, except for his ears, which were the color of beefsteak tomatoes. "Maybe the piss boy *enjoys* dirty work," he croaked. Then he did something I didn't expect. He spit in my face.

White noise filled my brain as I felt the slimy spittle roll down my cheek, and I'm not proud to admit that in the space of a heartbeat my anger bubbled over and I went a little crazy. Did something I don't think Stone expected. I took the advice of my old granddaddy—who always said if you were up against a man who could put your dick in the dirt, make sure to get the first lick, and make it count.

Before Stone could blink, I'd raised the blackthorn like a club and swung it down, full force, against his left knee. The sound of the blow was like a hammer on a coconut, and the shock wave traveled all the way to my elbow. Stone yelped in pain and surprise and staggered sideways, reaching out for the Jeep to keep from falling. He recovered quickly, though, and lunged at me with a choppy overhand right. Because he couldn't put much weight on his leg, however, there was no real power behind the blow. His knuckles raked the side of my head but didn't connect.

The momentum of his punch brought him within six inches of me. He was off balance, reeling. I brought the stick up sharply, where it connected with his testicles with a sickening thud. I hit him in the face again on the way down. Then, when he was on his knees, incapacitated, I walked around behind him, held the stick in both hands across his windpipe, put my knee in the middle of his back, and began to choke him. I stopped throttling when the vomit rose in his throat, grabbed him by the hair on the back of his head, and rammed him face first into the rear bumper of the vehicle.

Stone was on the ground, still trying to get up, mewling in bloody agony. I couldn't stop myself. I kicked him in the rib cage but I did it with my bad leg, so I imagined the effect was more humiliating than painful. I was cocking my foot for another punt when a big arm curled around my own throat and pulled me back. "That's enough, mister," a voice behind me growled. "You stop right now before I call the law."

I pulled away roughly and turned toward the man who'd broken my attack. It was Stan, the bartender, his face beet red, breathing heavily through his mouth. I didn't know where he'd come from. Maybe the motel. Maybe he'd been in Junior's car and I hadn't seen him through the tinted windows. "I am the law," I said menacingly. "And you know it."

Stan held his ground. "That don't give you the right to kill a man," he said. Stan looked down at Junior Stone and came up with a plan. "Why don't you *didi mau* before he gets up and cuts your lungs out," he said. "I'll take care of him."

Although my heart rate was about a million and six, the white noise was receding, and what Stan said began to make sense. *Didi mau*—Vietnamese for boogie time. The last time I heard that phrase I was in the navy, riding a gunboat on the Mekong River. I reached down and grabbed Stone by the collar of his suit, pulled him away from the Jeep, and let him fall face forward on the asphalt. I bent over and patted him down, took the six-inch folding knife I found in the pocket of his pants, and threw it in the front seat. I wiped the remains of Junior's spit from my face and his blood off the chrome bumper with my bandanna. Then I got inside the vehicle, started the engine, eased the stick shift into reverse, and backed up three feet.

Beside me, Stan had his arms under Stone's, helping him to his feet. Stone was mumbling something I couldn't hear.

I popped the car out of gear and stopped backing. "He have another smart-assed comment?" I asked.

Stan shook his head, puffed himself up. Defiant now that I was leaving. *Muy macho.* "Junior says you just made the worst mistake of your life," he said.

I pulled my hat low on my forehead, took my sunglasses out of my pocket, and put them on. "Nah, podna. *He's* the one made a mistake," I said. "And when he comes back to his senses, tell him this,

Stan: If he ever crosses my path again, I'll tie him down and slap wood on his ass."

I drove straight from the motel to the police station, where I found Al Kincaid in his office, his desk littered with the debris of his brunch, Egg McMuffins and hash browns in a box. I told him what I'd learned and done during my stay in his town. He winced when I got to the fight with Junior Stone. "Junior in the hospital?" he asked when I'd finished.

"I don't think so," I said. "He was standing when I left."

Kincaid scowled. "You want me to pick him up? Arrest him for assault?" he asked.

It was a tempting offer, but it would only make matters worse. "Nah," I told him. "Junior provoked the scuffle, but I threw the first punch."

"Well, I doubt he'll press charges against *you*," Kincaid said, smiling thinly. He tapped his pencil against the top of his desk thoughtfully for a few seconds. "I think I'll pick him up anyway, sweat him a little. We can both use the practice."

I shrugged my shoulders. Rock Springs was Kincaid's town. He could do whatever he wanted. "If you pick him up," I said, "you might as well ask him where he was the night Liam O'Bannion was murdered. Get his alibi on the record, if he's got one."

Kincaid stood, swept the trash from his meal into a wastebasket, and took his pearl-handled .45 from the hat rack where it was hanging, strapping the leather holster around his waist.

"I'll do that," he said, "and I'll keep him occupied for a couple hours." He reached to shake my hand. "But if you won't let me charge him, Harry, I suggest you use the time and take that bartender's advice. Put some highway between yourself and Harvey Stone. He's not the type to forget this."

I stopped by Pantaleo Trucking on the way out of town, to pay my personal respects to Sam Pantaleo and thank him for enabling me to make the acquaintance of Junior Stone. But considering my bloody frame of mind, I suppose it was just as well that his daughter, the receptionist, told me he was out of the office for the day and couldn't be reached, under any circumstances.

It was about twelve-thirty when I finally pointed the Jeep east on I–80, and with the wind whipping my face I spent most of the long drive back to Victory thinking about what I'd learned in Rock Springs, trying to make the connections that would do Curly Ahearn some good.

I'd learned a lot about Liam O'Bannion in a short period of time. He was a woman beater who stole from his girlfriend and owed a lot of nasty people money. He was an ex-con, a gambler, and a fence who dabbled in drugs—a man continually on the make. He'd been tilling the hardscrabble ground of crime for most of his life and had become a fairly energetic predator, always looking for his next meal. At least he was a man of apparently diversified business interests, even if some of them were unsavory and illegal—which meant he must have had decent organizational skill and with one exception had been smart enough to keep himself out of jail. That fact alone set him apart from the majority of crooks I'd come into contact with over the years. He had a legitimate import-export business and sometimes dealt in jade, although his income from that enterprise was marginal. It looked as if the import business was probably a cover for other activities—the sale of illegally poached bear parts to the Asian market, and maybe other rackets I wasn't aware of.

In Wyoming, he was involved with Sam Pantaleo, who might or might not have mob connections, and was thought to be involved in a host of illegal activities to supplement the princely living he made from his trucking company. I knew O'Bannion had been in Rock Springs to see Pantaleo and his henchman, Junior Stone, on more than one occasion, and I thought he'd probably come to Wyoming with the intention of seeing them again. If my hunch proved accurate, I thought Curly's telephone records would probably show that O'Bannion called Pantaleo the day he was murdered. He'd been upset by that call and had told Faith to pack her bags because they were going back to San Francisco instead of to Rock

Springs, where he'd hoped to straighten out his business dealings.

That implied there was trouble between O'Bannion and Pantaleo, and although I didn't know what it was, I suspected it had something to do with his death. Pantaleo didn't like the fact that I was looking into the matter and had sent Junior Stone to scare me off—a plan that had backfired because it had only served to confirm my belief that Pantaleo had something to hide and make me more determined to find out what it was.

There was still plenty I didn't know, however. Most important, I didn't know who killed O'Bannion. If he'd had a falling out with Pantaleo on the morning of his death, it was unlikely Pantaleo had made the long drive to Victory to kill him on the mountain that night. Junior Stone was a possibility. Maybe I'd discover that he'd been in or near Victory on the day of O'Bannion's murder. If he had an alibi, though, I was right back where I started.

Short-term, I needed to make a visit to the Wind River Indian Reservation and speak with Andy Patti, see if he could fill in the details of the poaching scheme. Beyond that, I figured I'd have to visit San Francisco, where there might be any number of people who wanted O'Bannion dead I wasn't yet aware of. I wasn't especially looking forward to that trip. For starters, I don't know San Francisco very well, and I had no idea who O'Bannion's business associates were in that city. Second, I'd be more than a thousand miles beyond the limit of my jurisdiction, working essentially as a private citizen. The principles of homicide investigation are the same whether you're in a city of a million people or a backwater like Victory, but it's always easier to investigate when you have the law's muscle backing you up. Cops have powers and access to information that ordinary citizens don't, and we get used to it. Eventually I'd probably discover what I needed to know in San Francisco, but it would take a lot longer without my badge and gun.

I stopped for take-out burgers at a fast-food place in Rawlins, and passed the city-limit sign in Victory a little before six. After crossing the desert in the heat of the day, it felt good to be back in the foothills of the Snowy Range, where the temperature was fifteen degrees lower than it had been on the open road. To the north, a bank of pewter-colored clouds were building over the peaks of the Snowies, clouds that might bring rain after sundown. The parking lots at both Gus Alzonakis's steak house and the Trails End were nearly full, but there wasn't much traffic on Main Street. There were a few cars in front of Ginny Larsen's Country Kitchen and Shapiro's Hardware, a few more parked in front of the Silver Dollar. A dozen people, tourists mostly, ambled down the sidewalk, window shopping and licking ice-cream cones. One man was dressed in purple-and-green shorts, a Hard Rock Cafe T-shirt and a brand-new pair of lizard-skin cowboy boots so tight they made him limp. Definitely a tourist. Probably bought the boots that very afternoon, and after shelling out at least $300 to acquire them was beginning to regret his purchase. When he got home, I predicted they'd go to the back of his closet, where boots made of anything but soft cowhide belong.

At the police station, I found a note on the door from Frankie, saying he'd be back in twenty minutes, so I went inside to see what had been happening during my absence. There were a few copies of speeding citations he'd written in the basket and an incident report detailing a fender bender that had taken place at the town's only traffic light. Among the reports was an envelope from Danny King, and inside I found the copy of O'Bannion's fingerprints I'd requested from the NCIC and a note. "Hey, Hollywood," the note read. "Now that you're a nationally famous lawman on television and all, do you think I could have a copy of your autograph? I'm gonna use it to impress waitresses." I chuckled, tucked the prints away in a file cabinet, and threw the note into the trash.

In a manila folder on my desk was a copy of O'Bannion's autopsy report, faxed over by James Bowen that morning. According to Bowen, the autopsy was incomplete because so much of O'Bannion's body had been eaten by the bear. Based on his stomach contents and the stage of rigor mortis, he believed O'Bannion had died between 7 P.M. and 9 P.M. Sunday night, almost thirty-six hours before his corpse was discovered. Besides the bruises that resulted from O'Bannion's fight with Curly earlier in the day, there was no fresh bruising or self-defense wounds to indicate that he'd struggled before his death. There was enough alcohol in his system to make him legally intoxicated, and Bowen found that O'Bannion had also used some sort of amphetamine shortly before his death. There was a lot of the drug in his body, Bowen said, although it was unclear whether he had swallowed or snorted it. Damage to his nasal membranes indicated that he'd inhaled drugs over a long period of time, however, so Bowen suspected the latter method of ingestion.

O'Bannion's death, Bowen wrote, had been instantaneous and caused by a single gunshot wound to his right temple. Scorching and powder burns indicated that the round had been fired from point-blank range. The bullet entered his temporal bone and traveled through his skull at a slight upward angle until it exited. The gas and flame expelled from the bore of the weapon had followed the bullet on its journey, turning most of O'Bannion's brain to mush. More than 30 percent of his brain tissue had been blown out through the opening of the exit wound. A test to determine if O'Bannion had fired a weapon prior to death was inconclusive, since the bear had eaten most of the skin and flesh on his hands and arms. Because there wasn't enough flesh to test, Bowen didn't rule out the possibility that O'Bannion had killed himself but noted it was unlikely, since no weapon had been found near his body. It was more likely, he wrote, that O'Bannion had been killed by someone else. For the time being, he was ruling the death a homicide.

In a second folder were copies of all the long-distance phone calls that had been made from the Ahearn residence in the last three weeks. During the period that coincided with O'Bannion and Faith's visit, nine calls had been made to the same number in Rock Springs, two of them on the day of O'Bannion's death. I made a note of the number and called Rock Springs information to get Sam Pantaleo's home number and the main number of the trucking company. All of the calls from Curly's phone had been made to Pantaleo's home number, which meant that O'Bannion had been in contact with him during the entire course of his visit. It was a call to Pantaleo that had upset O'Bannion on the last day of his life, caused him to tell Faith they were leaving Wyoming for San Francisco as soon as possible.

I put the phone records back into the folder and called Leo Becker, who told me he'd been in contact with Andy Patti, and that the U.S. Fish and Wildlife investigator had agreed to meet me the following afternoon at two o'clock in Fort Washakie on the Wind River Indian Reservation. Unless he heard from me to the contrary, I was to meet him at the tribal police station, where he had something he thought I'd be interested in. I told Becker that sounded fine, and he agreed to relay the message to Patti.

Next, I called Al Kincaid, who told me he'd picked up Junior Stone for questioning within a half hour after I left town. Junior, he said, looked as if he'd been worked over with a ball bat and was in a murderous funk.

"Did you ask him where he was the night O'Bannion was murdered?" I asked.

"Of course I asked him," Kincaid replied. "He says he spent the night with a local hooker name of Shawna Tinsley."

I knew Shawna, Cherry's friend from the bar. "You check it out?" I asked.

"Yep," said Kincaid, "and for what it's worth, Shawna swears Junior was with her all night. She says they had an early dinner and went back to his house. Says they stayed up most of the night screwing and slept till after one the next afternoon."

"You believe her?"

"I have to," he said. "I talked to one of Junior's neighbors and he confirms that Junior was home that night with a woman, because he heard them arguing and playing the stereo so loud he couldn't sleep. Says he went over to Junior's about midnight to ask him to keep it down, and Junior threatened him with a rake."

I felt a stab of disappointment. So far, Junior Stone was the best candidate I had in O'Bannion's murder. Shawna might have covered for him if he'd asked her, but the neighbor's corroboration seemed to clear him of the actual killing. I realized I was a long way from proving why O'Bannion had been murdered, or who had pulled the trigger.

I thanked Kincaid and hung up, brooded for five minutes, and then dialed my ex-wife's number in Denver. Nicole answered on the third ring, out of breath because she'd been working out on her treadmill when I called. She sounded distant and not particularly glad to hear the sound of my voice, but we made chitchat for a couple of minutes and I filled her in on O'Bannion's murder and my effort to keep Curly out of jail. I told her about my visit to Rock Springs and my plans to visit the Indian reservation the next day.

"I guess that means you won't be coming to pick the boys up after all," she said when I'd finished, her voice laced with anger.

"What?"

"Come on, Harry," she snapped. "You were supposed to come here tomorrow and take them back to Victory for a long weekend. They've been looking forward to it for weeks."

She was right, of course. I'd promised my two youngest sons a camping and fishing trip to Ryan Park and had been looking forward to it myself. In all the excitement, though, I'd lost track of time. Worst of all, there was no way I could cancel my trip north to the reservation. The fishing excursion would have to wait.

"I'm truly sorry, Nicole," I told her. "But this reservation thing is important."

"It always is," she said icily. "Your work is always more important than your family. Has been for years."

"Come on, Nicole, you know that's not true," I said, but I had learned from experience that there was no percentage in arguing. She might eventually forgive me. She might not. But the only thing that might make her forget her anger was time. "Listen, are the boys around? I'll explain what's going on to them, and I'm sure they'll understand. We'll only have to postpone for a couple weeks, tops."

"They're not here," she said. "They rode over to the mall to buy new fishing poles. They've been saving their allowance."

Ouch. "Oh, man," I groaned. "How soon do you think they'll be home? I'll call them and—"

"Don't bother, Harry," she broke in. "They've heard one version or another of that story a thousand times. They'll take it better coming from me."

With that she hung up, and I sat with the receiver in my hand, the empty line crackling in bitter accusation.

I didn't have time to sulk for long, because Frankie Tall Bull blew through the office door five minutes later—the storm clouds on his face matching those I'd seen scudding across the peaks of the Snowies. His long black hair was wind-blown, and there were circles of perspiration on the white long-sleeved cotton shirt he wore beneath his leather motorcycle vest. He sailed his wide-brimmed black hat to the top of his desk and wiped beads of sweat from his forehead with the sleeve of his shirt. Stood in the middle of the room with his hands on his hips, glowering.

"Hello, Frankie," I said cordially. "Wherever you've been, it doesn't look like it was a pleasure trip."

He grumbled an acknowledgment. "We've got trouble, Harry," he said, clearly in no mood for small talk.

His muscular body looked like coiled steel, and it was all he could do to stand still. I sat forward, told him to make himself comfortable. He reluctantly took a seat on the edge of his desk but kept both booted feet planted on the floor. "You better tell me about it," I said.

Frankie ran a hand through his hair and grimaced when it got caught in a tangle. "You remember I told you Baldi had asked Curly for that pistol? The one Curly misplaced?" he asked.

Frankie frowned. "Well, he couldn't do that," he said. "Told Baldi it was gone, maybe stolen."

I didn't say anything but waited for him to go on. "Naturally, Baldi didn't believe him," he said. "Showed up at the Ahearn place about an hour ago with a search warrant." He paused. "That's where I've been."

"A search warrant?" I asked. "What was he looking for?"

Frankie could sit no longer. He stretched himself up to his full six three and began pacing the small area between our desks. He looked like a Kodiak bear in an undersized cage. He stopped momentarily. "He had a warrant to search the house and take spent slugs from Curly's shooting range," he said. "You know what that means, don't you, Harry?"

I knew only too well what it meant. Two years ago, Curly and I had purchased a few pickup truckloads of untreated railroad ties and used them as backstops for the shooting ranges we built behind our houses. We used the ranges frequently when we got together to shoot our black powder muzzle-loaders. I used mine to keep in practice with my .357 Blackhawk and my old World War II–era military .45. Curly used his to plink with his tube-fed .22 semiautomatic and his vintage German Luger. I imagined he'd used it to sight in his missing .38.

The railroad ties were so thick and strong they trapped the bullets from those weapons, and every round fired on the range would still be embedded in the heavy oak. I started laughing, and Frankie looked at me as if I'd been nibbling locoweed. "Mind telling me what's so funny?" he asked.

"I thought you said we had trouble," I said, chuckling.

"We don't?" he asked.

"Nah," I said happily. "Baldi's got dick."

He gave me a puzzled look and waited for me to go on. "Here's the deal," I said. "Tony Baldi is *not* gonna find a slug in Curly's backstop matching the one that killed O'Bannion. That means the good sheriff is right back where he started, with nothing against the mayor but circumstantial evidence. All he was doing out at Curly's was showing off, blowing smoke rings out his butt."

Frankie was still dubious and gloomy. I stood up and clapped him on the back cheerfully. "The only way we'd have trouble is if Baldi found a slug in the backstop that matches, which would indicate O'Bannion was killed with Curly's gun," I said. "I'll bet dinner they ain't gonna match."

Frankie didn't answer. Native American pessimism, I suppose. He always expects the worst.

By the time I got to Curly's house, Baldi's deputies had already finished looking through the house for his .38 revolver—a weapon they didn't find—and had taken a number of spent slugs from the oak backstop of his shooting range. They were in a hurry to get them to the Department of Criminal Investigation's ballistics lab in Cheyenne to see if they could be matched to the slug that killed O'Bannion. Before he left, Tony Baldi warned Curly against leaving town in the next twenty-four hours. We all knew what that meant—the sheriff believed he'd have enough evidence the next day to arrest the mayor for murder.

I found Curly sitting on the deck in his going-to-work clothes—jeans, boots, long-sleeved T-shirt, and a Colorado Rockies cap—sipping iced tea from a mason jar; his two dogs were curled at his feet. As I trudged up the stairs, their tails thumped against the planking of the deck in welcome. Music was playing on the radio in the kitchen, and through the open screen door I could hear the sweet voice of Mary Chapin Carpenter—an artist on whom I have a horrible crush—singing about Lyle Lovett's hand on her thigh. Lucky man, Lyle Lovett. First Julia Roberts, now this. Guy's an inspiration to homely men everywhere.

Curly's expression was mean as snakes, and his jaw muscles flexed as he crushed whole ice cubes in his mouth. It sounded like rocks in a grinder. "The son of a bitch threatened to shoot my dogs," he rumbled before I'd even had time to say hello.

It wasn't the greeting I'd expected. The mutts, apparently aware that he was talking about them, thumped their tails even louder. "Who threatened to shoot your dogs?" I asked.

"Baldi," he spat. "Came out here with that damned warrant and the mutts did just what they were supposed to, wouldn't let him out of the car. He pulled a gun on them, for Christ sake. Woulda killed 'em, too, if I hadn't been around to call 'em off."

"The man's a menace," I agreed. I went into the kitchen and found a mason jar of my own, filled it with ice cubes and tea, and took it out to the deck.

My friend was obviously angry and not in a particularly conversational mood, so I took a seat and let him brood while I told him what I'd learned so far about Liam O'Bannion and what I suspected after my trip to Rock Springs. He seemed impressed that I'd been able to learn so much about O'Bannion in such a short time, and disgusted that he hadn't taken the time to check the man out himself before things got out of hand. Guy was living with his daughter, after all, could have become his son-in-law.

"I knew he was a no-good prick when I first laid eyes on him," Curly said angrily. "My biggest mistake was ignoring my instincts and letting him stay at my house in the first place. I shoulda turned him away at the front door and kicked him so hard he didn't quit bouncing till he hit Nevada."

When he was done stewing, he asked me what I planned to do next, so I told him about my trip to the Wind River Reservation the next day and my belief that I'd eventually have to make a trip to San Francisco. When I finished, he nodded in agreement, stood, and disappeared inside the house for five minutes. When he came back, he was holding a thick wad of cash. He straightened the bills and handed them to me.

"What's this for?" I asked. I didn't count the money, but I figured it was close to a thousand dollars.

"Expenses," he said simply. "Plane tickets to San Francisco aren't cheap."

I shook my head and handed the money back, but he waved me off. "Keep it, Harry," he said sharply. "You're doing me a big favor here, and I won't have you paying for it out of your own pocket."

I took the money reluctantly and slipped it into my front pocket. "I'll keep receipts," I assured him. "Give you back whatever's left over."

He shook his head sadly. "I have a feeling this thing may go on for a while," he said. "You let me know when you need more."

We drank our tea and watched the sun set behind the rocky wall of the Snowy Range, the shadows of the lodgepole pines lengthening tenfold before the deep greens and browns of Victory Valley turned to variegated shades of gray. The thick clouds that had been building over the mountains in the late afternoon finally rolled over the granite peaks and flowed down the wooded slopes toward us, filling the air with the smell of rain. A couple of miles away, a jagged bolt of lightning cracked the pewter sky, filling our ears seconds later with the sound of rolling thunder. The dogs perked up their ears at the noise and whimpered softly in fear of the coming storm. In Curly's corral, his black Thoroughbred gelding whinnied and galloped the perimeter of the buck-rail fence, his midnight tail flying like a pirate's flag.

I was beginning to agree with the dogs. It was time to go inside, but Curly showed no inclination to seek shelter, looking as if he might ride the weather right there in his lawn chair. I looked over the deck rail and noticed that Curly's old Willys wagon was the only vehicle in the driveway. Maybe Madelaine's Neon was in the garage.

He answered my question before I even asked. "I sent them off to Denver early this morning," he said. "They both needed a change of scenery."

The breeze was rising, rattling the metal wind chimes on the deck, rustling the brittle-sounding leaves of the aspens and willows in the yard. I watched a tumbleweed blow across the drive until it got caught in the undercarriage of my Jeep. My eyes were beginning to water from the wind-driven dust. I wiped the tears away with the heel of my hand. "I need to talk to her again, Curly," I said.

He raised his eyebrows. "Faith?"

I nodded grimly. "She lived with O'Bannion for two years," I explained. "She had to know more about how he made his living than she told me the last time we talked."

"You saying she lied, Harry?" he asked. There was steel in his voice, and his eyes narrowed. He leaned forward, and I had the feeling it was all he could do to keep from jumping up and lashing out.

I shook my head. "I'm not saying that at all," I told him reasonably. "All I'm saying is that for whatever reason, she didn't tell me everything she knows. If I'm gonna keep you out of prison, podna, I gotta get her to open up. That's all there is to it, Curly, and you know I'm telling the truth."

He stood up and walked to the edge of the deck, his hands gripping the railing while he watched the approaching storm. He stayed that way for several minutes—like Ahab on the quarterdeck of the *Pequod*—until the first fat drops of rain began to splatter the planking. On the sunbaked redwood, they looked like drops of blood.

My knees creaked and popped as I pushed myself to my feet and picked up my empty glass. My idiot buddy could stay outdoors and get soaked if he wanted, wait for a bolt of lightning to fry his bony ass. I'd wait for him inside at the whiskey cabinet.

I stomped into the kitchen and helped myself to three fingers of Jack Daniel's over ice, took a long sip. The smoky bourbon tasted of licorice and burned the back of my throat. I closed my eyes and waited until the fire diminished to a warm glow in the pit of my stomach. Outside, the clouds opened up and rain began to beat on the roof, against the glass of the kitchen windows. In addition to the din from the downpour, Trisha Yearwood was singing on the radio, so I didn't hear Curly when he finally came in. "I'm sorry, Harry," he said, breaking my reverie. "I didn't mean to take it out on you. It's just that everything is—"

I opened my eyes and smiled. "Don't worry about it," I said. He laid his hand on my shoulder and let it stay there for a minute, heavy and warm. Then he poured himself a bourbon and took a chair on the other side of the table. I took a cheroot from my pocket and fired it with a kitchen match, inhaling deeply. "Did you do what I told you and hire a lawyer?" I asked.

Curly took a drink and grimaced. "Jackson Simpson," he said around the face he was making. "Put him on retainer this afternoon."

I mumbled approval. Jack Simpson is the best defense attorney in southern Wyoming, almost as good as Gerry Spence, the cowboy lawyer from Jackson Hole who represented white separatist Randy Weaver, defended Imelda Marcos, and won a gazillion dollars from Kerr McGee in the Karen Silkwood case—until the appeals court took it all away. Unlike Gerry Spence, Jack Simpson occasionally loses a case, but that doesn't happen often and his opponents always know they've been in a scrap. I wondered how much Simpson charged and whether Curly could afford him if his case came to trial, but I didn't inquire. If I did my job, it wouldn't come to that anyway.

Considering how protective Curly was of his daughter, I knew I should tread lightly, but there was a troublesome question I had to ask. If Baldi was so interested in Curly's missing revolver, I figured I ought to exhibit a passing curiosity—at least until the ballistics report came back to prove what I assumed, that his gun hadn't been used in O'Bannion's murder. I took off my hat and smoothed the hair on the sides of my head, smoked until I screwed up the courage to begin. "You're not gonna like this much, Curly," I said tentatively, "but I need you to tell me something."

Curly didn't answer. He tensed and nodded slightly for me to go on.

"That revolver of yours was locked up at the Silver Dollar," I said. "Who had access to it?"

Curly frowned and shrugged his shoulders. "Hell, Harry, we all did," he said testily. "I keep a key at the bar, another on my key ring, another here at the house. What are you getting at?"

He knew what I was getting at, but he wanted me to spell it out. "Is it possible Faith could have taken it without your knowledge?" I asked, laying it out. It was an obvious question. I had no reason to believe Faith murdered Liam O'Bannion, but it's a simple fact that most murders are committed by someone close to the victim. Husbands kill their wives, wives kill their husbands, parents kill children, children kill parents, lovers slaughter each other with depressing regularity. And if what I'd learned about O'Bannion so far was true, Curly's daughter certainly had a motive—O'Bannion was a woman beater who'd been going through her money like quicksilver. Even if she loved him as much as she said, she could have snapped and put a bullet in his brainpan in a moment of passion. Believe me, stranger things have happened.

I expected Curly to react badly to my line of questioning, but I was still surprised when he pushed away from the table so hard his chair tipped over backward. "Goddamn you, Harry," he said roughly. His ruddy face was flushed, and I could see blood pumping through the veins of his neck. "Faith had nothing to do with that bastard's killing, and if you don't believe that just stay the fuck away from us. I won't have you—"

"Then it's possible she took the gun," I broke in. I doubted he'd hit me, but I wasn't sure what I'd do if he tried. At that second, a bold of lightning struck close, illuminating his angry face in a strobelike flash of blue. The power flickered and went out.

When it came back on seconds later, Curly had his whiskey glass in his fist. He threw it toward the sink, where it shattered in a thousand crystal shards. "She was with Madelaine the night he was murdered," he said, enunciating each word carefully, his voice tight and soft—a near whisper. "All night. Do you hear what I'm telling you? There was absolutely no way she could have—"

"I need to ask her about it myself," I said gently. "Someone has to do it eventually. It might as well be a friend."

He looked at the broken glass with disgust, as if he couldn't believe what he'd done. "Suit yourself, Harry," he said. "As far as I'm concerned, you can wait around here and ask her when she comes home. Wait all goddamned night if you want to . . . I've got to go to work."

Then he banged out the kitchen door and into the face of the storm.

I'd been a guest in Curly's home so often I knew it almost as well as my own, the difference being that his refrigerator is usually better provisioned than mine. It was a little after eight, and I hadn't eaten since lunch, so I swept up the broken glass. Then I rummaged through his larder until I came up with the fixings for a quick dinner—a couple of pork chops that I fried in a cast-iron skillet, a microwaved baked potato with sour cream and chives, canned corn—the spicy kind with little bits of red and green peppers—and apple sauce. I would have liked to make biscuits and cream gravy to go with the pork chops, but I thought that might have been pushing the limits of the famous Ahearn hospitality.

The cloudburst had stopped by the time I finished cooking, so I started a pot of coffee. When it began to brew, I heaped my dinner on a plate and took it out to the deck so I could enjoy the cool, rain-washed mountain air while I ate. When I finished, I loaded the dishes into the dishwasher and retired with a mug of black coffee to the living room, where I enthroned myself in Curly's leather recliner and used the remote to punch up a baseball game—the Colorado Rockies in a home stand against Pittsburgh. By the bottom of the seventh, the Rockies were down by nine and even the most rabid fans were leaving the stadium in near manic depression.

I switched off the television and read the first chapters of a new Elvis Cole mystery I found on the coffee table. I like Elvis, but I like his taciturn pal Joe Pike even better; he's sort of a personal role model. Somewhere around page fifty, I must have fallen asleep, because the next thing I knew Faith and Madelaine were standing in the living room with their arms full of shopping bags, Maddy with an amused expression on her tired face and Faith looking vaguely perturbed.

"I'd call the police and report that a strange man invaded my kitchen and then fell asleep in my husband's favorite chair," Madelaine said, dumping her packages on the couch. One of the bags tipped over, spilling a blouse and several items of lingerie on the floor. She picked up the clothing and tossed them haphazardly on the love seat next to the recliner. "But it wouldn't do much good."

"I know," I said, rubbing my eyes. "I *am* the police."

Madelaine bent over the recliner and gave me a welcoming kiss on the cheek. Then she sat down and kicked off her shoes and socks, wiggling her toes in the carpeting. When my eyes had focused, I looked at the digital clock on the VCR. Almost eleven. I'd been asleep for over an hour.

I said hello to Faith, who was leaning against the frame of the door between the kitchen and the living room, and she answered with a wan smile and a greeting so soft I couldn't understand what she said. Dressed in high-heeled sandals, tight jeans that rode so low on her hips that her lace underwear peeked out from the waistband, and a purple halter that left most of her midriff exposed, she looked like one of those rail-thin models Calvin Klein is so fond of. There was a slender gold ring through her navel, and both her fingernails and toenails were painted a glossy black. I understand that color is all the rage these days in the big city, but with her jet-black hair and pale skin, the total effect was fairly Morticia Addams. Spooky, in fact—and quite a contrast from the last time I'd seen her, sobbing her eyes out in the basement.

She still looked fragile, but not quite the delicate hothouse flower her father wanted to believe she was. There was something about her that bothered me, but I couldn't put my finger on what it was. Maybe it was just a generational thing, I thought. Maybe I was having trouble matching the image I had of her—an image filtered through Curly's paternal perceptions—with the obviously sexual and world-wise woman who stood before me. I watched her until she grew uncomfortable and sat down on the couch across the room, where she started going through her purchases, ignoring me completely.

Faith acted as if she could have cared less, but Madelaine knew that I was hanging around for some reason besides raiding her refrigerator. "You must have seen Curly before he left for work," she said. "How was he doing?"

I shrugged my shoulders, and I'm sure the expression on my face told her everything she needed to know. "He's stressed, Maddy," I said. "And he doesn't know who to blame for his problems, so he's—"

"Blaming everybody," she interrupted. A small grin crinkled her face. "He's absolutely insufferable when he gets like that. If I didn't love him so much, I think I'd probably have to whack him upside the head with a nine-iron."

"Waste of a good golf club," I chuckled. "The man's like an old plow mule, so knobby-headed you'd have to use a steel cheater bar just to get his attention."

We laughed a little, and then Maddy reached over and put her hand on my knee. I laid my hand on top of hers and gave it a squeeze. She returned the pressure, but she was watching my face intently. Our eyes met, and her soft gaze was probing, worried. "What's up, Harry?" she asked softly. "Do you have bad news?"

I shook my head and gave her hand a reassuring pat. "No," I said. "But I've started trying to find Liam's killer, and I need to ask some more questions. I waited around this evening to talk with Faith."

Faith looked up nervously when she heard that news, but her mother only nodded, as if she'd been expecting it. "Alone?" Maddy asked.

I shrugged. "It doesn't matter to me," I said. "You're going to hear about it eventually anyway."

A look passed between Faith and Madelaine. Like many mothers and daughters, they could almost communicate without words. "Do you want me to stay?" Madelaine asked. Faith nodded, and Madelaine got up from where she was sitting beside me and moved to her daughter's side on the couch, putting her arm protectively around Faith's shoulders. "What is it you need to know, Harry?" Maddy asked.

I sat forward and balanced my hands on my knees. "I'll tell you in a minute," I said, "but first, let me fill you in on what I've learned."

For the next ten minutes, I told Faith and Madelaine about Tony Baldi's visit to their house that afternoon, and what he thought might come of it. Then I told them what I'd discovered about O'Bannion from the National Crime Information Center and my trip to Rock Springs. Maddy listened intently, the frown lines on her gentle face deepening with concern. A couple of times, she held her hand over her mouth and shook her head as if she couldn't believe what she was hearing.

Faith, meanwhile, seemed to withdraw inside herself as I spoke. She looked down, with her chin resting on her chest, her arms wrapped around herself, and turned away from us slightly, using her small body as a shield to shut us out. More than once, it seemed she actually winced in pain when I dragged out an unpleasant tidbit of information about her deceased lover, but I forged ahead until it was all on the table. When I finished, the room was eerily quiet for several minutes, the silence broken only by the ticking of Maddy's grandfather clock and the creaking of the house.

Finally, Maddy took her arm from Faith's shoulder and stood up to face her daughter. "Did you know any of this?" she asked. There was understanding in her voice, but also firm determination. She wanted an answer, and she wanted it now.

Faith looked accusingly in my direction, then back at her mother. Her bottom lip trembled and she licked her dry lips before she spoke. "Some of it," she said quietly. "I knew he'd been in prison. I suspected about the poaching thing. I knew he was mixed up with bad people." Her voice took on an almost pleading quality. "But I don't know who might have killed him," she said. "I swear it."

Maddy's face fell while Faith was talking, and she looked as if she'd been punched in the stomach. She sat back down on the couch and stared at her feet until she'd gathered the inner strength to go on. She looked at her daughter, but Faith avoided her gaze. "Why didn't you tell us before?" Maddy asked.

Faith didn't answer, just threw her arm over her eyes and turned her face toward the wall.

Maddy grabbed her arm and shook it roughly, her long fingernails digging into the flesh of her daughter's upper arm. "Why, Faith?" she persisted. "Your father's in trouble. You can't keep any more secrets."

Faith's face flushed and she was breathing deeply, fighting back tears. When she spoke, her voice was thick with pain. "At first, I didn't say anything because I was afraid that if Daddy knew about Liam he wouldn't want anything to do with him," she said plaintively. "And I loved Liam. I wanted him and Daddy to be—"

Maddy cut her off in midsentence. "But what about *after* he was killed?" she asked. "Why didn't you tell us about him then? Why did you make Harry dig it all up by himself? Didn't you want to help your father—"

"Of course I wanted to help," Faith said. "But I didn't know what to do." She broke into tears then, but Maddy did nothing to comfort her. "He was dead," she said through her sobs. "I couldn't drag his memory through the mud."

That reasoning might have worked with someone of a more sentimental vein, but it cut no ice with Maddy Ahearn, whose husband was the primary suspect in O'Bannion's murder. "Bullshit," she said tautly. "You'd better understand what's going on here, girl. You brought this man into our lives and now it turns out he was nothing but a criminal."

Faith cringed at her mother's anger, but Maddy ignored it. "I don't know who killed him," she went on, "but I know one thing for certain: Your father didn't do it, and I'm not going to see him in jail under any circumstances. That means we don't have time for any more of your wounded-dove act. You're going to tell Harry everything you know, and you're going to do it right now." Maddy turned toward me. "Where do you want to start, Harry?" she asked.

I hadn't expected this to be a particularly cheerful conversation, but I was more than a little relieved that Madelaine was doing the dirty work. "To begin with," I said, "I need to know the names of

O'Bannion's associates in San Francisco, and I need to know anything Faith can tell me about them. Then I need to know about his business dealings, both in Wyoming and on the coast."

Faith didn't open her eyes. "I told you once, I don't—"

Maddy leaned forward, grabbed her daughter by the shoulders, and shook her roughly. "Weren't you listening?" she asked. "Tell him." Faith didn't answer. "Tell him!" Maddy commanded again.

Faith opened her eyes and looked at me. I saw a growing hatred there. "Fang," she said. From her mouth, the name sounded like a curse. "His partner in San Francisco is a guy named Tommy Fang. Liam sold him jade. Once in a while, some other stuff."

"Gall bladders?" I asked. "From bears?"

Faith nodded. "I think so," she said.

"How would I find this Tommy Fang?"

"I don't know exactly," Faith said. "He's got an import-export business in Chinatown. I only met him once, about a month ago. He came to the apartment to see Liam and they went outside to talk. I didn't hear much, but from what little I heard, I knew they were arguing about money."

"Liam owed him money?" I asked. "Or the other way around?"

"It was Liam," she said. "He owed money to Fang. A lot of it. It bothered him, what might happen if he didn't pay it back." She looked at her mother, then back at me. "That's all I know."

I figured she was still holding out, but I wasn't ready to press. Not yet, at least. "What about Sam Pantaleo?" I asked. "What can you tell me about him?"

"Who?" she asked.

"Sam Pantaleo," I said. "The man I told you about a few minutes ago. Owns a trucking company in Rock Springs. It was him Liam came to Wyoming to see. He called him from this house two times the day he was killed. Something about their last conversation upset him. What was it?"

Faith thought about the question for a full ten seconds before she answered. "I knew Liam was in trouble here, too, because he was so worried and angry all the time," she said. "But I don't know what the trouble was or who he was involved with. I never heard of Sam Pantaleo. It wasn't a name Liam mentioned."

I thought Maddy might reach down and shake her again, but I stopped her with a wave of my hand. "How about Junior Stone?" I asked. "What do you know about him?"

Faith shook her head to let me know the answer was absolutely nothing. Then she wrapped her arms around herself again and turned her face back toward the wall.

I felt a familiar knot of frustration growing in my stomach. There was something here I was missing, something I didn't see. "Why are you lying to me, Faith?" I asked gently. "Are you afraid of something?"

Faith flinched at the question, then she reacted in a way I hadn't expected. She stood up, pushed past her mother and faced me, her tiny hands balled on her hips. "I'm not lying," she hissed. "And the only thing I think I should be afraid of is *you.*"

With that, she spun on her heels and nearly ran from the room.

We didn't follow Faith when she stormed off because we both knew that she was done talking for the time being and pushing her further would be pointless. Before I left, however, I spent a few minutes with Madelaine, who was pained by my question but confirmed Faith's alibi. There was no way her daughter could have killed O'Bannion because she was with Maddy for the entire twenty-four-hour period after Curly's fight with the young man at the restaurant.

I thanked her with a hug and left her standing on the deck in her bare feet as I backed out of the driveway for the short drive into downtown Victory.

It was nearly midnight, but I was too wired to go home. Trouble was, I didn't know where else to go. The Silver Dollar was out because I wanted to mull things over in my mind and I didn't want to do my mulling in Curly's vicinity. Victory is a small town, so that reduced my remaining options considerably. It was either the Trails End or Gus Alzonakis's, the twin steak houses on Victory's southern periphery.

I ruled out the Trails End because most of my friends go there when they aren't at the Dollar, and I was in a solitary mood. Which left Gus Alzonakis's, perhaps the strangest bar-and-restaurant in the entire Rocky Mountain time zone.

It wasn't that Gus had started out to build a completely bizarre and geographically inappropriate eatery. It's just that in a town of 650 people with two huge steak houses across the street from each other, you've got to have a gimmick if you want to attract enough tourists and college folk from Laramie to pay the bills—a fact that had eluded the previous owner of the place. He'd gone backrupt fifteen years earlier, and Gus had picked up the property at a sheriff's auction. Straightaway, Gus realized that he needed something to set his new enterprise apart, and since Robbie Moore had the Western motif pretty well sewed up across the road at the Trails End, he set out in search of the perfect theme.

He found it at a Polynesian restaurant in San Diego that was going out of business and had its entire stock of South Sea paraphernalia for sale. Gus bought it all—everything from the bamboo paneling on the walls, to the little grass roofs over the tables that made them look like islanders' huts, to the outrigger canoes and stuffed marlins, to the lifebuoys, harpoons, and netting, to the 500-gallon saltwater aquarium full of miniature sharks and shellfish, right down to the glasses shaped like happy Buddhas and about a thousand cases of those little parasols you get in your drink at Chinese restaurants—and toted it all back to his new place in Victory.

After the locals got over their shock, the redecoration of the steak house tickled the heck out of them, and Gus does a good business, despite the fact that he doesn't have a single South Sea entrée on his menu and offers only one kind of seafood—coconut-batter-fried shrimp. The distinctive ambience might get them through the door the first time, but his customers come back for the sixteen-ounce mesquite-grilled porterhouse and to dance to the country-and-western bands he hires every night of the week.

When I walked in that night, the restaurant portion of the establishment was done serving, but the dance floor was full and there was a crowd of people in the bar. I hitched myself up on a stool and ordered a Baileys from Randy, the bartender, who was decked out in shorts that came to his knees, sandals, and a violet-and-green Hawaiian shirt so big it would have been baggy on Hulk Hogan.

When the rich liqueur came, I lit a cigar and sipped my drink while I watched the rituals going on around me and replayed my short conversation with Faith Ahearn in my mind. On one level, I was disappointed. Faith obviously knew more than she was telling but was keeping the information to herself. I didn't know why—maybe she was involved in his illegal enterprises and was keeping quiet out of an instinct for self-preservation—but I knew I'd eventually have to find a way to open her up, especially if Curly's situation deteriorated.

On the other hand, she'd given me something—the name of O'Bannion's business associate in San Francisco. At that point, I knew absolutely nothing about Tommy Fang, but at least I had another lead to follow, a place to start my inquiries on the coast. I made a mental note to call Danny King and have him run Fang's name through the NCIC as soon as possible. After that, I'd tap my old network of police associates and see if they could set me up with a contact in the San Francisco police department. Maybe the local cops had information on O'Bannion and Fang's activities in that city and would be willing to point me in the right direction.

I was ransacking my memory for people I might have known in the San Francisco police department when I smelled perfume and heard the rustle of feminine clothing as someone took the barstool next to mine, someone with very nice legs. I looked up from the legs and into the smiling face of Cindy Thompson, a face that had inspired and bedeviled a hundred hormone-ravaged football players back in the days when she was head cheerleader for Laramie High School.

Most recently, her face had graced political posters nailed to almost every flat surface in Victory as she campaigned for reelection to the town council. She'd won handily and, as president of that august body, was second in command after the mayor, Curly Ahearn. As such, she was one of the people responsible for my continued employment.

She was also the recent ex-wife of Harv Thompson, my friend and personal banker. I'd known the two of them since I first moved to Victory, and liked them immensely, so I was distressed when I heard about their breakup, and even more by the reason behind it. According to Victory's gossip pipeline—which transmits information faster than the Internet—she threw Harv out of their four-bedroom home less than an hour after catching him in flagrante delicto with a twenty-four-year-old teller who was bent over the large walnut desk in his office at the bank. Local wags said Harv maintained that he was only giving the young woman some advice on her golf swing— a defense that might have been more plausible had he been wearing pants at the time instead of a tequila-induced grin, a fluorescent green condom, and the teller's pantyhose wrapped around his neck like an aviator's scarf.

As I've often told him to his face, Harv Thompson is a pig, and certainly not deserving of his wife, who that evening looked as if she'd just stepped from the pages of *Ladies Home Journal*. About thirty-six years old, she probably carried less than 120 pounds on her five-foot-seven frame. Her strawberry-blond hair was cut to her shoulders and set off a face that belonged on a shampoo bottle— even if her nose was a little too large and her eyes a tad too close together to be considered a classic beauty. Dressed in a simple sleeveless black sheath dress that came to her knees, black pumps, and a single strand of pearls, Cindy Thompson was the best-looking woman in the room. "Hey, cowboy," she said, adjusting her skirt. "Mind if I join you?"

I gave her the patented Starbranch smile and, remembering that she didn't smoke, stubbed my cigar in the ashtray. "I'd be offended if you didn't, ma'am," I said. I motioned to the bartender. "Buy the lady a drink?" I asked.

She ordered something called a mudslide, which looked suspiciously like a milk shake and left a little mustache on her upper lip after she took her first drink. She patted it off with a napkin. "Looks like you've had a tough one, Harry," she said.

I agreed. "Feels tough," I said. "It's that body we found on the mountain the other day. I'm sure you've heard the rumors."

She nodded soberly. "That Curly's a suspect?" she asked. "Yeah, I've heard those rumors. You know how fast news like that travels around here—it's all Victory's talking about." She leaned toward me and spoke softly so she wouldn't be overheard, not that anyone seemed to be listening. "What's the deal?" she asked. "Is he going to be arrested?"

I answered with more conviction than I felt. "Not if I can help it," I said. There was no reason to keep her completely in the dark, so I spent a few minutes telling her as much as I could about Baldi's suspicions and my efforts to clear the mayor before the sheriff acted on those suspicions.

When I finished, Cindy looked saddened and obviously worried. "Poor Curly," she said sincerely. "Is there anything I can do to help?"

I told her there wasn't much she could do to aid the investigation but Curly needed all the support from his friends that he could get. "When you hear all the stories in the next few days," I told her, "you might remind the people telling them that it's Curly Ahearn they're talking about here, not Jeffrey Dahmer, and that people are innocent until proven guilty, even in Victory."

She smiled sweetly. "I can do that, Harry," she said. "I'm real convincing when I preach from the high ground." She thought for a minute. "I just hope it all works out."

We sat in companionable silence while we finished our drinks. When the bartender came back I declined a refill, but Cindy told him she'd have one for the road. When it came, she swiveled around on her stool to survey the diehards and finally shook her head in disgust. "When you got divorced, Harry," she said thoughtfully, "how long did it take you to get used to being single again?"

"About five minutes," I said, laughing. "And then I sobered up."

She patted my arm. "You still love her?"

"Nicole?" I asked. "Of course. I miss her all the time. She's my best friend."

"That's the problem for me, too," Cindy agreed. "Harv was always a better friend than he was a husband. It isn't that hard to throw a man who thinks with his penis out into the street, but slamming that door on your best friend—that's a bitch."

Onstage, the band leader announced last call and then broke into a slow buckle polisher of a song. All around us, people started pairing off, some of them heading toward the dance floor, others toward the door. A college type who'd been watching Cindy from a table in one of the darkened booths stood up and started meandering in our direction with a hopeful look on his face, but I glared at him until he took the hint and went off in search of other game.

Cindy watched impassively as her would-be suitor skulked off like a hungry jackal, the same way I imagined she'd look at a bug under a magnifying glass. "I'm afraid I'm not very good at this," she said.

"What?" I asked. She looked at me, and I noticed that her eyes had that slightly unfocused look that comes from too many hours in a smoky saloon and too many sweet drinks.

She waved her hand at the couples on the dance floor. "Putting myself back in circulation. I meet a man and we go about this far," she said, holding her thumb and index finger about an inch apart. "And then I think to myself, What do I really know about this loser, and why would I possibly want to have sex with him?" She smiled sadly. "I've slept alone every night since Harv left."

I reached over and took her hand. "You get used to it after a while," I said. "One evening you'll realize your own company ain't so bad after all. Then, when the time is right, you'll discover you're ready for that other stuff again, and it won't seem like a big deal. Natural as air."

Cindy stood up and took me by the arm. "I'm sorta into more immediate gratification, Harry," she said with a laugh. "I don't think I want to wait that long." She looked at me for a few seconds and then leaned forward so she could whisper into my ear. Her breath was warm and moist and smelled like chocolate. "You're the nicest guy I know these days, so here's an idea," she said. "Why don't you come out to the house and I'll run us a nice bath. Pour you a nightcap. After that we'll have meaningless sex." She paused, winked. "Think of it as therapy, Harry. It'd be great for my self-confidence."

Cindy Thompson and I had always engaged in some harmless, low-voltage flirting, and I'll admit that once or twice I'd imagined having a wild sexual encounter with the lady, but I'd always done my imagining in the privacy of my own mind—and that's where I expected the fantasy to stay. A concrete offer from the flesh-and-blood woman caught me by complete surprise and left me scrambling for an answer as I felt a warm blush creeping across my cheeks. She must have thought my discomfort was funny, because she laughed. "What's the matter, Harry?" she asked. "Cat got your tongue? Don't worry, podna . . . I'd still respect you in the morning. If you want to, we can just pretend it never happened."

"No, Cindy," I sputtered, "it's just that you and Harv. Well, Harv, he's . . . And you're . . . well, you're—"

"In need of a friend," she broke in, pulling me to my feet. Cindy chuckled some more and then she gave me a feathery kiss on the cheek. I started to protest again, but she held a finger to my lips before I could form a word. "That offer took all the courage I have at the moment, Harry," she said, suddenly very serious. "If you're any kind of gentleman, you'll just shut up and come on."

8

I woke the next morning before the sun was fully up and, for a few terrifying seconds, had no idea where I was. In the half-light of dawn, I could tell I was in a large bedroom with floor-to-ceiling windows, rich draperies, heavy wooden dressers, and a bed nearly as big as the deck of an aircraft carrier. Next, I realized I had absolutely no feeling in my right arm, which at that moment was wrapped around a woman snuggled up to my side with just a thatch of blond hair sticking out from under the covers.

I stayed right where I was for a few minutes, enjoying the radiant heat of Cindy's body and the cozy warmth of the feather comforter that covered us. Then, when I was fully awake, I carefully inched my arm out from under her and sat up to rub the sleep from my eyes. When I could wiggle my fingertips again, I tiptoed into the bathroom to shower and dress so I could be on the road before she woke up.

By the time I finished, she was up and on her way back into the bedroom with two steaming mugs of coffee. "Good morning, Harry," she said happily, handing me one of the cups. "Did you think you could sneak out of here without saying goodbye?"

I took the coffee and sipped gratefully. Then I sat back down on the bed and balanced the cup on my knee. "Listen, Cindy," I said sheepishly, "it isn't that I was sneaking out. It's just that—"

"Oh, cut it out, Harry," she said with a chuckle. "You wanted to get out of here before anyone noticed your car in the driveway."

I shrugged.

"Maybe I *want* people to see your car out there," she said playfully. "Maybe I want 'em to talk."

I shook my head in disbelief. "Trust me when I tell you that's a bad idea, Cindy," I said. "This town is so small you could fit it on a postage stamp, and we're both public officials. People see my car out there and they're gonna get the wrong idea. They're gonna think—"

I stopped talking when I realized she was laughing like a maniac. She sat down on the bed, put her arm around me, and gave me a kiss on the neck. "You have nothing to worry about, Mr. Starbranch. Your manners were impeccable." She paused and winked. *"Damn it."*

Which was the unvarnished truth, not that anyone in Victory would believe it. I'd followed her home the night before, and we'd taken a nice, leisurely soak in her hot tub. After that, she'd poured us both snifters of brandy, but instead of doing anything we'd have been embarrassed to tell our mothers about, we'd curled up on the couch in the family room and held each other while we watched a late-night showing of *The Big Sleep*. We both conked out during the movie, and when it was over we stumbled upstairs and fell into bed—our relationship unconsummated by mutual decree.

I winked back. "I know what you mean," I said. "Sometimes I even surprise myself."

She laughed again. "It was just what I needed, Harry," she said. "Thanks."

I left Cindy standing on her front porch and whistled to myself all the way out to the farm, where I dropped by my new house to see how the construction was coming along. After that, I stopped by Edna's to tell her I'd be out of town for a day or so. I found her in her backyard dressed in her work clothes—bib overalls, University of Wyoming sweatshirt, and knee-high rubber boots—watering her tomato plants. She raised an eyebrow when she saw me coming through the gate. "You're worse than a damned tomcat, Harry," she said archly. "Staying out all night, doing who knows what. Who you takin' down the road to ruin now? If you don't mind my askin'."

"None of your business, you old snoop," I grumbled good-naturedly. "You're just jealous, that's all."

Edna hooted. "Of course I'm jealous," she said. "It's been more'n forty years since I had to sneak in at the crack of dawn."

"More like fifty," I said, and then dodged out of the way as she shot a spray of water in my direction. To change the subject, I motioned at her plants. "Wish you'd hurry up and get those grown so I can come over and steal 'em," I said.

She gave me a toothless grin. She'd neglected to put her dentures in again. "Try to steal my tomatoes and I'll fill your sorry butt with buckshot," she said. She closed the nozzle on the hose and wiped her hands on the front of her overalls. "That plumber working on your house was over yesterday afternoon," she said. "Told me to ask you if you wanted a bidet in the bathroom. I told him to go ahead."

"You what?"

"You heard me," she said. "I told him to put that sucker in."

I sat down on her back-porch steps and reached over to shut the water off, in case she took a notion to spray me again. "Now what the hell do I need a bidet for?" I asked the old woman reasonably.

She shrugged her bony shoulders. "You never know when one of those doodads will come in handy," she said mischievously. "Who knows, maybe I'll come over and borrow it sometime. Give myself a thrill."

The mental image of ancient Edna Cook on a bidet was so amusing it put an added shine on the whole morning. When I got her grudging promise to watch over the place while I was gone, I went inside my own home and slipped into fresh clothes. Then I hopped back into the Jeep and buzzed into Victory, where I stopped by Ginny Larsen's Country Kitchen for a western omelette and home fries.

By the time I finished with breakfast it was a little after seven, and when I looked down the block toward the office, I saw that Frankie

Bull's cruiser was already in its parking space out front. I wheeled into the space beside his and let myself into the office, where I found him drinking a cup of coffee with that morning's edition of the *Laramie Boomerang* spread out over his desk.

He looked up when I walked in, just long enough to give me a disapproving cluck of his tongue. "You ought to have a little more regard for the lady's reputation," he said reprovingly and without preamble.

I was getting ready to sail my hat at the hat rack, but I stopped in mid-fling. "What the hell are you talking about?" I asked.

"The woman you were with last night. You ought to be a little more discreet."

I knew it, I thought. I should have gotten up at four o'clock instead of sleeping until five. "What did you hear?" I asked testily.

"Nothin'," he said, looking back down at the sports section. "I'm Sioux. We see signs that tell us everything we need to know."

"Don't give me that mystical bullshit," I said. I took the newspaper off his desk. He grabbed for it, but I held it just out of reach. "How'd you find out?"

He smiled then and yanked the paper out of my hands, smoothed the wrinkles out on his desktop, and went back to reading. "The lipstick on your neck," he muttered. "It's a dead giveaway."

I went into the bathroom and looked in the mirror. Sure enough, there was a pair of red lipstick lips on my neck, just above the collar. No wonder people were giving me funny looks in the restaurant at breakfast. I dabbed water on a paper towel and washed myself clean.

When I came back out, Frankie was closing the blinds at the window. "Going out?" I asked.

He finished with the windows and clicked on our answering machine. "You're going up to the reservation today, aren't you, boss?" he asked. I noticed that he was dressed a little more sedately than usual. Instead of his customary motorcycle vest and black Stetson, he was wearing a T-shirt with old-time Indians decked out in sunglasses on the front, faded jeans, and hard-soled moccasins. His hair was braided, with otter fur wrapped around the bottoms of the braids. His hammered-silver arm bands, ear cuffs, and aviator sunglasses set off the ensemble.

"That's the plan," I said. "I'm supposed to meet the Fish and Wildlife investigator up there around two."

"In that case," he said, "I thought I might ride along with you."

I looked at him questioningly, since I knew Frankie had few fond memories of the Wind River Reservation. He'd moved there shortly after he married his wife, Frieda, a Shoshone who was taking part in the Miss Indian America pageant in Sheridan. Frieda had insisted on living on the reservation in order to be close to her family, but the experience had been difficult for Frankie. The reservation was set aside for the Shoshone and Arapaho tribes, and as a Sioux, Frankie was something of an outsider. Even though he had been a tribal policeman when he lived on the Pine Ridge Reservation in South Dakota, he'd had a tough time making ends meet as a newlywed in Wyoming. With the exception of odd jobs as a handyman, he'd been unemployed for the better part of two years before they moved off the Wind River Reservation so Frieda could get her teaching degree at the University of Wyoming and Frankie could look for a job in law enforcement, a position he found in Victory. Although joblessness had given him plenty of time to work on his sculpture, I knew he'd been happy to see the reservation in his rearview mirror. To my knowledge, he hadn't been back to visit since the day they packed up their U-Haul and moved south.

"You afraid I'm gonna be lonely?" I asked.

He shook his head. "Nah, Harry," he said, chuckling. "I know you're never lonely as long as you've got yourself to talk to. I just have a little business up there to take care of. You remember me telling you about John Thorpe?"

"That Shoshone elder whose house you remodeled?" I asked. "The one who let you use that little cabin for a studio?"

Frankie nodded. "That's the one," he said. "His wife died a couple days ago, and John is having her ceremony this afternoon. Thought I'd pay my respects."

It wasn't that Victory was a hotbed of criminal activity, but I didn't like both of us to be out of town at the same time.

"Sorry, Frankie," I said. "I need you to hang around here in case Rollie Swenson sees flying saucers landing in his wife's vegetable garden again."

Frankie rolled his eyes at the very mention of Swenson's name. Rollie had been reporting visits from space aliens on a regular basis for the last six months—both at his small ranch outside Victory and his home in town. Once he'd even awakened me at three in the morning to let me know that on their most recent visit the aliens— short big-headed fellows with no hair and black eyes—had abducted him and performed a series of experiments that included extracting his semen with a six-inch needle hooked up to some kind of nuclear suction pump. We always answered Rollie's calls, but so far neither of us had gotten a glimpse of the alleged perpetrators of the latest intergalactic outrage.

"Oh, come on, Harry," he said. "If the Martians come while we're out of town, we'll just have Rollie's wife get their license number and put out an A.P.B. when we get home."

I chuckled and shook my head. "Sorry, Frankie," I said. "Whether the space aliens come for Rollie or not, I still need you to stay in Victory and mind the store. I especially need you to keep close tabs on Curly. If Tony Baldi comes poking around here today, I want one of us on hand to make sure he minds his manners."

Frankie wasn't happy about it, but he saw my point. "I suppose you're right," he said. He reached into his desk drawer and drew out an envelope with John Thorpe's name written on the front in his rounded script. He handed the envelope to me. "If you get a chance, would you mind delivering my condolences?" he asked. "The ceremony's scheduled to start around noon at the Fort Washakie pow-wow grounds, right down the road from the police station. You'll know it when you see it."

I filled my thermos with coffee and was on the highway by seven-twenty, happy to be on the open road on such a fine summer day. I traveled west on I–80 until I came to Rawlins, then turned north through the Great Divide Basin, drove past the rocky humps of the Ferris Mountains and the gas stations and liquor stores at Bairoil and Lamont, past the rolling Green Mountains and into the modern-day ghost town of Jeffrey City, the most depressing town in Wyoming.

A few miles northwest of Jeffrey City, the scenery begins to improve; the land is greener, awash with wildflowers in the spring and early summer, with the Wind River Mountains rising majestically to the west. I dropped over Beaver Rim and down the steep grade into the valley of Beaver Creek, slowing to let a couple of eighteen-wheelers pass me so I could enjoy the pleasant drive through the foothills of the Wind Rivers into the mountain town of Lander. From Lander, it's only a short hop north to the boundary of the reservation and the tribal center at Fort Washakie.

It was nearing noon when I arrived at the heart of the reservation, feeling—as I always do when I travel there—like I was visiting a Third World nation.

Larger than most counties in the state, the Wind River Indian Reservation boasts some of the most beautiful vistas imaginable. Set aside for the Shoshone because of the tribe's general friendliness to the whites who settled the West, the reservation was now shared by the Arapaho, the Shoshone's hereditary enemies, who were moved onto the reservation in the late 1870s. After killing each other on sight for most of their collective memories, the two tribes lived in uneasy proximity for decades, their sections of the reservation divided by a highway known among tribesmen as the Mason-Dixon line.

These days the Shoshone and Arapaho get along fairly well and share common goals—the primary objective being the continued economic and cultural survival of their people. Although the reservation is one of the more prosperous in terms of agricultural and mineral wealth, and members of both tribes receive a modest monthly living allotment, that prosperity is relative compared with the predominantly Anglo settlements of Riverton and Lander, which border the reservation to the east and south.

Driving down the highway into Fort Washakie, you feel you could be driving the back roads of the rural South. Although some homes are bright and well kept, cars and pickup trucks on blocks litter the driveways and front yards of many others. Rooflines sag, shingles buckle, concrete cracks and swells, almost everything needs a fresh coat of paint. In one home, a tract dwelling that looked as if it had been built within the last two years, a horse stood in the living room, poking its head through the empty space where the picture window used to be. There were two goats sunning themselves on the front porch, and chickens scratched the weedy, sunbaked earth at the edge of the drive. Naked children played around the broken hulk of a refrigerator in another, watched over by a group of hard-eyed young men drinking beer on the front stoop. The young men eyed me suspiciously when I passed, as did the drivers of most of the vehicles I met on the road. The drivers of others seemed to look through me as if I didn't exist.

I had plenty of time to kill before my two o'clock meeting with Andy Patti, so I stopped at a trading post and purchased some hanks of elk fur, horsehair, and pheasant feathers that would come in handy the next time I had time to tie a few trout flies. Then I found a lunch counter and ordered an iced tea and a bacon cheeseburger, which I munched while I read that morning's edition of the *Riverton Ranger.*

When I finished my lunch, I walked out to the parking lot and followed the sound of Indian drumming a quarter mile to the pow-wow grounds, where I found a dusty parking space among forty or fifty other vehicles, most of them older four-wheel drives with dried mud caked on their dented quarter panels. I skuffed through the parking lot and followed a small group of older men and women to the dancing area, where about sixty or seventy people were milling around, waiting for the ceremony to begin. To the right of a small set of bleachers, four Indians in T-shirts, short-sleeved Western shirts, and ball caps beat a communal drum in a slow, mournful rhythm while a group of women sang a tremolo accompaniment. Several people in the crowd glanced at me curiously as I took a seat on the bleachers and settled down until the time was right to deliver Frankie's envelope.

During my years in Wyoming, I'd visited the Wind River Reservation twice to watch the tribe's annual Sundance in July, but I'd never been to a "giveaway" before, although I knew in general terms what to expect because Frankie had described it. The ceremony, presided over by a close family member to honor a loved one who has died, consists largely of that person's giving away nearly everything he or she owns. This accomplishes two things. First, it's a dramatic testament to the insignificance of material possessions in the face of such unimaginable personal loss. Second, it allows those who are left behind to begin anew, unfettered by the possessions that bound them to the past.

Before long, the drummers increased their volume and intensity and the procession began, led by a barrel-shaped man with mahogany skin and close-cropped iron-gray hair, who I assumed was John Thorpe. He carried a large portrait of a woman I imagined was his deceased wife in a gilded frame and began leading the assembled relatives and friends in a slow procession around the dance area. When the mourners had gone entirely around the enclosure in time to the song played by the drummers and singers, Thorpe broke away from the line and took his place at a long table that had been set up in the middle of the arena, a table overflowing with towels and blankets, cookware, appliances, radios, a television set, and assorted household goods. Behind the table was the couple's furniture—chairs, tables, bookcases, bed frames, and dressers.

The first person in the line was given a dresser, which he carried away after speaking briefly with Thorpe. The next person was given a stack of bedding. The next, a box of pots and pans. The next, a blue Hudson's Bay blanket. And so it went, with some of the mourners going through the line a second time, until nearly all of the furniture and household goods were gone.

It was nearing the time when I was expected at the tribal police station to meet with Patti, so I stood self-consciously and took my place at the end of the line, keeping my eyes down until I reached the table. Thorpe obviously didn't know me, but that didn't keep him from observing the protocol of the occasion. When I came abreast of him, he picked a five-dollar bill from a small stack of cash at the end of the table and placed it in my hand. I didn't want to insult him by refusing the money, so I closed one hand around the bill and removed Frankie's letter from my pocket with the other.

"This is from Frankie Bull," I said. "He would have been here himself if he could."

The old man nodded in recognition of the name, took the letter, and tucked it unopened into the inside pocket of his corduroy dress jacket.

"I'm sorry for your loss," I said, but by that time Thorpe was already handing a toaster oven to a woman who had come late and taken the place behind me in the snaking line.

I turned away from the table and walked back toward the bleachers and the parking lot, my boots sending up small clouds of gritty dust with every step. In a grassy area at the edge of the parking lot, a group of men erected the poles for a tepee they were setting up, while two men erecting another pole adjusted the smoke poles on its canvas shell. Nearby, a couple of young Indian youths rode Appaloosa ponies around the grounds, their bare backs soaking up the heat of the afternoon sun. A group of women preparing the food they'd serve at the conclusion of the giveaway gossiped and talked quietly. I savored the aroma of fried bread and coffee that filled the air, the tangy smoke from someone's pipe, the clean scent of grass and pine.

When I passed the bleachers I looked over to see a man with his ropy, muscular arms resting comfortably on one of the wooden planks, watching me with amused curiosity. I nodded hello as I passed, and he turned away from the bleachers and fell in beside me. "You must be Harry Starbranch," he said, holding out a callused hand. "I'm Ben Moss."

I stopped and shook his hand, felt the strength of his rough grip. At about five eleven and 170 pounds, Moss looked to be in his early thirties. Dressed in jeans, a flannel shirt with the sleeves cut off at the biceps, and a straw cowboy hat with a rattlesnake band, he had a lanky runner's frame, a gaunt face with prominent cheekbones, and large brown eyes. He was wearing a military-looking 9-mm automatic on his hip and carried a good pair of binoculars around his neck. "I'm a tribal game warden," he explained, smiling. "Andy Patti and I have been expecting you." He looked at his watch. "Don't want to keep the man waiting."

He walked away, his long legs eating ground. I struggled to catch up. "Did Patti send you to meet me?" I asked curiously. I wasn't late for the meeting and couldn't figure why I'd needed an escort.

"Nah," Moss said, pulling a ring of keys from his pocket. He stopped beside a green Ford four-wheel-drive pickup with the tribal insignia on the side, unlocked the door, and hopped in. "I was just driving by and saw you hanging around out there. Figured you might have gotten lost."

I blinked my eyes. I didn't know whether to be grateful or insulted. It was nice to rate a personal welcome, but I was surely too old for a baby-sitter. "How'd you know who I was?" I asked. For a couple of seconds, I imagined he'd spotted my Jeep in the parking lot and picked out the Albany County plates. Then it came to me. Mine was the only Anglo face among the throng of Shoshones. I shrugged my shoulders sheepishly. "Never mind," I said.

Moss smiled crookedly and shook his head. "Cops," he muttered, but he meant morons. Then he peeled away, peppering my legs with a spray of gravel.

9

I followed Ben Moss a quarter of a mile to the tribal headquarters at Fort Washakie, the relatively new administration buildings a striking contrast to the slightly down-at-the-heels look of much of the rest of the reservation. By the time I found a space in the crowded parking lot fronting the reservation police department and switched off my engine, Moss had already parked his green Ford and gone inside. I walked up the short walk and into a small reception area, where a secretary with thick black hair to the middle of her back pointed me down a tiled hallway to the police department and the tribal jail.

I turned off the hallway into the police department's bull pen, and recognized the ambience immediately. The place looked as if it had been on the receiving end of a paper blizzard that nobody had bothered to clean up because they were waiting for federal disaster-relief funds. The dozen or so institutional-gray metal desks varied widely in size and shape, and none of the chairs matched. The bulletin board was cluttered with so many layers of memos and cartoons that I imagined the junk hanging there would fill an entire dumpster. Although it was a beautiful summer day outside, the windows were closed and dust motes danced in the light filtered through the blinds. Each desk carried an assortment of chipped mugs and Styrofoam cups, and the aroma of charred coffee and tobacco was so pervasive that its atomic residue had probably permeated the Sheetrock on the walls. The only way you'd ever get rid of that smell would be to rip everything out, right down to the studs, fumigate, and start from scratch.

All of the desks except two were empty. At one desk in the far corner, an earnest young man in a white Stetson with a tribal police badge on the front of his shirt typed reports on an old electric typewriter using only his index fingers, his lips pursed in concentration. Moss sat on top of another, sharing a joke with the man who sat in the chair with his stubby legs propped on the desktop. When they saw me standing in the doorway, the man in the chair stopped laughing, but the amusement didn't leave his eyes. In his mid-forties, he was rounding in the belly and cheeks—and because his Marine Corps cap was pushed back on his head, I could tell that he was fighting a losing battle with male-pattern baldness. He had an old tattoo of the Marine insignia on one forearm and a bloody dagger on the other, both of them blue and blurring with age—the kind of tattoos laser surgeons live to remove. The .44 magnum he was wearing was all business, however, and I had a hunch he knew how to use it. For a few seconds as I stood there, he took my measure, as men do, then he smiled and nodded a cheerful hello.

"You Andy Patti?" I asked.

He stood and crossed the room, his hand extended. "That I am," he said. "And you'd be Harry Starbranch." He hooked a finger over his shoulder toward Moss. "I was just telling Ben here to be nice, since we're in the presence of an honest-to-God legend."

I thought he was poking fun at me, so I didn't answer. Patti was quick to explain. "That business with the white supremacists last year," he said. "You did good work."

"I was lucky," I said. Mr. Humility.

Patti chuckled again. "I doubt it, Mr. Starbranch," he said. "I truly do."

He motioned me to one of the empty desks and, noticing the box of cheroots in my shirt pocket, told me I was welcome to smoke if I liked. He pawed around on one of the desktops until he came up with an ashtray brimming with the butts of Pall Mall unfiltereds and set it in front of me. Then he found a fresh Styrofoam cup and poured me some of the vile black sludge that was simmering on the hot plate of the stained coffeemaker on a table at the end of the room.

I thanked him for the coffee and took a sip. The brew was luke-warm and every bit as disgusting as it looked. I winced in agony, then I drained the cup, crushed it, and pitched the ruined hulk into a trash basket. The stuff was so strong, I guessed I probably wouldn't need another caffeine fix for at least six months. "Some things never change," I observed. "That stuff's the reason you never see many really old cops."

Ben Moss laughed out loud. "Don't say that in this office, Mr. Starbranch," he said. "That's not your ordinary cop coffee—it's a secret Shoshone recipe supposed to put lead in your pencil. The elders around here swear by it."

"Perfect," I said. "If it ever looks like I'm gonna get laid again, I'll call you for the ingredients."

We spent a few minutes breaking the ice, talking shop, and a few more while Patti told me how he'd come to work with Ben Moss. The Shoshones and Arapahos have a fine big-game management program on the reservation, he said, and their wardens, like Moss, don't need much outside help when it comes to enforcement. But when poachers in the backcountry cross the boundary between the reservation and the national forest, the crime becomes multijuris-dictional. That's when the state Game and Fish Department comes in. The U. S. Fish and Wildlife Service becomes involved if it looks as if Native American poachers are selling their reservation kills out of state, or if white poachers are involved on reservation ground. "There's a lot of country out there, and the reservation boundary is just an imaginary line," Patti said. "We wind up working together fairly often."

Patti opened a battered leather briefcase, pulled out a file folder, and flipped it open. The top sheet was an arrest report with a book-ing photo that had been attached with a paper clip. I learned the trick of reading upside down years ago when I was a beat cop, and I saw that the arrest report was for a man named Pius Franklin, dated about ten days previously. "Which brings us to the reason for your visit," he said, spinning the folder around and pushing it in my direction. "I understand you're investigating a subject very dear to my heart—these assholes who're selling bladders from illegally slaughtered black bears on the Asian market."

I told him that was becoming a tangential part of my investigation, although it wasn't the main focus. Primarily, I said, I was working Liam O'Bannion's homicide, trying to learn as much about him, his business, and his associates as possible in hopes of finding his killer. So far, I told Patti and Moss, I'd heard a lot of rumors and unearthed some promising leads, but I had nothing I could take to court. I'd learned from Al Kincaid and Leo Becker that Patti was interested in both Pantaleo and O'Bannion, I said, and I was hoping they could help me fill in a few of the blanks.

Patti looked at Ben Moss, who nodded in agreement to some unspoken question. Moss stood and excused himself from the room through a side door. "I could probably tell you some of what you want to know," Patti said. "But I think we'll introduce you to Mr. Pius Franklin and let him do it for us. It's so much more fascinating when it comes from the horse's mouth, don't you think?"

Five minutes later, I was seated in the police station's small interrogation room with Andy Patti, going over the file on Pius Franklin, when Moss led Franklin in and motioned him to take a chair across the wooden table from us.

Franklin, dressed in an orange jumpsuit and flip-flops, with handcuffs on his wrists, looked to be in his mid-twenties. His long hair was greasy-looking and his broad face was pockmarked from adolescent acne. His fingernails were caked with dirt and he smelled of rank body odor and about a thousand cigarettes. His surly coyote eyes glanced around the room suspiciously, and he sat forward on his chair, muscles tensed, feet flat on the floor, as if he planned to bolt at the first opportunity. I gave him a dismissive once-over and went back to my reading.

According to his file, Franklin had an arrest record going back almost a decade. He'd spent time in juvenile detention for stealing a car. As a teenager, he'd also been locked up for suspected burglary, selling alcohol to minors, possession of drug paraphernalia, and simple assault. When he turned eighteen, he'd been arrested in Riverton for possession of narcotics with intent to distribute, and had served three years in the state penitentiary in Rawlins. He'd spent the two years since his release getting into more trouble—two arrests for drunk driving and resisting arrest, three for reckless driving, one for beating his mother with a rolled-up magazine over money, and one for pulling a knife on a friend at the tribal recreation center. Either of the last two arrests could have put him back in the pen, but his mother refused to press charges, and the victim in the knife incident recanted his story before the case went to trial.

Ten days earlier, Franklin had been arrested by a reservation police officer near the St. Stephens Mission with nine ounces of methamphetamine in his glove compartment—more than enough to warrant a charge of possession with intent to distribute—and was looking at hard time.

He was also looking to make a deal. According to the file, he'd agreed to roll over on everyone associated in his various schemes if the drug-dealing charge could be reduced to simple possession, which might put him behind bars for a couple years, maximum.

To his credit, the prosecutor hadn't bitten, but had told Franklin and his attorney that if his information was good enough, he'd give some serious thought to the bargain. So far, Franklin had apparently given up the names of two burglars, a car thief, a livestock rustler, three big-game poachers who worked with him to kill wild game on the reservation and sell it to out-of-state buyers, and a half-dozen petty drug dealers. He'd also named his source for the methamphetamine that he had in his possession at the time of his arrest, and the person who bought gall bladders and paws from the bears he and his pals gunned down in the Wind River Mountains and the neighboring Shoshone National Forest. He claimed that the source of the speed and the person who bought his bear bladders for $90 apiece was the same individual—a guy from San Francisco named Liam O'Bannion.

I closed the file and stared at Franklin until he began to fidget. Beside me at the table, Patti tried to hide his amusement, leaned forward and made a little tent of his fingers. Ben Moss walked behind Franklin and glared at the back of his head. Having him back there made Pius Franklin a very anxious man, and he kept glancing nervously over his shoulder at Moss's imposing form.

"I want you to tell me everything you know about Liam O'Bannion and your business with him," I said quietly. "Start right at the beginning."

Franklin blew air from his lips and gave me the kind of look that said I was wasting his precious time. When his mouth cracked in a half smile, half sneer, I saw that one of his front teeth was broken so it ended in a point and the rest of them were yellow and had food caked in the spaces. Man was in serious need of a Water Pik. "I already told these guys everything there is to tell," he said. "I don't see why I have to go over it all—"

Ben Moss's open palm lashed out so fast it was only a blur, but when it connected with the back of Franklin's head the noise sounded like a gunshot in the small room and snapped Franklin's face so far forward that he almost smacked face first into the table. "Because we asked you to, you miserable cocksucker, that's why," Moss growled. "If we want you to tell it a million times, then that's how many goddamned times you'll tell it." He grabbed Franklin by the hair and held his head in place while he leaned his face in close to Franklin's. Franklin wanted to look away, but his eyes were drawn back to Ben Moss's, the way a rat's are to a cobra just before it strikes. "Do we understand each other?"

Although it can be an effective technique, I've never believed in beating a prisoner for information, and Moss's quick resort to violence made me uncomfortable. I looked at Patti to see if we should jump in, but he waved me off with a subtle hand gesture. I sat back uncomfortably and waited for Pius Franklin's response.

Franklin's jaw muscles bunched in anger, his hands clenched, and the tendons in his forearms twitched with isometric tension. It didn't take a mind reader to know what he was thinking: If he ever had the chance to kill Ben Moss, he'd do it in a heartbeat. Slit his throat and watch him bleed. For the time being, however, he was helpless. He finally nodded acquiescence. "We understand each other," he said, the words soft and wet, dripping bile.

Moss released Franklin's hair, but he gave his head a forward shove as he did it. "Then get to it, Pius," he said, "before I lose my patience." Then he walked over to the door and stood there glowering, his arms folded across his chest like clubs.

Now that the immediate danger had passed, Franklin turned surly again. He shrugged his shoulders and sighed. Doing us a big favor.

"What can you tell me about him?" I asked.

"Huh?"

"Tell me about him," I said. "What kind of man was he?"

"Smart," Franklin said. "And mean, at least according to his own reckoning." There was an evil gleam in his eyes when he looked at me. "One time, he told me he cut a guy's dick off with a pair of pruning shears 'cause the guy owed him 500 bucks."

"You believed him?" I asked.

Franklin laughed. "Man was white, wasn't he?" he asked, as if that explained everything. "Of course I didn't believe him. To my way of thinkin', he was nothin' more than a pale blowhard in a good suit of clothes—kind of man who talks a rough game but starts cryin' the first time you land one on his nose." He shrugged, a real man of the world. "Still, he had his uses—number one bein' a real entrepreneurial spirit, number two bein' his connections, and number three bein' that in spite of the fact I wouldn't trust him to empty my piss bucket, he always paid cash. We did a little business together from time to time."

"Where'd you meet?"

"Met him about five years ago," he said. "Up at that elk antler auction the Boy Scouts have every year at Jackson Hole. You know what I'm talking about?"

I said I did. Every year the Scouts and other volunteers collect antlers dropped by the thousands of elk that winter on the National Elk Refuge and bring them to downtown Jackson Hole, where the horns are auctioned off by the pound, mostly to buyers who grind them up and sell them on the Asian medicinal market. The auction draws bidders from around the world, some of them directly from the Orient, others American middlemen who supply the Asian market. It's a highly publicized and aboveboard auction, with most of the proceeds going to feed elk on the refuge. "Liam was a bidder?" I asked.

"Nah, he was there sellin' Amway," Franklin snorted. "Of course he was bidding. Antlers was one of his sources of income. He said he came there every year."

I made a note in my notebook and waited for him to go on. "Anyway, I ran into him in a greasy spoon the next morning, and we got to talking about how little dropped antlers were worth—at that time about nine bucks a pound—and how much more money he could make if he had a supply of blood-velvet antlers. You havta get those from the critters while they're still alive, and you gotta take 'em in the summer months before the legal hunting season, but you can get twenty-five bucks a pound."

As if that made it acceptable to slaughter a 600-pound bull elk in the prime of life, I thought angrily. A few hundred dollars more for liquor and drugs. Leave the carcass to scavengers. I held my tongue, but Patti didn't. I could tell he wanted to jump across the table and grab Franklin by the throat, but he restrained himself. Instead, he attacked verbally, his words short and sharp, like punches. "So you told him you knew where you could get plenty of velvet antlers, didn't you, Pius?" he hissed. "You and your buddies would shoot them right here on the reservation."

Franklin looked away, picking at one of his teeth with his fingernail. Letting Patti know he wasn't scared. "Yeah, I got him a few horns," he said. "We made a little money together." He looked challengingly at Ben Moss. "It ain't like we was killin' anybody. It ain't like we was robbin' banks."

According to Franklin, who told the rest of his story grudgingly, O'Bannion had seemed content with the velvet-horn trade for the better part of a year, but then he started dropping hints that he'd be interested in other commodities. In particular, the Asians he supplied wanted bear paws and bladders. They wanted a lot of them, and they wanted them fresh. For that, he promised, he'd be willing to pay top dollar. It was a risky proposition, after all, and risks deserved compensation.

Franklin, the budding entrepreneur, thought about it for a while and then figured what the hell. It took him a little time, but he eventually put together a loose coalition of Shoshone and Arapaho hunters who scoured the Wind Rivers for black bears. When they found them, they killed them on sight, removed the valuable parts, packed them on ice, and brought them back to Franklin. Sometimes they kept the hide and claws for themselves. Most times they left the meat on the ground to rot.

"Bear's greasy meat," Franklin observed by way of explanation.

For his part, Franklin made sure the bladders and paws were picked up and everyone got paid. It was good money, he said proudly, sometimes 300 or 400 bucks a month, once in a while more, especially if the hunters found a den with cubs.

I swallowed my disgust and tried to keep my face blank. Patti was trying to do the same, but I figured if he ground his teeth much harder, they'd probably break off at the roots. "Did O'Bannion come to collect the organs and paws himself?" I asked.

Franklin grunted. "First coupla times," he said. "After that, somebody else came. I met 'im at a motel in Riverton and he took the stuff away." He laughed wickedly. "Bastard's so ugly, though, I doubt he did much traveling in the daytime."

Bingo, I thought. "You wouldn't be talkin' about Junior Stone, would you?" I asked. Franklin looked impassive, so I went on. "Short guy, face looks like somebody mashed it with a tire iron?"

Franklin used the heel of his hand to squash his nose against his face. "Snout like this?" he asked. "Like a pig?"

"That's him," I said. "Junior Stone."

"Whatever you say," Franklin chuckled. "Dude never told me his name, and I never asked. All's I know is he had Sweetwater County plates on his big-assed car. Figured he came from Rock Springs."

I looked at Patti, who'd already made the connection. "We did some checking and came up with Stone's name on a motel receipt," he explained. "Checked a little more and found out Stone works for Pantaleo," he said. "That's why I called Becker."

I wanted to ask Patti a question, but I didn't want to ask in front of Pius Franklin. I stood and motioned toward the door, and Patti followed me out in the hall while Moss stayed behind with the prisoner. Patti took some change from his pocket and dropped it into the coin slot of a soda machine, then pushed the button for a cold Dr Pepper. When the soda banged out, he popped the top and took a long swig, swished it around in his mouth like mouthwash, getting the bad taste out.

I thought about lighting a cheroot but gave the notion up. "You find evidence tying Pantaleo to any of this?" I asked.

He shook his head sadly. "Not yet," he said. "It's obvious to me that Pantaleo trucks are carrying this stuff out of state, and I'd bet a thousand bucks he's taking a big chunk of the profits . . . but I can't *prove* it. Franklin says neither O'Bannion nor Stone ever mentioned the guy's name, and he sure never saw him."

He finished his soda in two long swallows, crushed the can, and winged it at a trash container. It bounced on the rim and dropped with a clang. Two points. "That's the main reason Ben and I agreed to talk to you today," he said. "I figured if we did you a favor, you'd share any information you develop on Pantaleo and the other people involved with us." He cocked a thumb over his shoulder toward the door of the interrogation room. "Pius Franklin is just a cocklebur on my round butt," he said. "I want the big shots' heads on a platter, and I'll take all the help I can get to put 'em there."

Two minutes later we were back in the interrogation room, which was hot and dank, thick with the scent of Franklin's acrid sweat. A spider dangled from the metal shade on the light above the table. I swatted it away, but the web tangled in my hand. I grimaced as the spider scrambled up the sleeve of my shirt and brushed it off angrily. I sat back down and reopened my notebook. "So tell me this, Pius," I said. "When was the last time you saw Liam O'Bannion?"

Franklin stared at the ceiling for a few seconds. "Maybe eight months ago," he said. "After that, I talked to him on the phone a few times when we had some merchandise for him, but that was it. He didn't like to come around here and get his hands dirty if he could help it." He chuckled again. "Don't think he cared much for our company."

"Did he call you when he was in the state before he got killed?" I asked, although I thought I already knew the answer. There weren't any long-distance calls made from Curly's phone to the reservation.

"Nah," Franklin said. "I guess I wasn't on his list. Even if he called, though, I would make myself scarce, 'cause I owed him money. Even if I didn't think he'd cut my dick off with a pruning shear, there was no sense taking chances." He thought about that for a second and then smiled. "Guess I won't have to pay it back now, will I?"

I closed the notebook and sat forward. "Two more questions," I said. "First, do you know anybody who was pissed off at O'Bannion, anybody might have wanted him dead?"

Franklin picked at his nose for a second while he considered the question, studying what came out on the end of his finger. "I imagine there were plenty of people who fit that category," he said. "He was just that kinda guy." He flicked his nose prize away with a flip of his fingers. "Know what I mean, Chief?"

When I didn't answer, Franklin stood up, rubbing his wrists where they'd been chafed by the handcuffs. As far as he was concerned, our conversation was just about over and he could get back to his cell. If he was like most prisoners, he'd be anxious to tune in to the afternoon soaps. "You said you had two questions," he said. "That was only one."

I looked him in the eyes. I wanted to be away from him almost as badly as he wanted to be away from us. The man made me feel as if I needed a bath. "What about the drugs you were selling on the reservation?" I asked. "The file says you got those from O'Bannion, too."

Franklin raised one of his thick eyebrows. "Who says I was selling drugs on the res?" he asked. "Like I told the tribal cops, I was gonna use it all myself. Crank myself up like a jet engine and fucking *fly*."

I was beginning to think that Moss had the right idea. Maybe we should just beat the weak-kneed slobber out of this guy and get it over with. "Bullshit," I grumbled. "I want an answer."

Franklin ignored me, turned away and started walking toward the door, but stopped when he saw that Moss had no intention of letting him go without giving me everything I wanted. He looked back over his shoulder. "What's to tell?" he asked. "The man sold a little dope through the mail. Once in a while, I bought it."

His grin looked like a badly carved jack-o'-lantern. "You didn't think a white, moon-assed yuppie like Liam O'Bannion supported his lifestyle just by sellin' bear guts, did ya?"

When Pius Franklin was returned to his cell, I took a chair at one of the desks in the bull pen while Patti opened the blinds and stood looking out the window at a couple of young women drinking sodas at a picnic table at the edge of the parking lot. Moss put a fresh pot of coffee on to brew and sat down with his feet up and his hands clasped behind his head. "So what do you think, Harry?" he asked.

I rubbed my face with my hands. I really did feel gritty and unclean. "I think I feel a little better every time I see a skell like Pius Franklin behind bars," I said. "Reaffirms my faith in the value of police work."

"I just hope we can keep him there," Moss said. "We've got enough problems on the reservation as it is." He pulled his feet off the desk and leaned forward. "Did you learn anything useful in there?" he asked.

"Maybe," I said. "He can definitely tie O'Bannion and Stone to some interstate game violations, and it looks like he can put O'Bannion in the drug business as well. But did he give me anything that will help nail O'Bannion's killer?" I shrugged my shoulders. "I just don't know," I said. "About all I know is that it's beginning to look like I'll have a better chance of finding the answer in San Francisco than in Wyoming."

Patti turned away from the window and filled us each a cup of coffee, which looked just as disgusting fresh as it did several hours old. "So you're going to pursue this poaching angle?" he asked. "Keep us informed about what you turn up."

I took a sip and nodded. "No problem," I said. "But to tell you the truth, I just can't get too excited about the bear-bladder business." Patti frowned and I went on. "If I was a betting man, I'd say it's more likely O'Bannion's drug dabbling got him killed. But who knows? Maybe I'm wrong."

Moss shook his head sadly. "I'm a tribal game warden, not a cop," he said. "But even I know there are plenty of violent people in the drug business." He stood and crossed the distance between us, then sat down on top of the desk in front of me. "You need to understand something, though, Harry," he said seriously. "The people involved in this poaching ring aren't choirboys, either."

His face lit up as if he'd just had an idea. "You in a rush to get back to Victory, Harry?" he asked.

As a matter of fact, I'd been thinking that if I hopped into the Jeep and put the pedal to the metal, I could be home well before midnight. Still, I was interested in what he had to say. Frankie Bull could handle anything that came up, even if I didn't get home until the next day. "I wouldn't mind hitting the road," I said cautiously. "But I suppose I've got a little time. What do you have in mind?"

Moss stood up and pulled his hat from the rack and his sunglasses from his desk drawer. "Take a ride with us," he said. "There's something I want you to see."

The road from Fort Washakie into the high reaches of the Wind River range begins climbing almost immediately, the sagebrush and alkali flatlands, cottonwood hollows, and occasional irrigated farms of the Wind River valley floor giving way to rocky foothills dotted with scrub cedars and lodgepole pines. From the flatlands, I could look up and see the Wind Rivers sweeping across the entire horizon to the west and southwest. Once the blacktop ran out and the road turned to washboard dirt, however, the angle was too steep to see anything but the few yards of winding grade directly in front of our vehicle.

We were all crammed into the front seat of Ben Moss's four-wheel-drive pickup, but Andy Patti had graciously taken the middle so I wouldn't have to contend with the gear shift, which Moss worked continually as we negotiated the climb.

From the passenger's window, which I had open with my arm leaning on the doorframe, I watched nervously as we bumped along the narrow, rocky road at under twenty miles an hour, the old engine of the pickup straining to gain every inch in its battle against the mountain. I was hoping against hope that we wouldn't meet another vehicle coming from the opposite direction, because I wasn't sure the track was wide enough for two vehicles to pass. I certainly didn't want to die in a tangled heap of smoldering metal at the bottom of the mountain. My knuckles grew white as I held on to the doorframe with one hand and braced myself against the dashboard with the other, the three of us leaning into one another every time Moss took a curve.

After we crested the first ridgeline, the road became a bit more level, the incline more gradual, and I relaxed a little as we drove west for nine or ten miles, the burbling Little Wind River on our right and a series of small streams that cut the hill country on our left. At Timmoco Creek, we began angling southwest toward the craggy peak of Mt. Shoshone, Washakie Park, and the great St. Lawrence Basin. In one small meadow ringed with aspens, we jumped a small herd of mule deer lying in the tall grass on the banks of a brook. A mile beyond that, we passed a family Moss recognized as Arapaho cutting firewood with a chain saw, the father bare-chested while he worked the bucking saw, his wife and three children stacking winter wood in the back of their half-ton stock truck. Moss honked and waved as we passed, and though the father only acknowledged us with a nod, the kids waved happily, one of them yelling that Ben should stop by on Sunday because his mother was making her famous peach pie.

We didn't talk much on the drive because we were all too busy concentrating on the road, but eventually Moss plugged a tape into the deck. I was expecting something familiar, perhaps country music. Instead, the tape was Indian, haunting melodies played on wooden flutes that took my imagination back a hundred years or more, to the time when those mountains were dotted with buffalo-hide Shoshone lodges, smoke drifting through the flaps at the top in lazy curls, while the women cured skins and the men leaned against willow back rests, soaked up the afternoon sun and smoked—talked of hunting and boasted of many coups against their enemies, the merciless Blackfeet and the haughty Crow.

What I would have given to be one of the first white men in those mountains. A trapper in Stewart or Bridger's brigade, with nothing but a Hawken rifle, some flint and steel, a good knife, and the opportunity to see the country while it was fresh and new. See it when every pond held beavers and the buffalo were so plentiful the migrating herds stretched from horizon to horizon, a dusty sea of wooly humps and sharp horns. To be a man with no occupation but survival and nothing on my social calendar but spring rendezvous on the Green River. A man who could watch the sky without seeing the vapor trails of jets. A man who could look at the mountain peaks without seeing radio towers.

A man whose chance of survival was about one in three, I thought, bringing myself back to earth. A man who stood a good chance of losing his hair, and most likely his privates, to the blade of a warrior's knife.

I forced myself out of my daydream and looked out the window to see that we were less than three miles from the base of Mt. Shoshone. The graded dirt road crossed Washakie Creek and then ended abruptly. Moss eased the pickup onto a rocky Jeep trail that followed the southern base of the mountain for a mile or so into a small valley between Mt. Shoshone and Mt. Baldy, which rose about two miles to the south.

For several minutes, our vision was obscured as we drove through a stand of lodgepole pines so thick I could only see a few yards. Eventually, however, we emerged into a small clearing with grass as high as my knees and the smell of death in the air.

Moss switched off the motor, and we listened for a moment to the ticking of the engine as it began to cool and the buzz of bottle flies looking for a meal.

From the cab of the pickup, I could count seven brown and tan carcasses in the little meadow. They were elk, and judging from their size, all were mature or nearly mature bulls, some as heavy as 600 pounds. Three lay on their sides, their legs sticking out grotesquely, their bodies bloated nearly to bursting. Four were on their knees as they had fallen, almost as if they were sleeping.

None of them had antlers, though, and I could see the raw, gaping wounds at the tops of their skulls where the horns had been cut away. I knew immediately what had happened, and it made me viscerally angry. Elk drop their horns in the fall, and begin growing new ones in the spring. Their horns are in velvet through the summer months, from June to August, until their racks are fully grown. Judging from the state of decomposition, these animals had been killed in early June when their horns were immature. They'd been slaughtered for a few pounds of blood velvet, a pitifully small amount of money in some poacher's pocket.

Moss left the cab of the pickup, opened a tool box he carried in the back, and removed a set of pliers. "They didn't even take the ivory," he said, as if that was as great a sin as killing the magestic animals in the first place. He wrapped a bandanna around his face against the nearly overpowering stench of decay and walked off in the direction of the nearest bull.

I knew what he was doing, but I couldn't bring myself to watch closely. Elk have two ivory nubs—not really molars but more like rudimentary tusks—in their upper jaw. About an inch long, sometimes a little longer, and rounded at the crown, the ivory teeth have been used as clothing decoration by Native Americans for generations. In the early decades of the twentieth century, they were prized so highly by members of the Elks, a national fraternal organization, that the species was nearly wiped out by white hunters eager to supply the ivory teeth, which the membership turned into rings and tie tacks.

It took only a moment for Moss to wrench the ivories from the first elk carcass, and less than ten minutes for him to finish the entire job. He carried the bloody nubs back to the vehicle and deposited them, along with the pliers, in his tool box. I imagined they would eventually find their way onto some Shoshone woman's ceremonial buckskin dress. He wiped his hands on his pants leg and got back into the cab, his face clouded with anger and disgust.

"Sick bastards," I said quietly.

Moss nodded his head and started the engine, easing the truck into gear.

"That they are, Harry, and let me tell you something else," Patti said, looking out over the carnage as we began to pull away. "The kind of people who would do this—or pay to have it done—are capable of anything."

He reached over and gave my knee a pat. "You'd be wise to keep that in mind."

10

▲▲▲

Curly Ahearn was arrested for the murder of Liam O'Bannion at nine o'clock the next morning as he and his wife were sitting at their kitchen table eating breakfast, but I didn't hear about it for a half hour, when the jangling phone woke me from a fitful slumber.

My alarm had gone off at the appointed hour of six, but I turned it off and went back to sleep because I was exhausted, and with good reason. I should have started home the day before as soon as we returned from the killing ground and gotten a decent night's rest, but instead I'd dawdled.

When Patti left Ben Moss and me standing in the parking lot to return to his campsite near the southern border of the reservation, I'd accepted Ben's invitation to dinner and followed him to his home, a three-bedroom cabin on the banks of the south fork of the Little Wind River. While Moss played a game of catch with his oldest son, I made use of the tribal fishing permit he'd sold me. I pulled my graphite fly rod from the backseat of the Jeep, attached a reel and one of my Starbranch specials—a particularly effective version of the traditional stone-fly nymph—and began working a relatively calm stretch of the river a hundred yards downstream from his home.

The brook trout were ravenous, and in a little over a half hour I caught seven. I released them all, and when I finished I found a seat on the bank at the base of a pine and watched the sun set over the mountains. Then I walked back to Moss's home in the gathering darkness, where I took the seat of honor with his family around the kitchen table and enjoyed the delicious meal his wife had prepared—venison stew and fry bread smothered in chokecherry gravy, a Shoshone specialty made by adding flour and water to chokecherry syrup. After I'd had dinner and a smoke on the front porch, Moss's wife filled my thermos with strong coffee for the drive home and we said our goodbyes.

I didn't get back to Victory until well after midnight, and because of all the caffeine I'd consumed I didn't fall asleep until after three. I slept badly and dreamed the kind of dreams I imagine Stephen King has every night of his life.

As I sat up and reached for the phone, I felt the dull throb of a headache behind my right eye, the kind of headache not even fifty aspirin will cure. I groaned as I picked up the receiver. "Starbranch," I said, my mouth so dry and sticky the single word seemed to catch on my tongue.

The person on the other end of the line was Frankie Bull. "I just got off the phone with Madelaine," he said without preamble. "Curly's in jail."

I shook my head to clear it and took a long drink from the glass of water I keep on the nightstand. I had the same sinking feeling in the pit of my stomach that I have when I get to the first big dip on a roller coaster. "The bullets?" I asked. I knew what the answer would be, but I didn't want to hear it.

"Yeah, they got a match," Frankie said. "It looks like O'Bannion was killed with Curly's thirty-eight."

When I walked in an hour later, the Albany County sheriff's office in Laramie was hopping. The dispatcher's radio squawked, secretaries chattered, and deputies bustled in and out of the squad-room door. A couple of them glanced at me curiously, but I didn't recognize their faces.

When I served my short stint as county sheriff, I'd managed to hire a decent team of aggressive and intelligent deputies. Tony Baldi fired most of them within the first six months after he came to office and replaced them with a stable of lame-brained drones. The one person I recognized was Larry Rawls, the only deputy I'd hired who had managed to survive the purge. His face lit up when he saw me, and for a second it looked as if he might actually say hello. He thought better of it, though, and gave me a sheepish look before he buried his face in a stack of paper. I was disappointed, but I guess I didn't blame him. In that environment, friendship with me wasn't exactly conducive to continued employment, let alone career advancement.

Madelaine and Faith were sitting on a long wooden railroad bench at the end of the room. Madelaine, who had dressed hurriedly in jeans, a T-shirt, and white canvas boat shoes without socks, looked drawn and frightened. She wore no makeup and her eyes were red and puffy from crying. Faith was dressed in much the same way— except her jeans had a half-dozen strategically placed rips—and looked nervous. She didn't seem to know what to do with her hands, and her eyes darted around the room as if incredible danger lurked in every corner.

When Maddy saw me come through the door, she jumped up and threw her arms around my neck. "Thank God you're here, Harry," she said, her voice trembling. "I didn't know what to—"

I held her tightly and smoothed her hair with my hand. "It's gonna be all right," I said reassuringly. "Did you call Jack Simpson?"

She nodded, stood away, and wiped her nose with a tissue she had balled in her hand. "I called him before I left the house," she said. "He should be here any time."

I held her hands and led her back to the bench. I sat beside her and spoke quietly. "Tell me what happened, Maddy," I said.

Maddy grimaced as she replayed the memory in her mind. "It was awful," she said. "We'd just finished breakfast when Tony barged in without even knocking. He told Curly the bullets that came from his range matched the one that killed Liam, and he was under arrest for murder."

She bit her lower lip. "They didn't even let him get dressed," she said. "They handcuffed him right there in his own home and took him away." She paused. "He looked so embarrassed, Harry," she said, then she broke down and sobbed.

In the last few days, Madelaine Ahearn's whole world had been torn apart, but I respected her quiet strength. She was a fighter, and she'd stand by her husband no matter what. "Where is Curly now?" I asked.

She brushed away her tears angrily and looked upward. "Upstairs being processed," she said. "After that I'm not sure what happens."

The Albany County sheriff's department is in the basement of the antiquated granite county administration building. Across the hall is the county court. The county assessor and clerk are on the second floor, and the district court and county prosecutor's office are on the third. The fourth floor houses the public defender's office and the jail, which is run by the sheriff's department. It's a dismal facility that freezes in winter and swelters in summer. The county has been sued by the American Civil Liberties Union for conditions there so many times that the county commission finally decided to build a new jail across the street, which was still under construction. I hoped my friend wouldn't have to stay in that hellhole long.

I sat Maddy down and got her a soda from the machine, then I told her to wait there for Jack Simpson's arrival. She nodded gratefully when I told her I'd go upstairs and see what was going on. "We've got to get him out of here, Harry," she said.

I mumbled agreement, but I didn't tell her that wouldn't be possible, at least that day. Since Curly had been arrested on a Sunday, the earliest his arraignment and bail hearing could be scheduled was the next day. And if he was charged with first-degree murder as I feared, it was likely the judge would deny bail altogether. The best-case scenario was that Curly might be behind bars for several months waiting for a trial date and then be acquitted. Worst case: He'd never see his home again as a free man.

The courthouse building doesn't have an elevator, so I was huffing by the time I'd climbed the four flights of stairs to the jail. Turns out it was a wasted effort, because the deputy in charge of the jail wouldn't let me past the front desk. Tony Baldi and Curly were closeted in the interrogation room, where I imagined Tony was attempting to convince Curly to give a statement without the benefit of legal counsel. I figured my friend was smart enough to keep his mouth closed until Jack Simpson turned up, so I spun on my heels and headed back downstairs.

As I passed the county prosecutor's office on the third floor, I saw that Walker Tisdale's door was open and let myself into the empty waiting room. Tisdale is a fourth-generation Wyomingite whose great-great-grandfather began accumulating the family fortune by grabbing as much of the state as he could get his hands on before homesteaders started showing up and fencing off their sixty-acre plots. That fortune grew over the years to the point where the accumulated Tisdale holdings comprise more landmass than several entire states and a handful of European nations. Their political pull in regional Republican circles is immense, and it is rumored that Walker's father, Everet, had handpicked many members of the state legislature, Wyoming's lone delegate to the U.S. House of Representatives, and at least one of the state's two U.S. senators.

Always a kingmaker, Everet Tisdale was now trying to establish his family as a front-line political powerhouse by financing Walker's run for the U.S. Senate against a three-term Republican incumbent who had alienated himself from the party's hard-liners by his record of pro-choice voting.

Unfortunately for Everet Tisdale, Walker lacked statewide name recognition and was showing poorly in early polls. That's why it didn't take a genius to realize why Walker was in his office on a Sunday instead of playing golf with his rich cronies at Old Baldy in Saratoga. He needed exposure, and the successful prosecution of a local mayor for first-degree murder would keep him on the front pages of state and regional newspapers for months. I imagined he'd been orchestrating the investigation of Curly from the beginning, and was salivating like a redbone hound at the opportunity to start cashing in. I wondered how long it would be before the television cameras showed up to interview him on the courthouse steps.

Through the glass doors that separated the waiting room from his private office, I could hear Walker's voice, and since I heard no one answer when he spoke, I surmised that he was on the phone. I didn't bother to knock on his office door, just let myself in and plopped into one of the leather wing chairs in front of his huge glass-topped desk.

When I came in, Walker looked up with a mixture of revulsion and anger at my unannounced visit. Leaning back in his chair with his expensive black wing tips on the glass top of his desk, he was dressed in a painfully starched white shirt, a silk rep tie, and blue pin-striped trousers creased so sharply they could cut steak. The suit jacket that matched the pants was hanging on a bentwood coat rack by the door, Walker's concession to weekend casual. At least he wasn't wearing the idiotic golf clothes he turns up in from time to time. He gave me a look of disgust and pointed to the phone as if I was too dim to notice that he was busy.

A gentleman would have taken the hint and retreated to the waiting room until his highness was available to grant an audience. I'm no gentleman. I knew my obstinance would surely make him furious, but since we've never liked each other I didn't especially care. I pretended to ignore him, crossed my legs, and smiled serenely.

He scowled and tried to continue his conversation but gave that up when I picked up his crystal-and-gold desk clock and began turning it over in my hands as if I might take it apart to see how it worked.

"I'm sorry, but I'm gonna have to get back to you in a few minutes," Walker finally grumbled to whoever was on the other end of the line. Then he banged the receiver down, stood up, and yanked the clock from my hands. He slammed it back on his desk with such frustrated force that I was pretty sure it had suffered internal damage.

"Hi, Walker," I said, still smiling. I noticed with some satisfaction that the second hand had indeed stopped moving. "What brings you to the office on Sunday?"

A red flush bloomed on Walker's cheeks. "You know damned well why I'm here, Starbranch," he growled. "The fucking question is, why are *you* here?"

I'm no stranger to profanity, but coming from Walker Tisdale's mouth it just sounded silly. Imagine Prince Charles saying the word *fuck* and you get the picture. I laughed good-naturedly. "Actually, Walker," I said, "I came here to do you a favor."

Walker sneered. "And what would that be?" he asked. "Are you here to tell me you've finally decided to check yourself into the Betty Ford Clinic?"

Prick, I thought angrily. A biting reply was just forming on my lips when I choked it back. I couldn't let him get under my skin. "Nah," I said. "I'm here to keep you from looking like a jackass again." I leaned forward and picked up the abused clock. Shook my head in mock sadness, because it was well and truly broken. I put it back and looked him in the eye. "You got the wrong man," I said. "Curly didn't kill Liam O'Bannion."

Now it was Walker's turn to smile. "Why thanks," he said, his voice dripping with sarcasm. "I don't know what made me think that." He held up an index finger and started counting off reasons. "One: He made a threat to kill the man that a dozen people heard. Two: It looks like his gun was the murder weapon. Three: He has no alibi for the time of the killing." He looked up, down to his final finger. "And four: Someone saw him on the highway less than two miles from the crime scene the night of the murder."

Walker shrugged his shoulders. "Why would I suspect someone like that, Harry?" he asked sarcastically. "Guess I'm just not a trusting soul."

His final point surprised me. Curly told me he'd been nowhere near the crime scene the night O'Bannion was murdered. According to him, he'd been fishing on the Little Laramie River, almost fifteen miles south of where O'Bannion's body was discovered. Needless to say, I'd believed him without question. "He wasn't there, Walker," I said defensively.

Walker gave me a dismissive wave. "Well, I've got two witnesses say he was," he said. "As a matter of fact, he almost ran them off the road right near the turnoff to that campground where O'Bannion's car was discovered. Made a hell of an impression on 'em, let me tell you."

I didn't answer because my brain was racing with possibilities, all of them bad.

"I know what you're thinking," Walker said wickedly. "You're thinking my witnesses must be wrong because Ahearn was out communing with nature, miles and miles away. Am I right?" He paused for a second. "Come on, am I right?"

I tried to keep my expression blank, not give him an inch. It didn't work. Walker is an arrogant jerk, but he's no moron. He read the answer in my eyes. "Don't feel so bad, podna," he said. "He told us that lie, too. Difference is, we saw through it."

Just then there was a tentative knock on the door. I turned around to see a staff writer for the *Laramie Daily Boomerang* and the regional correspondent for KTWO, the largest television station in Wyoming. There was also a gofer whose arms were loaded down with cameras, lights, and assorted broadcast paraphernalia. Walker stood and puffed out his chest like a tropical bird, smiled a 1,000-watt smile at the reporters, and waved them in.

He motioned me toward the door. "Now, if you don't mind, Starbranch," he said through his teeth. "I've got work to do."

I found Maddy and Faith right where I'd left them, but before I even had time to sit down, Jack Simpson blew through the doors of the sheriff's department with the force of an Oklahoma twister.

A man who believes that image is every bit as important for a lawyer as talent, Jack had certainly dressed for the occasion. Instead of his usual Savile Row suit, he was wearing a black frock coat and black pants, black boots, and a wide-brimmed black cowboy hat with silver conchos. His only concession to variety was a starched white shirt with a banded collar and a kidskin leather briefcase that was at least fifty years old. With his long hair flowing out from under the brim of the hat in waves, he looked like one of the Earp brothers right before the gunfight at the OK Corral—but his sharp face burned with the righteous anger of a fire-and-brimstone preacher. That close to Jack Simpson, I could almost smell the stink of burning sulfur.

Simpson did a double take when he saw me standing with Maddy and Faith, but he nodded a perfunctory hello before taking Madelaine by the hands and leading her down the hall to an alcove, where they stood for several minutes in quiet conversation. I couldn't hear what they were saying, but Simpson's face was kind and reassuring. Several times he laid his large hand on her shoulder. Once he pulled a silk handkerchief from his inside pocket and let her use it to dry her eyes. When they were finished, he led her back to us, a ropy arm around her waist, Maddy leaning into him for support.

I'd run across Jack Simpson several times since I quit the Denver police department and moved to Wyoming, usually in a courtroom when he was representing someone I'd arrested. Our relationship had been an adversarial one, and several times he'd said things about me that were less than complimentary. Now we were on the same side, and it made me uneasy.

He gave me a cool smile. "Hello, Harry," he said, reaching out to shake hands. "Good to see you again."

I didn't imagine he was serious, but there was no reason to be rude. "Yeah, it's been a while," I said.

Simpson chuckled. "Last time I heard of you was that television special about your shoot-out with Kit Duerr. Can you imagine a professional football star getting caught up in that white-supremacist bullshit?"

I never have understood what drives people to political violence and terrorism, but I didn't particularly want to discuss it. I shrugged my shoulders noncommittally, but Simpson wasn't deterred. "I would have liked to defend him," he said, smiling thinly. "But you killed him before I got the chance."

I didn't know what to say, so I stood there for a few seconds wrestling the absurd urge to peel off my shirt and show Simpson the puckered bullet hole in my shoulder where Duerr had shot me before I put a slug of my own through his miserable heart. Pull up my pant leg and have him take a look at my shattered knee. "It was him or me," I said inanely. "I didn't have a choice."

The smile left Simpson's face. "Of course," he said, letting me know he'd heard too many similar stories from cops who sent their brutally beaten suspects to the hospital, or the cemetery in a pine box.

I'll say this for the man, he certainly knew how to push the right emotional buttons; it had only taken him five seconds to get to me. I felt like popping him in the nose, but that would only prove his point. I gave him a flat stare and waited until he was tired of the game. Finally, he motioned me away from Faith and Maddy. "Give me a couple minutes before I go upstairs?" he asked.

I nodded and followed him down the hall to a small room used by reporters who cover the courthouse. The room was empty and we took seats on opposite sides of a black conference table. Simpson popped the latch on his briefcase and pulled out a yellow legal pad, reached into a pocket, and came up with an expensive fountain pen. He uncapped the pen and got ready to write. "Maddy tells me you've been looking into Liam O'Bannion's murder on your own," he said. "What have you got so far?"

For the next ten minutes, I told Simpson what I'd learned about O'Bannion—his poaching and drug business, his connections to Pantaleo and Tommy Fang—and how I intended to proceed. He listened impassively, taking notes occasionally, as I told him I was heading to San Francisco in the next day or two. With any luck, I said, I'd fit some important pieces of the puzzle. Maybe I'd even discover who really pulled the trigger.

After he digested that information, I told him about Tony Baldi's investigation. I recounted the fight at the steak house, Curly's threats against O'Bannion's life, the discovery of the bullet, and the matching slugs from Curly's shooting range. Despite the growing weight of evidence, I expressed my firm belief that Curly was innocent and gave him my promise to do everything in my power to prove it. I did not tell him that Curly might have lied about being seen near the crime scene on the night of the murder. I figured he'd find that out soon enough on his own.

When I finished, Simpson sighed deeply, capped his pen, and leaned back in his chair, staring at the ceiling. I let him think until he had processed the information. Then he leaned forward and stood up, buttoning his jacket. He looked more than a little disappointed. "That's very interesting, Harry," he said. "What you know so far may come in handy if we ever go before a jury and need to establish reasonable doubt." He clicked his briefcase closed and tucked it under an arm. "It won't do me a damned bit of good now, though," he said. "I'm not going to get anyone out of jail with unsubstantiated theories."

First he'd made me feel like a cold-blooded killer, and now I was incompetent. Is it any wonder I hate lawyers in general and defense lawyers in particular? "Look, I know valid evidence when I see it," I said defensively. "And I know what I have so far isn't very solid." He was still listening, but his hand was on the doorknob. "But it's still better than anything you're gonna get from Tony Baldi," I said. "Eventually, I'll nail it down—and you can take that to the bank."

Simpson opened the door and began to walk out. At the last second, he paused and looked at me over his shoulder. "And what if you find out Curly is guilty?" he asked. "What will you do then?"

I'm glad he walked away without an answer, because I didn't have one to give him. Until my conversation with Walker Tisdale not thirty minutes before, the question had never crossed my mind.

I sat with Madelaine and Faith on the hard wooden bench for the next two hours while Curly gave his statement to Tony Baldi in the upstairs interrogation room. People who worked at the courthouse were coming back from lunch when Simpson finally clumped down the stairs looking fairly wilted. He was carrying his hat and briefcase in one hand, and held the jacket that was slung over his shoulder with the other. There was a grim look on his face that told us most of what we wanted to know before he even opened his mouth.

According to Simpson, Curly's arraignment was scheduled for

eleven the following morning, and Tony had decided that in the interim the mayor would be held without visitors. Maddy's face fell at that news, but it brightened a little when Simpson assured her that Curly was holding up well and had asked for some toiletries and magazines to get him through the night. He suggested that Maddy and Faith go home and get some rest. He also asked them to avoid speaking with reporters.

They agreed meekly, Maddy planted a kiss on my cheek, and the three of them started for the door.

As far as I was concerned, Simpson hadn't answered the most important question. I caught up with him and grabbed him by the sleeve. His face flushed, so I let go. Jack Simpson wasn't the kind of man who likes being touched. "What's he being charged with?" I asked.

Simpson looked kindly at Maddy and Faith and then glared at me. Too late, I realized that he hadn't wanted to burden them with that information just yet. Now that the question was in the open, however, he couldn't dodge it. He put his arm around Maddy's shoulders and drew her close. Like a horse whose sixth sense tells it a lightning storm is near, she was so frightened that I was afraid she'd collapse.

"First-degree murder," he said quietly. "He's going to ask for the death sentence."

I had no reason to stay in Laramie, so I followed Maddy and Faith on the thirty-minute drive back to Victory and made sure there were no news people waiting on their front porch. Then I stopped by the office to check in with Frankie Bull and get a feeling for the local reaction to the mayor's arrest. There was a note on the door from Frankie saying he'd be back in an hour, so I let myself in and sorted through the mail and the stack of message slips.

A half dozen of the calls were from reporters, whom I had no intention of calling back. I threw those into the trash. A few were from local residents, who I imagined simply needed reassurance that their community wasn't going to fall apart. I put those in the to-do-later pile. Near the bottom was a message from Lou McGrew, Curly's assistant manager at the Silver Dollar, who wanted me to stop by before I went home. I tucked that one into my pocket and read the last message. It was from Cindy Thompson, who asked that I call her at home as soon as possible.

I dialed her number and let it ring more than a half-dozen times before she picked up, breathing hard. "Sorry it took me so long to answer," she said when I identified myself. "I was on the treadmill." She coughed and cleared her throat. "God, I hate that thing."

"That's because it's good for you," I said. "God doesn't want us to enjoy things that are good for us. If he wanted it the other way around, asparagus would taste like prime rib."

She laughed good-naturedly and asked me about my trip to the reservation. I told her as much as I could, then I told her about my morning in Laramie.

"So it doesn't look like Curly will be coming home?" she asked when I'd finished.

"Not for a while at least," I said.

Cindy sighed audibly. "That's what I was afraid of," she said. She was quiet then, and I listened to the phone line hum for a few seconds before she went on. "Listen, Harry, there's something we need to talk about. What are you doing for dinner?"

As usual in my relations with women, I misinterpreted her intentions. I thought she wanted to talk about *us,* so I tried to distance myself gracefully. As far as I was concerned, there was no us, at least no conjugal us. And that's the way I wanted to keep it for the time being. "I don't know, I'm pretty tired," I said. "I'll probably just go home and make myself a fried bologna sandwich and fall into bed."

"How 'bout I drop by around six?" she asked. "I'm not much on fried bologna, but I wouldn't mind a grilled cheese and a bowl of tomato soup." She paused. "Would you prefer wine or beer? My treat."

It's *always* beer with fried bologna, but I didn't tell her that. Instead, I waited a beat too long to answer and she sensed my hesitance. "On second thought, how 'bout a rain check?" she asked. She didn't sound particularly disappointed that we weren't having dinner together. Sometimes I have that effect on women. "We can talk on the phone now if you've got time."

I heard a note of worry in her voice that I hadn't noticed before. "Is something wrong, Cindy?" I asked.

"I don't know," she said. "I guess there could be." The line popped a couple of times. Call waiting on her end. She ignored it.

"I don't know how to sugarcoat this, so I won't even try," she said. "There's a special meeting of the town council tonight to discuss the situation with Curly Ahearn and appoint an interim mayor. I imagine that will be me."

"Congratulations," I said. "Curly will be back eventually, but I'm sure the town will be fine in your capable hands until then."

She didn't acknowledge the compliment. "They also want to talk about you, Harry," she said.

That one surprised me. "Can you tell me why?" I asked. "Or is it a secret."

"Of course it isn't a secret," she said. The line clicked a few more times, and then the person who was trying to call her gave up. "They're concerned that you're conducting a private investigation on the town's payroll, and they worry what will happen if the voters find out their tax dollars have gone to investigate this homicide. They believe it's the sheriff's investigation, and we shouldn't have any part of it since the crime didn't happen in your jurisdiction—not to mention that you've got a conflict of interest the size of Nebraska, being so close to Curly and all. They think we should just order you to back off."

I thought about that for a whole nanosecond. "I won't do it, Cindy," I said. "Curly Ahearn is my friend, your friend, and a friend to this whole town. He's always been there for me, and I'm gonna be there for him. If those petty jerks think I'm gonna sit around Victory writing speeding tickets while Curly gets the death penalty they're—"

"I was afraid of that, too," she broke in. "I knew that would be your reaction."

I was angry, but trying not to take it out on her. I wasn't very successful. "Well, what do *you* think, Cindy?" I asked. "You think they're right?"

I could tell by her tone that I'd hurt her. "Of course not, Harry," she said angrily. "I just wanted to tell you the way things are and let you know that if they make me mayor, I'll hold them off as long as I can."

I should have thanked her and left the matter alone. Instead, I lashed out, knowing even as the words spilled from my mouth that I was being ungrateful and unfair, tarring her and the rest of the council with the same brush. That didn't stop me, though. Unfortunately, it seldom does.

"You do that, Cindy," I snapped. "Because as far as I'm concerned, clearing Curly Ahearn is the most important thing in my life right now. If those backwater bureaucrats try to tell me otherwise, they can take my job and stick it up their collective asses."

Cindy started to say something when I finished my diatribe, but I hung up before she got the chance.

Her line was busy ten seconds later when I called back to apologize. I had the feeling it would be busy all afternoon.

Frankie Bull came in from his rounds about ten minutes later with nothing to report but the fact that Dr. Edward "Fast Eddie" Warnock's pet skunk, Geraldo, had escaped his cage and caused a commotion when he wandered into the lighting section at Shapiro's Hardware.

Fast Eddie had the animal's scent glands removed when it was a kitten, so it was relatively harmless, but that didn't mean diddly to Howard Shapiro, who failed to recognize the intruder as the doctor's roommate and attempted to terminate Geraldo with what the CIA describes as extreme prejudice. Fortunately, Frankie was driving past the store and saw the fracas in progress through the window. He recognized Geraldo on account of his abnormal obesity and was able to rescue him from Howard, who was trying to decapitate the poor, defenseless creature with a shovel he'd grabbed in the store's home-and-garden department. He wasn't able to prevent Howard from ruining about $500 worth of lamp shades and hanging light fixtures as he flailed wildly with the long-handled weapon, however, so the intervention wasn't entirely successful.

Fast Eddie was reportedly ecstatic at Geraldo's return, but Howard was threatening to file a lawsuit for loss of business and emotional duress. I figured Howard would probably settle out of court, as long as I could convince Eddie to spring for a good bottle of French wine as an appeasement offer—instead of the $3-a-bottle swill he gives us at Christmas. I made a mental note to suggest that prudent course of action to Eddie the next time I saw him.

"Poor Howard," I said with a laugh when Frankie finished his tale. "Last year it was Bea Thackery's goat rampaging through the Easter display, and now this. I'd love to be a fly on the wall when he tells this story to his insurance adjuster."

"I'm sure they have a line item for that under 'natural disasters,' " Frankie said, chuckling. "Merchandise damaged by fugitive skunk."

Frankie and I chewed the fat for a few more minutes, then I filled him in on what had happened at the courthouse in Laramie. I told him it was my intention to proceed with my own investigation, no matter what the town fathers said to the contrary, and that I'd probably be leaving for San Francisco the next afternoon, or the morning after, depending on the availability of air connections out of Brees Field in Laramie.

He said that was fine. Frankie thought he could probably handle police business in Victory while I was gone, as long as people kept better tabs on their livestock.

With that assurance, I suggested that he go home to spend some time with his wife, and he jumped at the chance. "I've been threatening to make Frieda a nice bouillabaisse," he said happily. "But I haven't had time to prepare the squid." He looked at his watch and nodded appreciatively. "If I get started right now, I can go over to that fresh seafood place in Laramie and be back in time to have dinner ready when she comes home from the library."

I sent him off with my blessing and tried not to think of squid (I make it a practice to avoid all food with tentacles and suckers, one of my few dietary prohibitions) while I locked up the office for the day and fired up the Jeep for the short ride down Main Street to the Silver Dollar.

There was almost no traffic on the streets, and most of the town's parking places were empty with the exception of those in front of the hardware store, the only retail business that opens on Sunday. There were a few more pickups parked at the Dollar, where a good portion of the town's male population usually gathers on the Sabbath to watch sports on the large-screen television and eat Curly's famous nuclear holocaust chili, the main reason there are more bleeding ulcers per capita in Victory, Wyoming, than are reported in the entire state of Texas and most of northern Mexico.

I rolled into a parking place directly in front of the Dollar and strolled through the golden-yellow sunlight of late afternoon into the saloon, which seemed as dark as a coal mine until my eyes began to adjust to the change in brightness.

Shania Twain was playing on the jukebox, and a baseball game with the sound off was going on the television. As usual, the air in the Dollar was thick with the smell of stale cigar and cigarette smoke, fried hamburger, spilled beer, and traces of a dozen brands of cheap cologne and dime-store perfume. Collectively, those base scents comprise my favorite fragrance in the world, and it almost induced immediate sensory overload. I breathed deeply and glanced around the room to survey the crowd. A couple of lumberjacks were throwing darts at the back of the bar, and three cowhands I recognized as employees at area ranches sat around a table, their hat brims pulled low on their foreheads and draft-beer glasses in their hands.

Other than that, the place was empty—except for Lou McGrew, who was seated on a barstool drinking Budweiser from a long-necked bottle and smoking a thin brown cigarette. Usually the mere sight of Lou—who only a year before had won a Dolly Parton look-alike contest during Cheyenne Frontier Days—is enough to lift my spirits. That day, however, I could tell something was wrong from across the room. She gave me a desultory wave with her cigarette hand when she saw me standing in the doorway and didn't smile as I crossed the creaking floorboards to take the stool next to her.

When I was seated, she ground her cigarette into an ashtray already brimming with butts and tipped her beer bottle to her plum-colored lips. She drained it in two long swallows, hopped down off her stool, and gave me a pat on the knee. "Get you anything, Harry?" she asked. "A beer? Couple of pickled eggs?"

I shook my head. "No thanks," I said. "Think I'll try twenty-four hours of clean living. See if it makes me sick."

She smiled thinly. "In other words, you're on your way home, where you have a six-pack and a box of macaroni and cheese waiting," she said.

I shrugged my shoulders. "You know me pretty well, but not as well as you think, darlin'," I said. "You're right on the six-pack, but not the pasta. Actually, I'm cooking fried bologna." Most times Lou is charmingly appalled when I discuss my eclectic eating habits, but she didn't even make a face. She seemed preoccupied, nervous. I waited until she'd emptied her ashtray, dumped the beer bottle, and was wiping down the bar with a white rag. "I got your message," I said. "What's up?"

Lou looked past me at the few customers and—satisfied that they could fend for themselves for a few minutes—motioned me toward the back room. "Let's talk in there," she said. I followed her into the storeroom and took a seat on a stack of beer cases while she perched on the edge of the desk. Her legs, even in high heels, came a good four inches short of the floor. She stared at her toes for thirty seconds before she started talking. "I've been thinking about this for a while, and I didn't know what to do about it," she said. "I finally decided to tell you and let you figure it out."

I nodded for her to continue. "It's about the night that young man was murdered," she said hesitantly. "Nobody's talked to me yet, but I saw something that's been bothering me. I didn't think anything of it at the time, but now that Curly's been arrested I don't think I can keep it secret . . ." She paused and shook her head sadly, as if she couldn't believe what she was about to say. "I love him, Harry," she said, "but if he did it I . . ." She stopped talking, and stared into the middle distance, wrestling with her emotions.

"What would make you think he's guilty, Lou?" I asked gently. "What did you see?"

Lou bit her lower lip and rubbed her forehead. "He stopped in here about one in the morning that night, just as I was getting ready to close," she said softly. "He was drunk, Harry, so drunk he could barely walk, let alone drive." She looked me in the eyes, and I could see that she was frightened. "There was blood all over the legs of his pants."

My insides turned to ice at that information, and my throat seemed to constrict. I could barely get my next words out. "Did you ask him where it came from?"

Lou nodded. "He said he came across a deer that had been hit on the highway and stopped to drag it off the road," she said.

That happens from time to time on Wyoming highways, particularly after dark when nocturnal game animals like deer come out to feed. Lou was right; it wasn't the sort of thing you'd give a second thought to under normal circumstances. These, however, were not normal circumstances. "What happened then?" I asked.

She pointed to a closet at the side of the room. "He keeps some clean clothes in there," she said. "He came in the office to change, and then he went home."

I stood up from my beer-case seat and walked to the closet and opened the door. There was a pair of snow boots on the floor, and a battered pair of sneakers. A ratty wool sweater and a down vest were on hangers, and a couple of ball caps sat on the shelf. There were no bloody pants. "What happened to them?" I asked. "Did you see him carry them out?"

She shook her head. "I wasn't paying attention," she said. "All I know is they were gone when I came in to look this morning after I heard about his arrest." She began to sob quietly then, her tears streaking her mascara. She rubbed them away with her fingertips. When she looked up, my heart broke, for both Lou and my friend.

"Did I do the right thing by telling you, Harry?" she asked plaintively. "I feel like such a treacherous bitch."

I walked over to her and wrapped her in my arms. "Yes," I whispered reassuringly, stroking her hair. "You did the right thing." I could feel the warmth of her tears on my chest, her heart pounding through the thin fabric of her blouse.

It matched the hammered rhythm of my own.

11

It took less time for Curly to be arraigned on first-degree murder charges the next day than it takes to drink an icy draft beer on a scorching August afternoon.

Larry Rawls led the mayor into the courtroom at a couple minutes before eleven, where Jack Simpson and Walker Tisdale were already waiting for him at their respective tables. Judge Forrest Thomas came in a couple minutes later, called for a reading of the charges, took Curly's plea of not guilty, and listened to about five minutes of debate over the question of bail before denying it entirely due to the gravity of the charge and the fact that it was a capital murder case. He shuffled through the pages of his calendar, set a preliminary-hearing date three weeks later, and walked out with a flutter of long black robe before the echo of his gavel died away.

Jack Simpson—dressed for the hearing in a buttery suede jacket, a starched white shirt with a high banded collar, black slacks, and gray cowboy boots made, no doubt, from the hide of some endangered species—whispered something into Curly's ear. Then he jammed his papers into his briefcase, folded his arms across his chest, and glared at Walker Tisdale as if he were a bug that needed squashing.

Rawls ambled forward to lead Curly back to jail as soon as the judge left the courtroom, and the mayor—dressed in an orange jail-issue jumpsuit, with chains attached to his ankles and wrists—looked back at us with an expression that reminded me of those photos of coyotes and wolves that are caught in traps and know the end is near. He gave me a weak smile and took a step toward Maddy, but Rawls grabbed him by the elbow before he got far.

"Sorry, Curly," Rawls said apologetically. "I gotta take you back upstairs right now."

Curly looked as if he wanted to argue, but he let out an unhappy sigh, hung his head, and turned away from us to go with the deputy. His shoulders had the old man's slump, and he seemed to have diminished physically during his short stay in the slam, as if he were actually shrinking. I wanted to give him some reassurance that everything would be fine. Unfortunately, I couldn't afford the luxury of compassion. There were too many hard questions he had to answer.

I followed him and Rawls out of the courtroom and the three of us rode the elevator to the top floor without saying a word, Curly leaning against the paneled wall of the elevator as if he needed support to stand. When we got out, we trooped down the short hallway to the jail administrator's desk and he buzzed us through the metal security door into the lockup. Rawls, who's always reminded me of Ichabod Crane and who I once counted as a friend, was obviously uncomfortable about his present role as a lackey in Baldi's administration. He mumbled something about being late for a staff meeting and skulked away. I watched him go and then signed the visitors log while the jailer, a thick-jowled, sour-tempered man named Addy Lennahan—who used to run an auto-repair shop and gas station before Baldi got elected and put him on the public payroll—took Curly back to his cell and closed him in.

When he came back to the desk, Lennahan took my revolver and made a big production of patting me down before he led me into the jail. The jail holds twenty-six prisoners, but as many as thirty-five are often incarcerated there in cramped conditions. The air is always heavy with the smell of Lysol, cigarettes, and puke, and you can barely hear yourself think for the racket of men yelling and a dozen television sets and radios going at full volume. Country-and-western music and soap operas seem to be the entertainment of choice, but once in a while one of the younger inmates throws in a little rap music that drives everyone insane.

That afternoon, the air-conditioning was malfunctioning as usual, so in addition to the maddening din, the temperature was well over eighty degrees and the fans going in every cell did nothing but move the hot air around. In most of the cells, prisoners were lying lethargically on their bunks, dressed in nothing but their underwear and plenty of sweat. I recognized a few local drunks and troublemakers, men I'd arrested on a regular basis during my own brief term as sheriff. In the cell beside Curly's, an overweight man with ham fists and fleshy arms sat with his head between his legs, retching in a metal bucket and moaning. His knuckles were scraped raw, and there was an angry-looking gash on his forehead that was held together with a half-dozen black stitches.

Curly, who had a cell to himself, was sitting on his bunk with his hands clasped between his knees. He nodded at the ham-fisted prisoner. "That boy's not feelin' too well today," he said. "Last night he drank a quart of vodka and decided to redecorate Shooters Saloon with a baseball bat."

The man finished throwing up, then curled up into a fetal position on his mattress, groaning from somewhere deep in his belly. "I take it he was less than successful," I said.

Curly agreed. "He only busted a couple jars of pickled eggs and a Budweiser mirror before the bartender took his bat away and beat the livin' shit out of him," he said. "They brought the son of a bitch in here around two this morning—stinking of vinegar and screaming that there were spiders on the walls the size of house cats." He paused thoughtfully. "I didn't see 'em myself. A few roaches looked like they'd been nibbling steroids . . . but no spiders."

Curly was making a weak attempt at humor, but he must have seen something in my face that he didn't like, because he got to his feet and walked to the door of the cell and we stood there, him on the inside, me on the outside, with our hands gripping the bars. "What's the matter, Harry?" he asked finally. "Did you learn something up there on the reservation you need to tell me about? You look like you've got too much bad news to carry around by yourself."

I shook my head. "It was nothing I found out on the reservation," I said. "That all went pretty well."

He pursed his lips as if he didn't understand. "Then what's the problem, podna?" he asked. "Let me in on the secret."

I pulled away from the cell bars, went to the window, and looked out on the street. I watched the traffic for a minute or so—a couple of secretaries in summer dresses and high heels ambling up the sidewalk to the courthouse, returning from their lunch hour, a young guy in cutoff jeans playing Frisbee with a black Lab on the grass. When I turned back, Curly was still standing where I'd left him, hanging on to the bars. There was no sense in fooling around, I thought. Might as well get to the point. "There's no secret from anyone but me," I said bitterly. "I want to know why you didn't tell me the whole story, Curly."

The mayor's brow furrowed. "What are you talking about, Harry?" he asked.

"I'm talking about the night of the murder," I said. I got right in his face, so close he could feel the heat of my breath as the words exploded from my mouth. "I'm talking about the fact that Tony Baldi has a witness says you were seen on the highway near the site of the shooting. I'm talking about the fact Lou McGrew says you came in later that night with so much blood on your pants they were stiff with it. I'm talking about the fact you didn't mention either of those things to me, goddamn it . . . and I want to know why."

Curly backed away from the bars until the back of his legs touched his bunk and then he sat down heavily, shaking his head, his eyes so big and sad-looking they reminded me of a dog. "Jesus, Harry," he said softly. "You think I did it, don't you?"

I cursed and slammed an open palm against the metal bars. "I don't know what the hell to think," I said angrily. "I know a few things, though." I counted the damning items off on my fingers. "I know Tony Baldi thinks he can prove you had a motive to kill O'Bannion. We both know he can prove you threatened to do it. I'm afraid he can prove the bullet that killed O'Bannion came from your gun. Now I find out you've been holding out on me. I find out

Tony can put you at the murder scene the night of the killing. I find out you had enough blood on your pants that night you *could* have killed someone." I waited for a beat while that sank in. "I know it's lookin' pretty fucking bad when it comes to proving your innocence, Curly, if you want my professional opinion. At this point, yeah, I'm beginning to think you might have done it."

The wounded drunk in the next cell stirred at my tirade, tried to sit up, and fell back with a thump and a screech of mattress springs. Curly studied the legs of his jumpsuit for a few seconds and then looked up. His voice sounded as if it hurt him to speak. "It was like I told you. I went fishing that night and fished till sundown. What I didn't tell you was that I felt so bad about blowing it with Faith I started drinking heavy on the river and just didn't quit." He shrugged his shoulders, held his palms apart. "Hell, I got so drunk I don't remember exactly where I went after that—I just drove. I guess I could have been near the murder scene. Fact is, I just don't remember . . . and that's why I didn't mention it."

I clucked my tongue and grimaced. "Tell me about the blood," I said. "Unless you were too drunk to remember that, too."

Curly stood, balled his hands, and held them at his hips. He was getting angry, giving me a glimpse of the old Curly Ahearn. "The blood came from where I said it did," he told me. "I pulled a deer off the blacktop out where Highway 130 crosses the Little Laramie, and it bled on my pants. That ever happen to you, podna?" He didn't wait for an answer. "What about that time we pulled that buck off the interstate down by Rawlins? Christ, Harry, you had blood to your knees."

He was right, and he knew it. It *had* happened to me. "Where are the pants?" I asked crossly.

He looked at me like I was a twenty-four-carat gold-plated fool. "They were old pants and they were ruined," he said simply. "I threw them away."

I chuckled cynically. "That's all very convenient, Curly," I said, pushing the envelope. "Maybe too convenient."

Now he *was* angry. Furious, in fact. "It might be convenient,

Harry," he spat. "But it's also the truth." He stalked to the bars and gave them a slap of his own. "If you don't believe it, you can kiss my hairy ass."

I smiled in spite of myself. I knew my friend as well as I knew myself. He wasn't lying. I could feel it in the marrow of my middle-aged bones. "I don't think I'll kiss your ass," I told him. I stuck my hand through the bars and poked him in the chest with my finger. "But if I find out you've held out on me again, I'll kick it all the way to Nebraska."

By the time I was done talking to Curly, I couldn't find Maddy and Faith downstairs, and I figured they'd followed Simpson back to his office. I walked out of the courthouse, jumped into the Jeep, and drove down Grand Avenue until I came to a travel agency.

The woman behind the front desk was a little disappointed when I told her I had absolutely no interest in a cruise to Jamaica on one of those huge floating incubators for social disease that specialize in single people, but she perked up a little when I told her I'd pay cash for a round-trip ticket to San Francisco on the first available flight. She pecked at her computer for a few seconds before informing me that, if I was interested, she could book me on a commuter flight (on a tiny plane known affectionately in these parts as the Vomit Comet) from Brees Field in Laramie at four-thirty that afternoon. The Comet would take me to Salt Lake, where I could hop a connection on Delta that would have me in San Francisco in time for dinner.

I counted out $400 and change, thanked her, and stuffed the computer-generated ticket into my pocket. Then I jumped back into my vehicle and pointed it toward Victory, where I stopped at the house long enough to pack a bag and leave a note for Edna, whose own note tacked to my front door informed me that she and a couple of geriatric cronies had driven over to Cheyenne for a shopping spree at the Frontier Mall.

Those obligations fulfilled, I raced into town to find the office empty and a note from Frankie saying he was having a late lunch at Ginny Larsen's and would be back in a half hour.

I let myself in and took a quick peek at the morning's call sheets and incident reports, gratified to find that nothing of significant import had happened in Victory that morning, unless you counted the fact that Harley Coyne's Australian shepherd had given birth to four puppies underneath the county library's bookmobile while the librarian was having breakfast at Ginny's. Frankie had apparently assisted the mother during the final stages of her delivery, and his report noted that all were healthy and doing fine.

I dropped the reports back into the basket, sat down at my desk, and punched out Danny King's number at the Laramie police department. King, as usual, was at his desk and sounded as if he had a mouthful of food. I told him what I wanted, an NCIC check on Tommy Fang, Liam O'Bannion's business associate in the Bay Area. King groused about the fact that our relationship was becoming very one-sided, with him doing favors and me offering nothing in return, especially the hand-tied trout flies I'd promised, but he grudgingly transmitted the request.

A couple minutes later, I had my answer. Four Tommy Fangs had been convicted in San Francisco in the last two decades on felonies ranging from bank robbery to white slavery, prostitution, and narcotics violations. One of them, the bank-robbing Tommy Fang, was currently serving a life sentence in a federal penitentiary, but the other three were back on the streets.

"Which one you interested in?" King asked.

"I don't know," I told him. "My Tommy Fang lives in Chinatown and runs some kind of an import-export business."

"Well, I've got their last known addresses," King said, "but I don't know Frisco well enough to tell you if they're in Chinatown. How old is your guy?"

"I don't know for sure," I said. "He's young enough he does his own bill collecting, and young enough to be intimidating when he does it."

"That probably eliminates one of them," King said. "According to this, Tommy Fang number two is seventy-three years old."

He gave me the addresses of the remaining two Fangs and a run-down of their various crimes. I wrote them down, but I didn't know if the information would do me any good. There could be a thousand Tommy Fangs in San Francisco for all I knew, and there was no way of knowing if the Tommy Fang who'd been in business with O'Bannion had ever been arrested for anything that would put him in the National Crime Information Center's computer database.

I spent the next half hour networking, calling big-city cops I'd worked with over the years to see if I could come up with a contact on the San Francisco police department who might put me on the trail of the right Tommy Fang once I arrived in California. The two San Francisco homicide detectives I'd worked with during my career as a murder investigator had since retired, but John Bruno, my old partner on the Denver P.D., came up with the name of Joe Terrenzi, a captain in the homicide division he'd shared information with after I moved to Victory.

I called Terrenzi's number and caught him at his desk. He was distant and gruff at first, but he warmed up immediately when I dropped Bruno's name. I told him the little I knew about Tommy Fang and what I suspected about his criminal activities. "This character doesn't ring a bell with me personally," Terrenzi said when I finished. "But let me do some checking. Give me a ring tomorrow and I'll see if I can put you with someone who'll help you out."

I thanked Terrenzi and hung up. Then I dialed Cindy Thompson at home. She answered on the first ring, as if she'd been waiting for the call. She sounded relieved to hear my voice on the other end of the line. "I've been on the phone with reporters for the last hour and a half," she said with a sigh. "Most of it with Sally Sheridan from the *Star-Tribune.*"

"My condolences," I commiserated. "Is she gathering facts for a particular story, or is she just making it up as she goes along?"

"I got the impression it's a little of both," Cindy said. "She's got this notion we're trying to cover something up out here, that we know more about Curly's troubles than we're letting on." She paused briefly. "And she thinks you're involved in it up to your eyebrows."

"A cover-up?" I groused. "Now what the hell would give her the idea I was—"

Cindy didn't wait for me to finish. "Well, for starters she wants to know why the town is bankrolling its own investigation of O'Bannion's murder," she said. "Why we're paying your salary to look into the killing instead of letting the proper authorities handle it."

"What did you tell her?" I asked.

"The truth," Cindy said. "I told her the town council voted last night to order you off the case. That I planned to pass that order along as soon as I talked to you. That's what I'm doing, Harry. I'm ordering you to quit spending your time on Curly Ahearn and get back to the work we pay you for."

"That's impossible, Cindy," I said angrily. "I'm leaving for California this afternoon. I need to go out there and see if I can—"

"You're not going anywhere," she said tersely. "I tried to hold them off, but they made me interim mayor and then outvoted me when this matter came to the table. For the time being you work for me, Harry, and even though I don't like it, I'm telling you to—"

"I won't do it on your time," I broke in. "Starting right now, I'm on vacation."

"You don't have any vacation time coming," she said reasonably. "You burned it all up when you went to Boston in January."

"Then I'll take a leave of absence," I said. "Unpaid, if that's the way you want it."

She didn't answer for a second, but when she did there was sadness in her voice. "A leave of absence has to be approved in advance, Harry," she said. "You know that as well as I do."

"And how long would that take?" I asked acidly.

"I don't know," she said. "The next meeting isn't scheduled for another week. And even then I doubt—"

"No good, Cindy," I said. "I'm leaving at four-thirty this afternoon."

I listened to the phone line crackle for thirty seconds before she spoke again. "If you do that, Harry, I don't know if I can protect you," she said. "You may as well take as much time as you want, because I'm not sure you'll have a job to come back to."

"I guess I'll have to take that chance, Cindy," I said. "But you can give those jackals on the council a message for me."

"What message, Harry?" she asked in the resigned tone of someone who knows something bad is coming and has absolutely no way of stopping it.

"You can tell 'em to fire me if they want to," I said. "Tell 'em I was lookin' for a job when I found this one."

12

▲▲▲

In general, I despise California. Nuts live in California. Surfer boys. Silicone women. Rolfers. Astral projectionists and channelers. Vegans and Feng Shui decorators. Every weird movement, lame psychoanalytic theory, and bizarre trend in dress and habit can trace its roots to California. Too much sun for too long has fried this state's collective brain.

On the other hand, I like San Francisco. It's gloomy much of the time, and the lights from cars and beacons and boats cast interesting patterns in the fog. I like the big bridges and the smell of the bay and the view of Alcatraz. I can't think of a more exquisite punishment than to cage bad men where—each and every day—they can only stare at the distant shore and imagine freedom. It does a lawman's heart good.

In my younger days, I particularly liked the fact that San Francisco was a heterosexual man's paradise. When you met a woman in most parts of the country, her first question was "Are you married?" In San Francisco, it was "Are you straight?" Answer yes and her eyes lit up like sparklers on the Fourth of July. These days I don't pay as much attention to my hormones, and I mostly look forward to San Francisco for the food.

The flight into the setting sun was smooth and comfortable. Only one person became nauseous on the Comet, and once I made my connection in Salt Lake I was seated next to a blond computer analyst from the Bay City named Jessica (in California, what else would she be named?) who drank too much wine with her unidentifiable meal and flirted shamelessly until we touched down in San Francisco. She gave me a business card with her home phone number written on the back in case I needed a tour guide while I was in town, and promised she knew a place where they served sushi "to die for." I thought Jessica was fairly cute—in a distressingly perky, Kathie Lee Gifford sort of way—but she was much too young for me. And since I would rather eat poached Spam than raw fish, I dropped her card into a trash barrel as soon as we picked up our luggage. Who needs temptation?

The airport was efficient, which is the best thing you can say about an airport. Unlike Newark or Chicago, people don't push you out of the way to grab their own bags or fight you for a taxi. The cab drivers mainly speak English, and they don't make small talk, which makes the $30 drive to the city just about tolerable.

When I visit San Francisco, I stay at one of the hotels down by the wharf so I can ride the cable cars, which I've liked since I saw my first Rice-a-Roni commercial. I tipped my driver five bucks when we pulled up in front of the hotel, and he was so pleased with the gratuity that he didn't try to drive over my foot when he pulled away.

My room was standard issue—one double bed, exactly two towels, and the standard complement of teeny-weeny bars of soap. I carried my bag to the room, threw open the drapes so I could see the ocean, and raided the honor bar for a miniature bottle of Jack Daniel's and a can of 7UP that probably cost me fifteen bucks. I took my drink out on the deck, put my feet up, and watched the sailboats on the bay.

When I was finished, it was too late to call Captain Terrenzi, so I took a quick shower and left the hotel to do some exploring. From my hotel, it was a block to the cable-car stop. With rush hour over, the line was fairly short and a couple of scruffy guys with guitars were in full swing with some Jimmy Buffett–type music I would have liked better if it had been remotely on key.

The entrance to Chinatown is marked by a giant pagoda-style gate at the intersection of Grant and Bush. I got off the cable car and walked down Grant Street, drinking in the atmosphere and scoping out the Oriental bric-a-brac and sculptures in the store windows. I paid particular attention to the statuary.

Liam O'Bannion had provided Wyoming jade for Oriental buyers in San Francisco, but I doubted that any of the material for the sculptures and assorted paraphernalia in the shop windows had been supplied by him. You can buy lots of green rocks in Chinatown, but it's a toss-up how much of what's on display is really jade. A good percentage of it is really soapstone, which makes it much less expensive, and much less valuable to the eventual purchaser. Soapstone, intricately carved, is a pretty thing, but it is not the *real* thing. In the first two blocks, I passed at least a dozen stores that were selling carved dragons, horses, goats, and fat little statues of Buddha. All of them, from what I could tell, were soapstone.

I'd left Laramie without eating lunch, forgone food on the airplane, and gone without dinner up to that point. I was starving, but in San Francisco that's an affliction that's easily cured. I picked a restaurant where an old Oriental guy was enjoying the evening air on a chair outside the door and smoking a cigarette in a long black holder. A boy who might have been twelve or thirteen mopped the floor, wiped his hands on his apron, and told me to sit anywhere I wanted while a middle-aged woman holding a full platter watched from the kitchen door. Whatever was on that platter smelled so delicious I was practically drooling on my shirt. It was not white rice and chop suey from a can.

"What's good?" I asked.

The kid looked as if he didn't understand what I was saying, but he finally shrugged his shoulders. Recommendations were clearly beyond his field of expertise because he held a long whispered conversation with the woman, who put down the platter and began to set another table as they spoke. He returned to tell me that *everything* on the menu was good, but that his mother said she could serve me the same thing she had made for her own evening meal, if I wanted.

"Fine," I said, "as long as her evening meal was on that platter."

Dinner was hot-and-sour soup with some little turnovers filled with curried crabmeat that caused my sinuses to sit up and sing. Those were followed by a plate of shrimp and noodles cooked with peapods and carrots and some slimy black tidbits I couldn't identify but that were delicious nevertheless.

After dinner, I joined the throng of tourists and ambled along until I came to the corner of Broadway and Columbus, where the landscape changed to sex clubs and bars that cater to a different sort of clientele. Homeless people on the street begged for spare change, and I was propositioned by at least three scabrous-looking hookers before I'd gone a city block.

I walked into a store called Adam & Eve, which turned out to be a triple-X-rated establishment that sold dirty movies and magazines catering to every human debauchery, as well as a hundred varieties of sexual gadgetry, most of which required at least four D-cell batteries. The manager made me for a cop the minute I walked in the door and followed me around nervously until I left.

I popped into a few more sex shops and a nudie bar long enough to drink a $5 beer while a woman (at least I think she was a woman) with a sixty-inch bust danced to an old country song called "Funny Face, I Love You." She made a lot of eye contact while she danced, and I had the uncomfortable feeling that she'd chosen the song especially for me.

Before I finished the beer, a young woman wearing nothing but a pair of boots that came to her knees, rings through her nipples, and pubic hair shaved to look like an exclamation point took the stool next to mine and asked if I'd like to buy her a glass of champagne. She looked disappointed when I told her no and stood up to leave—but only until she spotted another potential sucker in the crowd.

Feeling gritty and in need of another shower, I bought a cappuccino at a coffee bar, parked myself on a wooden bench, and tried to look wide-eyed and naive. The act must have been convincing, because it only took about four minutes before the wolves began to circle.

A chicken hawk in high-top running shoes and a black leather trench coat stopped by to ask if I was interested in a "very special treat." The treat turned out to be a young girl he promised was only twelve. When I told him no thanks, he showed me a couple Polaroids of a boy who was about the same age. I showed him my badge, and he took off at a healthy clip without looking closely enough to see that I wasn't local heat.

A few minutes later, a black hooker in a shiny blue dress, platform shoes, and net stockings asked if I wanted to party. When I ignored her, she raised her skirt high enough for me to see the bulge of a penis in her underwear and was mightily offended when I started laughing. She (he?) huffed off, muttering obscenities about white peckerwoods with red necks and tiny dicks.

That's how it went for the next hour or so, an interlude in which I turned down propositions for everything from "that thing Hugh Grant wanted" to a young Oriental punk's offer to sell me a fifteen-year-old Chinese bride—"Very pure . . . you know what I mean?"—for only $2,000.

I was thinking of calling it a night when a cab screeched to the curb in front of my bench and the driver leaned over to open the window on the passenger side. In the light of the street lamp, I could barely see his features under the bill of his ball cap, but he was white and looked to be in his middle twenties. There was a thick stubble on the lower half of his hard face, and he was wearing dark sunglasses, even though it was night. He looked me over and chuckled. "You look like a man with a need," he said. His voice had the thick rumble of a heavy smoker.

I decided to take a chance. "I need to find Tommy Fang," I told him. "That's what I need."

He gunned the engine and waved me inside. "What you want that asshole for?" he asked. "My stuff's better than his any day. What you need, bro? Ecstasy? A little blow? How 'bout some speed, keep you going all night?"

I tossed my empty cup into a can beside the bench, opened the back door, and folded myself into the cab. The interior smelled of fast-food hamburgers, and my jeans stuck to something that had been spilled on the upholstery of the backseat. I poked forty bucks through the hole in the partition separating the passenger's compartment from the driver. "I need to find Tommy Fang," I said again.

The driver scrunched down in his seat and let out an exaggerated moan. "Oh, man, I don't think you're listenin'," he said. "You know Tommy Fang?"

"Nope," I said. "I've never made the man's acquaintance."

"Then I'll do you a favor and tell you he ain't gonna appreciate it if you just knock on his door wantin' to buy dope," he said. "Tommy don't sell that shit himself. He got people to do that." He took off his sunglasses and gave me a red-eyed stare. "Guy like you shows up at Tommy Fang's, Tommy gonna take out a nine and blow you back to Tombstone."

I shook my head and pulled another twenty out of my pocket. "I didn't say I wanted to walk up to his door and ask to buy dope," I told him patiently. "I just said I need to find him. You know where he lives?"

The cabbie grumbled a no, turned around, and started drumming his hands on the steering wheel. "Why don't you just let me find you some pussy, buddy? You look like you could use it. I know a little place over on—"

"Then show me where he works," I broke in. I held the extra twenty through the hole in the partition. "That's all you have to do."

He took it without looking at me over his shoulder, and it disappeared like magic. "What are you, some kinda moron?" he asked. "Pay me sixty bucks to drive by Tommy's store . . . which, by the way, is gonna be closed?" He put the transmission into park, letting me know we weren't going anywhere fast.

"That's what us morons do," I said. "And if you hurry, I'll let you keep the money instead of pulling your dumb, dope-pushing ass out of this cab and dragging it into the first police station I see."

I leaned forward, stuck my arm through the partition, grabbed him by the collar, and gave him a shake. I held my badge to the window with the other so he could see it in his rearview mirror. "How's that sound, Jethro?" I growled. "We got an agreement? Or do I come up there and see what kinda crap you got in the glove box and under the seat? You already offered to sell me the stuff, so I guess you know that gives me probable cause to search."

The cabbie looked as if he wanted to find a pit bull, chop me up, and feed me to the pooch in bite-size pieces, but he was smart enough to realize that plan had a few flaws. For all he knew, I was armed to the teeth—which of course I wasn't, unless you count the blackthorn. He muttered something incomprehensible, jammed the transmission into drive, and tore away from the curb with such velocity that it threw me back against the seat. I stayed there while he sped down the busy street, heading back to Chinatown.

Less than five minutes later, we pulled off Grant onto a dark side street that looked filthy and dangerous. The streetlights had either burned out and had never been repaired or they'd been shot out. Overflowing trash cans lined the curbs, and the street was full of garbage that had spilled out and had never been picked up. Young men sat on the hoods of cars and porches in front of a couple of dilapidated apartment buildings. They didn't even try to hide the marijuana joints they were passing between them as we drove by, and I saw at least three of them with pistols tucked into their waistbands. Nine-millimeters most likely, maybe forty-fives. I got the distinct impression that life was cheap on this block, and I began to feel naked without my Blackhawk, not that it would do much good against the arsenal these kids were packing.

Halfway down the block, the cabbie killed his lights, coasted to the curb, and pointed to a building directly across the street. The outside of the building was lit by a single bulb in a metal fixture above the door that cast a weak yellow glow on the cracked sidewalk in front of the establishment. A sign said PACIFIC RIM IMPORTS, with Chinese lettering below that probably said the same thing.

Pacific Rim Imports obviously wasn't a retail outlet, because the doors were metal and there were no storefront windows, just a couple of regular windows with bars across them to discourage burglars. There were two garage doors big enough for large delivery trucks at the front of the building and a loading dock at the side. There was no light coming through the ground-floor windows, but lights were burning on the second and third floors of the building. I imagined that's where the offices were. Maybe someone even lived there.

"There you are, Sundance," the cabbie said quietly. "You go there tomorrow, you'll find Tommy Fang."

I jotted the address in my notebook. It didn't correspond to any of the addresses for Tommy Fangs on the NCIC, but the computer database usually lists home addresses, not businesses. "This the only Tommy Fang selling drugs around here?" I asked.

The cabbie gave me a look in the rearview that let me know that he thought I was certifiably insane. "The only one who matters," he said. He clicked on the headlights and flipped a U-turn, heading back to Grant. "But do me a favor," he said over his shoulder. "You talk to Tommy tomorrow, don't say how you found him."

I leaned back in the seat, gave him the name of my hotel, and stuck an unlit cigar into the corner of my mouth. I'd get myself a brandy from the honor bar and smoke the stogie on the deck, enjoy the warm salt air. Maybe order a nice Reuben from room service and catch a movie on cable.

Damn, I thought happily, this might be easier than I'd expected.

The next morning, I rose early and was on the wharf as the sun was rising over the hills of the city. As far as I'm concerned, this is the only time to visit that part of San Francisco, because the wharf area has several distinct personalities, depending on the time of day.

Go very early in the morning, around five, and the place is furiously busy as fish handlers and truck drivers and restaurant owners unload the catch of the day and take care of business. You can hardly walk down the street for all the foot traffic and big trucks and hand-carts, and the smell of fresh fish is overpowering. That's also when the pleasure boats docked at the wharf take off, so you have fisher-men and captains and guys with coffee carts up and down the street. This is my favorite time. The place is alive and vibrant, and a million miles from the quiet mountains of Victory.

At seven in the morning, the fishermen are gone and the tourists aren't up yet. You could fire a cannon down the streets along the wharf and never hit a living soul. The only people out are runners and walkers, whom I try to avoid whenever possible on account of the fact that deliberate exercise makes me nervous. At ten in the morning, tourists are hip to thigh, and that's the way it stays for the rest of the day and well into the night. I never go to the wharf after ten.

I bought a coffee from a roach coach and took it to a sidewalk bench to enjoy while I watched the pier workers ice fish and eager tourists boarding charter boats for a day on the water. A little after seven, I went to the hotel restaurant and ordered a big breakfast of sourdough pancakes and sausage, which I dawdled over while I read that morning's *Chronicle* and the most recent edition of the *Guardian,* an alternative weekly with decent investigative reporting and a wealth of personals and 900-number sex lines.

By nine-fifteen, I was back in my room, showered, shaved, and on hold while I waited for a receptionist to track down Captain Ter-renzi. He answered after about five minutes, and apologized for the wait. "Every time I hit the crapper, the phone rings," he groused good-naturedly. I listened while he shuffled papers for a few seconds. "I got a contact for you," he said when he'd finished. "Guy's name is Ty Cooper, a sergeant works in the gang-task-force unit."

I took the phone number he gave me. "Gang task force?" I asked.

"Sure," Terrenzi said. "The only Tommy Fang we're interested in is the boss of a local gang called the Hop Sing Boys that works out of Chinatown. Cooper knows as much about him as anyone on the department."

I thanked Terrenzi and took Cooper's number. He answered his own line and seemed more than willing to talk, although our conversation was interrupted a half-dozen times by other calls. I told him what I was working on, and though he said he'd only heard of Liam O'Bannion in passing, he'd try to fill me in on Fang and on Chinese organized crime in his city.

According to Cooper, there used to be two Tommy Fangs involved in Chinese gang activity in San Francisco, one in the Flying Dragons and one—the one whose import business I'd found the night before—in the Hop Sings.

The Flying Dragon Fang had been killed two years ago when members of the Wo Hop To triad in Hong Kong sent a bunch of its gangsters to America in an effort to take over the loose confederation of independent Chinese gangs operating on U.S. soil and make them operate under the triad's umbrella. The takeover attempt was bloody and ultimately unsuccessful, and had cost the lives of a number of gang members, including the Flying Dragon Fang—whose various body parts turned up in dumpsters around Chinatown for the better part of two weeks.

Currently, Cooper said, there are lots of independent gangs operating in San Francisco with names like Kit Jai, the Jackson Street Boys, Wah Ching, and the Black Dragons, and those gangs are involved in anything that will make a buck. "Drugs, gambling, extortion, prostitution, murder . . . you name it, they do it," he explained.

Lots of them also run legitimate businesses, everything from video stores and restaurants to nightclubs and karaoke lounges. Fang, whose import-export business brought in a healthy income in its own right, was one of the more successful gang leaders, having survived a half-dozen assassination attempts, assorted runs on his enterprise by other gangs, constant surveillance by the gang task force and various federal agencies, and at least two short prison terms more than a decade ago for prostitution-related and narcotics offenses.

As far as Cooper could tell, Tommy Fang ran a crew of more than twenty gang members, and—taking a cue from his colleagues in the American mafia—had put so much insulation between himself and the actual crimes committed by the young toughs who comprised the Hop Sing's troop of street soldiers that it was almost impossible to prove him guilty of anything more serious than a parking violation.

"Not that we have enough resources to go after him anyway," Cooper said. "You know how it is, Starbranch, with budget cutbacks and whatnot. There used to be fifteen cops on this task force just working Asians in San Francisco, but now we're down to about five covering the whole Bay Area."

He chuckled cynically, noting that the Bay Area, which includes San Francisco's 700,000 residents, has a population of around 5 million, 37 percent of whom are Asian. "We've got what my boss likes to describe as a 'serious manpower shortage,' " he said. "But he's a politician. Down here, we call it a fuckin' disaster."

I asked if he had anyone working undercover in the Hop Sings who might be able to tell me what specific criminal enterprises the gang had been exploring in the last couple of years.

"Nah," Cooper said, "we don't do much undercover. They know who we are and we know who they are. Mostly, we just work off informants to get as much information on these mutts as we can. Then, when some cop in robbery or homicide or fraud catches a case looks like gangs might be involved, we know where to steer them."

I asked him about Liam O'Bannion, but he wasn't much help. "There isn't a lot of cooperation between Chinese crooks and white crooks," he said, "although there's more now than in the past, especially when it comes to dope. I think I heard this O'Bannion's name once, but I can't remember the context. You mind holdin' on a second?"

I said I didn't mind and waited patiently while Cooper rifled through a stack of papers, humming an off-key rendition of "You Are My Sunshine" while he looked. "Here we go," he said when he came back. "Liam O'Bannion. Three forty-nine Prospect Avenue.

Thirty-three years old when we brought him in for questioning last year on a gambling investigation. Our informant said he was running a sports-betting operation for Fang, but we had to cut him loose for lack of evidence."

"Any suspicion O'Bannion and Fang were hooked up with anything else?" I asked. "Methamphetamine, for example? Maybe selling illegal bear bladders on the Asian medicinal market?"

"Bear bladders?" Cooper asked, surprised. He rustled some more paper. "I don't have anything, but it's always possible—those bladders are big business in Chinatown." he said. "Says here O'Bannion had a record for all kinds of things, even did some time on a narco rap. I guess it's not that big a stretch to see him sellin' bear parts, although I gotta tell you, that particular crime would be a low priority for the task force. You wanta know about that, maybe you should call the U.S. Fish and Wildlife Service."

I thanked Cooper and offered to take him fly-fishing if he ever visited Wyoming.

"Wyoming," he said thoughtfully. "I've never been there, but every time I hear of it I think of that movie *Dog Day Afternoon*. You ever see that, Harry?"

"Yeah," I said. I knew what was coming, but I didn't let on.

"My favorite part was when the guys holding hostages in the bank demanded transportation to a foreign country and the smart crook asked the dumb one where he wanted to go." Cooper laughed. "The mutt said *Wyoming*. That's the only foreign country he could think of. It always cracks me up."

"Me, too," I admitted. "Listen, Ty, before I go I need one more thing, a little advice."

"Name it."

"I'm thinking of paying Tommy Fang a visit this afternoon," I said. "Any suggestions on how I should handle him?"

Cooper snorted. "Yeah," he said. "With a chair and a fucking whip."

His voice took a serious tone. "You kidding about that? About seeing Tommy Fang?"

"Nope."

He swore under his breath, and when he spoke again he was angry. "You want my advice, Harry, here it is: Stay as far away from Tommy Fang as possible," he said. "We got enough body parts in dumpsters around this city as it is."

13

▲▲▲

When the Russians invaded Afghanistan, they discovered a terrible reality: Getting in was easy, but getting out was a bitch. I began to understand their tactical dilemma about thirty seconds after I walked through the door of Pacific Rim Imports. No one challenged me when I sauntered in the open door at the front of the building, where a crew of workers with handcarts were unloading a rental truck with out-of-state plates, but my presence did not go unnoticed.

A group of four young Oriental men in tank tops and blousy black pants playing cards at a table near the back of the loading bay looked up from their game as I made my way through the warehouse. One of them—a tough with a sharp face, long, muscular arms, and an elaborate dagger tattoo on his right forearm—stood up from the table and began walking the perimeter of the bay, putting himself between me and the door I'd just entered. He did not look friendly. As a matter of fact, he looked as if he could break three or four boards with his face, if he took the notion.

Jesus, I thought, I've fallen out of the sky and landed on the set of a bad kung-fu movie. Trouble was, I'm no Chuck Norris. I'm a bum-legged Wyoming cop who at that moment had no gun, no warrant, no authority, and no backup. Seems there's never an Uzi around when you need one, I thought unhappily.

I did the only thing I could. I decided to bluff like hell.

I skirted the truck and wove my way through the hundreds of wooden and cardboard packing crates coming off the truck and stacked on the cement floor of the warehouse, heading for a stairway with a sign pointing up that said OFFICE. Before I got there, another of the young thugs from the table was up and moving to cut me off. I flashed my badge and he hesitated and looked back over his shoulder at the two remaining men at the table as if for instruction. The larger of the two just shrugged and went back to glaring. Not the first time those watchdogs had had their leashes yanked by a cop with a badge, I figured. I put the shield back into my pocket before anyone could get a close look and see that I was a thousand miles out of my jurisdiction. How many times would that dumb trick work anyway?

Since my tough-guy act seemed to be working, I gave him my best Rooster Cogburn. "Tommy Fang," I growled. "He upstairs?"

No one answered, so I took that for a positive response. Although I hated doing it, I turned my back on the four goons and started climbing the stairs. I could feel their eyes on my back, but as far as I could tell they weren't following. When I reached the top of the landing, I followed a short, dark hallway to a set of doors that separated the warehouse from the company offices.

The decor and ambience changed for the better as soon as I went through the doors. Where the warehouse was dark, cluttered, and smelled of diesel fuel and sweat, the office section was well lit and clean. There was a spicy smell in the air, as if someone had burned a stick of jasmine incense not too long before. The hallway was done in expensive cloth wallpaper and wool carpeting, all of it in warm earth tones. There were live plants in pots along the sides of the hall, Chinese watercolors on the walls, and soft classical music coming from speakers recessed in the ceiling. At the end of the hallway was another door, where the lettering etched on the frosted glass informed me that I was entering the worldwide headquarters of Pacific Rim Imports. I reached out for the door handle, but before I touched it the door was opened by someone on the other side.

The woman holding the door and looking at me with a puzzled expression was the most beautiful creature I'd ever seen, at least in the flesh. About five four and achingly slender, she was Asian with thick black hair that fell past her waist. Her flawless skin was the color of amber, and her eyes were almond-shaped and brown with sparkling gold flecks. Her high cheekbones accented a heart-shaped face that bespoke intelligence and sensual promise. Dressed in a floor-length sea-green silk dress with a high collar, her only jewelry was the jade bracelet on her delicate wrist.

I was so busy gawking that I didn't hear the door from the warehouse open behind us. The woman looked past me and made a dismissive gesture with her hand. "It's all right, Chao," she said. Her voice was as soothing and sweet as warm honey. "I'll handle the gentleman from here."

I looked over my shoulder to see the largest tough from the warehouse standing just inside the hallway door, nervously shifting his weight from foot to foot. I imagined either he or one of his pals from downstairs had buzzed the office to warn of my unexpected arrival. "He says he's a cop," the thug said. "Says he's looking for Mr. Fang."

He sounded as if he was begging forgiveness, but she didn't grant it. Instead, she completely ignored him, took me by the arm, and led me into a lushly appointed waiting room where the focal point was her desk, an oddly shaped thing with rounded corners and about a thousand coats of glistening black lacquer. There was nothing on it but a phone that controlled a half-dozen lines, none of them blinking to indicate use, and a computer terminal, whose screen saver was flashing the images of about a hundred flying toasters.

"I'm April Lin," she said once the door to the hallway had closed behind us. "Mr. Fang's administrative assistant. And you are . . ."

I took her small hand in my own. "Harry Starbranch," I said. "I need a few minutes of Mr. Fang's time."

She nodded, and the slightest trace of a frown crossed her face. "Was Chao correct? Are you with the police?"

I chuckled good-naturedly. "Well, yes," I said, "but not the San Francisco police."

I held out my badge and let her check it out. She looked confused. "You're a long way from home, Mr. Starbranch," she said. "What could Mr. Fang possibly—"

"I need to ask him about a case I'm working on," I told her. "I'll only take a few moments of his time."

She handed the badge back and shook her head. "I'm sorry," she said. "Mr. Fang is very busy today. Maybe if you leave your name he'll call you—"

I stopped her before the brush-off was finished. "Why don't we do this," I said. "Why don't you tell him I'm here to talk about Liam O'Bannion and let him decide? Either that"—I pointed at the door behind her desk, which I imagined was the entrance to Fang's inner sanctum—"or I'll just go in there and ask him myself."

At my brusque tone, her face hardened and her body stiffened. "Wait here, Mr. Starbranch," she commanded. Then she turned around, rapped twice softly on Fang's office door, and let herself inside.

I cooled my heels in the waiting room and listened to the muffled voices behind the closed office door—hers gentle and murmuring and a male voice, rougher and more forceful. Once a man laughed, and it sounded like a dog barking. Less than a minute later, the office door opened and April Lin beckoned me inside. Her face was flushed and her stony expression told me that she wouldn't soon forget the problems I'd caused. "Mr. Fang says he'll see you briefly," she said, her voice solid ice. "Please come inside."

I don't know what I'd expected Tommy Fang to look like, but I certainly wasn't prepared for the man seated behind the desk at the far end of the room. Tommy Fang appeared to be in his mid-thirties, but he didn't look much like the vicious gangster I'd been warned about. In fact, he looked a lot like my accountant—an impression that was only partially dispelled when he took off his thick reading glasses as I walked in and revealed a pair of eyes as black and empty as a python's. Although Fang was sitting, I figured he'd go about five six, maybe 140 pounds. His hair was sparse on top, his lips thin, and his cheeks pudgy. His hands were waxy smooth and soft-looking, and his nails had a clear-nail-polish sheen. Once you got past his eyes, he looked like a dork, but he was wearing good clothes—a nice blue pin-striped suit with a painfully starched white oxford shirt and a red rep tie with a diamond pin that must have gone for a half carat.

The other man in the room fit the gangster stereotype a little better. He was sitting on a leather sofa and seemed to take up half of it. The guy was a monster. Big and Mongolian-looking, his blocky head was shaved completely bald. His hands were as wide as garden spades, and the ring finger on his right hand was chopped off at the middle joint. He had the body of a heavyweight wrestler on steroids, thick and barrel-shaped, well over 200 pounds. He was decked out in black polyester pants about four inches too short, white socks, and ugly square-toed black shoes with the kind of gum soles preferred by beat cops and barbers. There were several blotches of what looked like pizza stains (blood?) on the front of his badly fitting white shirt. Odd Job from the James Bond movie *Goldfinger,* with a couple of important differences. Instead of expensive clothing and a bowler with a razor-blade brim, this slob dressed like a Chinese Gomer Pyle. He was also wearing a huge long-barreled revolver in a shoulder holster, probably to discourage people from making fun of his wardrobe.

Fang pointed to an uncomfortable-looking ladder-back chair in front of his desk, and I sat down, took a quick look around the room, and collected my thoughts—which didn't take long, since I had no plan whatsoever. Judging from the creature comforts, it looked as if Fang spent a lot of time in his office doing something besides work. The lighting was indirect, which reduced the glare when he watched the large-screen television and VCR in a hardwood entertainment center along the far wall. There was a CD player in the center and a collection of a hundred or so compact discs. He had an impressive selection of video tapes and seemed to be especially fond of Mel Gibson. He even had Gibson's *Hamlet,* which only the actor's most rabid fans can stand. There was also an old-time pinball machine next to the entertainment center that was lit up and looked functional. As much as I love pinball, though, my favorite part of the office was Tommy's wet bar, which had lots of single-malt Scotch and Irish whiskey. No blended Canadian swill for Tommy Fang; he only went for the best. Throw in a pool table and a popcorn machine and the place would be perfect.

Outside the entertainment equipment and the expensive office furniture, however, the office had little in the way of decoration. There were no photographs, no paintings on the walls, and only one piece of sculpture. Standing on an alabaster pedestal at the side of Fang's desk was a jade dragon, the identical twin of the one I'd seen at Sam Pantaleo's less than a week ago. Coincidence? I doubted it.

Fang let me look around for only a couple of seconds before he made a little tepee of his fingers and leaned forward to rest his elbows on the desktop. "Now, Mr. Starbranch," he began in a soft voice with no accent, "perhaps you can tell me what a Wyoming policeman would possibly want from me. I've never even been in Wyoming, so I can assure you I never broke a law there."

I crossed my legs and tried to get comfortable on the chair, but it was impossible. I imagined he'd told me to sit there in the first place because he didn't want me comfortable. I was watching the goon on the couch in my peripheral vision, and I think he was smiling. "Liam O'Bannion," I said without preamble. "I'm looking into his murder."

Fang nodded sagely. "Ah, yes, Liam," he said. "I heard he'd met with misfortune."

"You knew him, then?"

"Of course," Fang said. "I purchased jade from him on occasion. Not much recently, however. The market's soft."

I decided to go for broke. Maybe Fang's reaction would tell me something. "Was that *all* you purchased from him?" I asked, letting the accusation hang in the air.

Fang didn't bite. "Well no, it wasn't all I purchased," Fang said, chuckling. "Once in a while, he sold me other things he picked up in his travels. Artwork, especially. Mr. O'Bannion had an eye for quality." He gestured at the bare walls of his office. "You couldn't tell it from here, but I'm a big fan of Western art. James Bama and Bev Doolittle in particular. Do you know those painters?"

This was like asking a country-music fanatic whether he'd ever heard of Hank Williams, so I didn't bother to answer, even though I collect prints by those artists myself. Besides, I wasn't there to discuss paintings. I was there to discuss murder. "How about gall bladders from bears?" I asked. "He ever sell you any of those? I hear you and he had quite an enterprise going."

Fang smiled, but it was only a mask. "I don't know who told you that, Mr. Starbranch, but they were sadly mistaken," he said. "Of course he didn't sell me any bear bladders. That would have been *illegal*." He leaned back in his chair. "And even if it weren't, I hear he wasn't exactly the most reputable dealer in those materials."

I almost laughed at the irony. "Reputable?" I asked.

"Well, it *is* a matter of interpretation," Fang admitted. "I never bought them myself, but I understand Mr. O'Bannion occasionally sold those items to persons in Chinatown. And from what I hear, he wasn't above mixing a few pig bladders with the genuine bear organs." His smile grew even colder. "In my neighborhood, that's the sort of thing that can get you killed."

He was playing with me—his tone letting me know there was nothing I could do about it, even if he *was* buying illegal bear organs, even if he pulled the trigger on O'Bannion himself—and I didn't appreciate it. "Is that what got him killed?" I asked. "Or was it drug-related? I hear you might know something about that, too."

A quick look passed between Fang and the goon, but if Fang was upset by my line of questioning, it didn't show. "I think you've been talking to the wrong people," he said. "I have no idea why Liam was murdered, and I have no idea who killed him. I only heard about it myself yesterday."

"Who told you?"

"I don't know," he said dismissively. "Someone in the neighborhood. I can tell you this, however. Liam O'Bannion was the sort of person who made many enemies. He was a good businessman because he knew what people wanted and how to get it. Trouble was, he couldn't be trusted." Fang smiled. "Not that he ever stole from me, but I've heard he stole from many others, and he was so arrogant, he thought he wouldn't be punished." He gave a little wave of his hand, and the thug on the couch stood up. "If you have nothing more I—"

I glared at the muscle man, then back at Fang. "As a matter of fact, I do have something else," I broke in. Fang pursed his lips in irritation, but he nodded for me to go on. "I heard Liam O'Bannion did steal from you. I heard he owed you a lot of money. I heard you argued with him about it shortly before his death. I heard he was afraid of what you might do."

Fang stood up from the desk, picked up a letter opener that looked like a dagger, and tested its point against his finger. He pushed until he drew a drop of blood, then he put the opener down and licked the blood away thoughtfully. The Dracula imitation was blatant theatrics, but it had the desired effect. I felt a little flutter of revulsion, maybe fear, in my belly. "As a matter of fact, he did owe me some money," Fang said, still looking at his finger, hoping for another drop. "But he did not steal it, and he paid it back . . . every penny. Mailed me a cashier's check the next day. The argument we had was the last time I saw him alive."

I didn't believe him for a second, but I had no leverage to make him tell the truth. "How much money did he owe you?" I asked. "Enough to have him killed for?"

Fang looked as if he couldn't believe the question, and a flash of anger passed across his face. Like lightning, it was gone immediately. Still, I had the feeling I'd overstayed my welcome. "I'm afraid the sum of money he owed is none of your business, Mr. Starbranch," he said. "And as I told you, he paid it back. Why, then, would I have him killed?" His voice was reasonable and patient, as if he were explaining a difficult math problem to a slow student. I had to say one thing for Tommy Fang, he kept a tight rein on his emotions. "Now, if you don't mind," he said, "I really am busy."

When I made no motion to leave, he nodded at the thug, who walked to the chair and took me by the elbow. His hand felt like the jaws of a vise, and since the tips of his fingers were above a nerve bundle, my lower arm and hand began tingling almost immediately. I tried to pull away but couldn't. He lifted me to my feet. "Chin Lau will see you out," Fang said. He picked up the phone receiver and held it between his cheek and his shoulder, as if he was waiting until I was gone to dial.

I knew I couldn't stop Fang's chore-boy from pulling me out, but I thought I could delay it for a few seconds. I planted my feet and leaned against the pressure he was putting on my arm so there was no way he could budge me gracefully. If worst came to worst, I figured I could crack Godzilla over the head with my blackthorn, maybe stun him long enough to get out of the office. Then I remembered that there were still at least four thugs in the warehouse, maybe more, who'd be happy to take over where Odd Job left off. I decided to nix the blackthorn idea and keep talking. I looked Fang in the eye, gave him my gunfighter squint. "Sam Pantaleo says hello," I said, trying not to wince from the pain.

The squint sometimes works with drunks and speeders, but it made no discernible impression on Fang, whose benign expression didn't change. "Who?" he asked innocently.

"Sam Pantaleo," I said, grimacing. My arm really did hurt, except for my fingers, which had gone numb. "He said to give you his regards."

Fang blew air through his cheeks. "You're a rude man, Mr. Starbranch," he observed. "But if I knew who you were talking about, I'd have you deliver my regards to him as well." With that he looked down and started punching numbers on the phone.

I started to say something so Fang wouldn't have the last word, but Chin Lau was practically dragging me toward the office door. Oh well, I thought, giving in to his superior strength, at least I won't have to fight my way out.

It had been over twenty-five years since I was ejected from anywhere I didn't want to leave—the last place was a strip joint in Saigon—and the landing was harder than I remembered.

Chin Lau fairly carried me down the stairway to the office, bustled me through the warehouse to the jeers of the four young thugs I'd intimidated on the way in, and ushered me out the loading door with a shove so forceful that I tumbled in a heap on the pavement. He threw my walking stick after me, and it clattered on the asphalt. Then he closed the metal garage door with a bang, leaving me alone except for a couple of amused loafers leaning against the building while they smoked. One said something to the other in a language I didn't understand, and they both cracked up. Neither, I should point out, offered to help.

I stood up and dusted myself off, decided there was nothing bruised but my ego. It's not that I was embarrassed at being pitched out of Tommy Fang's like a sack of garbage. Even I'm smart enough to know that it would have been pointless—and painful—to resist. What really hurt was the smirk on April Lin's face as I was getting myself pitched. No man likes to be pushed around in front of a beautiful woman, even a modern, sensitive fellow like me.

I walked down the street until I came to Grant, then I sauntered back through Chinatown until I came to the pagoda arch that marks the boundary of the district. Then I hopped the trolley that would take me in the direction of my hotel.

Although my visit with Tommy Fang had not lived up to my most minimal expectations, I had gotten two new bits of information. First, Liam O'Bannion had been salting his shipments of bear bladders with bladders from pigs, a scam that could have netted him thousands of dollars. Tommy said that might have gotten him killed in Chinatown, but I didn't think it got him killed on a mountain in Wyoming. Second, Tommy and Sam Pantaleo shared the same taste in gaudy Oriental art. The fact that they owned identical, and very expensive, jade dragons would have absolutely no meaning in a court of law, but in my mind it linked them together. It didn't mean they were partners in crime, but it suggested that they knew each other because the pieces were so unusual. It was a very tenuous connection, but it was better than nothing, enough to suggest that I was on the right track.

I was at loose ends, undecided about my next step, so I got off the trolley and resolved to do my pondering over shrimp scampi at the Franciscan Restaurant, a three-tiered, glass-encased leviathan of an eatery on Fisherman's Wharf. I love the Franciscan because almost every table provides an unobstructed view of the bay, Alcatraz Island, and the city. The waiters are friendly, and the bartender makes a memorable Bloody Mary. I drank two of them with my scampi and then topped the meal with coffee and tiramisu, which I munched slowly while I watched sailboats cavorting on the bay.

It was a little after one when I finished lunch, and I spent the rest of the afternoon acting like a tourist. I took a walking tour of Divisadero, went through the Palace of Fine Arts, and enjoyed a lovely stroll through the waterfront section of the Presidio near the Golden Gate Bridge.

At around seven-thirty, I hailed a cab and had the driver—a tall black woman with mocha skin, five earrings, and a boom box blasting Motown beside her on the front seat—drive me by Faith's doll shop on Chestnut Street near the Russian Hill section. The shop was a hole-in-the-wall storefront that shared the ground floor of a refurbished nineteenth-century redbrick building with a travel agency and a unisex barbershop called Hair Today, Gone Tomorrow, both of which were closed for the day. Faith's shop was dark, but the front window was filled with beautiful dolls, some dressed in Victorian lace, others in complex ball gowns, and still others in lush velvet traveling capes and long opera cloaks. There wasn't a single Barbie in view. Above the door was a wood-cut sign that said DOLLS IN THE ATTIC, and on the door itself was a small hand-lettered card that said CLOSED UNTIL FURTHER NOTICE.

The cabbie was happy to wait on the street and let the meter run as long as I liked, which was about three minutes. Then I gave her Faith and Liam's address on Prospect and we headed south on Leavenworth Street toward Nob Hill and the theater district, the cabbie singing along with Martha and the Vandellas at the top of her voluminous lungs.

Prospect was a little cul-de-sac within walking distance of the theater district. The street was a collection of tall, narrow town houses—each painted in pastel shades with four or five colors of trim and all of them decked out in gingerbread and carved molding, with window boxes spilling flowers and vines down their fronts. Each house had a garage on the ground level, and I suppose folks parked their cars inside. Each entrance was protected by an elaborate grille, and most front doors sported discreet decals announcing that the house was guarded by an alarm system.

Three forty-nine was in the middle of the cul-de-sac on the right side, and differed from its neighbors only in color. The clapboard siding was painted periwinkle blue, the shutters hunter green with hints of lemon and lavender. I paid the cabbie and gave her a generous tip, and she left me standing on the sidewalk in the fading light. The beginnings of a plan were starting to percolate in my brain, but I needed darkness to carry it off. I trudged down to the theater district and found a movie house showing a Japanese art film with subtitles. I bought a ticket and found a seat, fell asleep for about ten minutes after the opening credits, and didn't wake until the movie was over and the house lights came up.

It was fully dark when I went outside and headed back toward Prospect, which was lit by old-fashioned gas lamps with modern bulbs. There was no one on the street, and none of the neighbors poked a head out the window to ask what I was doing when I walked up the front stairs to check the front door of Faith and Liam's house. The porch light was not burning, but the street lamps gave off enough light to allow me to peer through the grillework to the front door, where I saw the decal warning burglars that the place was electronically protected.

I didn't know whether Liam and Faith had invested in an expensive security system that detects motion, whether their system was wired only to the doors and windows, or whether it was even turned on. For all I knew, they didn't even have a security system and figured that the decal alone would deter crooks. Either way, I couldn't take that big a chance, which ruled out trying to jimmy the locks with the plastic 'loid—a handy celluloid substitute for a credit card—I keep in my wallet for the odd occasions when I have to break and enter. I had to come up with another plan.

I came down off the porch and followed the side of the house until I blended into the darkness at the rear of the building. I always carry a small penlight along with my pocketknife in my front pocket, and I shined it upward to scope out the second-floor windows at the back of the house, which I'd need a ladder to enter, even if they weren't wired. No good.

The garage took up half the ground floor, and it looked as if a small basement took up the other half. I started working my way along the cement wall, checking each of the small basement windows. The first was locked and in good shape, as was the second, but on the third I had a stroke of luck. One of the small panes that made up the sectioned window had been broken at some point, leaving a jagged hole in the glass.

I shined the narrow beam of light through the window and didn't see any security wires. The hole wasn't big enough for me to reach my hand through in order to unfasten the latch, however, so I looked around until I found a fist-size chunk of concrete that would finish the job. I broke the remainder of the glass with a minimum of noise, reached through the window, and quickly opened the latch.

I knelt down and tried to blend in with the shadows until I was sure the noise of breaking glass hadn't alerted any of the neighbors, then I scoured the small backyard until I found a plastic five-gallon garden bucket to stand on and raised the window. It hurt, but I lifted one leg through so I was straddling the sill. Then I ducked my upper body through the window and hoped for the best. It was a tight squeeze, but I finally got through the tiny opening and dropped into the basement. I crouched down in the dark and took a few deep breaths, thankful that so far, at least, the alarms weren't sounding.

The basement was full of empty cardboard moving boxes stacked along the walls, old furniture, and garments hanging from the beams, and I could see a wooden staircase at the far side of the room and a door without a lock leading to the main living area of the house. It was time to decide whether to gamble. If I went through that door and the security system was turned on and detected motion, I'd be spending some quality time in a San Francisco jail.

I decided to take the risk, followed the beam of the penlight to the stairs, and made my way up, one creaking step at a time. At the top, I wrapped my hand around the handle, held my breath, and slowly opened the door, which opened into the kitchen. Nothing. Cautiously, I took a few quick steps to the living room and paused in the darkness. Still nothing. It seemed that I was safe, unless the system was the kind that didn't make noise when it was tripped and was connected directly to the police department. If that was the case, I only had a few minutes to find what I was looking for and get out before the cruisers arrived. Trouble was, I had no idea what I was looking for.

I used the dim light coming through the gauzy curtains to make my way upstairs to the master bedroom—a large room with a beautiful bay window, a high double bed with a quilted comforter, two heavy oak dressers, and what looked like an antique vanity with a wild assortment of silk scarves dangling from the mirror.

I figured Liam's dresser was the one with the bottles of after-shave, the collection of ball caps, and the shoe-polishing kit on top, so that's where I started. The two top drawers held the usual assortment of junk—matchbooks, credit-card receipts, belt buckles, and such. I didn't have time to examine any of it carefully, but there was nothing that jumped out and caught my attention. The second drawer was a loser also, nothing but underwear and folded jeans. The third drawer was full of sweaters and a few more interesting items. I found three little vials tucked under the clothing, the sort of orange vials that usually hold cocaine or other drugs. Two of them were empty; the third was half full. There was also a sharp fish-filleting knife in a leather sheath and a small automatic pistol that fit into the palm of my hand, maybe a .25 caliber.

I left the drugs and weapons where I found them and turned my attention to Faith's dresser, which might have interested a pervert with a lingerie fetish but held nothing of importance for me. The vanity was a bust, too. On the theory that most people hide things close to their beds, I next checked under the mattresses, under the rug behind the bed, and in the drawers of the nightstand—where I found a tangerine-colored vibrator and a year's supply of condoms, but nothing else worth mentioning. Ditto with the closets.

Frustrated, I gave up on the bedroom and went to the room next door, which appeared to serve as a combination office and workout room. A heavy wooden desk with a personal computer on top shared floor space with a stair machine, a treadmill, a stationary bike, and an old-fashioned set of weights.

I skipped the rest of the room and went right to the desk. There wasn't much on top except a few pieces of mail—recent bills and a pile of catalogs. I ignored those and opened the first shallow drawer. The drawer was jam-packed with paper in no particular order— bank statements on top of old checkbook registers, tax returns on top of newspaper clippings, pocket-size date books on top of Christmas cards, letters, and credit-card receipts on top of old bills. It was the same in the second drawer and the one below that.

With a growing sense of urgency, I flashed the beam of the penlight around the room until I found what I needed, a small white canvas gym bag filled with workout clothes, toiletries, and a towel. I dumped the gym stuff on the floor and started filling the bag with the papers in the desk. When all three drawers were empty, I zipped the bag, took a final look around the room, and headed downstairs. I figured I'd take my time and go through it once I got back to the hotel. I might not find any clues, but I imagined the accumulated paperwork might give me a better idea of what Liam and Faith's lives had been like in the last year or so.

I gave the bathroom, the living room, and the kitchen a cursory once-over on my way out, and found nothing of note except a pair of airline tickets to La Paz, Mexico, on the kitchen counter and a few letters that had been delivered through the mail slot in recent days. I checked the tickets and found that they were made out to Liam and Faith, who'd scheduled their trip for the coming September. I left them on the counter. After a moment's hesitation, I jammed the mail into my bag.

Less than a minute later, I was climbing back out the basement window. Getting out was much easier than getting in, however. I threw the bag out first and, after some difficulty, got one leg through the window so I was straddling the sill again. When I swung my head and torso through the opening, a hand grabbed me roughly by the collar to pull me the rest of the way through and send me tumbling to the ground.

I was taken so completely by surprise that I think I actually yelped as I scrambled to my hands and knees, my heart pumping about a zillion times a minute. From that angle, I could see a man's thick legs coming toward me rapidly. I didn't have time to think, just react. I launched myself forward like a lineman, my feet digging for traction. I hit him hard, wrapped my arms around his knees, and brought him down with a grunt. You can't put a lot of power behind your punches when you're wrestling on the ground, but I did my best. I hit him three or four times in the ribs and gave him a solid elbow across the jaw. Then I brought my knee up as hard as I could between his legs.

My assailant moaned and doubled over in pain, but I wasn't finished. I stood up, grabbed him by the hair, and pulled him to his feet. He was three inches shorter than I am, maybe five nine, and a good fifty pounds lighter. Once we were on our feet, it wasn't much of a contest. I gave him a hard right to the nose that sent him stumbling backward until he crashed into the wall of the house with a sickening thud. Then he sort of slithered down the wall until he was sitting on his butt. He didn't make much of an attempt to get up, so I walked over to help him. Before I did that, though, I thought I'd give him a couple more whacks, just for good measure.

I never got the chance.

I was just reaching down to grab him by the collar when his hand came out of the darkness around his waist with an ugly-looking short-barreled revolver. I froze like a deer caught in the headlights, watching in horror as he pulled the hammer back with his thumb and trained the muzzle between my eyeballs. The bore looked huge, as black as eternity. The gun was wavering slightly. I hoped his finger didn't twitch.

I didn't know who he was, but I figured that if he worked for Tommy Fang I was in deep trouble.

Turns out I was partially right. I *was* in trouble, but he didn't work for Fang. He brought the back of his hand to his nose, and it came away bloody. He gave his head a disgusted shake and then looked back at me, leaned forward, and touched the cold metal of the barrel against my forehead. "Hit the dirt, you son of a bitch," he groaned. "Your sorry ass is under arrest."

14

Talking's hard when you're lying facedown on the backseat of a car with your lips mashed into the upholstery and a set of handcuffs digging into the flesh of your wrists. It's a good thing the cop in the front seat didn't really expect a response. "This isn't money!" he said, pulling paper out of my purloined gym bag by the handfuls and tossing it around like confetti. He sounded like someone with a bad head cold, but I was afraid that was only because I'd broken his nose. "You stole the fucking mail!"

I would have preferred the word *borrowed,* but I wasn't prepared to quibble—I didn't want to get punched in the head again.

After sticking his revolver into my face, the man who'd arrested me had slapped the cuffs on my wrists, pulled me to my feet, and marched me to the nondescript Ford Taurus he had parked about a half block from Liam and Faith's house, muttering curses and socking me in the back of the head about every other step. A couple of times, I tried to tell him who I was and what I'd been doing, but he wasn't interested, just swatted me again and told me to shut up. He wasn't hitting hard, just enough to keep me moving, but the cumulative effect made my ears ring by the time we got to the automobile.

Once there, he opened the back door and shoved me in, then he got in front, turned on the dome light, and started rifling the contents of the bag—the source of his current displeasure. When the bag was empty he threw it at me, whanged it off my shoulder. "Where is it?" he asked roughly.

I rolled over on my side so I could get a better look at him. Dressed in street clothes—jeans, high-top sneakers, and a Hard Rock Cafe T-shirt under a faded denim work shirt with the sleeves rolled up—his long dishwater-blond hair curled down to his shoulders and his natty goatee and mustache couldn't hide the residue of baby fat in his cheeks. His perfectly straight teeth were blazingly white and just a little too big for his mouth. I figured him for late twenties, early thirties. Handsome in a young Troy Donahue, corn-fed sort of way, he looked more like a slightly derelict college student than a cop. He hadn't gotten around to introducing himself, or to producing any credentials. On the other hand, he hadn't read me the Miranda. Maybe I could talk myself out of this yet. "Where's what?" I asked helpfully.

He reached over the seat, picked up the bag, and whapped me with it again. It hurt about as much as getting slapped with a rolled-up newspaper, but it was still annoying. "The money!" he snapped. "Where's the damned money?"

I tried to sit up, but he pushed me back down. "I have no idea what you're talking about," I assured him reasonably, "but if you'll just quit slapping me with that stupid bag, I'll tell you all I can." With some effort, I rolled over to expose my back pocket. "Reach in there for my wallet," I said. "My identification."

He tried to sniff air through his nose, but it didn't work. Too stuffy. "I know who you are," he said. "You're a stinking burglar who just assaulted a federal officer. What more do I need to know?"

Federal officer? Perfect, I thought miserably. If he'd only given me his gun at that moment, I'd have shot myself and saved him the trouble. "I'm a cop for Christ's sake," I muttered. "Look in my wallet."

I waited until I felt his fingers in my pocket, felt him slip the wallet out. Then I turned over on my back to watch him read. He saw my badge first and laughed out loud, then he pulled my driver's license out of the compartment and studied it. When he finished with that, he ran through my credit cards, my library card, my Social Security card, and counted my money. Less than 200 bucks. He wasn't particularly impressed, but something in his face changed, softened a bit. He threw the wallet on the dash. "Is that supposed to mean something to me?" he asked. "You think just because you carry a shield from some hick town full of Spam-eating hillbillies I'm gonna pat you on the back and send you on your way? Forget it, Grandpa. You're in the big city now. That badge means dick."

Considering the circumstances, I suppose I should have expected a certain surliness on his part, but his trash-talking, tough-guy routine was getting on my nerves and I was afraid that pretty soon I'd start shooting off my mouth and say something I'd regret. "I know what it means," I told him. "But it ought to be enough to convince you to listen to me for sixty seconds. At least let me explain why I was in that house."

He smiled thinly. "Forget it," he said. "I'm not interested in hearing you run off at the mouth. If you're really a cop like you say you are, give me some names, people who can vouch for you."

The way he said it was a challenge, like the last thing he thought I'd give him was names of cops, but I rattled them off. Terrenzi and Cooper with the San Francisco police department, my ex-partner John Bruno in Denver, Ken Keegan, an investigator with the Wyoming Department of Criminal Investigation, Danny King with the Laramie cops, Aaron Cohen with the Federal Bureau of Investigation, and finally Frankie Tall Bull. He looked dubious, but he scribbled their names and numbers on a pad. When I finished, he popped the glove box, pulled out a cellular phone, and got out of the car. "Wait here," he commanded.

Like I had a choice.

For the next half hour, I wallowed on the seat like a trussed hog while he sat on the hood of the car and gabbed. I could hear the muffled sound of his voice, but I couldn't understand what he was saying. Once or twice he laughed, but mostly he sounded more than a little pissed off. My legs had developed a world-class cramp, and my arms were sound asleep when he finally finished talking. He opened the back door of the car and unlocked the cuffs. He wasn't especially gentle about it, either. "I got a couple messages for you," he said.

I sat up and rubbed my wrists. It would be a while before the feeling came back.

"First," he said, ticking it off on his fingers, "Frankie Bull says you should call him as soon as possible 'cause you're in hot water with the politicians you work for." I rolled my eyes. "Second," he went on, "your buddy Ken Keegan says to tell you he thinks I should do myself a favor—throw you in jail immediately and swallow the key. Says putting you behind bars is the only way I'll keep you from screwing up my cases."

Not only did I still not know who the young cop was, I had no idea what he was talking about. "Screwing up your cases?" I asked.

"Yeah," he said. "Depending on what you said to Tommy Fang this afternoon, you could have screwed 'em royally. Care to tell me about that conversation?"

I thought back to my meeting with Fang, remembered I'd accused him of just about everything but white slavery and jaywalking. I wasn't ready to go into detail, however, so I answered his question with one of my own. "How'd you know I talked to Fang?"

He gave me a no-big-deal shrug. "I saw you going in there and followed you when you left," he said. "I've been following you all day." He held out his hand. "Jaime Pichette," he said, "Drug Enforcement Administration." He showed me a gold and silver badge and a fancy photo identification card in a slender leather case. Sure enough, he was DEA. "Mr. Bull tells me you're looking into the death of Liam O'Bannion?" he said. "I should have figured that out when I saw where you're from."

I nodded stupidly. If he'd been following me, I hadn't picked up the tail. Not that I'd been expecting one. And why should he have suspected I was investigating O'Bannion's murder just by looking at my shield and address? I hoped I'd have a chance to ask him. "Look," I said tentatively, "I'm sorry about popping you in the nose. If I'd known you were a—"

Pichette shrugged good-naturedly. "Don't worry about it too much," he said. "I guess I was too busy dragging you out that window to make a proper introduction." He helped me out of the car and waited patiently while I stamped some feeling back into my legs. "You a drinking man, Mr. Starbranch?" he asked.

I told him I've been known to indulge on rare occasions. Then I asked him to call me Harry.

He motioned to the front door of the Taurus. "Hop in, *Mr. Starbranch*," he said. Guess he didn't think we should be on a first-name basis yet. "I'm gonna find a dark bar with a back table where we can talk in private."

He smiled, and for the first time it seemed almost genuine. "The least you can do after busting my nose is buy me a beer and tell me what the hell you've been doing in San Francisco." His smile grew even wider. With his rapidly swelling beak and the puffy shiners sprouting under both his eyes, his whole face looked lopsided, like a demented raccoon. "After that, I'll decide whether to take your friend's advice and toss you in the can."

Pichette was as good as his word and took us to a dismal and cavernous bucket o' blood called the Happy Hour, a definite misnomer, since the dive looked like a rest stop for men with prostate trouble and women with penicillin-resistant venereal disease. Signs behind the bar advertised the fact that the Happy Hour cashed welfare and Social Security checks, but informed patrons in at least four languages that there was NO CREDIT, NO SOLICITATION, NO GAMBLING, and NO PROFANITY. There wasn't a happy person in the place.

The scruffy bartender nodded at the DEA agent when we walked in and motioned us toward the back of the establishment, past the dozen or so down-and-outers and tired hookers sitting at the bar drinking draft beer and plonk wine, none of whom looked up from their misery as we walked by. Not the sort of place where it's safe to pay much attention to other customers.

We found a table in a dark corner where the upholstery on the bench seat was held together by silver duct tape and Pichette signaled the bartender to bring us a round. He didn't bother to ask what we wanted, just arrived at the table a couple minutes later with glasses of lukewarm beer, shots of bourbon, and a bowl of stale-looking pretzels and nuts. If he noticed the fact that Pichette looked as if he'd been on the losing end of a fistfight, he didn't comment.

Pichette waited until the barkeep was gone, then drained his shot in a single swallow. He chased it with half his beer and wiped foam from his upper lip with the back of his hand. I seldom drink bottom-shelf bar whiskey and even the beer looked suspicious, so I took a sociable sip of the brew and gave the shot to Pichette. He took it almost gratefully.

I lit a cigar to mask the smells of urine, spilled beer, and dime-store perfume that were making my stomach lurch. Pichette graciously waited until I had it going before he got down to business. "Now, Mr. Starbranch," he said, "I'd like you to tell me all about your investigation of Liam O'Bannion's murder, every gory detail. And please, start at the beginning." He leaned back on the seat with his arms behind his head, an overgrown kid waiting for a good bedtime story.

I'd decided I didn't much like Pichette, but there was no reason to hold back. Over the next twenty minutes I gave him the whole sordid tale, from the fight at the restaurant and the discovery of O'Bannion's corpse to Curly Ahearn's arrest and my ensuing visits to Pantaleo, the Wind River Reservation, and San Francisco. I told him about my fight with Junior Stone, about my confrontation with Tommy Fang, about getting thrown out of his office on my face. I told him about my suspicions and theories. I told him that despite everything I'd learned, I wasn't that much closer to proving who pulled the trigger on O'Bannion than I'd been the day we found his body in the jaws of a grizzly bear. I explained the frustration that led me to break into the house Liam shared with Faith Ahearn and steal the couple's mail. I ended my tale at the point where Pichette jammed his revolver into my face and shackled my wrists but told him that I planned to stick with the investigation until I proved Curly was innocent, no matter the personal and professional consequences.

Maybe it was the calming effect of the whiskey, but Pichette listened with bemused interest until I got to the part about my visit with Fang. Then his brow clouded and he drummed his fingers impatiently on the tabletop until I finished talking. "So you accused Tommy Fang of being involved in drugs?" he asked tersely.

"I guess I did," I admitted.

"Did you happen to mention how you came by that information?" he asked. "Does he know other cops are interested in that particular aspect of his business? Does he know the DEA is involved?"

"I don't know," I said. "But if he does, I didn't tell him. Like I told you, it was a short conversation. And to tell you the truth, although I'd heard rumors, even I didn't know the DEA was involved for certain. As far as Tommy Fang knows, I'm working this all by myself, which I thought I was."

"And Sam Pantaleo?"

"Same story."

Pichette didn't look as if he disbelieved me, but he didn't seem to believe me, either. He mulled it over while he finished his beer and apparently came to a conclusion. "And you really weren't looking for the money at O'Bannion's house?" he asked. It was more of a statement than an accusation, just confirming something he already suspected.

"I have no idea what money you think I was looking for," I told him. "It was my impression Liam was broke."

Pichette laughed. "Was he?" he asked. "There are lots of people around here who'd like the answer to that question, Mr. Starbranch. Including me." The DEA agent finished the dregs of his beer, wadded his napkin into a ball, and stood up. "Thanks for the help," he said. "I'm not going to arrest you, on one condition. Catch the first available flight back to Wyoming and stay away from Tommy Fang and Sam Pantaleo. I don't think you blew my investigation yet, and I'd like to keep it that way. Don't worry, though. I'm as interested in finding out who killed O'Bannion as you are, and I don't think it was your friend Curly Ahearn." With that he held out his hand. "Can you catch a cab back to your hotel?" he asked.

His abrupt dismissal surprised me, and then it made me angry. If this young punk thought he could send me away like an errant schoolboy, he was sadly mistaken. Nor could he scare me off with the threat of an arrest. I figured I could explain my break-in if I had to. Even if I couldn't, I didn't think Faith would press charges. And I seriously doubted that the San Francisco P.D. would be too upset that I'd punched a federal agent. In some police circles, that would be grounds for a commendation.

So far, I'd cooperated with Pichette in good faith and he'd given me nothing but attitude in return. That was about to end. Instead of shaking his outstretched hand, I slapped it away. "I thought I made it clear to you I'm not going anywhere until I prove who killed Liam O'Bannion," I told him sternly. "And if that means stepping on your toes while I do it, that's just too damned bad." I threw $10 on the table and ground my cigar out in the ashtray. Then I pushed by him and made my way toward the front door.

He called me back before I'd gone a dozen steps. "Hold it right there!" he yelled. There was a note of desperation in his voice that caused a couple of the old coots at the bar to look up from their libations. This obviously wasn't turning out as he'd planned.

"Up yours, Buckwheat," I muttered. I hunched my shoulders and kept going.

I almost didn't hear him when he said "Please."

The deal was simple. In order to avoid jeopardizing a two-year investigation, I'd stay away from Tommy Fang and go back to Wyoming to continue my inquiries. In return, Pichette would save me a lot of shoe leather by filling me in on everything about O'Bannion, Fang, and Pantaleo that he thought might be important. He'd also let me in on anything germane that broke after I left town. His current information wouldn't clear Curly of O'Bannion's murder, he said, but he hoped it would make the trail a little plainer.

I didn't mention it to Pichette, but my first visit with Fang was such a washout that I hadn't planned on seeing him again anyway. I had nothing to lose and plenty to gain by agreeing to his proposal, so that's what I did.

We sat back down in the darkened booth, and this time Pichette went to the bar and paid for our drinks. He had another shot and a beer. I ordered a ginger ale on crushed ice.

We sipped them for a few seconds before Pichette looked around the room to make sure no one was listening, then leaned forward conspiratorially. "What do you know about methamphetamine?" he asked quietly.

"Speed?" I asked. The question was so basic that it took me off guard. "I've been a cop for a long time, Pichette, long enough to know elementary pharmacology. I know it's been around for decades, though its popularity comes and goes. Lately, I hear it's on the come."

Pichette nodded agreement. "That's about right," he said. "In the seventies and early eighties, it was mostly motorcycle gangs. They cooked it and sold it by the quart." He ran a finger around the edge of his glass thoughtfully. "The business has changed considerably in the last two or three years, though," he said. "Out there in Victory, you may not have realized just how much."

Just one of the joys of rural living, I suppose. We're not exactly on the cutting edge of national drug chic. Although his condescension grated, I nodded for him to go on, and he did.

According to Pichette, the use of methamphetamine spiked in the late 1980s when the lab chemists who work for drug dealers figured out how to make the drug from a legal drug, ephedrine. When the DEA succeeded in regulating ephedrine, those same chemists quickly substituted pseudoephedrine, a common drug found in over-the-counter cold and allergy remedies. The result was what Pichette described as a "hellish tidal wave" of speed—which can be snorted, smoked, or injected, costs half as much as cocaine, and provides a considerably extended high.

Now the illegal drug of choice on the West Coast, methamphetamine is spreading across the country like wildfire, he said, leaving a trail of human carnage in its wake. In 1994, seizures were up 88 percent over the previous year and dosages were more powerful, since the average purity had jumped from 46 to 72 percent in a little over twenty-four months.

In addition to the physical damage users are causing themselves with this increasingly powerful and plentiful drug, he said, they're doing horrific damage to others.

"In Contra Costa County, near San Francisco, methamphetamine is involved in 89 percent of domestic-dispute cases, and 63 percent of those cases are scarred by violence. Speed psychosis accounts for a major share of hostage situations in northern California—nineteen or twenty days of no sleep and these skells go completely crazy," he said sadly. "The only people who profit are the dealers, the morticians, and the grave diggers."

He paused, perhaps remembering a situation that went horribly wrong, one where innocent blood was shed. "This stuff is as bad as anything you've ever seen, Mr. Starbranch," he said. "The DEA is committed to stopping it . . . right here, right now."

"And Fang, Pantaleo, O'Bannion . . ." I asked, letting my question dangle.

"Are right in the middle of it," he said. He looked down to study the rings his glass had left on the table, then back at me. "Except that for the last year, O'Bannion was working for *us*."

He couldn't have stunned me more if he'd slapped me in the face. "O'Bannion?" I asked incredulously. "A DEA agent?"

Pichette dismissed that with an agitated wave of his hand. "More like a confidential informant," he said. "We busted him a little over fourteen months ago for selling $10,000 worth of product to one of our undercovers. He didn't care for prison the last time he was there, so he was anxious to avoid going back. We've been using him to make a case against Pantaleo and Tommy Fang."

Now he had my undivided attention. "You mind giving me the details?" I asked.

Pichette backed off a little, suddenly wary. "Depends on how you intend to use them," he said.

"Look," I said, "I'm not interested in making a drug case against Fang or Pantaleo . . . that's your job. All I'm interested in doing is getting my friend out of jail. If you can help me do that, I'd be eternally grateful, and I'll make you a promise. I'll give you every bit of cooperation I can, and I won't do a thing to get in your way or blow your investigation. You have my word on it."

Pichette didn't answer right away, just excused himself to visit the men's room. He was in there a long time, but when he came back it was obvious he'd made a decision. "I've got your word?" he asked. "Ken Keegan says that means something coming from you."

I promised him he did.

"All right, then," he said. He sat down and looked up at the ceiling, thinking about a place to start. When he found one, he looked at me and shrugged his shoulders. "We got lucky," he said simply. "We'd known that Fang and Pantaleo were working together for a long time. Fang's chemists make the speed here in San Francisco and sell a lot of it in California. Not all, though. A good deal of their product goes to Pantaleo, who's connected to the Denver and Phoenix mobs. Problem was, we couldn't prove they were involved themselves. All we had were their gofers.

"When we busted O'Bannion, it was perfect. He was already working as a middleman between Fang and Pantaleo, moving a lot of speed and everything else he could think of to make a buck, including those bear bladders you're so interested in, dealing with the head men personally. It was a golden opportunity for us to score a big one against both the Chinese gangs and the mob, take a couple of the key players out of action. All O'Bannion had to do was wear a wire and keep records, let us know when the deals were going down. When it was all over, he'd testify and walk away with a new identity, spend the rest of his life living on the government's tab in the witness-protection program."

Pichette downed the shot of bourbon he'd brought back from the bar and his boyish face contorted in a grimace. He shuddered perceptibly as the whiskey worked its way down his throat to his belly. He took a sip of beer to wash it down. "It was working pretty well, and we probably would have made our arrests in a few months," he continued, "but O'Bannion started getting greedy. We knew he had a gambling problem, but I guess we didn't realize how bad it was. After he tapped his own finances and his girlfriend's, he started looking around for other sources of income, and the people he knew with the most money were his cronies in the drug trade.

"Long and short of it was he started stealing a little money and lost it gambling, then he had to steal more to pay it back. Eventually, the whole thing snowballed. In the last four months, he took $50,000 of our money that he was supposed to use to buy drugs, took $150,000 from Pantaleo that was supposed to pay the Asians for meth, *forgot* to pay Tommy another $100,000 for product that had already been delivered, then ripped him off for another $50,000 by selling him a cooler full of pig bladders that were supposed to be from bears." Pichette paused, waiting for me to add it all up. "Christ, he was stealing from *everybody* . . . and everybody wanted their money back," he went on. "Trouble was, some of these guys have more aggressive collection tactics than those of us who work for Uncle Sam."

"You think they killed him?" I broke in.

Pichette shook his head. "I doubt it," he said. "They would have killed him eventually, but they wanted their money back first. What they did was more indirect. O'Bannion's got a kid sister lives in Wisconsin, a college student. They said if he didn't pay up, they'd kill *her.*"

"It was a good tactic," he said. "O'Bannion grew up on the streets around here. Parents were both alcoholics who died in a car wreck while Liam was in junior high. He raised the sister the best he could, but he didn't like to work. He started out in petty crime and gradually worked his way up, and he was pretty good. Fairly smart, you know? Always had big ideas, saw the opportunities and acted on them. It set him apart from most of the pond scum we see around here. You look at his rap sheet and read between the lines, you know there was lots of stuff he got away with. He was absolutely amoral about most things and I wouldn't want to turn my back on him in a dark alley, but he came across as real likable. Friendly, you know? And sharp.

"Trouble was, he wasn't quite as smart as he thought, and it caught up with him. The bad guys hit him where they knew he was soft, his sister. Knowing what I know about O'Bannion, Faith Ahearn was just the last in a long string of women he used and then got rid of after he'd sucked them and their bank accounts dry, so his sister was the only person he really cared about. We offered to put her in protective custody, but O'Bannion said no, he didn't want to scare her or get her involved. Said he had most of the money he needed to get himself out of hot water on his own, buy himself a little time. Told me he had a little over $200,000."

"What went wrong?" I asked.

"The fucking money disappeared before he could pay it back," he said. "At least that's what O'Bannion claimed. He went out to Wyoming to beg Pantaleo for a little more time, and Pantaleo gave him a week, told him to stay in touch and not even think about running. Told him Junior Stone would track him down and cut his balls off if he ran. Then he'd fly out to Wisconsin and go to work on his sister."

Pichette drained the rest of his beer. "O'Bannion was bat shit," he recalled. "Phoned me in a panic and wanted DEA to bail him out. But since he'd already stolen so much from us, and we really didn't need him to make the rest of our case—as long as Fang and Pantaleo don't get wind of what we're up to and bolt before we're ready to arrest them—we said no. Told him that if he didn't come up with the money he'd taken from us, we'd likely prosecute. I did try to talk him into protective custody for himself and Faith in the interim, but he refused. Said he'd work it out with Pantaleo, one way or another.

"I don't know how he intended to work it out, but he still had five days left on the day he was killed—and we hear he died without paying off a single cent." Pichette chuckled darkly. "Surprised the piss out of me, Mr. Starbranch."

"What was so surprising?" I asked.

"Knowing O'Bannion, I suspected he'd just hidden that money away till he figured out a way to keep it for himself," Pichette answered. "After we heard he was dead, I imagined that sooner or later somebody else would get the same idea, go looking for the money."

He paused briefly. "That's why I been watching Fang's. Hell, when I saw you coming out of Liam's house I thought *you'd* found it—although at the time, I didn't know who you were."

"And all I had was the mail," I mused.

"Yep," he said ruefully. "A real disappointment."

I took a long swallow of my ginger ale and crunched an ice chunk between my teeth. My mind was racing with possibilities, but every time I followed one, it came to an abrupt dead end. "I know O'Bannion wasn't killed by Faith or Curly," I said, thinking out loud. "But if it wasn't Pantaleo or Fang, then who was it? And why?"

Pichette stood up and pulled the tail of his T-shirt over the revolver that was stuck in his waistband, getting ready to leave. "As you pointed out, Mr. Starbranch, drugs are my business—homicide is yours, at least it used to be." He dug around in the hip pocket of his jeans until he came up with a rumpled business card with nothing on it but his name and telephone number and threw it on the table in front of me. "If you find the answers to those questions—"

"It'll be a miracle," I blurted.

Pichette grinned as if he thought I was joking.

Pichette drove me back to the hotel, but before I got out of the car we spent a half hour sitting under the big lights in the parking lot, going through the contents of the gym bag I'd filled during my burglary of Liam and Faith's home.

It was primarily the sort of stuff you'd find in anyone's home office—old check registers, bank statements, bill stubs, and the like. I was interested nevertheless, because the detritus painted a detailed picture of their financial lives, and that picture was ugly.

According to a copy of their tax returns from the previous year, Faith had made a profit of about $20,000 from her doll shop and Liam claimed an income of $38,000 from his import-export business. They were hardly high rollers, but you wouldn't know that from the amount they spent. Between them, Faith and Liam had almost a dozen credit cards, and all of them were charged to the max. They each had a Visa, a Discover, and a MasterCard with credit limits ranging from $3,000 to $12,000. Faith had an American Express on which—according to the last statement—she owed close to $1,200, as well as credit cards for clothing, hardware, and furniture stores. Liam had an Optima with a balance of almost five grand, a Diners Club card, and a credit card for an electronics store. They also had accounts with a couple of finance companies that charged high interest for personal loans, and owed the companies about six grand each.

Judging from the paperwork, the young couple weren't exactly prompt when it came to paying their bills. There were dunning letters from every credit-card company with which they had an account, and a few of them had canceled the cards altogether. One of the finance companies was threatening legal action, and the electronics store had turned Liam's account over to an attorney for collection. There were also angry letters from doctors, dentists, a florist, and the bank they'd used to finance their automobiles, which promised them a visit from the repo men if they didn't make up several missed payments immediately. A recent letter from their landlord gave them three weeks to come up with four months' back rent or face eviction proceedings.

It didn't look as if they'd paid anyone for several months, and taking into account the fact that their most recent bank statement showed an available balance of just over $500 (their $1,000 credit limit was used up), they wouldn't have been able to make across-the-board payments for the current month, either—unless Liam dipped into the ill-gotten gains Pichette believed he'd squirreled away. I doubted he'd have chosen that course of action, since banks and credit-card companies seldom send thugs to break your legs or murder your family. Maybe he figured that since he would soon be in the witness program, it didn't matter how much he owed when he dropped out of his old life and into a new one.

On paper, it certainly appeared that they were in way over their heads, just a hair's breadth away from bankruptcy. Which made two items in the drift of paper stick out as unusual, or at least hopelessly optimistic.

One was a letter to Faith from a local real-estate agent telling her that the owner of a newly refurbished building on Sacramento was eager to sign a two-year agreement on a retail property that would double the floor space she currently leased for her doll business. Although the rent was almost double as well, the agent assured Faith that the better location would give her a more upscale image and she would enjoy increased foot traffic from people with lots of disposable income. The agent urged a signing date at the end of the current month and noted that she would need her first month's rent, her last month's rent, and a sizable security deposit at the time of signing, close to $10,000 total.

The second item was a page that had been torn from the home section of the *Chronicle*, with pictures of several restored Victorian houses near the waterfront circled in red. Notes in the margins indicated that Faith had gone to look at many of the houses in person, and under one home listed at $270,000 was a sentence written in a feminine hand that read, "Agent says seller would accept offer of two-twenty."

Between the interest in real estate and the arrangements she'd made for a fall vacation, it was clear that Faith had no intention of moving from the Bay Area anytime soon. She was making long-term plans, so maybe she didn't know the full extent of Liam's involvement in criminal activity. She didn't seem to know that he was headed for a new identity in the relocation program. I wondered when he'd planned to mention it. Maybe never. Maybe he hadn't planned to take her along.

There was no way Pichette was going to let me keep anything in the bag, so I borrowed a pen and paper and made some notes about how much money Faith and Liam owed, and to whom. I jotted down the name of the agent who wanted Faith to lease the new retail space, and I noted the names and numbers of the companies responsible for listing the houses circled in red, including the home where the owner was prepared to accept a low-ball offer.

When I'd finished, I thanked Pichette for his information and apologized once more for breaking his nose. Then I said good night and made my way to my room.

It was half past one, but I was too wired to sleep. I peeled out of my clothes and stood under a scalding shower until my skin turned pink and began to tingle. Then I wrapped a towel around my waist and padded out to the bedroom to call room service and have them send up a turkey club with bacon and a huge hunk of hot apple pie.

The sleepy clerk who answered the phone told me room service had quit delivering at midnight, so I made do with about $20 worth of peanuts, cookies, and cupcakes from the honor bar. I washed my feast down with three tiny bottles of Jack Daniel's and a diet Sprite—which I polished off in front of the television while watching the start of an old John Wayne movie, *She Wore a Yellow Ribbon,* courtesy of Ted Turner, a great American.

That's how I fell asleep, with John Wayne and Joanne Dru chasing a pack of suspiciously Italian-looking Indians with five o'clock shadow across the badlands of southern California. Joanne had a great smile and a perky, fifties-style bosom.

The Duke was so busy shooting Indians that he barely noticed.

When the burring phone jarred me awake, John Wayne had been replaced by Jimmy Stewart and the red glow from the digital alarm said it was five-fifteen. I ran my tongue around the inside of my mouth, trying to dislodge the worst of the gunk. As a last resort, I swallowed a mouthful of flat soda and picked up the receiver. "Starbranch," I mumbled.

The voice on the other end belonged to Frankie Bull, who sounded as if he were frightened and out of breath. "Harry," he said without preamble, "you've got to get home."

My brain was muzzy, firing on half its cylinders. It was an hour later in Wyoming, a little after six. What was he doing on the job so early? And couldn't this wait till after breakfast? "I know. I got your message," I grumbled. "I'm in Dutch with the town council. But tell 'em to cool their jets, will you, Frankie? I'll be home tonight, tomorrow at the latest." I laid my head back on the pillow and closed my eyes. Maybe if I just ignored him, he'd let me go back to sleep.

"That isn't it," he said. In the background I could hear voices, excited ones. It sounded like they were coming from a public-address system. Where was he? The airport? A hospital?

I tried to open my eyes, but the lids were sticking together with sleep. "Then what is it?" I demanded. "What's so damned important you've—"

A riot of noise erupted on his end of the line. A woman screaming. A man with a stern voice, giving orders. "I don't know how to tell you this, Harry," he said hesitantly. I could barely hear him above the din. "But someone burned your house last night."

At first I thought I must have misunderstood, but when I realized I hadn't, I sat up in bed, my head spinning with the effort. "What?"

Frankie yelled at someone to be quiet. "Someone burned your house," he repeated when he came back on. "But that isn't the worst part. We think your landlady must have caught them in the act." He paused. My mind was reeling. "Whoever torched your house beat her pretty bad, Harry," he said sadly. "We found her lying in her driveway. Blood all over the place."

My stomach rolled, my heart pounded. "Edna?" I asked. The name came out in a croak. "Is she—"

"Alive, but just barely," he said. "The doc says she's asking for you."

15

Edna Cook had been beaten so badly that the doctors who worked on her at the hospital made her look like a hundred-pound version of Boris Karloff in *The Mummy.*

Within an hour of Frankie's call that morning, I was on a plane heading back to Denver, then I caught the Vomit Comet to Brees Field in Laramie. I survived the bumpy ride over the Colorado Rockies, arrived a little after noon, and went directly to the hospital. The still-smoldering ashes of my home could wait.

I found Edna in the intensive-care unit at Ivinson Memorial Hospital in Laramie, with tubes in her arms and nose and a bank of electronic monitors keeping track of her heartbeat, her blood pressure, and maybe her brain waves, for all I knew. Her tiny body was covered by a thin blanket, and I could distinctly make out the bony knobs of her knees and elbows beneath the covering. Her head was completely encased in bandages, and stray wisps of her silver hair escaped in places, stood out from her head like strands of wayward silk. The only features visible through the wrappings were her mouth and eyelids. Her eyelids were bruised, and there was dried blood on her lips. She was unconscious, and her breath rumbled wetly in her chest.

Dr. Edward "Fast Eddie" Warnock sat slumped in a blue vinyl chair at the side of her bed. Frankie Bull was perched on the windowsill, worrying the brim of his hat. Both of them had been up most of the night, and fatigue was evident on their faces. The front of Fast Eddie's white lab coat was spattered with blood. There were dark circles under his red-rimmed eyes.

I stood at Edna's bedside with my hand below her breast so I could feel the faint thumping of her heart, trying desperately to control the grief and passion that threatened to overwhelm me. It would have been so easy to give in, but I forced myself to choke it back, to disassociate myself from my emotions so that I could think clearly. It was more difficult in that sterile and medicinal-smelling hospital room than it had been on the trip back to Wyoming, when the attack and its resulting damage had been abstract. The reality was worse than I'd imagined.

According to Frankie, the county firemen had discovered Edna, unconscious and sprawled on the gravel of the driveway between our houses, about fifteen minutes after a trucker passing the turnoff to the farm reported a structural fire in progress on his CB radio. By the time the firefighters arrived, there was nothing they could do to save my old wood-frame home, which had already begun to collapse, but they were in time to save Edna, who would have died from her wounds had she gone without help until morning.

The first fireman on the scene told Frankie the blaze was no accident, since an empty five-gallon gasoline can was lying in the driveway near Edna, and he suspected that she had seen the arsonist at work and tried to stop him. There was a shovel near her body that she might have been using as a weapon, but bloodstains on the wooden handle suggested that the arsonist had taken it away from her and used it, along with his fists, to bludgeon her senseless.

An EMT told Frankie that she regained consciousness briefly on the ambulance ride to the hospital, and in between asking for me and her dead husband, had babbled almost incoherently about the beating and the person who'd dealt it out—someone she called a monster with the face of a pig.

I didn't need another detail to know she was talking about Junior Stone, and I made a vow that if my old friend lived, I'd make Stone suffer every bit as badly as he'd made her suffer. He'd feel her every pain. Bleed from the same wounds. If she died, I would kill him. I'd look in his eyes when I did it so my face would be the vision he took with him on the long journey to hell.

I looked up at Fast Eddie, who was watching the assorted monitors with the absorbed fascination I reserve for sudden-death overtime on Monday-night football. "Is she gonna make it, Eddie?" I asked.

He shrugged his shoulders. "I don't know," he said. "Her cheekbones are shattered, her jaw is broken. Her skull was fractured in two places, she has four broken ribs, one of which punctured a lung. She has kidney damage, spleen damage, a bruised liver, and who knows how much internal damage we aren't even aware of yet. She's in a coma, so we don't know the full extent of her brain injury, or whether it will have any lasting effects."

He fiddled with the dial on one of the machines, followed the lead from the gizmo to the place where it was attached to Edna's chest, and made sure it was working properly. "This was a brutal assault, Harry," he said. "He meant to kill her."

"Is she gonna make it?" I persisted.

He rubbed his bloodshot eyes. When he spoke, his voice was gentle, preparing me for the worst. "That beating would probably have finished you or me," he said. "How many ninety-year-olds could live through something like that, do you think?"

I knew what he was saying—that Edna would likely die—but I refused to accept it. "Not many," I said, "but if anyone can do it, it's Edna." I smiled affectionately. "She's a hard-boiled old crow, Eddie. Life's been trying to kill her for decades without any success. Hell, she'll probably outlive the both of us."

"Maybe so," Eddie allowed. "We'll see what happens in the next twelve hours. If she makes it that long, I'd say she has a 20, 30 percent chance of pulling through."

He seemed so professional, so dispassionate, it pushed me over the edge. I stood up and grabbed him by the collar of the shirt. "You do whatever you have to do to increase those odds," I told him roughly. "Don't let her die!"

He slapped my hands away, a pained expression on his kind face. "Jesus, Harry, you think you have to tell me that?"

I let go, embarrassed. Looked at my hands, at the toes of my boots. I was acting like some sort of psychotic. "I'm sorry, Eddie," I said. "It's just that I—"

He put his hand on my shoulder. "I understand, Harry," he said. "She's your friend. I'm worried about her, too."

I wanted to stay at Edna's bedside, but Eddie wouldn't allow it. Nonfamily visitors weren't permitted in intensive care, and he'd broken the rules by letting us stay as long as we had. We could wait in the lobby or in the cafeteria, but he said there wasn't much point in that. He promised to call immediately if there was any change in her condition, told me he thought I ought to go home and see if I could salvage any of my belongings from the rubble.

I agreed reluctantly, declining his offer of a sedative to calm my nerves. Then I kissed the top of Edna's head through the bandages and followed Frankie out of her room and down the long hallway to the elevator that would take us to the hospital entrance. Outside, the temperature was in the low seventies with no humidity, the cloudless sky a sapphire blue. I walked with Frankie to the parking lot, where I'd left the Jeep in a fire lane.

Frankie pulled his keys from the pocket of his leather vest and spun the ring on his thick index finger. "We need to talk for a minute, Harry," he said.

Now that we were out of the hospital, I was in a hurry to make the thirty-mile drive back to Victory and take care of business at the farmhouse, see if there was anything to salvage. Then I'd be ready to go after Junior Stone. I turned toward him impatiently. "I know, I'm in trouble with Cindy Thompson and the town council," I told him. "Pichette gave me your message. I just didn't get the chance to call you back. Don't worry about it, Frankie, there'll be plenty of time to sort that out after I—"

"No, there won't," Frankie broke in. "I'm afraid things have gone a little farther than they were yesterday."

The tone of his voice was firm but a little apologetic. I could tell that he hated being the bearer of bad news. "What is it?" I asked. "Did they suspend me?"

"Worse than that, Harry," he said. "They fired you."

Those miserable, petty-bureaucratic sons of bitches. "On what grounds?" I snapped. "Failure to empty the parking meters?"

"For cause," he explained. "They said you continued a private investigation against direct orders. Said you were absent without leave." He paused, waiting for that news to sink in, see how I'd react. When I didn't erupt, he went on. "Cindy Thompson was the only one who argued against it," he said. "But they outvoted her. Gave you sixty days severance and terminated you as chief of police immediately."

"And who's the new chief?" I asked. "You?"

He nodded that it was so. "Interim," he said. "I told Cindy this morning I wouldn't accept it until I talked to you."

"Well take it, and best of luck," I told him. I turned away and started for the Jeep, but I couldn't resist a bit of pettiness. "I've got more important things to do anyway," I grumbled.

"There's something else," he called before I'd gone five steps.

I was so angry, I didn't know how much more I could handle before I started taking it out on him, so I decided the best course of action was to go off by myself for a while and simmer down. "It can wait," I called over my shoulder. "I'm gonna head out to the house, but I'll stop at the office when I'm finished. You can give me the grisly details then."

When he realized that I wasn't going to stop, he ran until he caught up, grabbed me by the elbow, and held on. "Faith Ahearn was kidnapped this morning," he said. "A couple hours after your house burned."

At first I didn't think I'd heard him correctly. Then my chest tightened and my breath caught in my throat. "Kidnapped? How?"

Frankie's shoulders sagged and his whole body seemed to follow. He sat down on the curb and waited until I took a seat beside him. "It happened around six-thirty—just a few minutes after I called you in San Francisco," he said. "Faith went out for a run and someone snatched her about a half mile from her house."

"Anyone see who it was?"

Frankie nodded. "Yeah, one of the neighbors was out feeding his horses and saw it happen," he said. "It was a guy in a gray Lincoln Town Car. The neighbor had a pair of binoculars and even got his license number."

"Junior Stone," I said. "Same bastard who burned my house and beat Edna."

Frankie drummed his fingers on his knees. "That's what I told Baldi after he ran the plate number," he said. "He didn't know who the hell Stone was, but I filled him in on your history. I told him I figured Stone didn't know you were in California when he set the fire. He was in Victory to kidnap Faith and decided he'd even the score with you while he was in the area. Edna just got in the way."

Just got in the way? That beautiful, gentle woman just got in the way? "They catch him yet?" I asked. I really hoped they hadn't. I wanted that for myself.

"Nope," Frankie said. "They've got an all-points bulletin, but he hasn't turned up. Baldi brought in the Department of Criminal Investigation in Cheyenne, and they were talking about calling someone from the FBI office in Denver. I told Tony that Junior Stone works for Sam Pantaleo, so Tony had the Rock Springs cops talk to Sam a couple hours ago. Pantaleo swears up and down that he hasn't seen Stone for days and doesn't even know who Faith Ahearn is. Last I heard, they still had him in custody, but nobody thinks they can hold him."

The more he talked, the more agitated his finger-drumming became. I wished he'd either stop or find a rhythm I could dance to. "The funny part is, Tony Baldi just got it through his thick skull there may be more to this case than he thought," he continued. "He's starting at square one, and the thing he wants to know is why Stone would have kidnapped Faith Ahearn in the first place. He asked me about your investigation, but I didn't tell him any more than I had to—not that I know all that much. I told him he'd have to talk to you, and he said that was fine. He said to have you stop by the sheriff's department as soon as you finished here at the hospital."

I cursed and pushed myself to my feet. There was no way in hell I was going to Baldi's office because I really did have pressing business. For starters, I needed to arm myself. I'd left my .357 Blackhawk under the seat of the Jeep when I flew off to California and was anxious to get it back on my waist. I might not be a cop anymore, but in Wyoming, at least, there's no law says you can't wear a sidearm. You can even wear it concealed if it suits your mood. "How's Maddy taking it?" I asked.

Frankie shrugged. "Eddie gave her some medicine," he said. "She's probably sleeping by now."

"And Curly?"

"I imagine he's gone ballistic," he said. "But I wouldn't know for sure, since Tony wouldn't let me in to see him." Frankie stood up and dusted off the seat of his jeans. At a little over six feet, I'm not a small man, but he towered over me like a giant, blocking out the sun. "Do you have any idea what's going on here, Harry?" he asked.

"I still don't know who killed Liam O'Bannion, if that's what you mean," I said. "But I'm closer to finding out than I was a few days ago. Sit with me in the Jeep for a few minutes and I'll fill you in."

We climbed into the vehicle and I moved it out of the fire lane and into the main parking lot, where I found an empty space in the shade of a large pine. I killed the engine and spent the next fifteen minutes telling Frankie about my trip to San Francisco, about my humiliating run-in with Tommy Fang and his goons, what I'd learned from the local police and from Pichette. Frankie clicked his tongue in disbelief when I got to the part about O'Bannion working for the DEA, but by the time I'd finished, he was nodding as if part of the story made sense.

"So you figure Pantaleo had Faith kidnapped because of the missing money?" he asked.

"That's how I see it," I said. "O'Bannion stole a shit-load of cash and got himself killed before he paid any of it back. If he spent it all before he died, then it's gone. But if you assume he still had the money—which is Pichette's theory—then it's around somewhere. I'd guess Pantaleo believes Faith knows where it is."

"What do you think? Do you think she knows?"

"I don't know," I said honestly. "I've had the feeling several times that she's holding back, not telling me everything. But I know one thing for sure: Whether she knows where O'Bannion's money is or not, she's in terrible danger. If she knows where it is and tells Stone, he'll probably kill her to keep her quiet about the kidnapping. If she doesn't know where it is, who knows how much torture he'll put her through before he decides she's telling the truth? After that, he'll probably kill her anyway."

I turned the key and the engine roared to life. "I've got to figure out a way to find her before that happens," I said. "So I don't have time to dick around with Tony Baldi. Do me a favor, will you? Drop by his office and tell him everything I just told you. Tell him I'll holler if anything else turns up."

I put the transmission into drive, but instead of taking the hint that it was time to leave, Frankie reached over and turned the motor off before I could move. He pulled the keys from the ignition and tucked them into his shirt pocket, where it would have been as easy to get them back as to take a T-bone from a hungry Doberman. "I've seen that look on your face before, Harry, and it usually means you're gonna raise the black flag. What are you planning to do?"

The answer was so obvious, I didn't think he needed to ask. "I'm going out to the farmhouse," I said. "And then I'm going to find Junior Stone and bring Faith home."

Frankie shook his head vehemently. "In case you forgot what I told you just a few minutes ago, you're a civilian now," he said. "You keep bulling your way around this investigation and you're gonna wind up in deep trouble. I think you should just let the proper—"

I felt a stab of betrayal. "Not you, too, Frankie," I said angrily. "You think I should back off? Let Tony Baldi handle it? Sit around with my thumbs up my ass while Junior Stone slaughters my best friend's daughter? Just forget that monster almost killed Edna Cook, left her bleeding in the dirt? Let them give Curly the needle for a murder he didn't commit? Is that what you're saying? Jesus, Frankie, I thought I knew you better than that."

My words stung him. He flinched but pressed on. "I don't see you've got a choice," he said. "You've got no authority, and if you take matters into your own hands, you're nothing but a vigilante, a criminal. You've arrested people for doing that before, Harry. You can't do it; it goes against everything you—"

"Fuck authority," I broke in. "A goddamned badge doesn't give me the authority I need to protect my friends." I slapped an open palm against my heart. "That authority is right here. Inside. I gave it to myself."

I couldn't hurt him anymore. I softened, laid my hand on his shoulder. "Listen, Frankie," I said. "I'm glad Tony Baldi is finally starting to see the light, and I'm even glad he brought in the DCI and maybe the feebs. But the fact is, those guys aren't gonna find Faith in time, not by working inside the law. That means I gotta do this my own way. If they find her before I do, fine, but I just can't take the chance."

Frankie looked down at his lap, bit his lower lip. At least he was listening.

"You know what I'm telling you is the truth," I went on. "And you know something else, Frankie. You know that if you were in my position, you'd do the same thing."

I knew I was right, because we'd had a version of this conversation before. Sometimes, we both knew, it's necessary for a cop to bend—or break—the rules in order to obtain a measure of justice. He ruminated for a few minutes, wrestling with his internal demons, then came to a decision. He squared his jaw, reached into his shirt pocket for his mirrored sunglasses, and pulled them on. "Then I guess I'm goin' with you, Harry," he said. "You're gonna need someone to watch your back."

I was relieved and touched by his loyalty. "What about the town council?" I asked. "Aren't you worried they'll fire you, too?"

He smiled thinly. "They might," he allowed. "But I never liked those people anyway. In the meantime, at least one of us will have a badge."

That was a comforting proposition, but I couldn't accept the offer without conditions. I'd welcome Frankie's help with Stone, but I couldn't expose him to a prison sentence. "I wouldn't mind some backup once I learn where Stone is keeping Faith," I admitted. "But first I've gotta find out where he's hiding, and to do that I've got to go off the books. I don't want you involved in that."

"Pantaleo?" he asked.

I nodded. "I'm gonna make him tell me where they are," I said. "And I'm not gonna let him have a lawyer present when I do it."

"You could get hurt," he said doubtfully. "Sam Pantaleo's a mean son of a bitch."

"So am I," I told him, with more bravado than I actually felt. "I think he'll eventually listen to reason."

"You want to meet somewhere afterward?" he asked.

"Yeah," I said. "Why don't you go talk to Tony Baldi, then drive out to Victory and drop by the office, call your wife and let her know you'll be out of town for a while. After that, you can head on over to Rock Springs. Take a room at the Golden Spike. I'll follow you over, find Pantaleo, and have a friendly conversation with him. It might be pretty late, but I'll call you when I find out where Stone is holed up."

"Anything else?" he questioned a bit sarcastically. As if I'd already asked for plenty.

I pretended not to notice. "Ordnance," I said. "Bring some shot-guns, tear gas, cartridges, a good rifle with a scope."

"Your seven-millimeter magnum?" he asked. "I think you left that at the office."

My Remington 7 mm was just the ticket—flat trajectory, a Leopold Ultra sighting scope, pinpoint accuracy at several hundred yards, killing power to spare. A hunting round from that rifle will mushroom on impact and tear through flesh with enough wallop to shatter heavy bones. It will leave an exit wound in a man the size of a softball—collateral soft-tissue damage galore. "That ought to do, podna," I told him. "If we have to lay crosshairs on this bastard, I don't want him getting away."

The farm where Edna and I live is about thirty-five miles from the nearest hydrant, so the only water firefighters had to work with was what they carried in their pumpers. It was enough to keep the fire from spreading, but it wasn't enough to completely extinguish the embers of my home.

I knelt down in the smoking rubble and used a still-smoldering crossbeam to light a cigar. Then I took the stogie into the sage, prickly pear, and buffalo grass of the front yard and sat cross-legged while I puffed reflectively and surveyed the damage.

There wasn't much that was identifiable. Among the hodgepodge of burned timbers and what was left of the collapsed roof, I saw charred lumps that might have been furniture, the metal legs of my kitchen table and chairs, the iron headboard and box spring from my bed, the carcasses of my appliances, a blackened bathtub and commode, a deformed spherical thing that might have been a bowling ball, the water heater tilting crazily due to a collapsing floor, like the Leaning Tower of Pisa.

My wood stove sat virtually unharmed in the middle of what used to be my living room. As soon as it cooled down, I could probably have someone move it to the new house I was building on Coyote Butte. Beyond the stove, however, it looked as if every material possession I owned had been destroyed. My clothes, my photographs and Western-art prints, my music collection, my guns, my fly-tying equipment, my graphite fly rods, my books, my television, my sheepskin moccasins, and my terry-cloth bathrobe. Every inanimate object that ever gave me a moment's comfort.

All gone. All charcoal.

It was strange to sit there in the warm June sunshine, to hear the meadowlarks in the distance singing their prairie serenade, to feel the kiss of the north wind on my face, and smell the acrid scent of burned siding and shingles. If you've ever been to a garbage dump where trash is burned, or the scene of a building fire after the flames have been extinguished, you know the stench.

I suppose I should have felt something. Pain, a sense of sadness and loss. Grief, perhaps, or animal rage. But at that moment—face-to-face with the rubble of my life—all I felt was numb. Disconnected. Cut adrift from the only moorings I had known since I came to Victory. My home. My job. My best friends.

I stayed there, almost motionless, for nearly a half hour, until the ashes of my cigar had grown long and crooked. I watched tendrils of smoke curling up from the debris, paying no attention to my watering eyes, the cramp in my legs. I was only vaguely aware of Edna's horses watching me from the corral, of her cats waiting patiently on her back porch, of the crows hopping on the periphery, looking for something to steal, a hawk riding thermals in the blue sky overhead.

I dimly recognized the sound of tires crunching through the gravel of the driveway, the sound of a car door closing, footsteps approaching—but even the prospect of visitors didn't rouse me from my reverie until a shadow crossed my field of vision and I realized that someone was standing behind me. "I called the hospital a little while ago, and Eddie said you'd probably be out here," Cindy Thompson said. Her voice was soft and friendly, full of compassion.

I turned to look in her direction but didn't answer, just squinted up at her standing between me and the sun. She was dressed for business, in a crisp blue skirt and blazer, a white blouse with a frilly collar, and medium heels. The backlighting gave her a bright halo around her blond head but threw her face in shadow. Even through the biting and pervasive smoke stench, I could detect the fragile scent of her perfume. Musky, with just a hint of spice.

"Well, Eddie was right," I said bitterly. "Here I am." I figured she'd driven out to commiserate about the loss of my house, share my anxiety for Edna, maybe to soften the blow of my firing, but I wasn't ready to be comforted. I turned away, resuming my sulky contemplation of the ruins.

I didn't expect the message she'd come to deliver.

"I'm afraid I've got some very bad news, Harry," she said gently. She sat down beside me on the ground, drawing her knees up to her chest. "Edna Cook died a few minutes after you left the hospital."

I heard her words, but my mind refused to process them. Instead, I had the fleeting thought that the dirt in the yard would probably soil her skirt, that the cactus would run her hose.

Soon, however, reality began to intrude. Edna Cook died, Cindy said. Edna *died.* The words were razor-edged and cruel. Final. Like a wave crashing onto the beach, my numbness was replaced by a sense of grief and loss so profound that I couldn't breathe. I felt it first as a fist in my belly, hard and bony and malignant. It rose to my chest, squeezed my lungs and heart, made my throat so tight that when I tried to speak—to shout an angry denial to the heavens— the only sound that came from my mouth was that of a wounded animal. I felt tears puddling at the corners of my eyes and brushed them away with the back of my hand.

I loved that cantankerous old woman, and now she was gone. Beaten to death by a piece of human garbage named Junior Stone.

Cindy put her arms around me and drew me close. I could feel her moist breath on my cheek, the gentle caress of her fingers on my temples. "She apparently went into cardiac arrest," she said. "Eddie was able to bring her back once, but the second time he lost her. He said to tell you she never came out of the coma, so she didn't suffer at the end."

I buried my head in her shoulder, suddenly racked by guilt and regret. "I shouldn't have left her," I muttered. "I should have stayed at the hospital and—"

"She knows, Harry," Cindy whispered. "Wherever she is now, she knows you were with her. She knows you came to her as quickly as you could."

At some level, I knew she was telling the truth, but it didn't help, because my absence from the hospital when Edna died wasn't the real issue. The real issue was the inescapable fact that the whole thing was my fault. If only I had kept my temper instead of giving in when

I beat Junior Stone for spitting in my face, if I had only acted like a professional lawman instead of an adolescent thug, Edna Cook would still be alive. My actions brought this horrible sentence down on her, and my actions alone.

I imagined I'd pay for that indiscretion to the end of my days.

I pulled away from Cindy's embrace and brought myself to my feet, my chest heaving, my face hot with fury and impotence, fists balling at my sides. In my frustration and self-recrimination, I wanted to lash out. To hit something. Anything. Typical Starbranch reaction—inappropriate and counterproductive.

Cindy didn't understand. She thought I was angry with her. She stood and pressed herself against my back, put her slender arms around my middle. "I'm so sorry, Harry," she said. "I'm sorry about Edna, sorry about Curly, sorry about the business with the town council. If I could have prevented any of it I—"

"I know that," I told her harshly. "None of this is on your head, Cindy. It's all on mine." I looked beyond the blackened rubble of my house to the driveway separating my home and Edna's and saw dark stains on the gravel. Edna's blood. One of her house slippers was at the side of the driveway, ground into the dirt when someone ran over it. Something white caught my eye, so I left Cindy and walked in that direction. The bottom half of Edna's dentures was lying at the base of a clump of rabbitbrush. She seldom wore them around the house, and why she'd put them in to confront an intruder in the middle of the night, I'd never know. I picked them up and tucked them into my pocket.

When they buried her, I wanted to make sure she had a full set of teeth. I'd hate to think of her meeting her several late husbands in heaven without them. She'd never forgive me.

I was so absorbed in my own misery, that I hadn't noticed Cindy following me. "Why don't you come with me?" she asked. "You can stay at the house until your new one is livable. I even think Harv left some clothes behind that might fit. They'll do until you can re-stock your own wardrobe."

"What?" I asked. I hadn't been paying attention.

Cindy misinterpreted my confusion. "It doesn't have to mean anything, Harry," she said. "You don't have to sleep with me if you don't want to, but you are going to need a place to stay. Take the guest bedroom if it makes you more comfortable—"

I gave her a weak smile. "It isn't that, Cindy," I said. "I appreciate the offer, but I've got something I have to do first."

She took me by the arm. "It'll keep for a while," she said. "Right now, you look exhausted. Come with me. I'll fix your favorite lunch and then tuck you in for a few hours. When you wake up you can—"

"I don't have time for sleep," I snapped. "I've got to go after Faith Ahearn, and I've wasted enough time already."

Cindy's brow knitted and she shook her head to clear it. "Faith Ahearn?" she asked. "Why would you have to go after Faith?"

"You haven't heard?" I asked.

"No," she said. "Why don't you tell me?"

I took her by the hand and led her to the lawn chairs on the shady side of Edna's house. When we were comfortable, I told her everything I'd learned since I began my investigation of Liam O'Bannion's death. She listened intently, nodding occasionally to let me know she was following the story, but she didn't interrupt. When I finished, she sat quietly for a few minutes, digesting it all.

"You were right about this whole thing, Harry," she said. "We should have listened to you."

Her apology was genuine, and there was no reason not to accept it. "I know you did what you could, Cindy," I said. "No hard feelings—but I've got a lot of unfinished business. I still don't know who killed O'Bannion, so I can't get Curly off the hook. And I've got to find Faith before Stone does something ugly."

Cindy stared across the rubble of my house to the sunbaked brown prairie beyond, lifted her eyes to the sky to watch the contrail of a jet passing overhead. "You're going after him?" she asked quietly.

I nodded. Cindy started to protest but thought better of it. "I don't know how long I'll be gone," I told her. "But I'd appreciate it if you'd look after things out here while I'm away. Edna's horses need feeding. So do her chickens, and all those cats."

"Of course," she said. She took one of my hands in both of her own, stared into my eyes. "But you've got to make me a promise first."

I didn't answer, just waited for her to go on. "Don't try to do this by yourself. It's too dangerous."

"I won't be alone," I told her.

"There's something else," she said. She bent toward me and kissed me full on the mouth. Her lips were soft, and her breath smelled like fresh mint leaves. When she pulled away, her cheeks and neck were flushed.

"Come back safely, Harry," she said quietly. "We've got some unfinished business of our own."

16

▲▲▲

I scorched asphalt on the drive from Victory across the Red Desert to Rock Springs, stopping only once at a truck stop in Rawlins for gas and a couple of microwaved burritos to go.

It's a good thing Interstate 80 is such a straight road, because I could barely concentrate on my driving—and was surprised more than once when an eighteen-wheeler materialized out of nowhere to pass me like I was behind the wheel of a geriatric Yugo, even though I was clipping along well past the seventy-five-mile-an-hour limit.

It was a fine summer afternoon, absolutely no humidity, only a few gauzy clouds in the sky, temperature in the low eighties. The air was spiked with the pungent smell of greasewood and sage, and the yellow afternoon sun turned the badlands into a shimmering palette of earthy reds, variegated browns, and muted greens. Herds of Pronghorn antelope grazed along the roadside, and wild horses raced across the barren alkali flats. A pair of bald eagles soared above the highway near Bitter Creek, sharp eyes scanning the blacktop for roadkill or a slow jackrabbit.

The majesty of the desert was lost on me, though, because all I could see was images of Edna on a cold metal table at the mortuary and other, even more frightening ones of the horrible things Junior Stone might be doing to Faith at that very moment. I'd been a cop for a long time, so I have lots of bad memories in the bank to draw from whenever I'm feeling paranoid, but in this case I had the suspicion that Stone was the sort who could come up with a few perverted tricks I hadn't seen before. My stomach tightened at the thought of him having Faith completely at his mercy, and I knew that even if she lived through the ordeal, her life would never be the same.

For most of the day, I'd been operating on emotion and adrenaline, reacting but not thinking rationally. As I passed the turnoff to Point of Rocks, about twenty-five miles out of Rock Springs, however, I realized that I had no idea what I planned to do once I got there.

First of all, I needed to figure out how to get Pantaleo alone so we could talk. I didn't think I'd have much success just marching into his office and escorting him out at gunpoint because I'd never get past his receptionist. If she didn't have a handgun tucked away in a desk drawer, she was perfectly capable of eviscerating me with her clawlike fingernails.

Beyond that, I had to have a way to make him talk once I had his undivided attention. In order to accomplish those objectives, I was prepared to break the law if I had to, but there was a limit to how far my conscience would let me go. Besides, I didn't want to end up in jail myself.

I needed a plan that was like one of those neutron bombs the Pentagon brass says will kill the enemy without destroying his buildings. I needed to destroy Pantaleo's faith in himself, all his courage and will, if I had any hope of making him tell me where Stone had taken Faith Ahearn. I needed to extract the information without really harming the bastard—not the easiest task when you're dealing with a hard case like Sam Pantaleo, who I imagined would respond only to the most excruciating pain or overwhelming terror. And I needed to do it all in a way that would keep him from blabbing to the police afterward.

That meant rubber hoses, shards of glass under his fingernails, and jumper cables alligator-clamped to his scrotum were out, not that I've ever resorted to those draconian interrogation tactics anyway. I needed something more elegant, more subtle. More *embarrassing*.

That part of the scheme came to me just as I crossed the Rock

Springs city limits, so I stopped at a couple places to pick up the necessary accoutrements—a roll of silver duct tape and a half-dozen two-liter bottles of soda pop, heavy on the 7UP and Dr Pepper, and one sparkling grape soda, just for whimsy.

"You havin' a party?" the pimple-faced cashier at the convenience store asked as he rang up the soda. Dressed in a Megadeth T-shirt, pants so baggy that four of my closest friends and I could have fit comfortably inside them, and a backward ball cap that didn't cover his stringy mop of blaze-orange hair, he was snapping a walnut-size wad of pink gum in time to the electronic mayhem blaring from a boom box behind the counter.

He bore an uncanny resemblance to my oldest son, Robert—right down to the Twisted Sister temporary tattoo on his right forearm and the scent of patchouli that emanated from his skinny body. I wanted to grab him by the shirt and shake some sense into him, the same impulse I have whenever I see my son—an unfortunate urge that leads him to avoid me whenever possible. Luckily for me and the kid, I resisted temptation. "You might say that," I told him. I threw a small bag of corn chips on the pile.

The cashier shot me a surly look. All that soda and one fifty-cent bag of chips? Guy thinks he's Donald Trump, the look said.

"In case we get hungry," I chuckled darkly. He must have seen something in my face he didn't like, because he looked down and wouldn't meet my eyes as he counted the change and bagged my purchases. Then he found some incredibly interesting feature on his feet to stare at until I was out of the store.

As my first order of business, I needed to find out where Pantaleo was, so I stowed the shopping bag in the Jeep and used a pay phone outside to call his home number. The woman who answered told me Sam wasn't back from work yet, and she didn't know when to expect him. I declined to leave a message, thanked her, and hung up.

Five minutes later, I was driving by the grounds of Pantaleo Trucking, where the activity at the loading docks was just as frantic as it had been on my first visit. The redbrick office, however, seemed to be closed for the day. Although I couldn't see inside lights burning through the tinted windows, there were only a half-dozen cars remaining in the parking lot, including a black BMW sedan in the reserved spot closest to the front door. I figured it belonged to Pantaleo, which meant he was still inside. All I needed to do was wait for him to come out and follow him. I figured if I was patient and he didn't make the tail, an opportunity to take him might present itself between the office and his house. If it didn't, I'd just have to think of a way to snatch him once he got home for the night.

I realized, of course, that forcing Pantaleo to give up Stone's location might mean he'd never be convicted for his role in Faith's abduction, but I was more than willing to make that trade-off. I'd simply trust fate—and Jaime Pichette—to make sure Pantaleo paid for *something,* even if it wasn't kidnapping. If that didn't happen, I'd eventually get around to collecting the debt myself.

I didn't want to risk parking on the street, so I pulled into the lot of an abandoned service station across the road from the trucking company and parked the Jeep in the shadows at the side of the building. I cut the engine and pulled my binoculars from the glove box, focused them on the front door of Pantaleo's office. Then I fired a stogie, popped Ry Cooder's *Borderline* album into the tape deck, and settled in to wait.

As darkness gathered over the next hour, most of the remaining employees in the office called it a day. A couple of young men with their suit coats slung over their shoulders strolled out and drove off together in a Toyota station wagon. Three secretary types came out individually and left the lot. Pantaleo's daughter—the receptionist—came next, her high heels clacking on the sidewalk as she made her way to the white Camaro convertible parked next to the Beemer. Her short skirt rode high enough to give me a nice glimpse of thigh as she got behind the wheel and started the big Detroit engine. She backed up without looking in her rearview mirror, cranked the wheel hard, and burned rubber leaving the lot. As she passed the station, I saw an ugly dent in the front fender on the passenger side of the expensive hot rod. I wondered how many new cars she went through in a year.

By the time Pantaleo let himself out the front door five minutes later and jiggled it to make sure it was locked, the office lot was empty. I watched him through the binoculars as he pulled a little thingamabob from his pocket, pointed it at the BMW, and pressed it with a beefy thumb. His car gave a couple of high-pitched beeps as the antitheft device deactivated, and he opened the door, threw his briefcase in the back, draped his suit coat over the passenger seat, and folded his thick body inside. He started the engine, turned around, and came to a full stop before he left the parking lot.

I gave him a few seconds before I started after him, time enough for a smoke-belching semi pulling a trailer with the Pantaleo logo to pull out of the warehouse lot and get between us. The truck gave me cover until we turned onto Dewar Drive, heading toward the center of town, and it kept me out of Pantaleo's rearview for five or six blocks until he peeled off and turned into the parking lot of a liquor store. I parked next door in the lot of an auto-parts place and waited for a few minutes until he came out with what looked like a bottle of wine in a brown paper bag.

From the liquor store, I followed him another few blocks before he made a left turn into a residential district—lots of split-level ranch houses, several multiunit apartment buildings, and a few new-looking duplexes. There weren't any other cars on the street, only a few kids standing under a light at one corner smoking cigarettes, and I worried that Pantaleo might notice me when I turned into the development behind him. As it turned out, he must have had other things on his mind, because he drove right into the driveway of one of the duplexes and cut his engine. He was just getting out as I drove by, and he didn't notice me then, either. By the time I got to the end of the block, he'd already gone inside.

I pulled over to the curb, cut the lights, and waited for a couple of minutes. Then I flipped a U-turn and drove slowly past the building. The front shades were drawn, so I couldn't see inside, but I could see light leaking out through the cracks in the drapery. The residence Pantaleo had entered was the right-hand unit of the duplex, and I noticed there was a fenced backyard behind the place accessed by a redwood gate at the end of the driveway. Too risky to go in that way. I'd have to try something else.

I drove to the end of the block, turned left, and found the entrance to the alley behind the duplex about twenty yards from the turnoff. I eased into the alley, drove slowly until I figured I was directly behind the duplex, and turned the engine off. The alley was overhung with branches from the cottonwoods and willows in the residential yards, so it was completely dark, and quiet except for the muted sounds of televisions and radios playing in some of the homes on the block. I took the keys from the ignition, hopped out, and let myself in through the alley gate into the backyard, thankful that I wasn't met on the other side by a ninety-pound watchdog with fangs.

There were plenty of dark places in the yard to hide in, so I found one next to a huge evergreen shrub and had a look around. There was a sliding glass door leading from the living room of the duplex to the patio in the backyard, but unlike the living-room drapes, these were open—and what I saw going on in the living room made me feel like a Peeping Tom.

I'll say one thing for Sam Pantaleo: The man didn't waste time when he was horny. He'd only been in the duplex for about five minutes, but he was already shirtless. His pants were bagged around his ankles and his left hand was tangled in the dark hair of a topless woman who was on her knees in front of him, engaged in energetic fellatio. The young woman giving Sam Pantaleo a hummer was definitely not the gray-haired matron whose photo I'd seen on his office desk. The middle-aged woman in the photo was his wife. This one was his girlfriend. No wonder the little woman didn't know what time to expect him home from work.

The opened wine bottle was in Pantaleo's right hand, and he occasionally took a long swallow as he looked over the bulge of his belly to contemplate the top of the woman's head. He wasn't smiling, and didn't even look as if he was having a particularly good time. As a matter of fact, his expression was sort of bored, maybe a little irritated, as if he thought he was doing her some kind of a favor. He was an arrogant, disgusting son of a bitch, and he needed to be taken down a peg.

I figured I was just the man to do it.

I was still engrossed in the X-rated tableau when a plan popped into my head with such speed and clarity that I almost laughed out loud. I reached down to unsnap the safety strap on my holster, made sure my handcuffs were ready. Then, holding my blackthorn in front of me to steady myself, I rocked back on my haunches to wait.

After a few minutes of intense oral ministration, the young woman stood up and wrapped her arms around Sam's neck, ground her hips against his crotch, and kissed him hard on the mouth. He pushed her black lace panties down, picked her up, and sat her on the back of the couch. He pulled the panties off her ankles and tossed them over his shoulder. Then he spread her knees apart and entered her, his heavy buttocks clenching with each thrust. She wrapped her long legs around his back and held on tight, fingernails digging into his shoulders, eyes squinched closed in what might have been passion but might have been pain.

They coupled like that for a spell, then Pantaleo picked her up and carried her around to the front of the couch. The two of them sank down toward the floor together until they were out of view, most likely working on a painful case of rug burn.

It's now or never, Starbranch, I thought.

Quickly and quietly, I skittered through the backyard to the gate leading to the driveway and the front of the house. I let myself out, darted to Pantaleo's BMW, planted my hands on the hood, and jumped up and down a couple of times, rocking the big car on its shock absorbers. The alarm began whooping immediately—loud and obnoxious like one of those European police sirens. I didn't want to be spotted by Pantaleo looking out the front window, or by any of the neighbors, so I scurried back into the darkness at the side of the duplex and found a good spot to lurk.

I didn't wait long.

A couple of the neighbors' porch lights kicked on because of the racket, and I'm pretty sure they got a good look at Sam Pantaleo when he charged out the front door fifteen seconds later wearing nothing but a pair of boxer shorts, tented in front by his rapidly shrinking erection.

I don't think they could see my hand coming out of the shadows, wrapped around the handle of my Blackhawk. I rested my wrist on the top of the fence and steadied it, drew a bead on Pantaleo's head.

Pantaleo didn't see it either, because he wasn't looking in that direction. He took a quick gander around his car to make sure nobody had jimmied the doors, and another up and down the empty street. False alarm. He cursed loudly and punched his thingamabob until the alarm shut off.

In the ensuing silence, the metallic click of the Blackhawk's hammer locking into place was as loud as the jaws of a spring-loaded bear trap snapping closed. Pantaleo froze, looked in the direction of the sound. When he saw the black hole of the bore, the barrel, the blade sight zeroed on his forehead, he drew a sharp breath. At that distance, I couldn't miss.

"Do you see how easy that was?" I asked.

He nodded rapidly. His hooded eyes flashed anger, but that was quickly replaced by something else: raw fear. In the blackness of the bore, Sam Pantaleo saw the great abyss, yawning and malevolent. I've enjoyed that view myself, and I'll tell you what I learned: It definitely gets your attention. "What do you want?" he asked quietly.

"I want you, Sam," I replied. I sounded menacing, even to myself. "I want you to walk through this gate and come with me, and I want you to do it without making a sound. If you don't . . ." I let the threat dangle for a heartbeat. "I'll bust a cap on your miserable ass."

He didn't hesitate, did exactly what I said.

It's amazing how fast most men—even case-hardened mobsters like Sam Pantaleo—will crumble when they find themselves standing alone . . . in the dark . . . in their underwear . . . looking down the muzzle of a .357 magnum.

Nothing to shoot back with but their own limp dicks.

I marched Pantaleo through his girlfriend's backyard and into the alley where I'd parked the Jeep without being seen by the woman or any of the neighbors. Sam was barefoot, so he walked gingerly, stubbed his toe on some decorative brickwork lining a flower garden, and hopped into the alley on one leg. I jabbed him in a kidney with the barrel of the Blackhawk every time he showed signs of slowing down.

At the Jeep, I cuffed his hands behind his back, took a couple of turns around his head with duct tape to keep his big mouth shut, and made him lie facedown on the floorboard of the vehicle with his legs scrunched up so he'd fit. It's a very small space and the transmission hump makes it worse, so it would be an uncomfortable ride. That was fine with me. I imagined I could find a few extra potholes and bumps to make the journey even more pleasurable.

I threw a blanket over Pantaleo, started the engine, and drove out of the alley with the lights off. I didn't turn them back on until I was back on Dewar Drive, heading out of Rock Springs toward the empty darkness of the open road. Pantaleo made a few muffled noises in the first mile or so, but I reached over the seat and whacked him on the head with the knobby end of the blackthorn. He gave that up soon enough. I put a Garth Brooks tape in the deck and turned it up loud so nobody would hear him if he got chatty again.

I wasn't heading anyplace special. All I needed was a secluded dirt road where I wouldn't be bothered for an hour or so. Fortunately, Rock Springs is surrounded by about 10,000 square miles of nothing but cactus, tumbleweeds, and Jeep trails that seem to lead nowhere—that's why they call it the desert. Finding a secluded place isn't as much of a problem as finding a place where something is going on. Bury a body out there and chances are good it will never be found by anything but hungry coyotes.

Not that I'd be burying any bodies.

I settled back in the seat and let the warm evening air wash in through the open windows, drummed my fingers on the steering wheel in time to the good music, and watched the barrow pits for deer and antelope eyeballs reflected in the headlights. I opened the bag of corn chips and popped a few into my mouth. Pretty soon, I'd have a soda to wash them down. Top it off with another cigar.

So far, I figured my first kidnapping had gone pretty well, considering that I'd gone into the operation without a coherent plan. Even improvising I'd gotten into town, located my target, made the snatch, and gotten out without being spotted or caught—all in less than four hours. Not bad.

I followed I–80 east for fourteen miles and then turned north on the two-lane blacktop that leads toward the old mining town of Superior, which these days is nearly a ghost town. About three miles later, a small, rutted road led off to the right toward Horsethief Creek, a miserly little trickle through the flats that's dry for most of the year. I turned off the highway, shifted into four-wheel drive, and eased down the rough pathway for a few hundred yards until I was out of sight of the road. Then I cut the engine and had a look around. Perfect.

The moon was nearly full, so there was plenty of light. I could hear the faint rumble of big trucks on the interstate, and on the far horizon I could see the twinkle of lights on an oil rig. The relative proximity of the rig didn't bother me. Pantaleo could yell as loud as he wanted and the roustabouts on evening tower would never hear him over the roar of the huge electric-diesel engines turning the drill string. We were all alone, Sam and I. Might as well be on another planet.

Just the way I wanted it.

I got out of the Jeep and stretched, took a deep breath to savor the subtle aroma of the desert at night, listened to the chirping of the crickets and the ticking of the engine as it began to cool. When I'd had my fill, I yanked the blanket off Pantaleo and pulled him out of the backseat, led him to the top of a small hillock, and made him sit down. Then I went back to the vehicle and got my bag of soda.

Sam watched me suspiciously as I carried it back and sat it down beside him, and it occurred to me that in his present condition he didn't look so tough after all. His black hair, with the impressive shocks of white on the sides, was mussed and sticking up at all angles, as if he'd combed it with a weed whacker. The moonlight turned his skin a sickly shade of pale blue, and his bare legs, though still muscular, were out of proportion to the rolls of flab on his belly. He was still a powerful man, but the way he was going he'd be as fat as Marlon Brando in ten years.

I took a bottle of 7UP out of the bag and held it up so he could see it. "You thirsty, Sam?" I asked cordially.

Sam didn't answer, of course, because his mouth was taped shut. He mumbled something and gave me a feral glare. I didn't pay any attention whatsoever. "Well, I am," I said. I uncapped the bottle and took a long swig, smacking my lips in appreciation. "And I think you are, too. Trouble is, all taped up like that, I can't get to your mouth." I gave him a wicked grin. "Guess we'll have to find another way."

Sam humphed through the tape and looked away, but I imagined he'd start paying attention soon enough, because what I had planned was fairly nasty.

Several years ago, I read a book by Joseph Wambaugh about the United States Border Patrol that talked about the interrogation tactics used by guards in one of the more notorious Mexican prisons. Seems these Mexicans had devised a simple, festive method of obtaining information from even the most reluctant and willful prisoners—the Bubble-Up party. What they did was this. They tied the prisoner's hands and put duct tape around his mouth. Then they pinched his nose shut until he really needed to take a breath. All the while, they were shaking the hell out of a bottle of Bubble-Up. When they let go of the prisoner's nose, he drew a deep reflexive breath through his nostrils, but instead of air, what he got was a shot of Bubble-Up foam from the agitated bottle. The carbonation played hell with the sensitive tissue of the prisoner's sinuses, causing a pain so intense that even the toughest dog in the pound would break down after a few doses and tell them everything they wanted to know.

That's what I had in mind for Sam. Without further ado, I pushed him down on his back, and even though he struggled and squirmed, I managed to hold his nose shut with one hand until his beady eyes bugged out, shaking a bottle of 7UP with the other. When he was ready, I gave him a good shot of foam and then held his nose shut again while it did its work.

After ten or fifteen seconds, I let go so he could draw a breath.

Then I did the whole thing again. And again. And again. And again. And again. Six times in all, until his chest and hair were soaked with sticky soda, until he was writhing on the ground in agony, until great tears were flowing down his sloppy cheeks.

Then I stopped and slowly opened a new bottle. I squatted down beside him on my haunches, grabbed him by the hair, and forced him to look into my eyes. "Here's the deal, Sam," I said matter-of-factly. "I know Junior Stone kidnapped Faith Ahearn on your orders. I know that, so don't even bother denying it unless you want another treatment. You with me so far?"

Pantaleo nodded grudgingly.

"Good," I said. "Then when I take the tape off your mouth, you're going to tell me where they are. If you don't"—I gave the bottle a vigorous shake, and it started to fizz out through the neck around my thumb—"I'm going to let you enjoy every last drop of this stuff, even the grape soda. I won't quit, Sam, no matter what. You believe me?"

He nodded again.

"Fine," I said. I found the end of the tape and peeled it off his head. It took a lot of hair as it came off. "Where are they?"

Pantaleo sputtered, blew pop through his nose. "You son of a bitch," he growled. "You're gonna be sorry you ever—"

I grabbed him by the hair again, tilted his head back, and shook the bottle. "I guess you didn't believe me," I told him. I brought the bottle toward his face and let it start to spurt.

He thrashed, shaking his head violently from side to side. I let about half a bottle squirt on his face, and even though he could now breathe through his mouth, he coughed and snorted like a patient in the tuberculosis ward.

When I reached for the tape to do his mouth again, I guess he finally decided I was serious. All the fight seemed to leave him, and his whole body sagged in resignation. "In a trailer house on Sweetwater Creek about four miles south of Rock Springs off Highway 430," he croaked. "You can't miss the turnoff. There's a gate and a cattle guard at the driveway. Big sign says Sweetwater Estates."

"Which trailer house?"

"The only one out there," Pantaleo said. "We're just starting the development."

I let go of his hair and he fell to his back with a thud. I rolled him over on his belly and removed the cuffs. "That's a good boy, Sam," I said. "But understand this. If you're lying, I'll come back and get you. If he's harmed her, I'll come back and get you." I started walking toward the Jeep. "And next time," I said over my shoulder, "my hospitality won't be this cordial."

I hopped into the vehicle, started the engine, and flipped on the lights. On the hillock, Pantaleo was sitting up, rubbing his offended nose. He looked up at me when he heard me shift into gear. "You're not gonna leave me here, are you?" he asked incredulously.

"Afraid so," I said, "but it's a nice night for a walk." I let out the clutch and started to back away. "Just watch out for rattlesnakes, Sam," I called cheerfully. "Little buggers love to hunt at night."

Twenty minutes later, I was knocking on the door of Frankie Bull's room at the Golden Spike.

Frankie opened it, ready for war. Dressed in a black T-shirt and a black leather vest, his hair was tightly braided and his black Stetson rode low on his forehead. He was wearing a buckskin medicine bag and the skull of some critter around his neck on a leather thong.

Badger, by the looks of the teeth. His .44 magnum was holstered on his right hip, and he wore his Bowie knife in a beaded sheath on his left. He was carrying a 9-mm Beretta with a fifteen-shot magazine in his waistband.

Behind him on the bed was the rest of our arsenal: two twelve-gauge pump shotguns loaded with double-aught buck, my 7-mm magnum, a half-dozen canisters of tear gas, and a couple more pistols—my old World War II .45 Colt automatic and another 9 mm, this one the SIG-Sauer P-226 I'd taken away from a drunken lumberjack at the Silver Dollar the previous winter.

There was also plenty of ammunition. A full box of 150-grain rounds for the 7 mm, two boxes of shotgun shells, extra clips for the .45 and the nines.

He even brought the pair of night-vision goggles we'd taken in trade from a local sergeant in the Wyoming National Guard. He gave us the goggles when we spent an entire weekend digging postholes on his ranch.

Frankie let me in without a word and waited silently while I looked over the weaponry. "You find out where she is?" he asked when I was satisfied.

"Yeah," I told him, "but you don't want to know how I did it."

"I didn't ask," he grumbled. He handed me an armful of hardware, stuffed the extra pistols, ammunition, and tear gas into a nylon duffel bag, and grabbed the rest himself. Between us, it looked as if we had enough firepower to overthrow a Third World country.

"Put your game face on and let's go get this bastard, Harry," he said. "Take him off the streets."

We were almost out the door before I finally came to my senses. I stopped, then turned around slowly, walked back to the bed, and laid the weapons down.

Frankie, standing in the doorway, was anxious to get under way. "What's up, boss?" he asked impatiently.

I picked up the receiver on the bedside phone, thumbed through the phone book until I found my number. "Be right with you, podna," I told him. "Soon as I make this call."

17

▲▲▲

Our convoy rolled from the Rock Springs police department forty-five minutes later with twenty-two heavily armed officers from Al Kincaid's staff and the Sweetwater County sheriff's department—a lethal force of men and women, many of them trained in special weapons and tactics, that Kincaid had assembled on very short notice by calling in off-duty backup. We traveled swiftly, without emergency lights or sirens. Kincaid, grim and uncommunicative, was at the wheel of the lead vehicle, with me riding shotgun and Frankie taking up most of the backseat.

Kincaid hadn't been particularly happy when I called him from the Golden Spike, and had demanded to know how I'd discovered Faith's whereabouts when his own efforts earlier in the day had failed so miserably.

I'd been more than evasive. I'd dodged the question entirely and told him he'd just have to trust me for the time being. He couldn't afford to ignore me since a young woman's life was at stake, but he'd made it plain there'd be a reckoning between us when this was over. I didn't know what I'd tell him when the time came. Maybe I'd just smile and say the answer came to me in a psychic vision. I wasn't eager to tell him the truth—that I'd tortured Sam Pantaleo by squirting soda pop up his nose until he broke down and gave Junior up like a bad habit. Then again, maybe telling the truth was the best option. Who'd believe a story like that? I didn't think Sam would be particularly anxious to corroborate it.

Despite Kincaid's chilly demeanor, I was glad I'd made the call.

A dark part of me wanted Stone for myself, but that's the part that always gets me in trouble. It was time to stop thinking of myself as a latter-day Wyatt Earp, notching my six-gun every time I took a criminal down. Frankie was right. It was time to ignore my overdeveloped thirst for revenge. Time to grow up and start doing things right. By the book.

We rolled down Highway 430 until we came to the turnoff to Sweetwater Estates, a narrow dirt road leading east through a stretch of sagebrush-dotted flatland that appeared to terminate at the base of a somber bluff about a quarter mile away. We didn't pull off the highway, just coasted to the side of the road, our tires crunching gravel on the shoulder. Kincaid killed his headlights and the drivers of the other vehicles followed suit. Then we got out to look around.

From our vantage point, we could see one lonely trailer house and the outlines of several silent pieces of heavy equipment that were being used by the construction crew at Sweetwater Estates—a road grader, a front-end loader, dump trucks, a water truck, a couple things I couldn't identify. There was a car parked in the shadows at the side of the mobile home that might have been Stone's Lincoln. Yellow light came from the picture window of the trailer and from one window in back that probably served as the bedroom.

Kincaid studied the approach to the mobile home for several minutes before he let his binoculars drop to his chest. "No fuckin' way," he muttered, and we all knew what he meant. We couldn't drive any closer without alerting Stone to our presence, and the moon was so bright that we couldn't go in on foot without serious risk of being spotted. If Stone was looking out of a window and paying attention, he could escape out the back or try to pick us off before we gained the protection of the heavy machinery.

Kincaid squatted down and checked the clip in his pearl-handled .45. Then he jacked a round into the chamber, eased the hammer down, and set the safety. The other cops and sheriff's deputies gathered around him in a huddle, inspecting their own weapons and bulletproof vests, some of them nervous, others almost preternaturally calm.

I stood at the edge of the group loading the short-barreled shotgun I'd chosen because a scatter gun is best for close work. If you're on the receiving end, a fat round being pumped into the chamber of a shotgun can be one of the most frightening sounds imaginable, and sometimes that alone will stop a criminal in his tracks. If not, there's always the weapon itself. Loaded with double-aught buck, a twelve-gauge will inflict devastating damage, and your aim doesn't have to be precise.

Most of the police officers were similarly armed, but there were several with assault weapons—a couple of Heckler & Koch MP5 9-mm submachine guns, three or four M16A2s, one man with an M24 sniper rifle, basically the military version of my Remington, outfitted with a lightweight synthetic stock and a Zeiss sighting scope.

Frankie, wearing the night-vision goggles around his neck, was loading the magazine of the 7 mm. I noticed that the other law-enforcement officers gave the formidable Sioux plenty of breathing room. I guess I didn't blame them. Absent the goggles and modern rifle, he looked as if he might have just popped through a time warp, a fierce, hulking warrior from another century. If I didn't know him, he'd scare me, too.

When we were ready, a few of the officers lit smokes and talked among themselves, while others surveyed the ground between us and the trailer house, committing to memory every bit of cover, every bare stretch where they'd be vulnerable.

Kincaid pondered the approach for five more minutes before he came to a decision. "There's no other way to do it," he said, telling us what we already knew. "We'll break into two groups and go in on foot. Half of you go around the back way and find some cover. The rest of us'll take the front and get behind that machinery.

"Keep low and move slowly. Stay on your walkie-talkies so we'll know when everyone's in place. If it looks like we can open some negotiations or even break in and take him, we'll make the decision then. If it doesn't"—he paused, stood up to his full height—"at least the son of a bitch won't get away."

When he was finished, the assault force broke into two clusters of about a dozen each. Most of the deputies from the sheriff's department went with the bunch heading to the back of the trailer. The Rock Springs cops would go with Kincaid to the front. Frankie and I were odd men out, but not for long. "You two come with me," Kincaid grumbled, "where you won't get in any trouble." With that, he spun on his heels and walked off into the moonlit prairie without another word.

I did what I was told without comment and followed his group when the other band split off, cradling the shotgun in my arms and watching the ground carefully so I wouldn't trip over an exposed root or stone. We moved purposefully and quietly. The only sounds of our passage were the scuffing of our boots on hard-packed earth, our huffy breathing, and the creaking of our leather holsters and hardware.

When we'd gone fifty yards, we spooked a jackrabbit that bolted away from us as fast as it could go. In the quiet, the sound of its small, muscular legs thumping the ground as it escaped through the brush was as loud as rolling thunder. Considering the tense atmosphere and our jumpy trigger fingers, it's a wonder a dozen guns didn't turn it into atomic residue.

When my heartbeat returned to normal, I chuckled softly, turned around to whisper something to Frankie—see if he'd been as startled by the bunny as I was. There was no one there. Frankie Tall Bull had been only a few steps behind me when we left the road, but now, like a spirit wraith, he was gone. The prairie shadows had swallowed him whole.

Junior Stone saw us coming long before we reached the safety of the heavy machinery parked on the construction site.

Luckily for us, the man was a lousy shot with a pistol.

We were still twenty yards away from cover, moving in a line with thirty feet between each officer, when the lights in the mobile home suddenly went dark. Seconds later, the first long bolt of blue muzzle flame shot from the front window, followed immediately by the popping report of the weapon.

Like everyone else, I put my head down and ran for cover in a mad sprint. Stone fired in our direction five more times before I found protection behind the blade of the road grader, but I had no idea where he was aiming, or if his bullets had found a target. All I knew for sure was that he missed me. I didn't know where the hell Frankie had gone, but I hoped he'd missed him, too.

When I was hidden, I hunkered down until the adrenaline level in my system dropped below red line and caught my breath—getting shot at always has a negative effect on my metabolism. Then I jacked a round into the chamber of the scatter gun, removed my Stetson, and poked my head cautiously over the edge of the blade. I could see nothing inside the darkened mobile home, just the curtain flapping through the open front window, but at least the shooting had stopped. In the shadows around me, I heard the metallic sounds of weapons being cocked, bolts slamming home on live rounds. Given the slightest encouragement from Kincaid, I'm sure the trailer would have been blown to dust.

Kincaid heard it, too. "Hold your fire!" he called. I couldn't see him, but his voice came from the vicinity of a dump truck parked a few yards away. "Was anyone hit?"

"Nah, he missed every time," called another gruff voice, this one from the darkness around the big rear tire of a water truck.

"Good," Kincaid said. For the next few minutes, I heard the muffled sound of his voice as he spoke on the walkie-talkie, then nothing for several minutes but the chirping of crickets and the sound of the gentle breeze whispering through the remaining stands of buffalo grass on the construction site. When Kincaid spoke again, he was using a bullhorn. "All right, Junior," he said, sounding like the voice of doom. "I don't need to tell you you're in a world of shit here. Why don't you just pitch your weapons through the window and come on out before it gets worse?"

Stone answered him with another shot that pinged harmlessly off the heavy-metal bumper of the truck. "I don't think so, Al," he called back, almost cheerfully. "As a matter of fact, I think I'll stay right where I am." He paused, and when he called again, his voice was full of menace. "And if you want to see this bitch alive again, you'll stay right where you are, too."

Kincaid didn't hesitate in reassuring him. "We're not going anywhere, Junior," he said. "All we want to do is talk."

I could swear I heard Stone laugh. "You and me have nothin' to talk about, Al," he hollered. "But if that was Harry Starbranch I saw hobblin' around out there, you send him in. He and I have a few things to straighten out."

Kincaid didn't answer, but even in the darkness I could feel his eyes searching me out. Overhead, a gauzy cloud scudded across the face of the moon, casting an eerie moving shadow over the construction site. I looked up and saw a larger cloud bank closing in from the north. Within fifteen minutes or less, it would cover the moon and throw us into darkness. That was good in that we'd no longer be such inviting targets for Stone's fire but bad because he might use the absence of light to make an escape. I didn't know about Kincaid, but the thought of all those tense, armed people stumbling around in pitch darkness trying to catch a killer was enough to make the short hair on my neck stand up. I hoped we could end it soon.

If Stone really wanted me inside, I decided I was willing to go along with his demand. Once I threw down my weapons and became a hostage, I'd be in a great deal of danger, but that was a situation I'd faced before. At least in the trailer I'd have a better chance of doing Faith some good than I had where I was. If I could get him talking, sooner or later he might drop his guard and give me the opportunity to take his gun away and keep the promise I'd made at our last meeting—to slap wood on his murdering ass. If I could do my slapping in the course of a legitimate police operation, that would be dandy.

I had the feeling Kincaid would tell Junior to pound sand, though, so I acted before he had a chance. I rested my shotgun against the blade of the grader, laid the Blackhawk on the ground, raised my hands above my head, and came out where Stone could see me. Kincaid was not pleased by my initiative. "Get back behind that grader, you dumb son of a bitch," he whispered, "or I'll shoot you myself."

I hesitated briefly, and Stone noticed. "Too late, Starbranch," he called through the window. "You start walking this way, and don't even think of turning back. I'll tell you when to stop."

I'd committed to a course of action, and now I couldn't turn back. I started walking, shuffling forward carefully so I didn't trip over my own feet. I'd only gone a few steps when Stone's voice rang out again. "Leave the cane, Starbranch," he said. "I learned my lesson about that last time." I did as he said and dropped the blackthorn walking stick in the dirt. Now I had nothing to fight him with but my wits and my fists, not even a pocketknife. I felt naked, and things were about to get worse.

It was only fifty feet from where I was standing to the stairs leading to the door of the mobile home, but it was the longest walk I'd ever taken in my life. I couldn't see anything inside the darkened interior, but there was a space at the right side of the picture window that seemed blacker, more malevolent, than the rest. I sensed that was where Stone was laying in wait, and it might have been my imagination, but I thought I could actually feel his gun sight playing across my chest, his finger exerting increasing tension on the trigger, taking up the slack. I hoped the porker didn't sneeze.

I was at the bottom of the stairs when he finally told me to stop. "That's about right, Starbranch," he said. I stood quietly so he could get a good look. "You carryin'?" he asked. "Maybe a little belly gun tucked in your boot?"

I shook my head. "Nothin' that could hurt a big, strong boy like you, Junior," I said disdainfully. "Not even a bad thought."

Stone chuckled wickedly. "It's not that I don't trust you, Starbranch, but why don't you prove it? Drop them clothes."

"What?"

"You heard me," he snapped. "Peel."

Junior let me keep my underwear, but that's the only decent act he had in his repertoire. When my clothing was lying at my feet in a puddle and I was down to my boxers, he ordered me to come inside. Then he made me kneel on the living-room floor while he taped my wrists and mouth, just as I'd done to Sam.

That's when the beating began. He started with his fists, quick shots to my back and kidneys, the back of my head and upper arms. He worked silently, only letting out a little whoof of breath every time he connected. By the tenth punch, I was lying on my stomach, fighting the black whirlies. By the twentieth, I was sliding into unconsciousness, no longer feeling the full force of the blows. The last thing I remember was a fist slamming into the back of my neck and what looked like a shower of meteors across my field of vision.

When I came to, he was no longer using his hands, he was using a piece of wood, maybe a broom handle. It made sharp snapping sounds as it connected with the heavy muscles of my shoulders, the backs of my legs. By then he was breathing heavily, grunting every time he brought the handle down again. My whole body felt numb and bruised. My mouth was full of bile. I couldn't call out, couldn't scream. All I could do was moan behind the tape. I wondered if the armed men and women outside could hear what he was doing. If they could, I wondered why they allowed it to continue.

Maybe Kincaid read my mind. "What's going on in there, Junior? Talk to me now, boy," he called through the bullhorn, his deep voice echoing through the misty fog of my agony.

Junior, out of breath and wheezing from exertion, stopped his assault, crabbed over to the window. It was too dark to see his features because the incoming clouds had blocked out the moon, but I could just make out his brutish outline as he peered over the sill. "Nothin' at all, Chief," he yelled back. "Me and Harry are just havin' a little chat."

"Let me speak to him," Kincaid demanded.

"Nah, he's busy," Stone answered.

"Damn it, Junior . . . let me talk to him or we're comin' in there right now."

Junior thought the matter over, decided he didn't want to find out if Kincaid was serious. "Hold on," he answered sullenly.

He duck-walked away from the window to where I was lying on the floor, grabbed a hand full of hair, and raised my head. "You be quiet when I take this tape off, understand?" he whispered.

I muttered something that might have been an affirmative response. My stomach was churning, like I might vomit. I was having trouble focusing and there was a loud humming in my ears, like feedback through an amplifier. The world felt fuzzy, surreal. I barely felt it when he yanked the tape from my head and dragged me to the window. He sat me up and leaned my back against the wall. "Talk to him," he said. When I didn't respond, he dug the barrel of his pistol into my temple, cocked the hammer for emphasis. "Talk to him."

I tried to do what he said, but the only sound that came from my mouth was a groan, like the noise you make when you wake from a deep sleep and your throat is full of phlegm.

"That you, Harry?" Kincaid asked from somewhere in the shadows.

I cleared my throat, took a deep breath, and let it out slowly. "Yeah, it's me," I croaked. My voice sounded different, the way it does when I hear myself on tape, soft around the edges the way it is when I've had about ten drinks. At least the nausea was going away.

"You all right?"

As a matter of fact, I was. Although I hurt all over, I didn't think anything was broken. Tell the truth, Junior Stone wasn't as tough as his reputation. I'd been hit before by men whose punches broke bones, ruptured organs, shattered knees, but Junior wasn't one of them. Stone dug the barrel of the pistol a little deeper into my scalp. Much more and he'd break skin. "Just fine," I managed. It was an answer to Kincaid's question, but it was also a taunt. I was telling Junior what I thought of him: not much.

Stone read me loud and clear. He backhanded me across the forehead with the butt of the pistol and I slumped sideways. The carpet burned my battered back and legs as he pulled me away from the window. "Satisfied now?" he yelled. "He's alive. You want to keep him that way, just stay put."

"Be calm, Junior," Kincaid called. "We'll stay here all night if you want."

Stone didn't intend to hang around that long. He rolled me on my stomach, grabbed my wrists, and pulled me roughly to my feet. I grunted in pain because it felt as if he was about to dislocate my shoulders. I've been a prisoner before, but I'd never felt so impotent in my life. I guess that happens when they take away your clothes. "You feel like a little ride, Starbranch?" he asked. "You're gonna get me out of here."

I stiffened my body, pulled away from him, but he yanked me back. "What about Faith?" I asked.

"What about her?" he growled. "She's already told me everything I wanted to know. I don't need her anymore, and she's in no condition to travel to the land of fruit and nuts with me even if I did."

I felt a righteous anger building inside my belly, drowning the pain—and with that anger came strength. "Is she alive?"

He raised his arm and hit me in the back of the head with his elbow. I stumbled forward, but he pulled me back before I fell. "Good question," he said. "But not one you'll have to worry about for long."

With that he pointed me toward the door, threw one thick forearm across my throat, and held the pistol to my head with his other hand. "If you hurt her—" I threatened through clenched teeth.

"What is it, big shot?" he growled. That close, his breath was rancid. It smelled of rotten teeth. He stank of something else as well, the acrid scent of fear. Beneath his bravado, Junior Stone was afraid. That made him dangerous and even more unpredictable, but the knowledge was something I might use to my advantage. "If I hurt her, you'll what?" he persisted.

"If you hurt her, you'd better kill me," I said, "because I'm gonna tear you apart."

He thought it over for a second. "It ain't an issue, Starbranch," he answered simply. Then he walked me through the front door and onto the stairs. He was behind me, using my body as a shield, but he needn't have bothered. With the cloud cover, it was so dark I could barely make out the location of the heavy equipment. Unless there was an unexpected break in the clouds, there was no way Kincaid or his officers could get a clean shot.

It was up to me to come up with something soon if I wanted out of my predicament alive. Whatever I dreamed up, I hoped it would work out better than my spur-of-the-moment plan to make myself a hostage and engage Stone in conversation until he dropped his guard. That brainstorm had turned into a disaster. The man had no desire to talk, exhibited no curiosity. He hadn't even asked how we'd found out where he was hiding. Maybe he didn't think it was important.

Stone, panting through his mouth like a dog, stood behind me on the porch for several long minutes, scanning the inky darkness of the construction site for motion. Unless his eyes were a lot better than mine, it was a wasted effort. "You out there, Al?" he finally yelled.

"We're here," Kincaid responded a second later, no longer using the horn.

Stone increased the pressure around my throat. "Here's how it's gonna go," he called. "Starbranch and me are gonna get in my car and drive outa here, and none of you are gonna follow. I see anybody in my rearview and Starbranch dies. We clear on that?"

There was a long pause. "What about the girl?" Kincaid asked.

"She's inside," Junior said. "You can get her when we're gone."

"You're not gonna get away with this, Junior."

"You let me worry about that," Junior said. He pushed me toward the first step, pressing his body against my back so we moved as one. I picked my way down the metal stairs, exploring with my toes before I put any weight on my legs. At the bottom, we shuffled through the dirt toward the side of the trailer where the Lincoln was parked. Cactus barbs pierced the tough soles of my feet, sharp rocks poked my tender insteps. It was only a few more feet to the car, and once we got inside I'd be completely at his mercy.

It's now or never, I thought.

There was no way I could beat Stone with my hands taped behind my back, so the best I could hope for was to create a diversion that might allow me to get away from him in the darkness.

Before we took another step I turned my head, opened my mouth, and bit down on the bicep of the arm he had around my throat. I felt my teeth pop through his skin, tasted a salty spurt of blood as they sank into heavy muscle. I held on like a pit bull, shaking my head from side to side, ripping flesh.

Stone howled, relaxed his grip.

It was enough.

I lunged forward and broke free. Then I put my weight on my good leg and spun around in a snapping back kick. He doubled over when my heel found the muscles of his lower stomach, but he held on to his pistol. I tried to run, but I was off balance, lurching. I tripped before I'd gone three steps, crashing to the ground, face first in a jumble. I tried to get up, my legs and feet thrashing for purchase.

Stone was on me before I could move. He grabbed me by the hair, pulled me over, and threw me to the ground on my back. Then he knelt on my chest with one knee and forced the muzzle of the pistol into my mouth. "I hope you enjoyed that, asshole," he hissed. "Tell O'Bannion hello when you see—"

I closed my eyes, ready for the end—but instead of a lightning bolt tearing through my mouth, I heard a soft thudding sound and Stone flinched, seemed to hesitate. He coughed, tried to clear his throat. Then he began to gag, like he was choking. The pistol jerked from my mouth, and Stone's knee came off my chest. He stood up, dropped the weapon. Clawed at his gullet with both hands.

Four rapid gunshots exploded from the darkness near the Lincoln, and the impact of the heavy slugs spun Stone away from me like a top. He completed his macabre pirouette, then crumpled in a gurgling heap at the foot of the stairs, his last breaths rattling in his ruined lungs.

I listened to Junior die until Frankie's voice came from the darkness, the sweetest sound I'd ever heard. "You all right, Harry?"

I tried to blink the afterimage of the muzzle blasts from my eyes. No good. I muttered something, still too stunned to speak coherently. I lay back and looked at the sky, took a deep breath, inhaled the sage perfume, drifting.

Seconds later, I felt Frankie's strong arms around me, lifting me up. He peeled the tape from my wrists and I turned around. He was wearing the night-vision goggles and his .44 magnum was tucked into his waistband. When Kincaid and his officers arrived a few seconds later with flashlights, they found his Bowie in Junior's neck—buried nearly to the bone handle in back, a good four inches of pointed, razor-sharp blade sticking out in front, right to the left of his Adam's apple.

Hell of an arm, that Frankie Bull.

Faith Ahearn was still alive, but not by much. She was in the back bedroom of the trailer, spread-eagled, facedown on the bed. She was naked, and her wrists and ankles were tied to the metal bed frame.

Her back, legs, and buttocks were a mass of red, angry welts and dark-blue bruises. Her eyes were blackened and puffy, her nose was swollen, and there was crusted blood around her nostrils. There were blisters on her arms and the bottoms of her feet that looked as if they were made by cigarettes. There was blood on the insides of her thighs from the violent rapes. A blow-dryer was abandoned in the tangled bedding between her legs. I hated to even think what he used that for.

I worked on Faith's arms and Kincaid freed her legs. She moaned when we rolled her over and opened her eyes to slits, but she didn't appear lucid, didn't seem to recognize me. Maybe she expected more punishment and was too far gone to care. She was breathing shallowly through her broken nose, but when I put my hand beneath her breast, I could feel a regular heartbeat. That, at least, was encouraging.

By then, there were more than a half-dozen cops crammed into the small bedroom with Kincaid and me, so I found a thin cotton blanket in a wadded ball on the floor and used it to cover Faith's abused body. I brushed a strand of sweaty dark hair away from her face, leaned down, and whispered into her ear. "You're safe now, sweetheart," I told her. "He can't hurt you anymore." Her eyelids fluttered at the sound of my voice, but that was her only response. I cradled her frail body in my arms and rocked her gently until the blue and red emergency lights from the vehicles Kincaid had sent officers to fetch began to dance across the wood-paneled walls and the night quiet was broken by the wailing sound of sirens.

Kincaid laid a rough hand on my shoulder. "We'll take her from here, Harry," he said. "We've got to get her to a hospital."

I nodded and helped lift Faith into the arms of two waiting officers, who carried her out of the trailer and laid her gently on the backseat of a waiting police cruiser. We watched it travel swiftly down the quarter-mile dirt road to the highway, then disappear over a rise seconds after it hit blacktop.

When it was gone, I went back inside the trailer on the off chance there was a working phone. I needed to call Maddy and Curly, who would be mad with worry. No good. There was a phone, but it wasn't hooked up. I slammed it down and stomped outside, where I found Frankie leaning against the front of the trailer, staring contemplatively at Stone's corpse, which was lying, still uncovered, at his feet. I looked down at Junior's porcine face, his small eyes staring sightlessly into the middle distance, the spreading pool of dark blood at his throat, the breastplate of blood on his bullet-riddled chest.

"She gonna be all right?" he asked quietly.

"She'll live," I told him. "What she went through in there, I don't think she'll ever be all right."

He nodded sadly, prodded Stone's body with the toe of his boot, and studied it closely for several long minutes. He squatted down on his haunches for a closer look, burning the image of Stone's face in his mind. "It's the first time I've ever killed anyone," he said. "It's not how I imagined."

I knew what he was feeling, because I've felt it myself more times than I care to remember. Taking another life changes your own irrevocably. No matter the circumstances that caused you to take the life, you see your victim's face in your dreams, often your nightmares, until the end of your days. You share your waking and resting hours with his ghost. It hovers in the background, never letting you forget. There are several ghosts haunting the darkened corners of my life. "He was a bad man," I said. "There was nothing else you could do."

"Maybe not," he said uncertainly. "Then again, maybe I could have—"

I didn't let him finish, told him the only thing I knew that might help. "If you had done it any other way, I'd be dead." I rested my hand on his muscular neck. "You saved my life, Frankie, and for that I'll be eternally grateful."

I heard the sound of boot heels on the ground and turned around to find Kincaid standing beside us. He flared a kitchen match with his fingernail and used it to light a smoke. He smoked it to the filter, then flicked it away. It landed in a shower of sparks.

"What now, Chief?" I asked.

"Pantaleo owns this property, this trailer house," he said. "Now I'm gonna bring him in again for questioning." He looked at me thoughtfully. "Anything you can tell me that'd help me make a case?"

"I know a few things, Al."

"Why'd he kidnap her?"

I walked to where my clothing was still lying in a heap, picked it up, and carried it to the stairs, sat down, and began to dress. "He kidnapped her because he thought she knew the location of some missing money," I said. "He tortured her to find out where it was. I don't know if he got what he was after."

"On Pantaleo's orders?" he asked.

"Of course," I said. "But I can't prove it." I remembered my last words to Pantaleo: "If he's hurt her, I'll come back and get you." I wouldn't need proof to do that if my words were anything but empty threats. Then again, maybe I had enough blood on my hands already.

"How did you know they were here?"

"Lucky guess," I said. I stood to tuck my shirt into the waistband of my blue jeans, sat down again, and pulled my battered Justin cowboy boots onto my sore feet.

"Bullshit, Harry!" Kincaid said angrily. "I was born at night, but not last night. It was a hell of a lot more than a lucky guess."

I shrugged, didn't answer. Stood up again and buckled the Blackhawk's leather holster belt around my waist. There was comfort in the weapon's solid weight. "I can't tell you exactly how I knew," I said. "It's enough that I did."

Kincaid snorted through his nose. "Oh, you'll tell me all right," he said. "Soon as we bag this prick and stop by the hospital, you're gonna come to the office and tell me everything you know, even if it takes all goddamned week."

I felt better with my clothes on, more like my old, surly self. Handful of aspirin, couple shots of Rebel Yell and I'd be good as new—until the next day, at least. I imagined I'd be hurting something fearsome then. "I'll tell you as much as I can," I promised. Then I limped off to find my blackthorn, my shotgun, and my hat.

18

Faith Ahearn was in bad shape—but she'd suffered no serious internal injuries —so the doctors told us her physical recovery would be fairly rapid. She needed rest and treatment for a concussion and a host of superficial wounds and bruises, but she was a healthy young woman. Barring complications, they thought she'd probably be released from their care within twenty-four hours.

I called Maddy in Victory as soon as we arrived at the hospital, and she called back within minutes to tell me that Cindy Thompson was driving her to Rock Springs to stay with her daughter and bring her home. If they made good time, they'd probably arrive shortly after sunup. We made arrangements to meet at the Golden Spike later that afternoon.

When we hung up, I tried to call Curly, but Addy Lennahan, the jailer, refused to bring him to the phone, even when I told him it was an emergency. I left a message telling my friend his daughter was safe and that I'd try to call back later.

"Don't bother," said Lennahan. "We revoked his phone and visitor privileges."

"Why?"

"He got a little crazy yesterday when he heard about Faith," he said. "Demanded we let him out and tore up his cell when we said no. He's in isolation now, except for his lawyer."

"He was just worried about his kid, Addy," I said. "You'd probably have done the same thing in his place."

"Well, I ain't in his place," Lennahan said. "He's in jail and he broke the rules. Far as me and Tony Baldi are concerned, that's all there is to it—least until we get a court order tellin' us otherwise."

"You're a real compassionate human being, Addy," I said bitterly.

"I'm tryin', Harry," he said, chuckling. "I truly am."

Then he hung up in my ear.

It was almost six in the morning when we left the emergency room for the police department, an exhausted bunch with dark circles under our eyes and plenty of stubble. Once there, Kincaid sent one of his officers to the corner diner for take-out breakfast—heaping portions of scrambled eggs, sausage and bacon, pancakes, muffins, and extra-large cups of strong black coffee. We wolfed our food in the squad room sitting around the department's collection of industrial-gray desks. When I'd finished, I borrowed a fistful of aspirin and a couple of Tylenols with codeine from one of the cops and washed them down with the dregs of my coffee. Then I laid my head down on my arms to catch a quick nap.

Al Kincaid had other plans. As soon as he finished his own breakfast, he detailed two officers to Sam Pantaleo's home to bring the man in for questioning. He sent another just coming on shift to the hospital with instructions to call as soon as Faith was awake and coherent. He wanted to take her statement while the events of the previous night were still fresh in her mind. He sent one more officer to the mortuary to watch Junior's autopsy, and another to search the dead man's house.

Then he slapped the top of the desk to get my attention and hooked a thumb over his shoulder toward his office. "Now it's your turn, Harry," he said gruffly. He turned to Frankie Bull, who was just finishing his second heavily buttered blueberry muffin. Killing Junior had shaken him badly, but at least he still had his appetite. "You wait here," he said. "I'll get to you when we're finished."

I followed Kincaid to a small office barely big enough for his desk and one uncomfortable-looking chair for visitors. He closed the door behind us, but the place was so tiny that I had to remain standing until he was seated behind his desk. I moved a stack of newspapers and magazines off the seat of the chair, put them on the floor, and sat down heavily. My bruised back screamed in anguish, and I couldn't rest it against the metal slats on the back of the chair. I sat stiffly, leaning forward with my hands on my knees, like a teenage truant in front of the headmaster. I hoped the drugs kicked in soon.

Kincaid put a small tape recorder on the desk between us and punched it on. Then he found a notebook and pen for backup. He rubbed his temples thoughtfully, then scribbled a couple of notes at the top of the first page. When he finished, he looked at me for a long moment before speaking. "Don't string me any windies now, no cock-and-bull stories," he said. "I want the whole sordid saga."

"It's a long one," I said.

Kincaid smiled thinly. "I've got time."

It had been my intention to tell him almost everything but to hold back the part where I committed kidnapping. In the end, I told him more than I planned. Not much of a liar, I guess. He listened patiently for the next half hour while I went over the background of my investigation, most of which he already knew from our previous visit. He scribbled furiously when I recounted my trip to San Francisco and my late-night meeting with Pichette. He grimaced when I told him how Stone had murdered Edna Cook and torched my house, and his brow furrowed when I gave him a sanitized and sketchy version of Pantaleo's abduction and the method I'd employed to encourage him to tell me where Junior was holding Faith. I couldn't tell whether he was angry or just concentrating, so I pressed on.

When I finished my tale, he leaned back in his chair and stared at the ceiling. When he was done cogitating, he sat forward and turned the recorder off. "I can understand why you wanted Stone for yourself, Harry," he said. "But you did the right thing, calling me in."

"I know," I said. "Unfortunately, I think I blew any chance of prosecuting Pantaleo for his part in Faith's abduction. The courts don't take kindly to information given under duress. I'm sorry about that, Al, I—"

He held his hand up to stop me from going on. I got the message: He didn't want to know any more details, didn't want me to incriminate myself further. I shut my fat trap, and was surprised when his mouth cracked in a huge grin. "Christ, Harry," he said, "you've been a cop so long, you see everything you do in that light. Didn't you tell me just a few minutes ago you're unemployed? Did you forget you're a *civilian?*"

I should have been quicker on the uptake, but I was so tired my brain pan felt as if it were full of fluffy cotton balls. "Yeah, I did . . ." I stuttered, "but . . ." His point hit me like a brick before I finished the sentence, and I felt my own grin threatening to split my face in two. The Constitution protects people against police officers who coerce information, but it doesn't protect against private citizens who do the coercing. Since I was now a civilian, I could testify against Pantaleo, and the fact that he told me Stone's location could be used against him in court. It would be dicey, of course. Pantaleo's lawyers would argue that I was acting under color of law, and might win. On the other hand, they might not.

There was one hitch. My testimony might help convict Pantaleo, but I'd just admitted to kidnapping and assault myself, two major-league felonies by anybody's reckoning. The consequences could be decidedly unpleasant.

Kincaid read my mind. "I know what you're thinking, but it might not be as bad as it looks," he said. "Going after Pantaleo on your own and doing whatever malicious thing you did once you had him was damned stupid, but it isn't necessarily the end of the world. I'm the one who would have to file charges against you if I feel there's sufficient evidence, but at this point I'm real ambivalent about pursuing that aggressively, because you were trying to save an innocent young woman's life." He waited for a beat while I digested that happy tidbit. "Also keep in mind that Stone worked for Pantaleo, but even if we can't prove Sam ordered the kidnapping, your testimony shows he had prior knowledge of a felony being committed on his own property," he continued. "That's the sort of thing gonna make him look real bad in front of the county prosecutor or a jury, so even if he makes a formal complaint against you and forces me to look into his accusations, it's—"

"My word against his," I broke in, finishing his thought. There were no witnesses, after all. No way for Sam to prove he didn't make the whole thing up to save his own skin.

"Exactly," Kincaid said smugly. "I don't think it'll ever come to that, though—which is a good thing, since you're obviously the kind who'd have trouble lying under oath." He was stating a fact, and didn't expect a response. I didn't give him one. "You think Sam will want the whole world to know who he was boinkin' when you found him?" he asked. "You think that's the kind of thing he'd want his wife and kids to hear in open court? You think he wants the people he's in business with to know he was so bone-headed he let you snatch him in his underwear? I don't know exactly how you broke him, and I don't want to—but I don't imagine he'd want his enemies to know how easy it apparently was. Do you?"

I'd already considered those very questions, albeit briefly. I shrugged. "Maybe not."

"Well, I know Sam a little better than you do," he said, "and I can guarantee that's the kind of information he'll take to his grave. Those things became public knowledge, he'd have people lining up to take him down first chance they got, including most of his own family."

Kincaid stood and clapped me on the shoulder. "I wouldn't worry about it too much, podna," he said. "Everything's gonna work out fine."

I felt a genuine flush of relief. "Thanks, Al," I said.

Kincaid stood and threaded his way past me, opened the door, and gestured me out with a formal sweep of his arm. "Sam's had a long night of it, but if you left him where you said you did, he oughta be trailin' in any minute," he said. "If you and Mister Bull will excuse me, I think I'll go keep my officers company at his house. I can't wait to welcome him home."

Frankie hit the road for Victory as soon as Kincaid left the police station, so I took his room at the Golden Spike, put the DO NOT DISTURB sign on the door, closed the drapes, unplugged the phone, and conked out with my clothes on.

I slept deeply, without dreams, until an insistent rapping brought me back, kicking and screaming, from the land of nod. One of my eyes felt as if it was almost swollen shut, but when I got the other one to focus properly, the bedside clock told me it was four-thirty in the afternoon. I dragged myself off the bed and to my feet, but I almost fell down again as soon as I stood up to answer the door. My battered muscles had plenty of time to stiffen up while I was snoozing, and they had risen to the challenge. I felt like one giant, throbbing mess from the back of my neck to the bottom of my calves, and I knew it would take a whole bottle of Tylenol with codeine just to take the edge off. Unfortunately, I didn't have a single one.

I hobbled to the door like a decrepit Miami pensioner and opened it a crack, holding the Blackhawk out of view at my side. Maddy Ahearn and Cindy Thompson were waiting in the hall, and both of them winced when they saw my face. "My God, Harry," Cindy said, "you look awful."

I removed the security chain and opened the door for them to come in. "You oughta see the other guy," I said automatically, before I remembered what the other guy looked like. Thanks to Frankie, the other guy looked dead.

Maddy didn't say a word, just grabbed me in a miniature bear hug and held on as if she feared that a big hand might come down from the sky and snatch me away. It hurt like hell, if you want to know the truth, but I didn't try to stop her, just hugged back. I looked over the top of her head at Cindy, who was standing a few steps away, the question in her eyes as plain as if she'd spoken it aloud: Are you okay?

I nodded and went on hugging, letting my sore eyes feast on

Cindy's charms. Dressed in a pantsuit that flattered her natural curves and open-toed leather sandals in rich mahogany, she looked as if she'd just stepped from the pages of the Lord & Taylor catalog. The cream-colored natural cotton fabric of the suit complemented her honey-colored hair, offset her deep, early-summer tan, and the scooped neckline of the loose sleeveless blouse would have stopped traffic if it scooped a half inch lower. She was wearing a single strand of pearls, and aside from a few laugh lines at the corners of her mouth and a couple of crinkles around her eyes that were hardly worth mentioning, she could have passed for twenty-five, thirty tops. Not bad for a woman who had been dragged out of bed at the crack of dawn and had spent the day at a hospital.

I caught my own reflection in the mirror—hair sticking up at a thousand odd angles, two days growth of salt-and-pepper beard, filthy clothes, a purple patch on my swollen cheekbone that was turning into an impressively grotesque contusion, puffy, bloodshot, eyes, a vivid scarlet scrape right in the middle of my forehead where Junior whacked me with the butt of his pistol—and nearly jumped. I was pretty sure I didn't smell like a rosebud, either. People see us together, they'd think Beauty and the Beast, for sure.

I felt the warmth of Maddy's tears on my chest and waited patiently until she pushed away to arm's length and wiped her nose. "Thank you, Harry," she said. "I can't tell you how frightened I was, how much it means that you—"

I kissed her cheek, dabbed a tear from the corner of her eye. "It's nothing, Maddy," I said. "I'm just happy she's alive. You've been with her, did the doctor say—"

"She's going to recover physically," Maddy said. "I don't know about the rest. I'll just take her home tomorrow and hope for the best, no matter how long it takes."

I got the women seated and poured them cold drinks from the honor bar. There was a little machine in the room that made enough hot water for two cups of instant coffee, so I turned that on for myself. When it was ready, I sat on the bed and sipped gratefully. It tasted bitter and disgusting, but I needed the caffeine. Maddy waited until I'd finished half a cup.

"Do you know why he did that to her, Harry?" she asked. "Why he kidnapped her in the first place?"

"He thought she knew about a lot of money Liam stole from some bad people," I said.

"Does she?"

"I don't know for sure," I said honestly. "What Stone did after he kidnapped her, he did because he was an animal."

"It always comes back to Liam, doesn't it, Harry," Maddy said. It was a statement, not a question.

"Yeah."

"Do you know who killed him?" she asked hopefully. "Was it Stone? Did this Pantaleo have something to do with it?"

I shook my head sadly. "It wasn't Stone," I said. "I don't know about Pantaleo. In spite of all that's happened, Maddy, I still haven't found anything that'll help Curly. Trust me, though. I'll see this thing through to the end. We'll get your husband out of jail."

We sat in thoughtful silence for several minutes until Cindy finished her soda. Then she stood up and opened the drapes. It was a beautiful summer afternoon, not a cloud in the sky. "Al Kincaid stopped by the hospital after lunch," she said. "Told me he'd been trying to call you."

"I unplugged the phone."

"That's what he figured," she said. "He asked me to tell you he arrested Pantaleo shortly after he left you this morning. Said to tell you Sam had a long walk home. When they found him, his feet were full of cactus barbs and he was ranting about snakes." She watched me curiously for an explanation, but I only smiled. "He wants you to call him first thing tomorrow."

I said I would, and we talked for another fifteen minutes before Maddy stood up and smoothed her blue knee-length skirt. "Now that I know you're all right, I think I should go back to the hospital. You don't mind?"

"Of course not, Maddy. That's where you belong."

She bent over and hugged my neck, kissed the sore spot on my forehead. "Cindy?" she asked.

Cindy shook her head. "I think I'll stay here for a while," she said. "Harry looks like he could use a good meal."

I saw Maddy to the door, and we stood together for a long moment, holding hands. "I'm sorry about Edna, Harry," she said. "I know you loved her."

"That I did." I bit my lip, felt my throat constricting. "I'm gonna miss that old woman."

"Me, too," she said. She laid her hand on my cheek. "When you come home to Victory, you'll stay at our house until your new one is finished."

"I don't know, Maddy, I—"

She quieted me with a look. "You're family, Harry," she said, smiling softly. "Looking out for each other—that's what families do."

When Maddy was gone, I told Cindy to make herself comfortable while I cleaned up. Then I went into the bathroom, stripped out of my foul clothes, and ran a shower so hot it filled the room with billowing clouds of steam. My abused back couldn't stand the massage setting, so I turned the showerhead on gentle, closed my eyes, and stood under the healing spray for a long time.

I didn't hear Cindy open the bathroom door, or slip into the shower. The first I became aware of her presence was the feathery touch of her fingertips on my shoulders, moving downward across the welts and bruises on my lower back and legs. "Oh, Harry," she whispered. "Kincaid told us Stone beat you, but I didn't know how bad it was. Does it—"

"It looks worse than it is," I lied. I rubbed water from my eyes and opened them cautiously. She was still wearing her bra and panties.

"Modesty," she explained, smiling. "You just hold still and let the nurse do her job." She turned me around so I was leaning against the tiles at the side of the shower with my arms resting above my head. Then she washed me carefully, starting with my hair and ending with my feet. When she was finished, she dried me with a thick towel and led me to the bed. She closed the drapes, and I lay on my stomach quietly while she took a bottle of aloe lotion from her purse, squirted some into her hands to warm it, then slathered it on my back. Her hands were tender and comforting, and my damaged muscles tingled at her touch.

My muscles weren't all that tingled. She rolled me on my back and rubbed lotion on my chest, even more on the area around my groin and the sensitive skin of my inner thighs. "That's not sore," I said.

She smiled. "But it's responding to treatment," she said. She stood at the side of the bed, unhooked her damp bra, let it fall to the floor, and stepped gracefully out of her panties. She was a beautiful woman—healthy, glowing, ripe. No question, I wanted her, but things were moving too rapidly, beyond my control. "Cindy, I don't—"

She bent over, held a finger to my lips. "I know, Harry," she said. "I know you're still in love with your ex-wife, but I'm here and she's not. With all the brutality in your life, even a man like you needs some tenderness once in a while." She kissed me full on the mouth, tongue darting across my lips, then pulled away. "Let me make love to you," she said. "Limited-time offer. No strings."

When she put it that way, what choice did I have? I put my hands on her shoulders, let my fingers drift to trace the outline of her breasts, her erect nipples, the feminine flare of her hips. I guided her down as she straddled me, entered her slowly. She put her hands on the sides of my head, held herself up, and looked at me with liquid blue eyes. "If it hurts too badly . . ." she whispered, rocking gently.

It had been a long time since I was with a woman. Too long. "At this point," I said, bringing her close, absolutely lost in her musky scent, the firm, velvet slickness of her sex, "I think it would hurt to stop."

We made love once, too quickly. Then we rested and did it again, this time without the urgency, drawing it out, fingers and tongues exploring, bringing each other to the edge, then backing away. We built to a sensual crescendo that left us both gasping in the tangled mass of bedding, legs entwined, her skin bonded to my own by a fragrant sheen of sweat.

We stayed that way for fifteen minutes, gathering our breath, our strength, letting our superheated bodies cool. Then she pulled away from me with a little pop and led me back into the bathroom for a quick, businesslike shower. I tried halfheartedly to get something going again—something involving soap—but she slapped my hands away and continued scrubbing herself briskly. "Later, gator," she said. "If you want to try anything like that, you've got to feed me first."

Fair enough.

When we were showered and dressed, Cindy accompanied me without complaint to a corner drug for toiletries and the local Corral West Ranchwear, where I used my credit card to buy the beginnings of a new wardrobe.

She didn't comment when I threw a couple pairs of jeans and a selection of boxers and white athletic socks on the pile, but she voiced her preferences cheerfully and often while I picked out a half-dozen Western-cut shirts and a gray corduroy jacket that could go casual or dressy, depending on the occasion. I balked when she threw in a black silk bandanna to go with the outfits, started to put it back on the shelf. She took it away and jammed it back on my pile. "Make you look like an outlaw," she said, as if that was the last word on the subject. It was.

I changed into some of my new duds in the dressing room, then we hopped into the Jeep and headed to a supper club I remembered a few miles west of town called the Log Inn. We lingered over cocktails at the bar, then got a table and treated ourselves to a fine, high-calorie meal. She had some sort of chicken and pasta thing in fettuccine sauce. I had a thick rib eye, medium-rare, and a baked potato smothered in sour cream. We both had chocolate cake for dessert. She had Irish cream with her coffee. I had brandy with mine. Topped it off with a nice cigar. Cindy said she liked the smell.

Throughout dinner, I enjoyed the openly appreciative looks of the other men in the restaurant, the sly, envious glances of the women. "They hate you," I told her when she caught one middle-aged matron staring.

"It's because they can tell I just got laid," she whispered. "They're jealous."

"Nah," I said. "I took a good look at myself in the mirror, so I know they've got nothing to be jealous of in that department. Christ, Cindy, it must look like you're on a mercy date with the Hunchback of Notre Dame." I paused, blew a perfect smoke ring, and watched it float upward. Pronounced judgment. "They hate you because you're so skinny you can afford to eat a meal like the one you just put away, and they can't."

She brushed off the compliment with a wink. "You look fine to me," she said lasciviously. "And even if you didn't, it's not your face I'm currently interested in."

I felt my cheeks warming in a blush. "Speaking of which, you hussy," I said, "I believe I've kept my end of the bargain."

She wrinkled her forehead curiously. "What bargain?"

I gave her a wicked grin. "I fed you," I told her, reaching for the check. "Now it's time to pay for your supper."

I suppose it's no surprise that we went to bed early and fell asleep late, and all I can say for sure is that we were both smiling when we finally drifted off.

I can't speak for Cindy, but I was feeling pretty decent. My libido was in better shape than it had been in weeks—okay, months. My stomach was full of rich food and drink. There was a gorgeous, interesting woman snuggling beside me, who'd still be there in the morning. Although I hadn't solved Liam O'Bannion's murder, I had saved Curly's daughter from almost certain death. While I was lying in a cozy bed, Sam Pantaleo was spending the night on a lumpy jail cot, courtesy of information I'd provided.

Those were all good things, right?

The bad things didn't come back until around four in the morning, the hour of the wolf, the hour when my demons always come to visit. My eyes popped open at the appointed time, and I awoke with a feeling of low-level anxiety in my belly so pervasive I knew I'd never get back to sleep.

I lay there in the dark, feeling Cindy's sleep-warm breath on my chest, staring at the ceiling and trying to catalog and explore the potential reasons for my disquietude. There was a long list of possibilities.

For starters, now that I was fully sated, I was beginning to feel more than a little guilty—not just for sleeping with Cindy Thompson but for enjoying it so much. Even though I was a divorced and available adult male whose ex-wife was decidedly pessimistic about our chances of getting back together, I still couldn't shake the feeling that I'd committed adultery, cheated on Nicole. It was irrational, but there it was.

I chewed that bone until about four-thirty, determined to do my spiritual penance in advance, because I knew I was certainly going to sin again—hopefully as soon as Cindy woke up.

After that, I worried about my kids, my job, my unfinished house, and the uncertain state of my finances.

At around five, I moved on to my ghosts. Edna Cook. My father and mother. Faces from the war, from the streets, bedrooms, and gutters of Denver during my days in homicide. Kit Duerr, the man I'd killed the winter before in a cabin in the Snowy Range. Jerry Slaymaker, Bobby Snow, and Ray Bolton—men who'd wanted to kill me, men I'd either killed or watched die.

Junior Stone, the newest member of the unearthly group, arrived last and stayed longest. "Maybe the piss boy *likes* dirty work," he'd taunted. As he strutted the late-night stage of my imagination, Frankie's knife was still lodged in his throat, and his spectral voice was a mockery of the day I'd given in to my base emotions and beaten him in Rock Springs.

The sun was coming up when Junior finally went away, forcibly banished by the delicate pink rays to the brimstone of my own personal hell. Sooner or later, he'd be back.

Carefully, I extricated my arm from around Cindy, sat up quietly, and pulled on my pants. Then I padded out through the sliding doors and onto the balcony overlooking the parking lot. I sat in a cold metal chair, put my bare feet up on the railing, and tried to focus on what I suspected was the most compelling reason for my anxiety and restlessness—the case.

Now that the sun was coming up and Junior's shade was gone, I was alone to examine something he'd said that had been floating around the darker waters of my brain for the last twenty-four hours, percolating just below the level of awareness.

We were standing in the living room of the trailer, moments before Stone led me outside and met his own death on the point of Frankie's blade. I asked him about Faith and he answered honestly, because he didn't think I'd live long enough for it to matter. "What about her?" he'd said. "She's already told me everything I wanted to know. I don't need her anymore, and she's in no condition to travel to the land of fruit and nuts with me even if I did."

Under the circumstances, I hadn't paid much attention to his remark because I was busy thinking of a way to stay alive. After that, I'd simply been too stunned by the violence of the experience, too exhausted and too concerned with my roiling hormones for the significance of his throwaway comment to register. Now it hit home with a vengeance. I gasped at the clarity of the insight, stood up, and grabbed the railing so hard my knuckles turned white, holding myself steady.

The land of fruits and nuts? In the clear light of dawn, the meaning of his trite, red-neck reference was obvious. He was planning a trip to California, because he'd raped and tortured Faith Ahearn until she gave him enough good reasons for the journey.

About 200,000 of them, in fact.

19

▲▲▲

It's no easier getting out of Rock Springs by air than it is anywhere else in Wyoming, but by ten-thirty that morning I was on a cramped commuter flight to Denver, where I'd made hasty reservations on the noon flight back to San Francisco.

Cindy was surprised when I told her my half-baked plan, but she'd agreed to follow Faith and Maddy back to Victory in my Jeep as soon as Curly's daughter was released from the hospital, which would probably be that day. She'd even volunteered to pick me up at Brees Field in Laramie when I finished my business on the coast, and told me I was welcome to park my boots under her bed until my house was finished or hell froze over, whichever came first.

I'd accepted the former offer and dodged the latter. I'm not opposed to unmarried couples sharing a roof, but I'm old-fashioned enough to think they ought to date more than once before they set up housekeeping. Besides, it wasn't fair to drag her further into an uncertain relationship with someone lugging as much emotional baggage as I was. Before we spent many more nights in the same bed, I needed some closure with Nicole. For more than five years, I'd been nursing hopes that we could eventually smooth out our differences, live as a family again, and it was time to press the issue and find out if I was wasting my time. If my ex-wife turned me down once and for all, I knew I'd be devastated, but I also knew the wounds would slowly heal, the hollow places would begin to fill. Eventually, I'd want to start over, and maybe I'd start with someone like Cindy Thompson.

When she drove me to the airport in my Jeep, Cindy had dropped me off in the loading zone with a steamy kiss on the lips that was chaste in comparison to what we'd been doing in bed an hour before. She wiped the lipstick smudge off with her thumb. "Thanks for yesterday . . . and this morning," she said. "It was just what I needed."

"Me, too," I admitted. "But I want you to know that . . ." I stalled, my tongue in knots.

"You want me to know what?"

I knew it would probably come out wrong, but I couldn't help that and just blurted it out. "I want you to know I hope you won't think I took advantage of you, just to get you in the sack," I told her. "It meant a lot to me, Cindy, but I don't want you to think that's all I—"

She laughed and laid a finger across my lips to keep me quiet. "Sometimes you have a tendency to think things to death, but where you come up with some of these wrongheaded notions I'll never know," she said. "I seduced *you*, Harry. I don't remember you inviting me to get in the shower in my bloomers. In that case, it's me who owes an apology if one's due. Would that make you feel better?"

"No . . ." I stammered, "that's not what I . . ."

"Didn't think so," she sniggered. She reached across me and opened my door. "Have a safe trip, chico," she said. "And don't stew over what happened between us last night. You've got enough on your mind as it is."

I got out and closed the door, then leaned my head down to talk through the open window. "I'll call as soon as I know when to expect me home," I said. "If you're not busy, I'll buy you dinner at the Trails End."

"That sounds nice," she said. She ground the gears when she shifted the Jeep into first. I winced, but stopped myself from giving her advice on using the heavy-duty clutch. She pulled forward an inch or two, then stopped when she saw the uncertainty on my face. "You're a true gentleman and a good lay, Mr. Starbranch," she said.

"But if you don't quit fretting about your car and your untarnished reputation, you're gonna miss your flight."

I didn't get the chance to protest. I don't know what the woman found so damned amusing, but I could still hear her laughing as she squealed the tires and drove away.

Because of the time difference, it was only a little before one in the afternoon when my United flight touched down under pewter skies at San Francisco International Airport. The small hard seats in the tiny commuter plane and only slightly larger ones in the passenger jet had been murder on my back and legs, and it felt good to stretch and walk the kinks out. I took my single carry-on bag and made my way through the terminal to the car-rental agencies. Fifteen minutes later, I was heading north on Highway 101 toward the city in a non-descript blue Chevrolet sedan with an engine so puny that pulling out of the merge lane onto the highway was an exercise in terror matched only by my annual visit to the proctologist.

Once on the highway, though, it was a straight shot into town, so I turned the wipers on against the gentle drizzle, edged into a travel lane, opened the window a crack for the warm sea breeze, and sat back to enjoy the ride.

I didn't plan to be in the city long, and there was no one I needed to call. With any luck, I'd be on my way back to Wyoming by nightfall, or the next morning latest. I didn't think it would take much longer than that to check a theory I'd been stringing together that might solve one of the mysteries remaining on my plate.

During my last visit, I hadn't learned much that would help Curly, but in view of more recent events, I was thinking about some of the information I'd picked up in a new light. In particular, I was thinking of a couple items I'd snatched from Faith and Liam's house before Pichette caught me and threatened to throw me in jail for burglary—the letter from Faith's realtor urging her to sign a lease on a new store before the end of the month, and the newspaper clippings indicating Faith's interest in a new home.

Considering what I'd been told about the couple's dismal financial condition, at the time those items seemed to be nothing more than romantic wishful thinking. But if Junior Stone had been telling the truth, and Faith knew where the money was hidden all along, those discoveries took on a more sinister cast. If she knew about the money, there were several troubling questions—like whether she'd been involved in O'Bannion's criminal enterprises and whether she'd played a more active role in his death than I'd previously suspected. I knew she didn't kill him herself because Maddy had provided her with an alibi, but it wasn't out of the question that she'd had an accomplice, maybe even paid to have it done. A quarter-million dollars, give or take $30,000, is a compelling motive for murder.

If it turned out that she had been involved, that meant she had allowed her father to take the fall for O'Bannion's murder. Damn her, if it was true. Damn her for bringing this down on her parents' heads. My thoughts grew blacker and more vengeful as I drove, and I didn't like where they were leading. But in spite of my anger, there was nothing I could do but follow my nose and see what it turned up.

So where was O'Bannion's missing money?

If it was in a safe-deposit box, an offshore bank, or even an account they'd opened somewhere besides their regular bank, I was out of luck. I hadn't found a box key or an account number, and without the force of law behind me there was no way I could gain information about, or access to, the money, even if I found where it was located. If I had to, I supposed I could call Pichette and convince him to get a warrant, but I wasn't ready to call him in, and I didn't know if I ever would be.

Call it a hunch, but I doubted it was stashed in any of those places anyway, because it would have left a trail in a bank account and getting to it might have been a problem if it was stored in a safe-deposit box. Of course, it might still be at the house. Lord knows I'd only given that a cursory search. If worse came to worst, I figured I could wait until dark and break in again, spend all night if it took that long. Go over the place with a microscope.

My instincts told me that wouldn't be necessary. The San Francisco Bay Area is a huge metropolis with 5 million people and a billion hiding places, but one lesson about human nature I'd learned as a cop is that most people, especially women, tend to hide things close by, where they can keep an eye on them. Usually, that means their bedrooms—under the floorboards, sewn inside the mattress, behind the wall paneling, taped to the bottom of their dresser drawers. If that's too hot, if too many people suspect there's something worth finding in the bedroom, they'll pick the next best alternative—somewhere they visit on a regular basis, somewhere they feel safe and comfortable. If Faith had hidden the money, I figured that meant her store.

Because I usually rely on public transportation, I'd seldom driven myself in San Francisco, but it was impossible to get lost, even for me. The early-afternoon traffic was moderate, and I followed Highway 101 north through the heart of the city, past the Civic Center and Lafayette Playground. At the point where the highway takes a ninety-degree turn west toward the Golden Gate Bridge, I kept heading north toward Fort Mason and the Golden Gate National Recreation Area. Chestnut Street was only one block past the turn, and I found a parking place a half block from Dolls in the Attic and killed the engine.

I got out of the car and turned my collar up against the gentle rain, then I ambled down the sidewalk to the redbrick building that housed Faith's store, the travel agency, and the hair salon with the dumb name, Hair Today, Gone Tomorrow. The CLOSED UNTIL FURTHER NOTICE card was still posted on the front door of Faith's shop, but it was beginning to curl from the humidity. I could see through the window that there were several customers in the travel agency and most of the representatives were busy, but the beauty parlor was deserted except for a big-haired blonde in a blue smock watching me curiously from her perch on a stool behind the cash register.

I didn't want her to become civic-minded and call the police when I committed my daylight break-in, so I pasted on my most trustworthy smile and went inside. The beauty parlor smelled of shampoo and astringent hair dye, and the coffee tables were littered with ancient copies of *People* and hairstyle brochures. The blonde gave my bruised face and shaggy mane the once-over and clucked her tongue disapprovingly. "You cut your own?" she asked.

"Yeah," I said, chuckling. "With a pair of tin snips."

"That's what I thought," she said. She ran a long, lacquered fingernail down a page of her appointment book. From where I stood, it looked as if she had plenty of free time. "Looks like I can fit you in."

"I'm not here for a haircut," I told her. I took one of my cards from my wallet and passed it over. She held it gingerly, her lips moving as she read. "I'm here on business for the Ahearn family. I'll be in Faith's store for a while, but I didn't want you to think I'm a robber."

The blonde's face furrowed in a frown that threatened to crack the mask of makeup that covered her broad face like a plaster cast. "I don't know," she said doubtfully. "I been kinda watchin' the place for her, and you aren't the first person to come around. I run all the other ones off."

And if they had any sense, I thought, they didn't stop running until they got to Mexico. I wrote Maddy's phone number on a pad of paper and handed it over. "You can call her there if you have any questions," I said. I hoped she wouldn't bother, because they weren't home.

The blonde was lazy, so my ruse worked. She thought it over for a few seconds, then dropped the card and hunched her shoulders in a bored shrug. "Come on back when you finish up, and I'll fix that hair," she said. "I always rise to a challenge."

I stood with my back to the beauty shop so the blonde couldn't see that instead of a key I was using my plastic 'loid to jimmy the lock on the door to Faith's shop. She didn't have a dead bolt and I'm pretty handy with the 'loid, so I had the door open in seconds.

The air inside the shop was stale and musty, with just a subtle hint of dead mouse—and a fine layer of dust had collected on the surfaces of all the tables and countertops. I stepped over a pile of mail that had accumulated in front of the slot and locked the door behind me.

The main room of the shop was perhaps thirty by forty feet, and it was crammed with dolls of every size and color imaginable, including a stack of Barbies still in the box at least eight feet high. I don't know much about doll collecting, but I was surprised at some of the price tags. The day I pay $2,000 for a doll—or a baseball card, or an autographed football, for that matter—is the day I'll volunteer for intercranial liposuction and get the last smidgen of my brain sucked out.

At the far end of the main room was a little cubbyhole that doubled as an office, and behind that a storeroom filled with more dolls and doll paraphernalia on tall wooden shelves. That's where I started, using a carpet knife to slice the packing tape fastening more than a hundred boxes, all of them carefully packed with dolls. After that, I pawed through the trash barrels and poked through all the cupboards and cabinets, even took a peek in the packing chests on wooden pallets along one wall. They were filled with doll clothes.

There was no safe in the office, no strong box, and nothing in the drawers of the desk but invoices, bills of sale, certificates of authenticity, and one dog-eared copy of *Playgirl* magazine. I flipped the centerfold open and laughed when I saw that Faith, or someone, had drawn a handlebar mustache and a pirate's eye patch on Mr. November.

The answering machine was full, so I ran through the messages that had come in since Faith left for Wyoming. Most of them were from customers, a few were from friends wondering when she'd be home. One was an obscene message from a kid who sounded like his voice was changing, and there were a half-dozen hang-ups. Nothing of interest.

I'd been at it for more than an hour when I got to the main show room, and I started by moving the shelves in the front of the store away from the walls to see if anything was hidden behind them. There were lots of dust bunnies and a rumpled dollar bill, but nothing else. From there, I went on to the doll boxes, which took another hour. I left the ones that were factory-sealed alone, but opened each and every box that was hand-taped.

Zero.

I was just about to start ripping up the floorboards when I noticed two Victorian dollhouses, each of them about three feet high, at the back of the room near the door to the office. I hadn't paid them much attention up to that point, because they looked fairly derelict and were tucked away under a deep overhanging shelf. I pulled the first dollhouse out from under the shelf, lifted the roof away and found nothing but three floors of miniature furniture, paintings, and rugs—even a miniature ceramic cat curled up in front of a miniature fireplace.

The second house was full of cash.

I stared at the banded stacks of fifty and hundred-dollar bills crammed into the dollhouse for several seconds before my shock began to subside and I realized that anyone looking in the front window could see what I was doing. The wooden dollhouse was heavy enough by itself, but with that much money inside I figured it weighed well over 200 pounds. I dragged the dollhouse into the storeroom an inch at a time, gouging deep gashes in the hardwood floor and huffing like a locomotive on a long grade. When I was out of view, I closed the door of the storeroom behind me, spread a moving blanket on the floor to sit on, and began to count.

It took ninety minutes to tally the stash, because there was more than I'd expected. I counted once to get a rough idea of the total and once more to be sure. When I finished, I sat back against one of the wooden shelves and realized that I was looking at more money than I'd ever seen in one place in my life—a hundred dollars shy of a half-million bucks, almost twice as much as Pichette believed O'Bannion had stolen. No wonder the man was in deep shit, since all but the $50,000 he'd pinched from the DEA was drug money and other ill-gotten gains from Fang and Pantaleo.

Now that *I* had all their money, the question was what to do with it. I knew what I *should* do, of course. I knew I should walk into the next room, call Pichette, and turn the whole fortune over to him.

The only problem with that plan was that once I made the call, the results would be completely out of my hands—never an appealing prospect for a dyed-in-the-wool, anal-retentive control freak like myself.

I'd finally turned up some evidence that might help Curly at trial, but revealing that evidence meant implicating his daughter. If she'd been involved in O'Bannion's murder at any level—and it made me heartsick to realize that was very likely—I wouldn't protect her, even though I knew it would be just as hard on Curly and Madelaine to see their daughter in jail as it would to see Curly behind bars for a crime he didn't commit.

I just didn't want to set that legal juggernaut in motion until I was absolutely certain she was guilty—but to answer the questions still lingering in my mind, I needed to speak with her again. That meant I was prepared to bend the law and ignore its strictest interpretation of my responsibilities, at least for the nonce.

Although I didn't particularly like the idea of leaving the cash in the store while I was in Wyoming tying up the loose ends of my investigation, I didn't especially want to lug it around, either. A hoard of money the size of a dog house is the kind of thing that's difficult to conceal and draws the wrong kind of attention. Despite the risk that one of Fang's men would find the money while I was away (if I'd found it, it was idiotic to believe no one else would put the pieces together), I reluctantly decided I had no choice but to leave it where it was and hope it would keep for a few more days.

I stood up, put the stacks of cash back inside the dollhouse, and scoured the store until I came up with a plain white box, just big enough to hold $50,000 in five banded stacks of one-hundred C-notes each that I skimmed from the top of the cache. Then I fitted the top back on the house and pushed it back to where I'd found it, using a carpet runner to hide the gouge marks. When I was satisfied, I tucked the box under my arm, let myself out the front door, and waved to the blonde, who was still watching from the beauty-parlor window. If she realized I was leaving with more than I brought in, she gave no indication, just made a scissors pantomime with her fingers and pointed at me. I shook my head in an apologetic no and steamed off toward the gutless rental car, looking nervously over my shoulder to make sure I wasn't being followed.

Looked like I didn't have time for that haircut, after all.

It was a little after six when I left Dolls in the Attic, just in time for the worst of rush hour in San Francisco. I crept along at the rate of about six feet a minute all the way down Highway 101, the stink of burning clutch plate heavy in my nostrils. We don't have many traffic jams in Wyoming, unless you count the occasional herd of Black Angus crossing the highway, so I spent the entire trip to the airport cursing the glacial pace and wishing I could be home. By the time I made it to San Francisco International and turned in my rental car, I found that if I hopped the next available flight to Denver, I'd have to stay overnight since I'd already missed that day's last commuter flight from Denver to Laramie.

Faced with the prospect of flying to Denver and spending the night in a Holiday Inn or enjoying one last night in Frisco, I made the wise choice. I made plane reservations for the next morning, hopped a cab to Japantown, and took a room at the Miyako Hotel. When I'd dropped my overnight bag in the room and stored the box of cash in the hotel safe, I treated myself to the works at the Kabuki Hot Spring—fifteen minutes in the steam cabinet, a back scrub, a relaxing soak in a deep Japanese-style tub and a full-body shiatsu massage (ouch!).

When I left two hours later, my muscles felt like noodles, so I hopped another cab in search of sustenance, which I found a few blocks later at a Fisherman's Wharf restaurant called Bobby Rubino's that served a plate of baby-back ribs so huge it reminded me of dinner hour at the Flintstone's.

It was a fine evening, and I awoke the next morning so refreshed that I hardly noticed the heavy turbulence on the flight home, or the squalling of a couple of preschoolers in the next aisle who apparently belonged to a frazzled woman wearing so much perfume I figured she probably bought it by the fifty-gallon drum.

Cindy, who'd driven back to Victory with Maddy and Faith the evening before, met me at Brees Field wearing a pair of khaki shorts, a faded denim, shirt, and open-toed sandals. I took a deep breath of dry, smog-free air and basked in the high-country sunshine on my face. At least the rain hadn't followed me back from the coast.

I was distracted, so we didn't talk much on the way home after Cindy caught me up on the basics. Following a brief talk with Kincaid, Faith had been released from the hospital late the previous afternoon and was resting at Madelaine and Curly's house. According to Cindy, Faith told Kincaid she had no idea why she'd been kidnapped, and claimed to know nothing about O'Bannion's missing money when the Rock Springs cop asked about it. She also said she didn't remember whether Stone had mentioned Pantaleo's name at any time during the ordeal. Kincaid hadn't believed her, of course, and had made plans to drive over to take a formal statement in a few days when her strength, and hopefully her memory, had improved.

When we rolled down the sleepy Main Street of Victory, I saw Frankie's cruiser parked in front of the office. I was in a hurry and didn't stop, just dropped Cindy at her house with a kiss and a promise to call, or drop by that night.

"I'd rather have you in person, if you're giving me a choice," she said. "Why don't you plan on staying at the house?"

"Might be late," I told her.

"Doesn't matter," she said playfully. "There's a key under the ceramic dog on the front porch. I'll be the one in the bedroom, sleeping nude."

I watched Cindy until she was safely inside, then I gunned the engine and pointed the Jeep toward Curly's house. When I pulled into the driveway five minutes later, his red bulldog and the German shepherd came bounding off the deck to welcome me home. I scratched their backs and ears, then clomped up the stairs and into the kitchen, where Maddy was putting the finishing touches on a bowl of tuna salad. She licked mayonnaise off her fingers and gave me a muscular hug. "I'm just making lunch," she said. She turned back to the counter and began cutting a loaf of homemade bread into thick slices. "Why don't you pour us a glass of iced tea, and you can tell me about San Francisco while we eat."

"I ate on the plane," I said. "Is Faith awake?"

Something in my voice caused her to stop cutting in mid-slice. "I think so," she said apprehensively. "Why, is something—"

"I need to talk to her," I broke in. "Alone."

Maddy shook her head. "She's been through hell in the last couple of days, Harry," she said. "Whatever it is, can't it wait until—"

I took her by both hands. "Do you want your husband out of jail, Maddy?"

"Yes," she whispered.

"Then it won't wait," I said. "Not another minute."

Faith seemed small and lost in the huge bed. Dressed in a pink-and-white nightgown with a high collar that covered the bruises on her neck, she was propped up on two overstuffed pillows. A television was tuned to an afternoon soap opera, but she wasn't paying attention. She was looking out the window toward the green and blue mountains of the Snowy Range. I don't think she was staring at anything in particular because her eyes had the dull, glazed look of someone with a bellyful of sedatives. She didn't say hello when I came in and sat on the edge of her bed, just gave me a weak smile that must have hurt her cracked lips.

"They tell me you saved my life, Mr. Starbranch," she said. Her voice sounded flat and unemotional, the voice of someone who thought that life might not have been worth saving. "I want to thank you for what you did. I wanted to tell you yesterday, but they said you'd gone away."

I looked down at my hands for a minute, then into her eyes. "I was in San Francisco, Faith," I said gently. "I found the money at your shop."

She jerked as if my words were a hot poker in her guts, turned her head into the pillows, and closed her eyes so tightly her whole face trembled. "You've got to tell me about it," I said. "Do you know who killed Liam?"

"No," she said, her voice so quiet I had to strain to hear.

"No you won't tell me, or no you don't know who killed him?" I asked brusquely. She ignored me, so I went on. "I know what you've been through and I'm sorry to make it worse," I said. "But I'm not going away until you tell me what I need to know. It's time to quit screwing around, Faith. You're ruining your father's life. Do you want that on your conscience, too?"

"No," she whispered desperately. "I don't want that on my conscience. My father did nothing wrong."

"Then tell me."

Faith seemed to shrink even further into her bedding. "I took Liam's money," she admitted painfully. "But I don't know who killed him." She grabbed my hand and squeezed. Her palms were warm and damp. "Please, you've got to believe me."

I pressed on. "The money," I said. "Tell me about the money."

Faith started speaking, stumbling over the words. She paused until she'd gathered whatever meager strength she had left. "He'd taken all I had, and he was going to leave me," she said. "I found his money, and I took it. I didn't know it would get him killed."

"You're not telling me the truth," I said.

She sat up, breathing heavily. "What reason do I have to lie?" she asked. "Do you think I wanted him dead? Do you think all I cared about was the money?"

"I don't know," I said. "It's a lot of money. I've gotta tell you, Faith, I've seen people killed for fifty bucks. Hell, when you come down to it, I've seen people killed for telephone change."

She stopped me with an angry wave of her hand. "I *loved* him, Mr. Starbranch," she said. "I was angry when I took the money, but I wanted him to *stay*. Don't you see that? I thought without the money, he'd have to stay because he couldn't afford to leave. I thought I could use it to buy us a better life. I know it sounds crazy, but I wasn't thinking of what might happen. I was only thinking of us. He never even suspected what I'd done."

She broke down in deep, rib-rending sobs, holding her hands to her stomach against the pain. "It's my fault Liam's dead," she whimpered. "My fault my father's in jail." She threw her arms around my neck and held on as if I were a life preserver in a stormy sea. "I'm so sorry," she said. "So very sorry."

There wasn't much I could say to comfort her, because if she was telling the truth, she was right in believing she'd set in motion the chain of events that had torn her family apart. When Faith took the money, she put O'Bannion at lethal odds with nearly everyone in his life—Fang, Pantaleo, even the Drug Enforcement Administration, which I suspected would have kept him out of the witness-protection program until he gave them back their fifty grand. Even if she had no direct part in his killing, as she claimed, she'd certainly drawn the bull's eye on his head. I held her until she quieted. Then I dabbed her eyes with a tissue and laid her back down on her pillows, straightening her blankets.

"I'll go to the police," she said. Then, almost as an afterthought, she asked, "Will I be in trouble?"

I shook my head. "It's drug money, most of it anyway," I told her. "If you weren't involved in selling narcotics, I don't think you'll be in any trouble."

Faith considered that for a moment. "You believe me, then?"

I wanted to, I really did. Truth was, I didn't know what I believed anymore. This wasn't shaking down the way I'd expected, and I was running out of ideas. "I wish I could," I said sadly. "But I still think you know something that could help me find Liam's killer, and for some reason you're holding back. If you want me to believe you, you've got to tell me everything."

She closed her eyes again. "I want to help, but I've told you all I know," she said.

"Maybe not," I said. I'd decided that even though I was uncertain about Faith's level of complicity, the facts suggested that she played a role in O'Bannion's death. I no longer had any choice but to take my evidence to Tony Baldi and Jack Simpson. Call Pichette and tell him where to find the money.

Before I did that, however, I still had one more question, one more possibility to explore. It was a long shot, but I'd gone about as far as I could. I'd eliminated every suspect I'd turned up but Curly and perhaps one other—one I'd so far overlooked, one who would be too painful even for Faith to contemplate. The more I thought about it, though, it made a sort of macabre sense. As Sherlock Holmes noted, when you have eliminated the impossible, whatever remains, however improbable, must be the truth.

I'd accepted Curly's innocence on faith. Absent suspects I was unaware of, that only left one option if Faith had no hand in O'Bannion's murder. If I was right, I knew the truth would clear Faith Ahearn, but at the same time it might crush her completely. Even as it proved her innocent of involvement in her lover's actual demise, it would fill her with guilt she'd carry to the end of her days. I pitied her, but in the end I had no choice.

"Think back to the days before Liam died," I began tentatively. "You were staying with Maddy and your father . . ."

20

▲▲▲

Ken Keegan looked as if he'd been wearing his suit in the sauna for about three months. An agent for the state Department of Criminal Investigation in Cheyenne, he's never been a particularly snappy dresser because it's almost impossible to buy clothes that hang well on his boxy frame. That afternoon, with the ever-present Camel unfiltered hanging from the corner of his mouth, he was even more rumpled than usual. He groaned his way out of his state-issue Ford, ran a hand across his square head to make sure his flattop was level, then closed the middle button of his wrinkled blue suit coat to cover the 9-mm automatic he wears in a shoulder holster.

Frankie Tall Bull, leaning against the fender of the Jeep, chuckled to himself when he saw Keegan's outfit, and seemed especially delighted by his down-at-the-heel black wing tips. "It doesn't look like Ken dressed for the outdoors," he said. "I think I hear L. L. Bean spinning in his grave."

"Be nice," I muttered under my breath. "Those *are* his hiking clothes."

Despite his sartorial squalor, it was good to see my old friend again. Keegan and I have worked on several cases together since I first moved to Wyoming, and despite some bumpy patches we've maintained a relationship based on trust, professional respect, and shared interests—mainly food, bourbon, and nicotine. At one point, he'd even offered me a job with the DCI, which I turned down because I was planning to ride out the rest of my career in Victory. I wondered if it was too late to change my mind.

Keegan smiled when I crossed the parking lot and offered one of his platter-size hands in greeting. I knew exactly what was coming, a variation on an old theme. "I heard you were unemployed," he said, nodding at my waistline, "but it doesn't look like poverty has affected your appetite."

"Just puttin' on an extra layer for the winter," I said. My turn. I fingered the lapel of his wrinkled jacket. "Armani?"

"No, it's all mine," he said, his face cracking in a grin that would frighten most children. Keegan shook hands with Frankie and then took a look around. "Not that I don't appreciate a chance to get out of the office once in a while, but would you mind telling me why I'm here?"

"I need someone with authority out here in the county," I said. "Someone who's objective."

I hadn't explained much when I'd called Keegan and asked him to drive over from Cheyenne and meet Frankie and me in the campground where O'Bannion had parked before he died. Ken had been curious, but he hadn't pressed. He knew I wouldn't bother him without good reason, and I thought I had one of those.

Before I told anyone about the money, I wanted to go over the killing ground one more time. There was a fair chance I'd turn up empty-handed, but if I found what I was looking for, I'd either have enough to free Curly or convict him. I knew I couldn't control the outcome, but if my search was fruitful, I wanted the evidence in impartial hands, and I didn't think Sheriff Anthony Baldi qualified. I didn't believe Baldi would tamper with evidence to get the result he wanted, but I've known him to destroy crucial evidence by carelessness too many times to trust him. Besides, whatever we found would be analyzed in the DCI's crime lab anyway, so it made sense to avoid the middleman and put it in Keegan's custody from the start.

Also, if the whole thing turned out to be a wild-goose chase, I'd just as soon my friends were the only witnesses. Tony Baldi already thought I was a moron, and I had no desire to remove all doubt.

Keegan and Frankie shot the breeze while I got the long nylon bag of equipment out of the Jeep, but when I started off down the trail toward the place where we'd found O'Bannion's body with it slung over my shoulder, Frankie took pity and carried it himself. That was fine with me, because the bag was heavy and the trail was steep.

It took us the better part of an hour to walk from the campground to the rocky ridge where we'd discovered the first pieces of Liam's corpse, and by the time we arrived, Keegan was limping from covering the rocky terrain in street shoes. He'd taken off his jacket, wadded it up, and was carrying it under one hairy arm. He'd pulled the knot of his tie away from his collar, his white shirt stuck to his back from sweat, and he was chewing an unlit Camel like a toothpick.

Except for my feet, I was in about the same shape. Winded. Bum leg throbbing. In need of a cigar, some horse liniment, and a cold Coors, I felt like the national poster boy for middle age.

Frankie, damn his eyes, looked as if he'd done nothing more strenuous than walk from his front door to the driveway. He sat the bag down on a rocky ledge and walked to the edge of the precipice to look out over the steep, forested slope where we'd found O'Bannion's leg and gnawed arm.

As soon as I could breathe without wheezing, I unzipped the bag and took out my prize, the GTA 1000 metal detector I'd borrowed from Howard Shapiro at the hardware store before I left Victory. When it comes to metal detectors, the GTA 1000 is pretty much state-of-the-art. It's got 2-D elliptical cross-fire search coils with smart sensors that can tell the difference between a piece of aluminum foil and a silver dollar, a slide-off battery clip, and a knife-edge scan pattern that, in theory, will enable a user to stand on a dung heap and discover every speck of metal buried inside. Shapiro made me promise that I wouldn't scratch it, or get it wet, and that I'd give him a piece of the action if I discovered gold. I naturally agreed, but that day I wasn't looking for treasure.

I was looking for a gun.

I knew enough about Tony Baldi's slipshod technique of crime-scene investigation to know that he would never have thought of looking for the weapon with a metal detector. From what I knew of his investigation, he'd been so cocksure he was dealing with a murder that he stopped scouring the crime scene as soon as he found the slug that killed O'Bannion. His pea brain was simply too small to consider the possibility that the slug was only part of the answer.

I flipped the gizmo on and waited until I started getting warm-up images on the amber screen that tells you the size, shape, and depth of the metal thing it's registering. Then I started working in gradually widening circles, beginning at the rocks where we believed the shooting took place.

Although I hadn't told either of them exactly what I was looking for, I could tell by the looks on their faces that Frankie and Ken thought I was insane. What little ground there was in the boulder field was as hard as concrete, and there was no way anything of importance would have gotten itself buried in the recent past. Luckily, I wasn't looking for anything that was buried—I was interested in the deep fissures of the granite ledge, some of which seemed to go down several yards. Drop a silver dollar down one of those cracks and it was gone forever, unless someone with a GTA 1000 came along to find it and bring it back.

It took less than five minutes before I got couple of little warning pings on the detector, and then the screen showed me the image of something metal lodged about thirty feet down the fissure I was searching. It didn't look like a gun, but that wasn't surprising since I didn't think I was looking at the object from the side. If the weapon was lodged vertically in the rocks, the image showing on my screen would either be a view down the bore or straight down from the handle.

I went to my equipment bag and grabbed a fisherman's magnet attached to a piece of stout, monofilament line, thinking that the location was perfect. If the bear had tugged O'Bannion's body down the slope to the place where we'd found his arm and leg, the gun could have been dragged along with him, at least until it fell into the crevasse.

I ran back to the crack in the granite and played the magnet out on the line until I'd released about twenty-five feet into the cranny. It caught a couple of times on protrusions in the rock, but I jiggled it until it came loose.

Even from where I was kneeling on the surface, I could hear the metallic clack as the magnet found its target and latched on.

My heart shimmied and I began pulling the line in. A few seconds later, I was holding a blood-stained .38 caliber Smith & Wesson with black rubber grips and a snub nose at the end of my line. I didn't touch the revolver because I didn't want to damage whatever fingerprints were on the grips, trigger, cylinder, and perhaps the barrel. I just held it up triumphantly like a trout on a string.

"Is that what I think it is?" Keegan asked. "The murder weapon?"

I nodded energetically. "I believe so," I said. "That's why I wanted you here. I want you to get this back to the state lab and run whatever prints you find on it."

He didn't look as if he understood. "What if they're Curly's?" he asked.

"I doubt they are," I said. "Right before I called you, Faith told me that the night before he died, O'Bannion was so wired on speed he couldn't sleep, so the two of them got Curly's keys and went down to the Silver Dollar after it closed and spent the rest of the night drinking whiskey and playing the juke. That means he could have taken the pistol without Curly knowing—and that means he could have—"

Keegan saw where I was going immediately. "Killed *himself?*" he asked incredulously.

"It's possible," I said. "When your lab techs run the prints on that gun, I think they're gonna find some of Curly's—but on top of those, I'm betting they're gonna find some other prints, too. I think when you run those other prints through the NCIC, you're gonna find they belong to one of the cons in their database, our old friend Liam O'Bannion."

Keegan shook his head doubtfully. "I hope you're right," he said. "It's gonna be hard on you if it turns out you found the evidence to put Curly away forever." He carefully wrapped the Smith & Wesson in a handkerchief and tucked it into his pocket. "Either way, I ought to have your answer by the end of the day."

We gathered our gear and were setting a brisk pace along the game trail back to the campground when Frankie caught up with me and began marching alongside, his long legs eating ground. "I read the coroner's report, Harry, and the wound certainly could have been self-inflicted, but I still don't get it."

"What don't you understand?"

"Why would he kill himself?"

I knew the answer, but I still wasn't quite ready to tell anyone the whole story, not even Frankie. "Maybe he didn't think he had a choice," I said. As I spoke, a prairie hen rose from a tangle of deadfall at the side of the trail, her brown wings flapping wildly as she struggled to lift her heavy body into the thin mountain air. I stood still and watched until the frightened grouse disappeared over the ridgeline, flying so close to the ground that her belly seemed to skim the tops of the purple sage. "Then again," I said, "maybe he just ignored the signs."

Frankie squinted against the bright-yellow afternoon sun. "What signs?"

Who says there's no such thing as karma? I pulled my hat low on my forehead and leaned against the blackthorn. "The ones at the campground, Frankie," I said, smiling at the irony. *Please don't feed the bears.*

Ken had the lab results by six that evening, but it was almost noon the next day before Tony Baldi and the county prosecutor, Walker Tisdale, finally admitted that their case against Curly Ahearn had gone up in a wispy puff of Rocky Mountain smoke. O'Bannion's prints, it turned out, were all over the revolver, even the cartridges. The man had almost certainly taken his own life—an opinion the Department of Criminal Investigation voiced in the strongest possible terms.

Walker dropped the charges quietly and then left for a weeklong fishing trip at Jackson Lake Lodge, leaving Tony to deal with the media. Baldi held a press conference and told the pack of assembled reporters, led by Sally Sheridan of the *Casper Star-Tribune* in all her aggressive, red-headed splendor, that no, he didn't believe the fact that he'd arrested an innocent man illustrated the general incompetence of his administration. Considering the budget cuts his office had suffered in the last year, they'd done the best they could.

Curly's attorney, Jackson Simpson, watching the spectacle from the periphery in a fringed buckskin jacket and a black hat with the diameter of a man-hole cover, disrupted the proceedings to inform Tony and the assembled representatives of the fourth estate that once he filed suit for false arrest, Tony's office would have to learn to live on even less, since he planned to liberate at least a million from the county's treasury on the mayor's behalf.

I watched the conference on the courthouse steps until I'd had my fill of hot air and bluster, then I went inside to find Maddy. The two of us were waiting in the lobby when Curly was finally processed and released from jail at about one-thirty. He came through the door of the elevator from the top floor dressed in faded jeans, a T-shirt that featured a bunch of old-time Indian warriors wearing red sunglasses, and his Colorado Rockies cap sitting squarely on his bald head. He picked his wife off her feet and whirled her in a clumsy fandango, then set her down and drew me into their circle in a three-way hug.

"I was beginning to think you forgot me," he said happily. "I was in there so long, I was even starting to look forward to the afternoon soaps." He gave Maddy a lascivious wink. "I learned a few tricks from the perverts on *The Young and the Restless* you're really gonna love, darlin'."

The crowd of reporters was still congregated on the front steps, waiting for Curly to make a statement. To avoid them, the three of us went through the sheriff's department and out the back door, where the Jeep was parked in Walker Tisdale's reserved space.

"Where to?" I asked as Curly climbed into the back seat, leaving the bucket next to me for his wife.

"Straight to the house," he said. "First I'm gonna take the world's longest shower. Then you're gonna help me catch up on all my bad habits."

I started the engine, popped the transmission into reverse. "I don't know, podna," I said. "I think you probably need some time to—"

He whacked me playfully in the back of the head to shut me up, and the force knocked my hat down over my eyes. He leaned forward and reset my Stetson at a rakish angle. "Thanks to you, Harry," he said, leaning down in the seat so he wouldn't be spotted when we drove away, "I've got all the time in the world."

Curly was as good as his word, and stayed in the shower until he'd used every drop of hot water in the house. Then he closeted himself in Faith's bedroom and stayed there talking with her for the better part of an hour.

I used the time to get a bed of charcoal going in the grill while Maddy made a salad. Then the two of us sat on the deck—me with a beer, her sipping red wine—shucking fresh corn and snapping green beans until we had enough vegetables for our meal. The phone rang several times, but we ignored it. Maddy wanted details of the case, and I told her about everything except the money. Then she started probing in her gentle way to find out what was up in my life, particularly my budding romance with Cindy Thompson and my uncertain relationship with Nicole. I didn't know where either of those was going myself, so I was reticent. She didn't push, just changed the subject and told me how happy she was to have her husband home, how worried she was about her daughter. I was content to listen to her ramble and watch the afternoon shadows lengthen across the valley floor, study the progress of the dogs as they hunted the chokecherry thickets of the stream bank in search of rabbits and the odd bull snake, for some reason one of their favorite meals.

Curly was subdued when he finally joined us on the deck, clearly disturbed by his talk with Faith. When Maddy saw the troubled look on his face, she made room for him next to her on the bench. They shared a look, and her eyes softened. She took his hand and pressed it to her cheek.

"Those sons of bitches," he said, a general indictment that could, and probably did, include nearly everyone associated with the case. "I'm worried she's not gonna make it out of this, Maddy. She blames herself for the whole thing, even O'Bannion's suicide. I can't understand why she blames herself for that. She didn't pull the trigger on that coward. He did it himself."

"I don't know, either," Maddy said. "But she does."

I turned my head away so they couldn't see the look on my face. If they saw, they'd know I was hiding something. At some point, I figured I'd have to tell them the truth—that O'Bannion killed himself in desperation because Faith had taken a half-million dollars of drug money that didn't belong to him, and he knew that if he didn't end his own life quickly, men like Tommy Fang and Sam Pantaleo would make him beg for a bullet. At the moment, however, they had enough on their minds without the added burden of that unsavory truth.

"Maybe I could talk to her," I offered. I knew I couldn't make it much easier on her, but at least I could assure her that the secret was safe with me until she chose to reveal it herself.

Curly shook his head. "I don't think that's a good idea," he said. "She's too upset, and I'm afraid she's not making much sense." He held his wife close. "Tomorrow morning, first thing, we'll find her a good counselor. Help her work through this. I don't think she can do it on her own."

I hoped Faith would eventually come to realize what fine parents she'd been blessed with. Whether she deserved them or not was another question.

I busied myself with the rib eyes while Curly and Maddy took a short walk, arm in arm, along the bank of the stream, their heads together, talking quietly. When the food was ready, we set plates at the wooden table on the deck and ate as evening descended over the peaks of the Snowies. Curly's joy at being released from jail was gone, and he ate absentmindedly, out of the conversational loop. Maddy glanced at him occasionally, and her concern was apparent on her face, although she tried to make small talk so I wouldn't feel like an oddball.

They needed time alone, I decided, and it was wrong of me to intrude, even though Curly had insisted. I finished my dinner as quickly as I could and turned down Maddy's offer of a Baileys and coffee in lieu of dessert. "No thanks," I said. "To tell you the truth, I want to make it an early night. I thought now that I'm a man of leisure I'd get up at the crack of dawn tomorrow morning and see if the trout are biting on the Little Laramie. I haven't been fishin' on a workday since I was a kid."

"Bullshit," Curly said, making a halfhearted attempt at humor. "You might be anxious to drown a worm, but from the gossip I hear about you and Cindy Thompson, you won't be anywhere near the river."

I didn't dignify that with a response, just stood up and helped clear the table, said my goodbyes to Maddy. When we were finished, Curly followed me outside to the Jeep and stood there with his hands in his pockets, looking down at his feet. "You have another smart-assed comment?" I asked, jangling my keys.

"Nah," he said, taking my hand in his rough grip. "I just want you to know I appreciate what you did."

"It was nothin'," I said. "You just go back in there and take care of your family."

He shook his head. "No, Harry, it was *everything.*" If I didn't know him better, I would have thought he was going to cry. Not Curly, though. He choked it back and opened the door of the vehicle, held it until I was inside. He closed it and leaned against the window. "Don't worry about your job, podna," he said. "As soon as I take care of my family business, I plan to run through those assholes on the council like shit through a goose."

"I wasn't worried for a minute," I said, cranking the engine. "But next time I go to work for this stupid burg, I want an ironclad contract."

Cindy, dressed in a gray sweatsuit, ugly sheepskin slippers, with some kind of green mud on her face, was watching a Clint Eastwood movie on the VCR when I got to her house, the one about the aging gunfighter who's lured back to the world of violence, *Unforgiven*. I'd already seen it at least a dozen times, so I left her and her bowl of popcorn in the den and made my way to the basement.

Harv Thompson is a very competent banker, but he was apparently a lousy husband and, worse yet, a miserable fly fisherman. Since my own gear had been destroyed in the fire at my house, I needed some temporary replacements if I intended to go fishing with the rising sun. Trouble was, all Harv had left behind when Cindy booted him out was a stiff Eagle Claw rod that doubled as a combination spin/fly caster and a box of factory-tied flies with barbed hooks that looked as if he'd purchased them in quantity from the five-and-dime.

I picked out a half-dozen flies that were adequate representations of real insects and spent the next half hour filing the barbs off so I could release the trout I caught without harming them. Then I dug around in his various plastic tackle boxes until I found a cheap fly reel with a windup action that felt like it had maybe three hours of use left before it went to the big scrap heap in the sky. Instead of Harv's leftover garbage, I thought I'd probably have better luck fishing with a stick of dynamite, or a .357, but beggars can't be choosers. I made a mental note to call the Orvis Company and have them Fed Ex their latest catalog. I didn't have more than two changes of fresh underwear or a set of sheets, but by God, I couldn't be expected to start a new life without a graphite fly rod and the makings for some Wooly Boogers and a few Zug Bugs.

Outfitted and prepared for the morning, I trudged back upstairs to find Cindy, absent the facial mud, waiting in the kitchen, sipping a cup of hot tea. "Sorry you had to see that," she said. "I didn't expect you for a couple of hours."

"See what?"

"My *Creature from the Black Lagoon* impersonation," she said. "I usually save that one for the third date."

"No problem," I said. "I've got a few plans for our third date, too, but mine involve Jell-O. Grape, I think."

"Sounds yummy," she said, laughing. She poured me a cup of tea, and then she did something that made me realize how much I missed being in a comfortable relationship with a woman. She helped me off with my boots. I wriggled my toes in her plush carpet, leaned close to inhale the fragrant steam coming from my cup. Cindy stood behind me and rubbed my shoulders, her fingers strong and probing. "I'm happy this is over, Harry," she said. "Glad it's at an end."

I leaned back into her ministrations, closed my eyes. I felt sad, more than a little hollow. "These things never end, Cindy," I said. "At least they never end well."

"What do you mean?"

"It's fairly simple, really," I said. "Everybody's been changed by this for the worse. Almost everyone I care about lost more than they could spare. Edna lost her life. I lost my house. Frankie killed a man, so he lost what was left of his innocence. Maddy lost. Even Curly. He got out of jail, but the circumstances that put him there may have destroyed his daughter. She believes she's responsible for O'Bannion's death, and no one will ever convince her differently."

Cindy stopped rubbing and sat beside me at the table, sipping her tea reflectively. "I know what you're saying, Harry. There's not much to feel good about," she said. "But why would Faith think she's responsible?"

She'd asked the question of the hour, but I hadn't answered it for Curly and I wouldn't for Cindy, either. "I'm not entirely certain," I answered evasively. "Maybe a good therapist can help her straighten it out."

I think she sensed that I was being less than truthful, but she didn't press. She just pulled me to my feet and wrapped her arms around my middle. I nuzzled the top of her head gently. Her hair smelled like almonds. "Looks to me like you could use a little therapy yourself, cowboy," she said. "Why don't you come to bed?" She took me by the hand and began leading me upstairs. "I don't have a Ph.D., but I work cheap."

That sounded like a good prescription to me. At the moment, making love was the most optimistic, life-affirming thing I could do.

Faith Ahearn tried to kill herself around midnight with sixty Seconals, a half bottle of Valium, and an undetermined number of Percodans. She almost succeeded. Maddy woke about two in the morning with a feeling of free-floating anxiety that first caused her to check the locks on all her doors and then, as an afterthought, to look in on her daughter.

She found Faith in a heap on the floor, covered in vomit and breathing erratically. She didn't wait for the ambulance crew from Laramie, just woke Curly and the two of them bundled Faith up in the car and raced her thirty miles to the hospital. They were almost too late. By the time they reached the emergency room, most of the drugs were already in Faith's bloodstream and her vital systems were shutting down. She went into cardiac arrest twice, but the emergency-room doctors were successful in jump-starting her both times.

I didn't hear about the suicide attempt until I got back to Victory from the Little Laramie River, where I'd spent most of the morning pulling rainbows and brookies from the icy-blue water. When I caught enough fish, I took my thermos of coffee and sat looking out over the prairie with my back against an aspen, watching hawks ride the thermals while I decompressed.

For me, a few hours on a trout stream, thinking like a fish, is better than six months on a head shrinker's couch—and I had plenty of personal issues to settle. I didn't resolve a single one, but I made a start. A few more days on the river and I imagined I'd be healthy enough to do something productive, like figuring out how I was going to earn a living. Perhaps it was time to give up police work altogether and find a less stressful occupation. Maybe I'd become a fishing guide. I wouldn't make much money, but I'd never have to worry about getting fired—unless I got mad and terminated my-self.

I toyed with that pleasant notion all the way back to town, where the only traffic was Ray Hladky driving a green John Deere tractor with a brush-cutting blade down the center of Main Street. I followed him as far as Ginny Larsen's Country Kitchen, then peeled off into a parking place and killed the engine, my mouth already watering in anticipation of lunch—chicken-fried steak with cream gravy and mashed potatoes. Comfort food. It was a little before two, and most of the lunchtime regulars were already gone. Ginny gave me a wave through the window as I dropped a quarter into the parking meter and started inside. Before I got through the door, however, someone called my name and I turned to see Dr. Eddie Warnock running across the street in my direction.

For a second, I thought Fast Eddie was coming to remind me that it was time for my annual physical, but when I saw the worried look on his face, I realized his purpose wasn't something that would give him as much personal pleasure as the prospect of nagging me for an hour. His tie was undone and his white lab coat was flapping in the light breeze. His thinning hair stood out at the sides of his head as if he'd been brushing it with his fingers. "Where've you been, Harry?" he asked. "I've been looking all over for you. Even Frankie didn't know where you—"

I had my hand on the door to the café, but I waited for him to catch up. "Fishin', Eddie," I said. "Sorry I didn't check in with you beforehand."

He took me by the elbow and pulled me away from the door. "You haven't heard, then?" he asked.

"Heard what?"

We sat on the curb while Eddie told me about Faith's attempt to take her own life and the frantic efforts to save it. My stomach churned as I listened, and a black cloud seemed to cover the face of the sun that was even darker than the gray rain clouds blowing down from the north. The story only got worse. The doctors at Ivinson Memorial in Laramie had brought Faith back to life, and while they thought they could keep her that way, there was no telling what kind of life it would be. "There's usually some kind of brain damage in cases like this," Eddie explained. "But they don't know how much she sustained, because she's in a coma."

"She'll come out of it?" I asked, willing him to say yes. The wind was rising and a small dust devil twisted down the opposite side of the street, spinning papers and leaves in its wake. A tumbleweed blowing down the gutter caught against my leg. The dust burned my eyes and I rubbed it away.

Eddie shrugged sadly. "Maybe," he said. "But maybe not. I haven't seen many of them myself, but I've heard of cases where people like this remain comatose for years after an overdose. Think of Karen Quinlan. Once in a while, they come out of it." He clasped his hands in his lap and stared at his feet. The first fat raindrops splattered on the asphalt. He turned his collar up against the storm. "Most often," he said, almost to himself, "they just never wake up."

I watched the Life Flight helicopter carrying Faith Ahearn take off from Ivinson Memorial Hospital in Laramie to a more specialized-care facility in Denver at a little after noon the next day. Then I said goodbye to Curly and Madelaine, who were driving directly from the hospital to Denver, where they planned to stay with their daughter for as long as they possibly could.

I was standing in the parking lot of the hospital as they drove away, but before I could get behind the wheel of the Jeep, Frankie Bull pulled up next to me in his cruiser. "Did I miss them?" he asked.

I told him he had.

"How's Faith?"

"No change," I said. "Eddie thinks it could be permanent."

Frankie shook his head sadly. "I heard Faith doesn't have any health insurance," he said. "I hope Curly can afford it."

I knew where there was enough money to last a while, but I didn't say anything. Almost half a million dollars can buy a lot of treatment. The money was raised by men who traded in human misery. It seemed fitting that it be spent to heal.

"I got a call before I left Victory," Frankie said. "Pichette says to tell you his people nailed some of Tommy Fang's goons loading sixty kilos of methamphetamine into a Pantaleo truck this morning. Tommy and his boys are in jail, and the truck driver is already begging to give Sam up in exchange for immunity. Pichette figures he's got a strong enough case to put Fang and Sam behind bars for at least twenty years."

That was the best news I'd had in days. "Why did he call you?"

Frankie shrugged. "Because he couldn't find you," he said. "I'm just delivering the message."

"Thanks."

I wanted to get back to Victory as soon as possible, but before I left town I stopped by the post office and bought an overnight delivery envelope. I took it out to the Jeep and reached under the seat for the white box I'd been carrying there, the box filled with $50,000 I'd skimmed from Faith's hoard. I slid the box in the envelope and included a handwritten note. Three words: "From Liam O'Bannion."

I sealed the envelope and addressed it to Jamie Pichette, trudged back inside, and handed the package to a postal clerk at the counter.

In San Francisco, Pichette told me O'Bannion had taken fifty grand of the DEA's money before he died. Now—at least as far as the government was concerned—Liam's account was paid in full.

I bought a fifth of Rebel Yell and drank most of it that afternoon at the side of Edna Cook's grave.

I'd missed her service because I'd been in San Francisco when Edna's family buried her half a mile from her house in a willow grove on the banks of Antelope Creek. Now the family was gone, and the sprays of cheap funeral flowers were wilting, their petals dropping into the freshly turned earth of her final resting place.

I took some comfort in the fact that once my house was finished I could look out my front window and see her grave marker. But knowing she would always be close was small comfort, because I believed I should have prevented her death.

I should have done a lot of things.

For starters, I should have done more for Faith Ahearn. I'd taken her away from Junior Stone, but I hadn't saved her. I'd simply consigned her to a different but equally destructive fate.

Hell of a victory.

The whiskey caught up with me around four and I pulled one of Edna's cats—a tabby that had been lurking around her grave all afternoon—into my lap. I rubbed the cat's neck until it began to purr, and then I leaned back against the trunk of a willow and fell asleep.

I awoke an hour later to the sound of tires crunching gravel on the dirt road leading to the grave. The black Mercedes convertible stopped about twenty feet away and two people got out. The driver was a tall man with a receding hairline who looked to be about my age. Dressed in a purple polo shirt, white shorts and low-top sneakers with no socks, he wore a pair of expensive sunglasses held around his neck by a chain. The Colorado vanity plates on his car said TORT ACE. Definitely a lawyer.

The passenger was my ex-wife, Nicole.

I didn't know who her companion was, but the look that passed between them before she left the car told me he was more than her friend. The stranger put his hands in his pockets and leaned against the fender, watching nervously as Nicole walked to the side of the grave and stood, looking down at the top of my head. Dressed in a light summer floral-print dress that came to her knees, she looked beautiful as always, even more so with the golden evening sunlight dancing in the highlights of her auburn hair. My heart felt so heavy I thought it might fall from my chest.

"Do you mind if I sit?" she asked. I wondered if she recognized the place Edna's family had chosen for a burial site. Once, in happier times, we'd made love there after a long horseback ride.

"Of course not."

She sat, curling her feet under her on the ground. I felt like I should offer her something, but all I had was the bourbon, and Nicole was never one to drink from the bottle. The cat jumped off my lap and brushed its body against her thigh.

"I've tried calling you for several days," she said.

I nodded toward the ruins of my house. "Phone's out of service," I said.

"So I see." She picked up the cat and held it against her breast. Its yellow eyes closed in delight. "I talked to Frankie this morning, and he told me everything that's happened," she said. "I'm sorry about Edna and Faith. At least Curly's out of jail. That's something, isn't it, Harry?"

I shrugged. "How are the boys?" I asked, changing the subject.

"Fine," she said. "They all want to come up and visit. I told them they'd have to wait until your house is finished."

"No reason to wait. Send 'em up next weekend and we'll camp out. Maybe I'll even put 'em to work."

"They'd enjoy that," she said. She was quiet then, watching Edna's horses in the pasture, one of her dogs chasing a gopher. She put the cat down and smoothed her dress nervously. "I didn't think it would be this hard," she said.

"What?"

She nodded in the direction of her companion. My throat seemed to close. I couldn't breathe. I felt weak, growing ever weaker.

"We need to talk, Harry," she said softly.

In the pasture, Edna's old gelding raised his head, his ears straining forward, nostrils flaring. I don't know what he'd seen or felt that frightened him, but in less than a second he bolted off at a gallop away from us toward the piney foothills—head down, sharp hooves pounding antediluvian earth, black tail trailing like a pennant. He was nothing but an aging nag, I told myself, but with only a little imagination he could have been my Red Desert stallion—stretched out and racing toward the rimrock mesas on the far horizon.

Running against the wind.